THE
WICKED
HOUR

ALSO BY ALICE BLANCHARD

Trace of Evil

THE WICKED HOUR

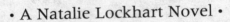

• A Natalie Lockhart Novel •

Alice Blanchard

MINOTAUR BOOKS
NEW YORK

Published in the United States by Minotaur Books, an imprint of St. Martin's Publishing Group

THE WICKED HOUR. Copyright © 2020 by Alice Blanchard. All rights reserved. Printed in the United States of America. For information, address St. Martin's Publishing Group, 120 Broadway, New York, NY 10271.

www.minotaurbooks.com

Excerpt from *The Witching Tree* copyright © 2021 by Alice Blanchard

The Library of Congress has cataloged the hardcover edition as follows:

Names: Blanchard, Alice, author.
Title: The wicked hour : a Natalie Lockhart novel / Alice Blanchard.
Description: First Edition. | New York : Minotaur Books, 2020. |
    Series: Natalie Lockhart ; 2 |
Identifiers: LCCN 2020031676 | ISBN 9781250205735 (hardcover) |
    ISBN 9781250205742 (ebook)
Subjects: GSAFD: Mystery fiction.
Classification: LCC PS3552.L36512 W53 2020 | DDC 813/.54—dc23
LC record available at https://lccn.loc.gov/2020031676

ISBN 978-1-250-77113-1 (trade paperback)

Our books may be purchased in bulk for promotional, educational, or business use. Please contact your local bookseller or the Macmillan Corporate and Premium Sales Department at 1-800-221-7945, extension 5442, or by email at MacmillanSpecialMarkets@macmillan.com.

First Minotaur Books Trade Paperback Edition: 2021

10 9 8 7 6 5 4 3 2 1

To Doug.
To the dream.

PROLOGUE

———⟋———

LAST APRIL IN UPSTATE NEW YORK

The man grabbed a towel, wiped his face, and caught sight of his reflection in the bathroom mirror. He felt odd. Not himself. His smile was strong and dazzling, but his eyes were couched and wary. He had holding-back eyes.

He went downstairs. The house was old. The banister creaked. He could feel his insides ripping apart. Time was slipping away. He felt an urgent need to do something.

In the sunny dining room, he drank his coffee and read the newspaper. He stared at the headline dominating the front page. COP KILLS CROW KILLER! First of all, she wasn't a cop, she was a detective—but that wouldn't have the same ring to it, he supposed. It was all about the clicks nowadays.

He fetched another cup of coffee, then read the sports page. He waited with mounting tension, expecting to be disrupted any second. It upset him that she was so silent this morning. He tilted his head and listened for the smallest sound coming from the basement. Nothing.

He found it difficult to stay focused.

The dining room was littered with fast-food containers, scribbled notes on lined yellow pads, and stacks of books. The house was silent, but the stillness had sounds running through it—innocuous buzzes and ticks you could trace to mundane realities, like the creak of a floorboard expanding; the rattling cough of a radiator; the scratch of a tree limb that needed pruning; the flap of a loose utility line against the siding. Eerie sounds that were little more than an irritation.

He paused. He listened. It worried him—this morning's silence. Shafts of golden light filtered in through the windows. It was going to be a beautiful day.

He put down the paper, went into the living room, picked up the remote, and selected Mozart's Violin Concerto in D Major. The house filled with beautiful leaps and trills. Piano concertos and operas moved him deeply, but he especially loved the violins. Sometimes he would stand in front of the speakers, rest his hands on the cabinetry, and feel the vibrations of the French horns and kettledrums pounding through the bones of his arms, until the music resonated inside his rib cage. He could feel the composer's fingers landing on the keyboard and the mellow notes of the violins squeezing through his veins, and he imagined that he was holding Mozart's or Stravinsky's bleeding heart in his hands.

Now a tormented cry pierced the loveliness. He released an unsteady breath and cranked the volume on the sound system. He lived on a dead-end street. People rarely ventured out this way, and the house was well-insulated. Nobody could hear the screams unless they drove past the property with their windows rolled down at just the right moment. Very rarely did anyone drive out this way.

He went outside and stood in his pajamas and slippers in the backyard, waiting for the next outburst. He let his eyes lose their focus until the landscape of overgrown gardens and trees became a blur of color and shadow, like an impressionist painting. He surrendered to a greater reality and listened to the birdsong in the woods, wishing that he could shake this version of events out of his skull. Perhaps a parallel universe was waiting for him around the next heartbeat?

An agonized scream pierced the morning calm.

Loud.

Terrifying.

It made him shudder.

The hairs rose everywhere on his body, and yet he did nothing. He remained motionless and waited for this delicious agony to subside. It always did eventually.

In the lull that followed, he could hear the wind in the trees. He could hear the waxwings and kingbirds deep in the woods. Birds were descendants of the dinosaurs, those massive killing machines that had ruled the earth once, but were nothing more than fluttering flowers now—singing their sweet, sad warrior songs in the treetops where the foxes and raccoons couldn't get them.

Another piercing scream.

Like a splash of cold water.

He went inside, locked the door, and paced back and forth, burning off excess energy. Today was the day. A smile plied his lips. Prickles raced up his spine. He listened to the combination of sounds coming from upstairs and downstairs, like musical notes with pauses in between.

Low groan.

A squeaky sob.

Rest.

Moan.

A stomach-churning wail.

Rest.

You could compose a concerto in A minor with these kaleidoscopic tones. One from above, the other below. He raised his arms slowly, his right hand holding an invisible bow, the fingers of his left hand pressing against invisible strings. He played to an invisible audience—his muscles moving with precision, greasy strands of hair falling across his face. The violins were grieving. The entire house was weeping. His shoulders fell earthward. Tonight, he would see those cloudy eyes in his dreams. And in the morning, he would wake up with the smell of death in his nose.

1

October 31. **The monsters** were out in force tonight. They'd taken over Burning Lake, New York, and Detective Natalie Lockhart was powerless to stop them. She adjusted her 99-cent eye mask and headed through a huge crowd of costumed revelers, making her way toward the town square. The night air was cool and sweet-smelling. Autumn leaves crunched underfoot. The annual ritual was in full swing—a monthlong celebration culminating in Halloween's Eve, a night full of dancing and drinking and having as much spooky fun as you could fit into one wild twenty-four-hour period.

"Love your costume!" a passing vampire shouted, and Natalie smiled back. She was dressed in her old police uniform. She'd pulled it out of mothballs, and it felt loose on her skinnier frame. All the detectives in the Criminal Investigations Unit had been assigned undercover duties tonight and were required to wear a costume, but Natalie didn't feel like parading around as a mermaid or a princess or a witch. After spending the past six Halloweens on foot patrol, monitoring the streets as a BLPD officer, she decided to do the same thing this year, minus her service weapon and duty belt. She would be a zombie cop. Before her shift began, Natalie let down her hair, put on a chalky foundation and dark lipstick, added a dribble of fake blood to one cheek, slipped on a blue eye mask and a plastic joke badge, and told anyone who asked, "This is my costume. Like it or lump it." Her fellow detectives had greeted her announcement with clammy silence. Only Luke had the temerity to ask, "Is that wise, Natalie?"

After thinking about it now, she realized no . . . it wasn't the wisest decision she'd ever made. But it represented a subliminal desire to be a cop again, not the tabloid-splashed detective who'd shot the Crow Killer point-blank. She wanted to turn back time and walk the beat again, like she had in the good old days before Grace died. Nothing positive had happened to Natalie since last April. She'd lost everything that ever mattered to her.

The downtown district was dazzling tonight, lit by thousands of twinkle lights. The sizeable crowds had no clue that Natalie and her fellow detectives were working undercover, communicating via their department smartphones using secure, encrypted software to disseminate real-time communications. Her phone with its earpiece disguised as white AirPods allowed her to go about undetected, transmitting video feed to the rest of the unit, who were spread out across town, monitoring for trouble spots.

By all estimates, more than a hundred thousand people had descended on this self-proclaimed epicenter for magic and witchcraft. With a little help from the surrounding jurisdictions, a total of two hundred and twenty-five police officers were safeguarding downtown Burning Lake tonight—cops on foot, cops on bikes, cops in squad cars—along with forty plainclothes officers and the BLPD's seven detectives. So far, the radio chatter had been nonstop—illegal drones were spotted flying above the fairgrounds, drunken tourists had broken through the barriers and climbed on top of vehicles, fights had broken out in multiple locations, shoplifters and pickpockets were having a field day. There were unexpected road closures and arguments over parking spaces. Most of the public lots and garages were filled to capacity, and traffic congestion was heavy in places.

"This is Command," Lieutenant Luke Pittman's voice sputtered in her ear.

Natalie tensed as she always did nowadays when she heard Luke speak and adjusted her earpiece. "CIU-seven," she responded, while the other detectives in the unit chimed in as well. *"CIU-four . . . CIU-two . . . received . . ."*

"We've got a boisterous crowd spilling onto Beulah Miles Road, which is supposed to be closed to pedestrian traffic," Luke told them from the nerve center of tonight's operation, the dispatch area of the station house with its telecommunications equipment and mapping software. "That street is officially closed, but a huge crowd is coming out of the Witches' Ball, and I need a couple of warm bodies down there to monitor the situation while we send over a few squad cars to clear it."

"I'm two blocks away, Lieu," Detective Augie Vickers volunteered, his take-charge voice booming in her earpiece. "You want me to head over there?"

"Go ahead, Augie."

"Me also," Mike Anderson chimed in.

"Go, Mike. The rest of the team continue along your assigned routes," Luke said.

"You don't need any more of us?" Natalie asked.

"Negative. Continue along your assigned routes. Out."

She signed off and grimaced at her phone. "Fuck you, too." Luke's cold professionalism wounded her, but it no longer surprised her. After Grace passed away last April, Natalie had done her very best to push him away. She didn't know why. It was just that Luke's sympathy, his kindness, only seemed to make things worse, like poking a raw wound and never letting it heal. The more he tried to help, the worse Natalie felt, until finally Luke gave up and complied with her wishes, leaving her to her grief. Now she missed him. Really missed him. They used to meet casually after work just to gripe and shoot the shit. Their friendship had spanned decades, reaching all the way back to their tumultuous childhoods, and Natalie had secretly been in love with him forever. Their mutual alienation was painful, and lately she felt a desire to move closer to Luke, but the misunderstandings had piled up and the cracks in their relationship had become chasms.

Not only was her relationship with Luke on the fritz but Detective Brandon Buckner was avoiding her, too. Brandon and Natalie had once been good buddies, but the tragic events of last April had torn them apart. He recently confessed he didn't *want* to hate Natalie—he just couldn't help himself. Whenever he looked at her, Brandon was reminded of his dead wife. He refused to talk to her outside of their official duties and had taken the night shift in order to avoid working with her. Every time she interacted with Luke or Brandon, she wanted to crawl home and pull the covers over her head.

Now her scalp itched beneath the sweaty hatband, and her feet ached. Natalie had been walking for three hours straight without a break. The air smelled spicy and greasy from the open-air market food carts. There were tacky storefront displays of broomstick-riding witches, swooping bats, and a mock-dungeon with skeletons chained to the walls. People screamed with delight at the Freddy Krueger and Beetlejuice look-alikes. The BLPD was stretched thin to accommodate long lines for various guided tours, museum exhibits, Halloween-themed balls, fortune-teller booths, haunted houses, and graveyard tours. Visitors could buy combination tickets, and comfortable shoes were recommended. For the kids, there were corn mazes, pumpkin-decorating contests, and other family-friendly activities.

Natalie wiped her sweaty hands on her pants. All she wanted was a small square of space to call her own—just for a minute. She hadn't taken a break in hours. She crossed the town square, past the filled-to-capacity pubs and neon-lit occult shops selling everything from mojo balls to freakish displays of "once-alive" things fermenting in glass jars. There were sightseeing double-decker buses, street performers, and barkers promoting guided tours. Merchants offered free samples of sugar skulls and sickly sweet candies, as much as you could eat.

A thousand overlapping conversations echoed across the square. Batman and Wonder Woman were extremely popular this year. So were Pennywise the Clown and all the Disney princesses—Ariel, Belle, Rapunzel. She spotted Lord Voldemort holding hands with Miss Dead Universe and Kylo Ren kissing Lizzie Borden, along with the usual contingent of ghosts, witches, ghouls, zombies, and murdered Victorian ladies.

On the next block, a group of teenage girls were huddled together at the curb, laughing and giggling. They'd gone full Goth—four of them were dressed in black, and a fifth wore a bloodstained white dress. The four Goth girls held rubber knives dripping with fake blood, and it took Natalie a moment to realize who they were supposed to be—Daisy, Grace, Bunny, and Lindsey, along with their unwitting victim in white, Willow Lockhart. The girls didn't notice Natalie, but she recognized them vaguely from Ellie's school. Chatting away excitedly, they crossed the street and disappeared around the corner.

Natalie felt loose as liquid, no bones to hold her upright. Her heart beat erratically as she ducked into the nearest bistro. She locked herself in the restroom and stood for a numb moment, shivering with surprise and anger. At home, there was a chart on the refrigerator door delineating the seven stages of grief. First came shock and denial; then came pain and guilt; followed by anger and bargaining; then depression and loneliness; fighting spirit; reconstruction; and finally, acceptance and hope. She couldn't wait to get to that last fucking stage. She figured she must be hovering over the fourth stage right about now.

Depression and loneliness.

She'd isolated herself from the people who mattered the most.

There was only one person she could turn to in times like this. Natalie took out her phone and called Dr. Russ Swinton, the wise old man of medicine, director of the bustling intensive care unit at Langston Memorial Hospital. A no-nonsense professional in his mid-fifties, saddlebag-tough and emotionless, which made him exactly the kind of person she needed right now. Twenty-one years ago, Russ had examined Natalie after she'd been attacked in the woods. Now he was helping her through one of the most difficult periods of her life.

After five rings, he picked up. "Yes?" he said in a crisp, intimidating tone. There were muffled hospital sounds in the background.

"Sorry to bother you, I know it's late . . ."

"Natalie, what's up?"

"You said I should call if I experienced any unusual symptoms . . ."

"Yes—why? What's going on?"

What's up? What's up? She suddenly wasn't sure how to answer that complicated question. Her mind filled with so many thoughts, it went blank. "My heart is pounding. Feels like it's skipping beats."

"Where are you?"

"Town Square. In Maurice's Bistro. I'm on duty tonight. Undercover."

"What triggered the palpitations?"

"I saw a group of teenage girls dressed up for Halloween as Grace and Daisy and Bunny, you know, carrying bloody knives . . . the whole bit."

"I see." He paused. "That must've been very jarring."

Six months ago, Natalie's older sister, Grace, had confessed to killing two people: first, her best friend, Daisy Buckner, who'd been threatening to reveal a horrifying secret they shared. When Grace and Daisy were teenagers, they formed a coven and killed Natalie's other sister, Willow, stabbing her twenty-seven times. Willow's boyfriend at the time, Justin Fowler, had gone to prison for it. And then last April, shortly after Grace had confessed these terrible things to Natalie, she'd taken her own life.

And so yes, it was rather jarring to see five teenage girls dressed up for Halloween like two of Natalie's beloved sisters, one of whom had killed the other twenty years ago.

Jarring.

"Are you experiencing any other symptoms, Natalie?"

"Shortness of breath." She swallowed a sob. "Do you think it could have something to do with the reduced dosage?" For a while, she'd been on antidepressants, and Dr. Swinton was helping her taper off them.

"It sounds to me like a panic attack. I can't be sure over the phone. The ER's a zoo right now, but if you can make it down here, I'll squeeze you in."

"No, that's okay," she backtracked, staring at her reflection in the mirror. She had stopped panting. Her heart rate was returning to normal, although her face was slick with sweat. She cleared her throat and said, "I'm feeling better now." She placed two fingers over the pulse point on her throat. "It helps to talk."

"You sure?"

"Yeah, I'm feeling much better. Thanks, Doc."

"No problem. Listen. Call Sofia in the morning and set up an appointment for this week, whenever you can make it in. I'd like to run a few tests. I think we should decrease the dosage by twenty-five milligrams every two weeks, instead of fifty milligrams like we've been doing."

"Okay," she said, feeling embarrassed because she shouldn't have panicked like that. "I'll call Sofia tomorrow."

"And Natalie, if you experience any other symptoms tonight, drop everything and get over to the ER. I'm leaving shortly, but Dr. Evander will be taking over, and I'll fill him in on the situation. Okay?"

"Promise. Thanks again." She hung up.

2

Natalie splashed cold water on her face, straightened her uniform, and headed out again, turning west on Eastham Street, where the carnival atmosphere was ramped to eleven—drunks stumbling out of the bars, music blasting from every venue.

She checked her watch. According to the duty roster, her next assignment was to join the team monitoring the large gathering on Abby's Hex Peninsula, where the mannequins were scheduled to burn at midnight. Abby's Hex was the last place in the world Natalie wanted to be. She could feel another panic attack coming on—that heart-skipping arrhythmia brought on by stress. Where were her boundaries lately? She used to have boundaries. Nowadays it was impossible to define the edges of her grief.

She turned west onto Sarah Hutchins Drive, then took a shortcut toward the rutted parking lot behind the Barkin' Dawg, where the CIU no longer had their weekly meetups. The Howard Street lot was one of Burning Lake's best-kept secrets, since it provided the fastest way out of downtown during the hectic month of October, bypassing the worst of the traffic. Only the locals knew about it.

There was a flyer stuck under the windshield wiper of her smoke-gray

Honda Pilot—a discount coupon for the Midnight Graves Tour. She crumpled it up and tossed it in back, then got in and rested her head against the steering wheel. She swam in a kind of waking dream, not fully present. The grief was always there like a clinging mist.

She powered down her window and let the night air cool her face. Like her father, Joey, used to say, "It's not the burden that weighs you down— it's how you carry it."

Five minutes later, she'd left downtown behind and was heading north into the woods. The northern quadrant of Burning Lake consisted mostly of conservancy lands and wealthy neighborhoods where the estates were passed down from generation to generation, and the driveways snaked elegantly into the woods. She would take Route 151 east toward the lake.

Now her radio crackled to life. "Calling all available units . . ."

Natalie scooped up the mike and responded, "This is CIU-seven."

"There's been a report of a disturbance on Hollins Drive," Dispatch said. "Private residence. A group of uninvited guests are demanding to be let into the party."

"I'm near that location now. ETA three minutes. What's the address, Dennis?"

"Seventy-three Hollins."

She knew who lived there. Hunter Rose, the founder of Rose Security Software. "Responding to the call," she said and dunked the mike back in its cradle on the dash. She was grateful for the diversion. Abby's Hex would have to wait.

She took the covered bridge across Swift Run Creek, then drove past turn-of-the-century homes nestled in old pine groves. There were ten historic covered bridges in Burning Lake, and at least half of them were in desperate need of repair. The town council recently insisted the bridges were safe, despite the large cracks in the concrete abutments. The Swift Run Creek covered bridge was in the worst shape of all, having been damaged in last year's spring flood. It was built in 1799, the year of President George Washington's death, and remained an iconic feature in the town's brochure to commemorate New York State's 1799 declaration to end slavery.

Now the old covered bridge was propped up with a bunch of rickety-looking scaffolding.

Natalie drove through the woods for another mile or so before pulling up in front of 73 Hollins Drive. She could hear loud rock music coming from inside the house. Thirty-three-year-old Hunter Rose lived in this nineteenth-century mansion on twenty acres of rugged wilderness. He was one of Burning Lake's most prominent citizens, as well as being an old flame of Natalie's. Not that it mattered. Their fling only lasted a summer after her sophomore year in college—they'd fucked everywhere inside that house—but she hadn't spoken to him in ages. They traveled in different circles now, and she remembered him being kind of a douche. He was very smart and good-looking, and so self-aware that he readily admitted he'd hurt people in his past, specifically women who'd fallen in love with him. He confessed to Natalie that he didn't think much of it because he hadn't promised them anything. She found his candor repugnant, but also refreshing, since most people would've gone to great lengths to hide their emotional cruelty, but Natalie and Hunter also shared a deeper history that felt like a soft bruised wound between them, and that was probably the main reason she'd broken up with him. Because he couldn't let go of the past.

Overhead, a few passing clouds briefly obscured the three-quarter moon. The sweeping gravel driveway was full of parked cars—BMWs, Bentleys, Lexuses—and there were more high-end vehicles parked on the roadside, where several valets were smoking cigarettes. Natalie spotted Brandon's black Jeep Cherokee parked at the base of the driveway and wondered what he was doing there. Two detectives on the busiest night of the year was a little excessive for a response to a relatively minor call. Brandon and two private security guards in blue jackets were busy corralling a dozen rowdy costumed revelers on the lawn's sloping incline.

Natalie got out. The rambling stone mansion was huge and creepy-looking, a Romanesque Revival folly constructed in the late 1800s by a Boston steel magnate, who had turned it into a luxury resort. In the 1920s, it became a sanitorium for tuberculosis patients. In 1935, it was abandoned and left neglected until the mid-1980s, when Hunter's father bought it and restored it to its former glory. Hunter and his brother had grown up there, which was something Natalie still couldn't imagine.

The clouds blew away and the moon shone down on the immaculate lawn. Festive hanging paper lanterns swayed in the mild breeze. The October air smelled of pine sap. As Natalie approached the group, Michael Myers started texting frantically, Spider-Man threw up on the grass, Esmeralda comforted a wilted-looking Ariel, and Chucky the Doll guzzled booze out of a paper bag. They were all complaining loudly, shouting questions at Brandon and not listening to his answers.

"What's going on?" she asked Brandon.

"They weren't invited. They're creating a ruckus. Mr. Rose doesn't want to press charges. He just wants them off his property."

Mr. Rose. Brandon always buckled to authority.

Floodlights with motion sensors lit the property, and there were at least three outdoor security cameras she could spot. Now Chucky the Doll and Michael Myers were hollering obscenities at each other. Natalie introduced herself and said, "What seems to be the problem here, gentlemen?"

"My girlfriend's in there!" Chucky the Doll shouted, whipping off his mask. Natalie recognized Cody Dugway, the owner of a popular tattoo parlor in town called Cody's Ink. A good businessman. Not a known troublemaker. "She called about twenty minutes ago and said to come over, and now these idiots won't let us in."

"What's her name?" Natalie asked.

"Isabel Miller. They won't let us in."

"It's a private party," Brandon told Cody firmly.

"But my girlfriend's in there," he said stubbornly. "I'm not going anywhere without Isabel."

Just then, a twentysomething woman in a short black dress came hurrying out of the house, clutching her handbag and shoes. She looked around blearily. "Cody?"

"Isabel!" Cody shouted, waving his arms.

"Hi, babe!" She waved back.

She was halfway down the stone path by the time Natalie caught up with her.

"Wait a second. Are you okay?" She took hold of Isabel's arm.

"Fine. S'nothing." Isabel tried to wriggle free. "Leggo. Wanna go home." She hurried down the sloping yard toward the road, where her boyfriend and his friends were waiting for her. A drunken cheer went up.

Natalie looked over at Brandon, who shrugged indifferently from the roadside, his face a blank in the moonlight.

Cody swept Isabel up in his arms and spun her around. Then the uninvited guests got back in their cars and the caravan pulled away.

Natalie turned toward the house, where the party continued unabated. Then she headed down the incline toward Brandon. "Crazy night, huh?"

He opened the door to his Jeep and got in.

"Hey, wait," she said.

His face was grim and rigid as hardened plaster. "What?" he said through the rolled-down window.

Her disappointment was so profound that her mind felt stuck. She leaned against his door and said, "I need something from you, Brandon."

"Yeah, what's that?"

"A little sympathy."

An enormous roar went up inside the house, accompanied by laughter.

"How long are you going to keep avoiding me?" she asked. "Why can't we talk about this? When are we going to move past it and be friends again? I miss you."

He looked away, and she could see a tear glimmering in the corner of one eye.

"When do you plan on forgiving me, you stubborn asshole?"

He turned to her with brutal honesty. "Do you know what I did yesterday, Natalie? I stood inside my house . . . in the kitchen, on the spot where it happened . . . and I tried to picture how it went down that day. And I swear to God, I could sense Daisy's presence . . . and it fucking killed me . . . the utter waste of it all. And I thought, How could this have happened? Why didn't we see it coming? How could I have been so fucking blind?"

Every word felt like the jab of an ice pick.

"And by we—you mean *me*?" she said pointedly. "*I* should've seen it coming? *I* should've known?"

He rubbed his eyes with his index finger and thumb, then heaved a tired sigh. "This isn't about you, Natalie. You've apologized enough. I'm not looking for any more apologies."

"Then what do you want?" she cried. "How am I supposed to fix this?"

He shook his head sadly. "Not everything can be fixed." He started the engine.

She wanted to say, "Fuck you." She wanted to say, "I understand." Instead she stood there feeling clammy and humiliated, and watched him go.

3

Natalie had never missed the burning of the mannequins in her life. But tonight, she didn't want to be there. She didn't want to see it. The spectacle. The scary buzz of the crowd. The raging bonfire lighting the faces of those closest to the pyre. The mannequins' skirts dancing in the flames, accompanied by raucous, drunken laughter.

Burn the witches.

The revelers were out for blood tonight. Everyone squeezed a little closer, straining to see over the heads of those in front of them. See what exactly? The sad spectacle of three female mannequins on fire. What if that was Grace up there in the straw hat and colonial dress? What if it was Daisy or Bunny or Lindsey?

Burn the witches.

Natalie felt a growing tightness in her chest, like fingers wrapping around her heart. She didn't want to revisit the place where her niece had been harmed by her so-called friends. She didn't want to stand on the spot where Abigail, Sarah, and Victoriana had been falsely accused of witchcraft more than three hundred years ago and sentenced to death for their so-called sins. She wondered what had happened to the people of Burning

Lake after 1712. How did the relatives of the accused handle it? How did they continue to live side by side with the judges who'd condemned their loved ones to death?

A burst of maniacal laughter snapped her out of her reverie. Natalie had been monitoring the crowd for almost an hour now, listening to the gleeful chatter of people celebrating other people's pain. She hated the concentration of bodies—too close, too warm, too loud. An ambulance was stationed at the entrance of the peninsula, just in case, and a handful of paramedics roamed the crowds, on the lookout for injuries or accidents. Sometimes people fainted or got too close to the flames. Sometimes they fell down and twisted an ankle. Every year around this time, the hospital emergency room would be clogged with visitors suffering from minor burns, cuts, alcohol poisoning, overdoses, nonlethal car accidents, food poisoning, sprains, and other complaints. During the entire month of October, Burning Lake bled Halloween through its pores.

A great cheer went up. The ceremony was over. An unsettled feeling tickled the back of Natalie's throat. She could sense the shift before it happened—hundreds of people turning around at once and heading back to town. She checked her watch. One o'clock. Her shift was over, but tonight's festivities would continue until dawn.

For the most part, the crowd was orderly and friendly, spontaneous conversations cropping up all around her as everyone made their way through the wooded peninsula back to their cars. These people weren't so bad. They were here to be entertained. They weren't thinking about the past. They were probably carrying around their own pain and needed a break from their routine everyday lives. Natalie straightened her shoulders, and a flock of birds exploded from the treetops as if she'd shaken them off.

Fifteen minutes later, she entered the police station. The dispatcher's phones were ringing off the hook. Hardly anyone was around tonight, except for the officers in charge of the jail and the booking process. There were plenty of drunks in the holding tanks. She could hear them caterwauling as she headed for the elevator bank.

Natalie sorted through her messages as she took an elevator to the third floor, which was overheated and stuffy. The hallway was dark, with stray slants of office light spilling out of open doorways. She dropped her message slips on her desk and removed the cheap eye mask. The unit was quiet tonight. The guys had either gone home or were still out in the field, depending on what shift they'd pulled. She sipped her coffee, took a seat at her desk, and started typing up her reports. After a few minutes, she heard Luke's mellow, confident voice echoing down the hallway. She wiped the fake blood off her cheek, tucked her hair behind her ears, removed the joke badge, and stood up. She followed the sound of his voice down the hallway to his office.

The door was open, a triangle of yellow light slashing across the worn carpet. Luke was on his phone. He glanced up and nodded. "Yeah, okay," he said into the receiver.

She crossed her arms and waited.

"Will do, Chief." He hung up and tossed the newspaper in the trash. "What can I do for you, Natalie?" he said politely. The new Luke. Stiff and formal. The guy she didn't like so much. Who created this monster? Oh, right. She did.

She took a seat and said, "So how was your day?"

He arched an eyebrow. "You want all the gory details?"

"Sure." She smiled. "Why not?"

"Tonight was a clusterfuck."

"Yeah, it was total chaos out there," she said vaguely, her mood toggling between hope and frustration that maybe the walls would tumble down, and they could be their old selves again. She missed their private jokes, traded smirks, and deep commiseration that came from their shared experience of the fucked-up-ness of humankind on this side of the law-enforcement line. When you stopped a guy for a broken taillight who had a severed deer's head bleeding all over the seat beside him, then you understood what it was—deep in your bones—to be a cop.

"Want one?" He offered her a packet of roasted sunflower seeds. He kept dozens in his desk drawer, along with protein bars and packets of granola.

"No, thanks."

"Actually, it was pretty civil compared to last year," he admitted, and she noticed the tiredness in his voice, the tiny etchings around his eyes. "Forty-two arrests, not including DUIs and traffic stops. Lots of alcohol-related transgressions, mostly bar fights, a few people selling souvenirs without a license, some property damage and random gunfire . . . in other words, not bad for this time of year."

"And now it's over."

"Almost." He smiled uneasily.

She didn't know where to put her hands. She crossed her arms and uncrossed them, while an awkward silence filled the room. She raised her chin. There was an unmistakable tension between them.

Tomorrow, November 1, the tourists would be heading home en masse. Order would be restored. The cleanup would begin. Brochures would litter the streets and dumpsters would overflow. Local merchants would close up shop for a few days and count their profits, and everyone would agree—this had to be the most successful Halloween ever. They said that every year. Except for a few hungover stragglers, peace and quiet would descend and the town of Burning Lake would return to normal again.

Except for Natalie, things would never be normal again.

Luke crumpled the packet of sunflower seeds and tossed it in the trash. "Anything else?" he asked. It was completely quiet up here. More desolate than on the first floor.

She cocked an eyebrow. "Anything else? Hmm."

He looked at her sideways. "What?"

"Yeah, okay, I've got a question for you. How long does it take to get over it?"

His eyes narrowed.

"Loss. Grief. How long does it take? When am I going to feel like a regular person again?"

He stared at her with a mixture of uncertainty and compassion. "I advised you months ago to get into grief counseling, Natalie . . ."

"I know, but I'm asking you. Personally. As a friend. All I feel is death all around me. Everything's frozen in time, like that kingdom in the fairy tale where everybody is sound asleep. Frozen. For years. Like ice sculptures. It's like . . . I reach out to touch things, but they're brittle. They break apart in my hands. Nothing moves forward—ever. Everything stagnates. Day after day. It's like I'm trapped inside a terrarium with my hands pressed against the sides, watching my own exhalations fog up the glass. What I mean is . . . tonight, for example, I was surrounded by people, and yet I've never felt so alone. And I didn't think . . . I mean, we've been friends forever."

"We're still friends," he said, looking down at his hands.

"Oh really? This is friendship? This professional, tiptoey politeness?"

He looked at her with such careful eyes, her stomach jumped. "I'm your boss. You work for me. And you know what, Natalie? You were right to create a distance between us. Your instincts were correct."

Fear flickered in her heart. Her lips parted, but she said nothing.

"We should keep our focus on the job, where it belongs. Don't you think?"

"Okay, so I pushed you away. I'm sorry. Can't we get back to the way it was?"

He rubbed his face and said tiredly, "Natalie."

"What?" she said, equally exasperated.

He crossed his arms. "You need to learn to trust yourself."

"What do you mean by that? Trust myself?"

"You know what I mean," he said firmly, forcing her to figure it out.

Her ears grew hot. She thought about it for a moment. "Okay. It's true, I guess, that I don't trust myself anymore. I don't trust my judgment. Because, I mean, how could Grace have fooled me all those years? Why didn't I suspect something?"

He nodded patiently. "But that's not the whole truth. We all slip up sometimes. You have good instincts, Natalie. You're an excellent detective. You can trust that."

"Right. Got it."

"Not everyone catches everything. Not every case gets solved. That's just life."

She pretended to suck it up, even though she felt a rock-hard disappointment in her gut. She should've known there was something wrong with Grace.

"And besides," he said, "you solved one of the biggest cases upstate New York has ever seen."

"Oh God. I'm so sick of hearing about the Crow Killer, Luke."

"I'm just saying . . ."

"Saying what? Win some, lose some?"

He looked away, his expression hardening.

Natalie wanted to cry.

She got up to leave, and it was as if he saw her vulnerability, and it made him want to protect her, because he leaned forward and said, "Natalie?"

She stood motionless. The room grew still.

"If Brandon has a beef with you, that's his problem. If he can't act like a mature, responsible adult and work things out, then let it go. Ignore him."

She nodded, tears tremoring in the corners of her eyes.

"My door is always open. And no matter what . . . I've got your back."

"I hope so."

"Don't hope. You can count on it."

"Thanks." She walked swiftly away from him.

4

Natalie drove home chasing the three-quarter moon. The car radio prickled with static, so she turned it off and listened to the crackling hum of the asphalt underneath her tires as she drove past old farmsteads and orchards. Finally, she was home.

The old house needed a lot of work. The gray paint was peeling off the siding in flakes as big as maple leaves. You couldn't tell what color it had once been—white or green or yellow—who knew? The windows were drafty and the window frames were warped. She needed to replace them with updated energy-efficient windows. The house bled heat. She couldn't stand the thought of going through another winter hopping from electric heater to the stove, crouching over inefficient heating vents and warming her hands on the toaster, for fuck's sake.

Moonlight invaded the interior of the big drafty house. She dropped her stuff on the living-room sofa and thought about moving across town to one of the nicer neighborhoods where it wasn't so isolated. She'd been thinking about renovating and selling this one. At the very least it would keep her busy, now that Halloween season was over and done with. Max Callahan, an old friend of hers from her high school days, had been advising her that she should probably work with a contractor, but she wanted to do it herself. It was liberating to think that no one would be able to stop her. She could strip off that fugly, faded-fucking-flowery wallpaper, replaster the ceiling, and repaint the walls. She could flip this house and relocate to a vastly more modern residence with up-to-date fixtures and a dishwasher that actually worked.

But deep down, Natalie understood why she'd probably never leave Wildwood Road. The house contained countless little mysteries, shiny beads of memory, dust particles of daydreams. The sun slanted down hard in the morning, highlighting the kitchen's cubbyholes for knickknacks and the little hideaway ironing board. The refrigerator magnets that once held Natalie's homework now displayed Ellie's postcards. Out back, past Deborah's overgrown garden, was the pet cemetery for the girls' goldfish, hamsters, and guinea pigs. In the living room, the old pine shelving her father had put up one long-ago summer still contained her and Grace's and Willow's favorite childhood books. Natalie cherished these memories and couldn't imagine her life without these daily reminders.

Now she wandered into the kitchen, thinking she should eat. She opened the cupboards—Kashi cookies, cinnamon Pop-Tarts, instant cocoa with baby marshmallows, Snapple iced tea. She didn't want anything. Just water. She fetched a glass from the cupboard and dropped it. It shattered on the worn tiled floor.

"Oh, shit."

She got the dustpan and broom from the narrow closet and swept everything up, then realized she'd broken one of her mother's prized possessions—it was probably a collector's item by now—those cheap Fred Flintstone jelly glasses Deborah inherited from her mother, Grandma Lilith, who used to save money in the early 1960s by purchasing Welch's grape jelly and using the jars as drinking glasses. There were only a dozen left—Pebbles, Bamm-Bamm, Dino the dinosaur, Fred, Betty Rubble. Scratch that. Now there were eleven.

Natalie burst into tears.

Everything she touched broke.

She cleaned it up, tossed it out, then went upstairs to bed. She got undressed, put on her extra-large T-shirt, slipped under the covers, and closed her eyes. Behind her eyelids, ghosts came to life.

Natalie, Grace, and Willow—the three of them hanging out in the backyard, swinging, and riding their bikes. Sometimes they had friends over, Daisy and Bunny and Lindsey and Bella and Adam and Bobby and Max.

Natalie's mental exhaustion was beginning to supersede her physical exhaustion. She didn't know if she would be getting any sleep tonight. She had to get up early in the morning, since she'd volunteered for the annual cleanup—another ploy to keep herself busy. The festivities had been going on for the entire month of October, and now thousands upon thousands of tourists would be packing their bags, and tomorrow's mass exodus meant that they would be leaving behind block after block of litter in their wake. Tons of it. In some areas, the trash would be so thick you'd have to wade through it. Mountains of trash bags would pile up on every corner. Recovery could take days. One year, it took an entire week. Natalie had signed up to help with the voluntary efforts, and the longer it took them to clean up, the busier she would be.

Oh God. Not another sleepless night.

She lay awake, staring at the green glow of the digital clock, impatient for dawn.

5

NOVEMBER 1, THE DAY AFTER HALLOWEEN

At 6:00 A.M., Natalie reached out and smacked off her alarm clock before it had a chance to blast in her ear. Still fuzzy from back-to-back shifts, she got out of bed, took a long hot shower, made a fresh pot of coffee, and grabbed a Pop-Tart. It was supposed to be her day off, but Natalie had signed up for the annual post-Halloween cleanup, and she didn't want to be late.

The job was voluntary, but it came with a lot of rules. You were supposed to dress down for the occasion, so she put on a worn pair of jeans, a paint-spotted T-shirt, a hoodie with holes in the elbows, and a ratty pair of sneakers—items of clothing she didn't mind throwing away. After eight hours of handling garbage, the smell would weave itself so thoroughly into the fabric that you couldn't salvage them. They'd have to be tossed.

Cleanup began at dawn and carried on until midnight, with crews working in shifts. It took a lot of manpower to remove the tons of rubbish left behind. Sometimes it took three or four days, but every single one of the volunteers agreed they would tough it out until the streets of Burning Lake were swept clean and businesses could reopen.

Not wanting to be late, Natalie loaded up the dishwasher, put on her mandatory orange safety vest over her hoodie, scooped up her keys, and drove into town, where she signed an attendance sheet and joined a hundred other volunteers.

Dozens of bright-eyed young members of several nonprofit organizations had shown up, along with plenty of local volunteers, including public works employees and off-duty police officers. Vans transported the volunteers to their assigned locations. Tons of trash filled the streets this morning. In places, huge overflowing piles of broken lawn chairs, overturned garbage cans, and large pieces of debris were blocking traffic, and the vans occasionally had to turn around and find another route in.

Natalie was assigned to a three-block section of Sarah Hutchins Drive, which looked like a hurricane had blown through. She was handed a pair of puncture-resistant gloves and a surgical mask for the dust before she got out of the van. She stood for a moment with her five-man crew, scanning the commercial district. On every corner, mountains of bulging Hefty bags waited to be picked up in front of the elegant Victorian buildings. The sidewalks and alleys were blanketed with fast-food wrappers, foam cups, discarded Halloween masks, sagging pumpkins, hand-painted signs, rumpled coupons, parking tickets, soggy french fries, and half-eaten turkey legs. It was as if the town was lying flat on its ass and clasping its hungover head.

One of the volunteers on Natalie's crew, a middle-aged man, had been assigned the task of shoveling trash into a wheeled garbage can. She listened to his raspy breathing as she got to work picking up beer bottles and filling one heavy-duty trash bag after another, until they were almost too heavy to carry. She dragged them over to the nearest corner and stacked them on the curb. Their goal was to empty these three blocks by three o'clock this afternoon, then move on to the next location. After they were done, a dump truck would swing by to collect the piles of trash. Once the dump trucks had carted the garbage away, a street sweeper would pass through.

It was a picture-perfect Monday morning. November 1. There was a frosty chill in the air. Church bells tolled, and pigeons scurried out of their way, flapping clumsily toward the rooftops. All the businesses in town were shuttered this morning, and very few people were out walking around besides the volunteers. NO PARKING signs covered the meters. No more activity. No more hustle and bustle.

It worried Natalie, because she welcomed the chaos. She coped with Grace's death by keeping busy. She'd volunteered for as much overtime as she could handle. It kept her from thinking. It exhausted her. She slept like a baby. Every night this month there had been drama. Sirens. Partying. People smoking weed in the cemeteries. Shoplifting. Drunk driving. Speeding. Jaywalking. Crowds of rowdy teenagers. But all good things had to come to an end.

Natalie wondered how she was going to fill her time going forward— maybe get started right away on renovating her house. She wanted to knock down a few walls. She didn't need so many cramped, boxy little rooms. She longed for plenty of space and lots of sun. Maybe buy the kind of plants you couldn't kill. Open up the place and let it breathe.

"Natalie?" Rainie Sandhill came out of the shop across the street. Everybody liked Rainie, the owner of Heal Thyself, a New Age boutique. She was a slender blond businesswoman with a wry smile and a big heart. "The party's over, huh?" she said, crossing her arms and surveying the lay of the land.

Natalie smiled. "Yeah, it's dead as a doornail around here." She couldn't prevent the prickles from rising on the back of her neck. Rainie's daughter, Angela, had been marginally involved in the tragic events of last April, but Rainie refused to hold anything against anyone—not India or Berkley, not Lindsey or Daisy or Bunny. Not even Grace. She never mentioned the horrible events of last spring and made it a point to talk about pretty much anything else besides the homicides and their reverberating echoes.

"How much tonnage of trash do you estimate we had this year?" Rainie asked, smiling at Natalie. "Maybe two-hundred-plus?"

"Gee, I don't know," Natalie said honestly.

"They say that's how you measure the success of the season. By the amount of trash that's left behind."

"Makes sense." Natalie wiped the sweat off her brow. "It looks pretty successful from where I'm standing."

Rainie laughed. "I don't get it, Natalie. Every year you're out here."

She shrugged. "It reminds me of my father. He'd take me to the soup kitchen whenever he volunteered. He used to say that love moves in two directions."

"Oh, that's sweet."

Officer Joey Lockhart was a funny guy with a long nose who liked to eat meatball subs for lunch. On those rare occasions when Natalie had gone with him on a ride-along, Joey would tear off one end of his sub and give it to her. He was generous and funny. He taught her how to keep her gloveless hands warm in the winter by folding her thumb under the rest of her fingers, like pigs in a blanket. "See that?" he'd say, showing her how it worked. "That'll keep 'em nice and toasty, so you can keep walking the beat without getting frostbite. Pro tip."

Now Natalie tossed another beer bottle into the trash bag.

"Well, anyway," Rainie said. "You guys are the unsung heroes of Halloween, if you ask me. Here you are, raking, sweeping, and hauling all this trash off to the landfills." She squinted down the street, where several front-end loaders and garbage trucks rumbled in the distance.

A cool breeze sent ribbons of glitter confetti snaking across the asphalt, and a shiver shot across Natalie's scalp. Traffic would have to be diverted, which meant more cops working triple shifts this week. She was grateful for the opportunity not to think. Hard work and no play didn't make Natalie a dull girl. It made her sleepy and blank, which was exactly what she wanted.

"Last year, it took five whole days to clean up this mess," Rainie said, biting her thumbnail and eyeing Natalie with concern in her pale hazel eyes.

"It'll be back to normal soon," Natalie reassured her.

"I hope so. Would you like a cup of coffee, Natalie?"

"No, thanks. Maybe later."

Dr. Swinton had advised Natalie to find somebody she could trust. Maybe Rainie was that person? After all, Natalie didn't have a whole lot of female friends. Most of her friends were guys. Maybe that was fucked up.

Rainie leaned forward and spoke to the rasping middle-aged man with the shovel. "Hello? Sir? Would you like some coffee?"

"Oh," he said, resting his shovel on the ground. "Thanks, Rainie."

"Cream and sugar?"

"Oh, yes. Please."

"Coming right up." Rainie hurried across the street and ducked into her shop.

Natalie spent the next couple of hours raking up refuse and tossing overstuffed trash bags into a big pile for the dump trucks to cart away. At ten o'clock, bells tolled all over town. The middle-aged man's breathing had grown increasingly ragged, and she finally urged him to go home. Trickles of sweat ran down her back. The sun was high in the sky. She picked up a crumpled brochure that said, "Looking for a wicked good time?"

"Detective?"

She glanced up and spotted a thirtysomething public works employee waving at her from an alley about a block and a half away. A nerdy-looking guy in coveralls. She set down her rake, took off her gloves, and went to see what he wanted. "Hello, there. What's up?"

He pointed into the alley behind him with a greasy thumb and said, "Something's down there. In the dumpster."

She frowned. "What do you mean?"

"At first I thought it was a mannequin. Just the arm part, because it was sticking out of the side door, you know? But when I pulled on the hand, I realized it was attached to a body." He grimaced and swallowed hard.

A tickle of nausea flared at the back of her throat. "Stay here," she told him, heading into the alley to investigate. It was narrow and littered with paper trash caught up in little whirlwinds of air. Matted patches of dead leaves had collected in the brick corners.

An eerie quiet pressed against her ears. Her hands were trembling. The sheer scope and horror of the events of last spring still paralyzed her sometimes. But as a detective, she couldn't let past events interfere with the task at hand. All her training kicked in at once.

The forest-green dumpster was a standard front loader with several welded steel forklift pockets on either side. The air around it was cloyingly sweet. On the left flank of the dumpster was a black ribbed sliding door, where people could toss in their trash. There was also a top access lid, but it was five feet or more above the ground and difficult for some to reach. Huddled around the dumpster like sleeping drunks were all the other trash bags that wouldn't fit inside. The dumpster was full to overflowing.

A distant door slapped shut, jarring her. Natalie bit her tongue and could taste the salty warm blood in her mouth. She had a flash of Grace lying in her casket. It was so surreal, to stand there looking at the dead. Where was her laugh? The glint in her eyes? Her joy? Her wry amusement? All gone. It was like staring at an old photograph and wishing it to life. There were only echoes of emotions left, concentric rings of memories billowing outward beyond your grasp.

"Check the side pocket," the public works employee said from the mouth of the alley.

Steeling herself, Natalie tugged on the black plastic handle, but the side door wouldn't budge. It was stuck a quarter of the way open. The air smelled putrid. There was too much trash jamming up the mechanism. She had to wiggle the plastic door, both pushing it open and pulling out stray pieces of trash, mostly flattened cardboard containers. Finally, the door slid all the way open, and the stench of rotting vegetables hit her. She could see a slender arm wedged in between the jammed-together trash—a female arm with grayish skin and delicate, purple-tipped fingers. Natalie felt for a pulse, but of course there was none. The victim was dead.

She stood blinking in the bright sunshine, all her thoughts dog-paddling backward into deeper water. A ripple of resistance blowing through her. No way was she going to get stuck with another drop-everything case. She'd had her fill of notoriety, thanks very much. She didn't want to go down that path again. She refused to stand in the media spotlight, so harsh and glaring. It was true, Natalie wanted to keep busy—but not this way. Let someone else do it. Let Augie or Mike or Brandon take the case. Six months ago, her life had morphed into a nightmare of tabloid headlines and aggressive reporters calling her all hours of the day and night. There was an aggressive journalist from Syracuse who'd practically insisted he was the only one qualified to tell her story—as if she wanted her story to be told. She'd had her fill of sensational articles and internet stalkers. She was sick of the trollish behavior and just-plain-weird serial killer fanboys. She didn't want to know how many bloodthirsty people there were in the world.

But Natalie was holding on to the dead woman's hand, so pale and fragile, and she simply couldn't let go. "Okay," she whispered. "I won't abandon you."

6

It took two officers in hazmat suits approximately thirty-five minutes to remove the body from the dumpster and place it on a tarp in the middle of the alley, and now the victim was hidden from view by a hastily constructed tent. Half a dozen officers were scouring the crime scene for physical evidence, while Natalie sent more officers out across the neighborhood to canvass for potential witnesses. The coroner was on his way. So was Luke.

The victim—Jane Doe, at this point—had been found stripped naked between several layers of trash. No clothes or jewelry had been found on her person. The plan was to take the dumpster and all of its contents down to the police impound lot for further scrutiny, once the coroner had performed his preliminary exam.

Jane Doe was a Caucasian female, five foot three, approximately twenty to twenty-five years old. She had a pretty face and a petite body, and the only identifying marks Natalie could find were a few moles, an old appendix scar, and a recent-looking tattoo of an unknown symbol on her upper left arm. The victim's hands were bunched into fists, clutching at stray pieces of trash—which meant that she may have been alive when she was tossed in the dumpster. Last but not least, there was a prominent hickey on the underside of Jane Doe's chin that reminded Natalie of her childhood friend Bella Striver.

Twelve years ago, Bella had run off to California on the night of their high school graduation, and Natalie had never seen or heard from her again. Bella used to have a similar mark under her chin, an oval-shaped callus about the size of a silver dollar. It wasn't a hickey, although it could've been mistaken for one. Natalie recognized this unique mark. On a hunch, she gently pried open the victim's left hand—leaving intact the cigarette butt and rumpled candy bar wrapper—and studied the victim's fingertips. Just as she'd suspected, they were hard and calloused. She checked the right hand—there were no such calluses on the fingertips of Jane Doe's right hand.

The muscles of Natalie's throat constricted. It was starting to make sense. She exited the tent and took a deep breath. She activated her phone and called Luke, but it went straight to his voicemail. "Hi, it's me," Natalie said. "I found something interesting. Call me as soon as you get this." She hung up.

The centuries-old alley was narrow and poorly lit at night. Yesterday, there had been a steady flow of foot traffic less than thirty feet away from the dumpster. If Jane Doe was attacked in the alley, then chances are she would've screamed. However, since it was Halloween, her cries for help could've been mistaken for mock terror. Halloween season was all about drunken shrieks of laughter. Would anyone in that rowdy, noisy crowd on Sarah Hutchins Drive have come running?

Natalie felt sick to her stomach. There was a faint smell of decomp on her clothes. When Willow was killed, Bella had come over to Natalie's house and stayed up with her all night long. They talked quietly, and Bella let Natalie cry on her shoulder as much as she needed to.

Now Natalie tried to shake off her sense of detachment, but it kept threatening to overpower her. Like her father used to say, "You have to be fully present at a crime scene. Alert and aware."

Focus, Natalie.

She ducked back into the makeshift tent and propped the tent flap open, letting in a swath of sunlight that illuminated Jane Doe's mahogany-colored hair. Her vivid blue eyes reflected the azure chill of the November sky. On the back of her hands were ink stamps from various local bars, clubs, and pubs—some recognizable, others blurry or smudged. Natalie took pictures, since they could use these stamps to track the victim's whereabouts last night.

Jane Doe's skin was cold to the touch, but no cooler than the surrounding air temperature. Since a naked body cooled faster than a clothed one, the estimated time of death should've been six to eight hours ago. However, although the victim was found naked, she was covered in garbage and not exposed to any air currents, which meant she would've cooled down at a slower rate than normal, approximately ten to twelve hours.

Natalie winced as she rolled the body over. She had seen fossilized and rotting cadavers and oozing remains at the police academy. Her own experience had taught her to pack a jar of Vaseline in her kit, which helped with the smell, but she'd forgotten to replace the empty jar. She knew a lot of facts about dead bodies. For instance, buried bodies decomposed seven times more slowly than a body dumped aboveground; the odor of death penetrated air-conditioned rooms and trash bags; the molecules escaping from a decomposing body often clung to your hair and clothes, so that hours later you could still smell the corpse. It was the gift that kept on giving.

Patchy skin discoloration, called lividity, covered a large area of Jane Doe's body where the blood had settled postmortem, or after death—on the backs of her legs, arms, and torso. It was proof she'd died lying on her back inside the dumpster, while more garbage was tossed on top of her. What a gruesome way to go. It made Natalie angry. Sweat trickled from her armpits. She would never get used to the horror of seeing someone so young and healthy dead, her life prematurely snuffed out.

Steeling herself, Natalie pressed her index finger into the back of Jane Doe's thigh. The skin's lividity remained. If you pressed your fingertip firmly against discolored skin, the pressure would cause blanching. Once the pressure was released, the discoloration would return. However, five hours after death, the discoloration would become clotted, and any pressure applied to the skin would no longer cause it to blanch. It was not blanching now, which meant that Jane Doe had been dead for five hours at a minimum.

With gloved hands, Natalie examined the victim's feet and hands for signs of rigor mortis. There was rigidity throughout the body, which suggested that Jane Doe had been dead for at least eight hours. When combined with the body temperature, Natalie felt fairly certain that the time of death was eight to twelve hours ago.

Now an alley cat slithered against the vinyl tent, meowing loudly. Natalie poked the cat's shadow, and it scurried away.

Who was Jane Doe? A tourist, a resident, or a hired performer? Was this a homicide, suicide, or accidental overdose? Natalie couldn't determine the method of death—there were no telltale needle marks, razor cuts, or strangulation marks. No bullet wounds, stab wounds, or signs of blunt trauma. There was some minor bruising on her arms and legs, along with a few cuts and abrasions on her knees, which could've happened during a struggle or from falling down drunk. Natalie would have to wait for the autopsy report to find out whether Jane Doe had been raped, and whether or not this was the result of foul play, but she couldn't rule out suicide or accidental death by suffocation, drug overdose, alcohol poisoning, or any other number of findings. Not yet.

Eight to twelve hours ago, there had been huge crowds on Sarah Hutchins Drive, a mere twelve yards away from the dumpster. If Jane Doe had walked into the alley naked, it would've gone viral by now. But if Jane Doe had been fully clothed when she walked into the alley, how did her attacker or attackers get away with it? Did people ignore her cries for help? Or maybe she walked into the alley with her attacker—perhaps a friend or someone she'd picked up at a bar. Maybe they were making love behind the dumpster when she was attacked?

Maybe someone heard the screams and brushed them aside. Not every witness came forward voluntarily. Fortunately, Natalie knew there were plenty of CCTV cameras in these turn-of-the-century buildings, storefront businesses like Rainie's New Age boutique across the street, the occult bookshop next door, the antiques store, and the Laundromat a few blocks down. Maybe they'd get lucky.

Jane Doe's makeup had been carefully applied, but after a night of partying, her lipstick was worn off and there were little glops of mascara under her eyes. Her layered haircut was a good one, and Natalie had noticed a smear of dried gel on a portion of her hair. She touched the substance and found it to be chalky and sticky. Was that semen or hair gel or something else?

Today's absence of people left a neglectful silence behind. A mild breeze sent loose swirls of dust spinning across the brick walkway. Jane Doe and her attacker weren't the only people to have entered the alley last night. Addicts used these alleyways to score drugs, to shit and piss and get drunk in, and anyone from last night's crowds could've come in here and trampled over potential evidence. An unknown number of employees from local businesses had dumped their trash here, depositing garbage on top of the body, unaware that the victim lay helpless or dead inside.

Natalie left the tent and stood with her face toward the sun. Soon the coroner would make his preliminary findings and remove the body to the morgue. Afterward, Natalie's team could take full control of the dumpster and transport it across town to the impound lot for further scrutiny. Maybe they'd find more clues inside.

In a typical crime scene, you'd find dozens of evidence cards dotting the landscape, but after forty-five minutes they'd accumulated well over eighty orange placards. Not a good sign. All this random trace would create time-consuming false leads.

She spotted the calico cat slithering along the sooty brick wall, braiding its way through the weeds that grew from the crumbling sidewalk. The cat paused to sniff at a patch of crabgrass, and Natalie went over to see what he was pawing at. She shooed the cat away and plucked a used condom from the weeds, studying it briefly before tagging and bagging it.

Luke pulled up in front of the alley in his midnight-blue Ford Ranger and got out. "Got your message," he said, walking toward her. "What's up?"

"She played the violin," Natalie told him.

7

Luke ducked under the yellow crime tape and joined Natalie inside the makeshift tent. Jane Doe floated like an ivory carving on a sea-blue tarp. Together they knelt beside the body, while Natalie pointed out the reddish mark on her neck. "It's called a violin hickey."

He leaned in for closer inspection, his frown deepening.

"Also known as fiddler's neck," she said. "It's a callus created by excessive practicing of the violin, due to constant pressure on the underside of the chin from where the violin rests." Still wearing gloves, Natalie lifted Jane Doe's left arm and turned it over so that her hand was palm side up. The dead woman's limbs were surprisingly insubstantial—as lightweight as a bird with its wings folded. "These calluses on the fingertips of her left hand are from playing the violin, depressing the strings on the fingerboard. My childhood friend Bella had similar calluses. The other hand holds the bow, so there aren't any calluses." She gently put the hand down. "Also, I found a gummy substance in her hair." She showed him. "Could be rosin. Violinists will rub rosin on their bows to make them sticky. The stickiness enhances the contact between the bow and the strings."

He sat back on his heels. "So she's a violinist. Was she a hired musician?"

"We're canvassing the area now, trying to find out. We could be looking at a street performer, or part of a string quartet."

Hundreds of musicians flocked to Burning Lake during the month of October, when dozens of venues featured rock bands, rhythm and blues, honky-tonk, rockabilly, house music, folk singers, classical chamber ensembles, soloists, string quartets, and madrigals. There was also an annual Halloween-themed music festival, which had been held in Percival Burton Park last Friday evening.

"Did you find any ID on her?" Luke asked.

"Nothing yet. After the coroner completes his preliminary, I'll have the dumpster hauled down to the impound lot, where we can forensically sort through the garbage. Hopefully, we'll find out who she is soon enough."

"What's your time of death estimate?"

"Eight to twelve hours ago."

He rubbed his jaw thoughtfully and studied the body. The victim's pale skin was smudged with dirt and grime from the dumpster. "What about method of death?"

"I couldn't find any strangulation marks or puncture wounds. No signs of blunt trauma, no evidence of violent assault. No needle marks. Just some minor bruising, and a few scrapes on her knees, maybe from falling down. There was a small amount of vomit inside her mouth, which could indicate an overdose. I can't tell if she was raped. We're going to have to wait for the autopsy."

Luke nodded. "Eight to twelve hours ago . . . so we're talking midnight to four in the morning. Why would she walk into a dead-end alley at that time of night? It's deep and narrow, not very well lit. The dumpster's a good thirty-five feet away from the street. Maybe the crowd size made her feel safe, but why come in here? For what purpose? Drugs? Hookup?"

"She doesn't look like a junkie," Natalie said. "No track marks or huffer's rash. No bags under the eyes. No gauntness. Her makeup was skillfully applied. She had a good haircut and appears to be in great shape physically.

A jogger, maybe. Her teeth are well-maintained. No infections or skin rashes." The victim's opaque gaze was fixed on the tent ceiling. "I found a used condom on the sidewalk a few yards from the dumpster, but it looks pretty old. I'm guessing she's a musician or music student. Bella used to train at the conservatory in Chaste Falls, if I remember correctly."

Luke looked at her. "The one up north?"

She nodded. "That's as good a place to start as any, if we don't find her ID."

Luke crossed his arms. "Check the missing persons reports for Upstate New York, starting with Chaste Falls. What about physical evidence?"

"The only problem is, we've got too much of it," she told him. "All this trash. And a lot of businesses in the vicinity use this dumpster for their refuse service, which means there were an unknown number of employees tromping in and out of the alley last night, dumping their trash here. At this point, I think we'd have better luck with the surveillance cameras. The guys are door-to-dooring now, talking to local store owners and asking for videotapes. We've also initiated a request for the traffic cams."

"Good. Maybe we can catch her on tape."

"If we only knew what costume to look for," Natalie added.

"Good point." He frowned. "Maybe her costume's still in the dumpster?"

"Could be." She studied Luke for a moment. He was freshly shaved this morning. He always wore crisp white shirts that were professionally steam cleaned and pressed. He must've spent a fortune on dry cleaning, she thought. He looked as if he'd been lifting lately. Taking care of himself. His face was drawn, and she knew they were both feeling it. A deep sadness, with a brooding, simmering anger underneath it.

"We'll need to do an extensive tox screen for prescription meds, illicit drugs, and roofies," she said. "The sooner the better." She picked up Jane Doe's left hand. "These calluses on the fingertips mean she's right-handed. She would've held the bow in her right hand. And check this out." She turned the pale hand over. "Ink stamps from all the bars and events she attended last night. We can ask the venues for their surveillance tapes as well."

"Which makes the tapes our top priority."

Looking at the body was exhausting, as if death could suck all the hope out of your heart. "Meanwhile, the guys are processing everything for prints, trace, and biologicals," she said.

The sound of sirens broke their concentration. They ducked out of the tent, and the sheer brilliance of the day made her go sun-blind for an instant. The pungent smell of rotting garbage filled her lungs. She waited for her pulse to slow. There was a tune playing inside her head she couldn't get rid of, an old Aerosmith song called "I Don't Want to Miss a Thing."

Natalie didn't want to miss a thing. Not a speck. Not a fiber. Not a hair.

A throng of curious shopkeepers and sanitation workers had gathered at the mouth of the alley, where an officer was posted. Bright yellow tape cordoned off the crime scene, and red leaves blew across the pavement. Natalie thought about Ellie. She thought about her sisters, so whip smart and funny and beautiful. She thought about all the girls who were dead or had gone missing. Life could be so unfair. Joey called it revolving-door injustice.

Now the coroner's maroon van pulled up and parked, its blue-and-reds flashing, and Coroner Barry Fishbeck stepped out. His silver hair and goatee shone platinum in the sun. He came striding over to them, never one for formalities, and got straight to the point. "Where's my Jane Doe?"

"This way." She nodded at the tent.

Natalie felt a creeping nausea and paused outside the tent, while Luke and Barry ducked inside. That song was playing in a loop inside her head. "I Don't Want to Miss a Thing."

Okay. What was she missing?

She crouched down at the tent opening, an early November cold creeping across the back of her neck, and listened to the two seasoned professionals discussing the case, while Jane Doe lay inert and vulnerable, the final kiss of her violin lingering on the underside of her chin.

Natalie looked across the street. Someone nearby must've seen something.

8

The hospitality industry was huge in Burning Lake, with plenty of historic inns and bed-and-breakfasts to choose from. The quirky art galleries, occult bookshops, and artisan bakeries gave the town its eccentric charm. Nestled among the upscale bistros and fortune-tellers was Heal Thyself, a New Age boutique owned by Rainie Sandhill.

Natalie walked in the door and was greeted with soothing music and the scent of patchouli. A hand-painted sign on the wall said, "Don't Divine and Drive." The shelves were stocked with everything from crystal balls to bundled herbs for smudging. You could spend hours thumbing through the self-help books and touchy-feely magazines.

Rainie snuck up behind her. "I saw the commotion outside. What's going on?"

Natalie jumped. "Oh, you startled me, Rainie."

"Sorry, I have a tendency to do that. My shoes." She pointed at her hemp-weave sandals. Her T-shirt said, "Make Pot Legal!" In her mid-thirties, with fashionably short ash-blond hair and clear hazel eyes, Rainie wielded considerable clout in this town. She was the associate director of the Chamber of Commerce, and whenever you walked into her store, you'd get an earful about zoning laws and business regulations. "What's going on out there, Natalie? We're all freaking out."

"We're not sure. That's why I'm here. Is there a place where we can talk?"

"Sure. Follow me." Rainie turned toward the employee behind the counter and said, "Ashley, do you mind taking over? I'll be in my office."

"No problem," barely-out-of-college Ashley responded.

Rainie escorted Natalie down a narrow aisle full of astrology guides, magic wands, ceramic pixies, and how-to books on witchcraft. The roomy office at the back of the shop got a lot of sun. Rainie closed the door behind them and told Natalie to take a seat. "So what happened? Who died?"

"We don't know yet. That's why we're asking all the merchants in the area for their surveillance tapes, if you have any."

"But someone *did* die?" she repeated.

"I can't validate any rumors." News traveled fast in small towns, but Natalie didn't want to cause a panic. "Can you keep it confidential?"

"Absolutely."

"We've had a fatality. A young woman."

"Oh my God." Rainie rubbed her lovely, unlined face. She had a ballet dancer's body under the turquoise yoga pants and tie-dyed tee, and she was what Natalie's mother used to call a careless beauty—the kind who smeared her lipstick on her teeth and pulled her hair into a messy ponytail to distract from her loveliness. "Well, of course, you can have our tapes. I'd be happy to hand them over, but my cameras only point into the shop. They focus on the cash register and the aisles. So I don't know how much help they're going to be."

"No views of the main entrance?" Natalie asked, disappointed.

Rainie shook her head. "Plus, I use an old analog system, and we recycle our tapes, so they can get pretty grainy. It's mostly for catching shoplifters, or God forbid if someone tries to rob us. Nobody's done that yet, but if they ever did, we'd have it on tape. I tell my girls, just hand over the money and let justice take its course."

Natalie nodded resignedly and checked her watch. "Okay, we'll need all your tapes from this past week."

Rainie furrowed her delicate brow. "I only have the last twenty-four hours. Like I said, it's an old system. I've been meaning to upgrade, but you know how it goes . . . time slips by so fast. Budget priorities. Listen," she said, leaning forward confidentially, "Angela's back at school, still struggling with what happened, but she's okay. She and Ellie have kept in touch. I'm so glad to hear Ellie's doing well. How is she?"

"Fine," Natalie said, shifting uncomfortably in her seat, because she didn't really know how Ellie was doing. Ellie was slipping away from her. "She likes Manhattan."

"Who wouldn't?" Rainie said with a lighthearted laugh. "Well, I guess that old cliché is true. Time heals all wounds."

Natalie nodded politely, but the thought of her niece hurt like a toothache. At first they'd been so close, texting and calling and emailing each other all the time, telling each other stories about the funny, smart things Grace used to do. Shared memories that made them laugh or cry.

But there were so many painful memories here in Burning Lake—Ellie's mother was dead, terrible secrets had been revealed, and her best friends had tried to harm her. No wonder Ellie was drifting away. And as she adjusted to her new life in Manhattan with her father, Natalie was unable to bridge the gap created by such an enormous loss. The path back to Ellie felt swampy at best, full of quicksand and slithery stages of grief.

"Angie told me she has a boyfriend now. How great is that?"

Natalie smiled blankly. Ellie hadn't mentioned any boyfriends the last time they talked. But it was a good thing that the girls were getting along. Angela Sandhill had been hauled before the police and interrogated, but she wasn't charged with anything. She became an important witness in Berkley's and India's trials, which had created a rift between the Sandhills, the Cochrans, and the Auberdines. Nowadays, those three families avoided one another, but Rainie never held a grudge. She wasn't a spiteful person.

"I told Angela the other day, whatever you do with your life, please *do not* open a boutique," Rainie said, casually brushing a few strands of blond hair out of her eyes. "With a brick-and-mortar business, you have to run things super-efficiently or else you'll fail. It's not like selling merchandise online. With square footage, you've got to hustle and move your wares.

Move, move, move. Sell, sell, sell. That's what it's all about, I told her. Not about witches or fairy dust or magic."

Natalie nodded, still thinking about Ellie and letting the conversation stray and unravel, unable to rein it in.

"I work all the time, every day," Rainie went on. "Even Sundays are for inventory. I almost never clock out, and it's not just me. We're all struggling—all of us small businesses here in town. That's why I'm so anxious about getting the streets cleaned up as soon as possible, you know? We need to open our doors again. I'm not getting rich off this shit. Don't get me wrong, I love my store. But come on . . . don't tell me we have to wait another three or four days before we can be open for business."

"We're doing our best," Natalie said, losing patience along with her focus.

"Oh, I'm sure you are," Rainie said, backpedaling. "I don't fault any of you. Least of all you, Natalie. I see you out there working your butt off. I don't blame the police. It's just my rotten luck that a dead body shows up across the street, and the cleanup in front of my establishment grinds to a halt."

"Everyone's being inconvenienced. It can't be helped."

Rainie placed her hand over her heart. "Oh, I sound like such a jerk. Don't mind me, Natalie. I'm a stress mess. You know what happened to Ned Bertrand, right? After last Halloween? He had a stroke. And I know why. I know what it feels like to wake up in the middle of the night, thinking you're going to fail. Or you're going to have to fire half your employees or else lose your business. It happened to Kathy Peterson, too, you know? Bell Book and Cupcakes? Everyone *loved* those cupcakes. How the hell could she have gone out of business?"

Natalie's phone buzzed, interrupting them. "Sorry, I have to take this. Hello?"

It was Luke. "Autopsy's in twenty minutes," he said.

"Be right there." She hung up. "Try not to stress about it, Rainie."

She gave an apologetic smile. "I'll try not to. Thanks, Natalie."

"I'll take those tapes now," she said, getting up.

9

Sixty-five-year-old Coroner Barry Fishbeck had a large head with fleshy cheeks and a prominent laugh line on one side of his mouth that gave him a permanently skeptical look. This afternoon in the morgue he wore a long-sleeved gown, a blue surgical cap, a splash shield, shoe covers, and a pair of latex gloves. The lighting inside the autopsy suite was harsh and bright. Merciless, really.

"Ready to proceed, folks?"

Natalie and Luke nodded from the other side of the autopsy table.

Barry adjusted his splash shield and studied the corpse. "We have an unknown Jane Doe," he said into his digital recorder. "Female Caucasian, five foot three and a quarter, weighing approximately a hundred and five pounds. I'm guessing she's twenty to twenty-five years old. Hair is a reddish brown. Eye color is blue. There's a fresh-looking tattoo on her upper left arm near the shoulder. It is inflamed and slightly raised. There's also a prominent red mark on the underside of her chin . . . which Detective Lockhart has identified as . . ." He looked up. "What did you call it, Natalie?"

"A violin hickey," she responded. "My friend Bella used to have one.

Also known as fiddler's neck. It's a callus that forms where the violin rests against the chin."

"So we're looking at a professional violinist then?" Barry inquired.

"I think so. Calluses on the fingertips of the left hand are from depressing the strings of the violin, which would make her right-handed."

"Very good," Barry said, studying Jane Doe's fingertips.

"She might be a performing artist who was hired to play at one of our venues during Halloween," Luke said. "I've asked Mike Anderson to compile a list of seasonal hires for us—any musicians who play the violin . . . a fiddle player in a band . . . a member of a string quartet or chamber ensemble. Hopefully we'll have a name soon."

"Fingers crossed." Barry leaned over Jane Doe and pried open her rigored jaw. It unlocked with a crackling sound that made Natalie wince. "In the meantime, let's see what else we can learn about her."

Natalie's hands gripped the edge of the counter as she steadied herself. The sterile countertop held a tray of surgical tools—forceps, scissors, scalpels, bone saw, a dish for weighing organs, a pair of rib cutters, an electric saw. Not very pleasant, these instruments of death.

"She's had some dental work done," Barry observed. "A root canal and six veneers—excellent work. Her overall health appears to be good. There's an appendix scar. Nothing on the radiographs. No broken bones, fractures, or other injuries. No needle or track marks. She isn't malnourished. No other scars or birthmarks. As to method of death, I'm not finding any overt signs of a struggle, although there are a few contusions on her limbs and abrasions on both knees. You could get those from falling down or from being pushed down. We did a nail scrape earlier, and there's something under the nails, but it could just be grease from the dumpster. Either she was thrown in, or she climbed in, or she tried to crawl out, I don't know . . . we should know more once we get the lab reports back."

Jane Doe's ash-gray hands were sealed inside two plastic bags, and they looked almost sculptural, like art pieces on display.

"What kind of Wiccan symbol is that on her arm?" Luke inquired.

"The tattoo?" Barry said.

"It looks like a witch's sigil," Natalie said, swiping through images on her phone. "It's a personalized occult symbol you can create yourself in order to change certain aspects of your life," she explained. She showed Luke and Barry the Google results on her screen. "It's like making a wish while blowing the candles out on your birthday cake."

"Only it's more permanent," Luke added.

"Right."

"Did you take the print cards yet?" Luke asked Barry, who nodded.

"I gave them to Officer Keegan twenty minutes ago."

"Which means Lenny should have them," Luke told Natalie.

"Hopefully we'll get a match," she said.

Detective Lenny Labruzzo was in charge of processing all trace evidence at the crime scene, but the victim's fingerprints took priority. Natalie knew he'd call them the instant he got a hit off the DMV database. In the meantime, Detective Augie Vickers was in charge of searching through the dumpster at the police impound lot, and they'd Express-Mailed the used condom to the state lab for DNA testing, since that was the one thing the unit wasn't equipped to handle. Natalie secretly wanted to be involved in every aspect of the investigation, but like her father used to say, "Ride the horse with loose reins, as long as it knows where it's going." These experienced detectives all knew where they were going.

Natalie narrowed her focus on random details—Jane Doe's unvarnished nails, her pierced ears, the sparkly silver glitter in her hair. The glitter looked deliberate—part of a costume she'd worn last night. The costume was still missing. Natalie couldn't help but think—*we care so much about how we look, making thoughtful decisions, but then death takes all control away from us.*

"No external signs of penetration, anal or vaginal," Barry said into his recorder. "No apparent trauma, abrasions, or contusions to the area. No semen stains showing up in the black light." He peeled off his gloves. "There's no overt evidence of rape, but I won't know definitively until we've done a complete rape kit and get the swabs back from the lab. I'd say that overall, these minor lacerations and contusions could've happened at any point last night, due to rambunctious partying, but it could also be due to physical assault. I haven't found any evidence to declare this a homicide yet. No broken hyoid bone or other evidence of strangulation. No blunt trauma to the head, no penetrating wounds, no deep bruising to the neck or abdomen. There was a bit of vomitus in her mouth. It's possible she died from a drug overdose or alcohol poisoning, but we'll have to see what the tox screen says." He pulled off his headgear. "During the next phase of the autopsy, I'll be collecting fluids for the toxicology report—blood, urine, vitreous. I'll be drawing blood from various parts of the body, including the eyeball, the femoral vein in the leg, and heart blood. I'll be collecting tissue samples from the liver, brain, lungs, and kidney, plus any stomach contents. We should know more once we get the toxicology results back."

"How long will that take?" Luke asked impatiently.

"Two or three weeks is standard, but since time is of the essence, I'm putting a priority rush on it. There's usually a backlog, but the mayor called this morning to inform me of the significance of the case . . . we can't have healthy young women dying on our watch during our biggest tourist season, now can we? That would be a disaster for the whole town."

"How extensive a tox screen are you talking about?" Natalie asked.

"Given the nature of the festivities . . . we'll be testing for opiates, amphetamines, sedatives, marijuana, alcohol, barbiturates, party drugs—in short, everything under the sun," Barry assured her. "Legal or illegal substances. We'll also be looking for any drug interactions that could've depressed her heart rate and breathing. It's the same kind of extensive drug-testing an emergency room might perform for a patient showing signs of an overdose. We'll be asking for a thorough clinical toxicology." Barry picked up a scalpel and made a deep Y incision across Jane Doe's chest. Then he picked up a pair of rib cutters and said, "This next phase is going to take a while."

Luke and Natalie exchanged a look. Neither one wanted to stick around for the procedure. Barry would spend the next couple of hours performing the rape kit and an internal exam, cutting through the viscera with a pair of scissors and weighing each organ before placing everything into a plastic bag for its return to the body. When that was done, he would sew everything back inside, then store Jane Doe in a refrigerated room until the investigation was over and the funeral home could collect the body for burial.

"Keep us posted," Luke told Barry, then motioned Natalie outside.

They found the exit door and stood on the cement steps, where they had a good view of the eastern end of downtown. Crews were still picking up garbage. The city was paying for the entire cleanup effort out of its annual budget. No one complained about the extra expense, since all those tourist dollars were a welcome boost to the town coffers. But today, the stores were shuttered and traffic was thin. Burning Lake was in recovery mode, with plenty of merchants sleeping in. Despite Rainie's concerns, most people preferred a few days off after four frantic weeks of rampant consumerism.

"We need to identify her as quickly as possible," Luke said. "Find out if any local venues are missing a violinist. Also, we should talk to all the local tattoo parlors . . ."

"You remember Bella Striver, don't you?" Natalie asked.

"Yeah, sure," Luke said with a nod. "I was a teenager when Joey invited me over for spaghetti dinner and Bella was playing the violin in the backyard. You and your sisters were sitting together on the hammock, swinging your legs in perfect symmetry to the music. She was like . . . what? Six years old?"

Natalie smiled. Bella was a pixieish beauty with sparkly eyes and a bouncy smile who used to spend three or four hours a day practicing her violin. The Striver family legend was that when Bella was a toddler, she picked up her father's violin and knew exactly what to do without being told. A natural. A child prodigy. Her father—a former wunderkind himself—was a strict disciplinarian who used to prompt Bella to show off her skills. "Play the Vivaldi for them, and then Rimsky-Korsakov's 'Flight of the Bumblebee.'" He was obsessively attentive and extremely harsh in his criticisms. Over the years, he lost sight of who Bella really was—a normal girl—and, in Natalie's opinion, that was what eventually drove her away from him.

"My violin is practically my *lover*," Bella once complained when they were hanging out as teenagers. "It's so stupid! Dad has big plans for me, but I just want to be a girl and do girlie things, like makeup and dating. Instead, I have no social life, because he wants me to be the next Hilary Hahn or Sarah Chang." Bella was hurt, more hurt than anyone Natalie knew, and that pain was in her music.

At their high school graduation ceremony, Bella played Bach's Chaconne in D Minor to wild applause. The Brilliant Misfits, five best friends, celebrated that night by meeting in the woods. They got drunk and stoned in Funland's old derailed train, slid down the infamous Tongue, and ended up perched on the edge of the Bridge to the Future, predicting where they'd all be ten years from now.

Bella's big dream was to become a pop star and travel around the world. Nobody really knew her, she complained that night—not the real Bella. Instead, all of the adults in her life projected their own hopes and dreams on to her. Her shyness and reticence created a blank canvas on which they splashed their own delusions—they told her she was a gifted prodigy, a future superstar, a blazing comet. "But I'm *not* who they think I am," Bella said bitterly that night on the bridge, one hand clutching the neck of her violin case. "I'm not this whimsical little sprite—this magical elfin genius. I'm a lazy slob. I'm a greedy monster. I want to conquer the fucking world. I want to lie in bed for a thousand years."

Bobby lit a joint and Max passed around a bottle of his parents' tequila, and the five of them got stoned and drunk together, laughing and reminiscing. Eventually Natalie and Bobby wandered off to make out, and at some point, Natalie could hear Bella playing Debussy in the woods, but she assumed that Bella was hanging out with Max and Adam. Then the playing stopped, and Natalie lost her virginity.

All hell broke loose when Bella went missing shortly after midnight. Natalie's father, Joey, became involved in the extensive search for the missing girl, and at one point Mr. Striver came under suspicion. But the prime suspect was Nesbitt Rose, Hunter Rose's younger brother, who'd had cognitive problems since birth and was by his own admission the last person to have seen Bella alive.

Hounded by the media, with the town in an uproar—three weeks after Bella's disappearance, on a drizzly rainy night—Nesbitt sucked on the nozzle of a vacuum cleaner and put an end to his misery. Three months later, Bella's father started receiving letters containing Polaroids that proved that his "missing" daughter was still alive. She was fine, she said. She just had to get away and be her own person. Natalie also received a few letters from Bella, explaining why she ran away. Mostly she blamed it on her ambitious, overbearing father. She said she didn't want to be a violin soloist anymore. As a consequence, the police labeled her a runaway, and the missing persons case was closed.

Eventually, the notes and snapshots from Bella stopped arriving, and no one ever saw or heard from her again. Natalie still missed her. There was a hole in her life where Bella belonged.

"Why do you bring that up?" Luke asked now. "Do you think it's related?"

"No. Maybe. It's too early to say. I just remember the pressure Bella was under to perform. To achieve. How hard her father pushed her, until he finally pushed her away permanently."

"Her father was a suspect, wasn't he?"

Natalie nodded. "Along with Nesbitt Rose. But they were proven innocent after the letters started to arrive."

Her phone rang. It was Augie.

"We hit pay dirt," he told her. "The victim's wallet and clothing were farther down in the dumpster."

"We'll be right over," she told him and hung up.

10

The **police impound** lot was located on the outskirts of town, where historic brick warehouses sat vacant and boarded up. The cement compound was surrounded by a ten-foot security fence. Vehicles were impounded for a variety of reasons, everything from criminal activity to parking violations, but the department also used the facility to store evidence that was too bulky to keep in the station house—things like safes and snowmobiles and dumpsters.

Natalie waited in her car for Luke to pull up behind her at the entrance of the multilevel parking garage. The guard waved them inside. They found parking on sublevel one and took an elevator to the ground floor. Luke accidentally brushed his hand against hers as they both reached for the button. "Sorry." His voice was tight. She could feel her face flushing as she depressed the button.

He studied her for a moment. "I saw Callahan's truck out by your place the other day."

She looked at him, startled, and then looked away, trying to hide her emotions, but she could feel her neck flush a deeper shade of red. "Max Callahan? Yeah, he fixed a roof leak last summer. I've been thinking about renovating the house. Maybe knock down a few walls. Open up the space. Max is advising me about which contractors to hire and stuff," she said awkwardly, more than a bit miffed at him for opening this topic of conversation right before the elevator doors dinged open.

Luke gallantly held the door for her.

"Why do you ask?" she said irritably, stepping out into the hallway.

"Just curious." His slightly amused smile bothered her.

She stored away her mixed feelings about their relationship and put on a take-charge expression. Together they walked through a maze of hallways toward the impound lot's processing center on the ground floor—a cavernous cement room with three large vehicle bays and a loading dock at one end. Today the air reeked of liquefied garbage.

"Lieutenant. Natalie." Augie greeted them at the door.

Detectives Augie Vickers and Lenny Labruzzo wore orange hazmat suits splashed with foul-smelling juices, and the stench nearly knocked Natalie off her feet—a tough combination of oniony sweat, dirty feet, and weeks-old garbage.

"I know, I know," Augie acknowledged with a chuckle. "Give me a root canal. Kill me quick." In his late forties, the hardworking detective was a lifelong bachelor who lived in a man cave of a house, crammed with sports memorabilia, comfortable broad chairs, and state-of-the-art electronics. He had a thick neck and broad shoulders from lifting weights—another fad he'd thrown himself into with abandon. Augie was dogged and methodical, and whatever he decided to do, he would see it through with grim determination to the bitter end.

Lenny, on the other hand, was more laid-back, the type of guy who took life's complications in stride. He'd just become a grandfather and was a few years away from retirement, and no one in the department knew what they were going to do without him. At work, Lenny and Augie referred to themselves as the Fossils.

Lenny was on his knees peering into the empty dumpster like a cave. A magnetized flashlight was stuck to the inside wall, illuminating the grimy interior. Lenny was absorbed with his task, using delicate brushstrokes to apply iridescent fingerprint powder to the metal surfaces.

"Check this out," Augie said excitedly, leading them through a maze of leaky trash bags and semi-organized stacks of garbage.

The main bay area resembled a mechanic's shop. The large open layout contained three vehicle bays equipped with air tools and work lights suspended from the ceiling. The closer they got to the dumpster, the more nasty undertones Natalie could detect—burnt pizza, raw garlic, human sewage. The two detectives had spent the last three hours raking and sifting through the foul-smelling stuff, differentiating the useless from the pertinent, the irrelevant from the potentially important evidence.

They stepped over assorted piles of debris—beer bottles, paper products, maggot-infested half-eaten sandwiches, clumps of human hair from a styling salon, shards of glass, broken umbrellas, fast-food containers, two dead rats, a ton of cigarette butts and scattered coffee grounds, empty pizza boxes, and jagged pieces of scrap metal.

"Now for the important stuff," Augie said, squatting down.

Natalie and Luke knelt down next to him.

Augie handed Natalie a sealed evidence bag. "We found this zipped leather purse with a set of car keys inside, along with some cash, her driver's license and registration, two credit cards, an ATM card, and her medical insurance card. As you can see, the picture on her license matches the victim. Her name is Morgan Chambers. She's twenty-four years old and rents an apartment in Chaste Falls."

"We need to get her picture ID out there as soon as possible to the officers who are door-to-dooring," Natalie said. "They can ask around and find out where she was staying here in town, maybe locate her car. Did you find her cell phone?"

"Not yet, but we're still looking. And get this," Augie said, picking up a large see-through evidence bag. "We think this is the outfit she was wearing last night—Wonder Woman. The shop's name is on the label. We also found a pair of gold hoop earrings, a watch, and a ring that might belong to her, plus a silver necklace with some sort of Wiccan charm on it. We're not positive all the jewelry's hers, but Lenny is going to take everything down to the station and process it for prints and trace later."

"Can I see that?" Natalie asked, and Augie handed her the bag with the jewelry inside. "If she was attacked, then her attacker didn't take any of her jewelry, cash, or credit cards. And in fact, someone must've removed all her jewelry and dropped it in the dumpster. Why?"

"It's pretty weird," Augie agreed.

Natalie swiped through the images on her phone until she came to a close-up of Morgan's tattoo, then held up the silver necklace for comparison. "The Wiccan symbol on the pendant and the tattoo don't correspond." She handed the evidence bag back to Augie. "So we're looking for a Wonder Woman on the surveillance tapes, then?"

Luke took out his phone. "I'll let Mike know. He's in charge of reviewing the tapes."

"And we have to look at the possibility that she might've been attacked elsewhere," Natalie said, "then was transported to the dumpster inside a trash bag." She shuddered at the thought. "Maybe she tore her way out of the bag before she died."

"We didn't find any torn-open trash bags nearby," Augie said. "We didn't find any of her belongings inside a trash bag, either. It was all scattered loose around the vicinity of the body where she lay in the dumpster. We photographed and documented everything as we removed it layer by layer. It's sort of like being an archeologist."

Natalie studied the evidence bag containing the Wonder Woman costume. "Nothing looks ripped or torn, except for the tights . . . small runs in the knees and a few spots of blood where she fell down or was pushed. It corresponds with the scrapes on the victim's knees."

"There weren't any corresponding scrapes on the palms of her hands, though," Luke said. "If she was inebriated and fell down, you'd expect to find scrapes or bruises on the palms of her hands, right?"

Natalie nodded. "Maybe the perp forced her to kneel." She cringed at the thought, goose bumps prickling her arms, and then studied the evidence bag. There was a pair of women's cotton panties inside sporting an illustration of a violin string with a few words printed above it: "This is my G-string."

"Huh. A violin joke," she said, remembering Bella's lame jokes. *Violinists*

aren't violint. Don't be an f-hole. A violinist never frets. This music is R-rated for
sax and violins.

The fluorescent lights buzzed distractingly overhead.

"Anyway, most of the trash in this dumpster came from nearby businesses," Augie said, waving his hand over the debris. "According to the canvassing officers, most of the local establishments typically toss their trash after closing time, but last night was exceptionally busy, so they had their employees do a couple of garbage runs. So far, none of them noticed anything unusual. That area is poorly lit, and they generally use the top lid to deposit the trash, since the side door jams a lot."

"We need to look more closely at those surveillance tapes for anyone carrying a trash bag, and interview every single person who threw away trash last night."

"I'll let Mike know," Luke said, taking out his phone.

"So none of the employees that the guys have interviewed so far used the side door of the dumpster last night?" Natalie asked Augie.

"It gets stuck, so they mostly use the top lid. And the later it got, the fuller the dumpster became, until they had to leave the Hefty bags on the ground. Most of the shops closed around midnight, but the pubs and bars stayed open until two or three in the morning. Some of them didn't close at all." He shrugged. "Halloween's Eve."

"Did you spot any other bloodstains on the clothing?" Natalie asked.

"Just what you see on the tights."

"Those are preliminary findings," Lenny said from the dumpster, his voice echoing through the bays. "I'll be testing everything with luminol back at the station. You can't block out the sunlight well enough here."

Outside, beyond the open doors of the bays, sunlight hammered down on the asphalt and the blue sky bristled with birds. "Looks like all the elements of the costume are accounted for," Natalie said, returning her attention to the evidence bag. "Tights. Dress. Belt. Armbands. Tiara. Everything's a size two. Size seven shoes."

"Did you find any weapons in the dumpster?" Luke asked.

"No, but we're still looking," Augie said.

Natalie and Luke both stood up and thanked them.

Out in the hallway, she told her boss, "Morgan's father is listed on her medical insurance card. I looked up his address online. The Chambers live in the same town, Chaste Falls. I need to drive up there and inform the family."

"Meanwhile, we'll start tracking her time line," Luke said as they headed for the elevators. "Find out exactly where she went last night, and who she talked to. How she ended up in this situation. I'll have Brandon follow up on the hand stamps. He can organize a team of officers to interview the staff of all the clubs, bars, restaurants, and events she attended. Then, as soon as you've informed the family, we'll get her image out to the media ASAP. We'll use her driver's license photograph." He depressed the elevator button—this time she let him. "See if any other witnesses come forward."

They stepped into the elevator together, and it seemed to take forever for the brushed aluminum doors to slide shut. They fell silent as the elevator descended. Luke stared dead ahead, while Natalie glanced at his profile, wondering if he'd changed his mind about them.

The first time she ever met Luke, he was a scrawny kid with a friendly smile, and every single one of his T-shirts had holes or rips in them. His sneakers were threadbare. He chewed on his nails. He was lousy at directions. He celebrated when he passed his driver's license test at sixteen. He bought a beat-up Chevy Nova and got lost on the country roads while blasting the B-52s' "Dirty Back Road" on his crummy RadioShack speakers.

When they were kids, despite being eight years apart, Natalie and Luke used to sit together in the hot summer sun or on a snow-dusted porch, just talking. Just shooting the shit. Luke was the mirror opposite of her ex-boyfriend Zack. He loved old-fashioned tales of heroism and held an image in his head of what a man should be. Strong. Brave. Daring. Sometimes he walked around as if he were wearing a superhero cape.

At the end of every conversation, he would hold out his thumb and Natalie would squeeze it. Thumb squeeze. Their old ritual. Offered instead of a hug. Sometimes Natalie held out her thumb and Luke squeezed it. A sign of loyalty and forever friendship between two mismatched kids—so close and yet years apart.

Luke never liked Zack, which should've been her first clue, since he was a great judge of character. Luke could find your inflection point just by looking at you too long. He could sense deception when you just had to look away. When you could no longer return the probing stare. When it came to Zack, Luke avoided the topic, as if it were off-limits for him to have an opinion one way or the other. But his body language spoke for him. At first, she thought he was being protective like a brother; only in retrospect did she realize he was perhaps a little jealous.

Luke was one of the few people in the world Natalie could honestly be herself around. They'd spent a lot of time together as kids, but whenever they met outside of the confines of the Lockharts' backyard, Luke pretended not to know her. Natalie caught on quickly. She did likewise, even though it confused her.

Now their ages didn't seem to matter. Adulthood leveled the playing field.

She sensed him now, his body, standing next to her in the elevator. She had to acknowledge there was something going on between them. Something old, but also something new. Each time she thought about it, her blood thrummed a little deeper.

The elevator bounced slightly as it landed on sublevel one.

They got out and walked to their respective vehicles.

"Call me if you need anything," Luke said, getting into his Ford Ranger and driving away.

11

Chaste Falls was located thirty miles north of Burning Lake, about a half-hour drive past leafy woods, sprawling farmsteads, and gray stone walls. Natalie tried to stay focused, but soon tendrils of self-doubt began to creep into her thoughts. All kinds of conflicting feelings nestled in her heart, and she burst into tears. Like a grief-stricken bratty kid, she'd dissolved all of her most important relationships, right when she needed them the most. She missed her family, which had been torn from her. She missed her friends. She imagined Luke kissing her with his soft warm lips and felt that tender spot she'd always had for him beginning to swell. He was loose-limbed and athletic, funny and ironic in just the right ways. She'd always had her pick of guys, but Luke was special. They fit perfectly together—she couldn't explain it. Put simply, he "got" her, and she "got" him.

Now a radical thought popped into her head. Part of her wanted to get married and have kids, to dive into a whole new life with Luke. This was no joke. She suddenly wanted the ring and everything. She almost laughed. How ironic. How corny. All her life, Natalie had strived for independence and strength. Back in elementary school, when every other girl wanted to be a princess, Natalie aspired to become like her dad, Officer Joey Lockhart, and catch the bad guys. She saw herself as the hero of her own story, not a princess bride. Certainly not a pregnant princess bride.

Now she brushed away her absurd tears and looked around for a tissue, but there weren't any, so she used the sleeve of her jacket to wipe her wet face. She detected a whiff of decay on her cuff and grimaced. Great, she'd forgotten to change after the autopsy. She berated herself for this oversight, then pushed aside her messy, contradictory emotions and took the next exit off the highway.

Morgan Chambers's parents lived in an upscale neighborhood nestled in the foothills of the Adirondacks. The view was spectacular—a backdrop of mountains veined with ridges and waterfalls. The Georgian-style house on Vista View Drive was flanked by sturdy oaks and well-tended gardens. There was a stained-glass fanlight over the antique six-paneled door.

Natalie rang the doorbell, and Mr. Chambers greeted her—a man in his mid-fifties with faded red hair and sharply focused eyes. He wore bland clothes—a beige sweater, tailored brown pants, comfortable canvas shoes. "Hello? Can I help you?"

"My name is Detective Lockhart," she said, showing him her badge. "I have news about your daughter, Morgan. May I come in?"

The pain in his eyes was staggering. "News?" he repeated softly.

"Yes. Can we talk inside?"

His shoulders sagged. He swallowed hard and looked as if he wanted to slam the door in her face—after all, the first stage of grief was denial.

"Please come in," he said, opening the door.

She followed him into a spacious living room with deep bay windows, mahogany-paneled walls, and a stone fireplace. Natalie sensed that if she ran her finger along the mantelpiece, she wouldn't find a speck of dust.

Now Ms. Chambers came downstairs—a fiftysomething, thin, intense-looking woman. She had a wary expression on her face. "What's going on?"

"This is Detective, um . . ." Mr. Chambers turned toward Natalie, baffled.

"Lockhart." She shook the woman's hand. "Hello, Ms. Chambers. I have some unfortunate news about your daughter, Morgan."

"Unfortunate?" Ms. Chambers repeated anxiously. "What do you mean?"

Natalie could hear the blood squishing through her heart, as if it were made of rubber. She took a deep breath and said, "We found a deceased young woman inside a dumpster in Burning Lake this morning . . . along with your daughter's wallet with her ID inside. I'm sorry, but I need you to confirm that it's Morgan."

They stared at her with crushed expressions. Ms. Chambers pressed her lips together and held herself erect, balancing her grief on her squared shoulders, while Mr. Chambers dragged a chair across the carpet and told his wife, "Have a seat, Heather."

She brushed his concerns aside. "I'm okay."

"Detective, have a seat," Mr. Chambers insisted.

This shiny house couldn't be more different from the one Natalie had grown up in, with its clutter and noise. Here the silence pressed against your ears. No music, no laughter, no barking dogs or raucous children. Natalie was afraid to sit on the antique Chippendale-style chair. Its elegant legs didn't seem capable of holding more weight than a sparrow's. She felt like a visitor at a museum where people just happened to live.

"Thank you." She took a seat and didn't know where to put her hands. There were no armrests. So she folded them in her lap, very ladylike.

Mr. Chambers ushered his wife over to the elegant antique sofa, where they sat side by side like two china cups shivering in their saucers. The house smelled of woodsmoke. The brocaded curtains were parted, allowing a gorgeous view of the backyard. Within all this beauty, ugliness had struck. Natalie had brought death into the house with her—an unforgivable sin.

"I'm sorry, but I need to show you her picture," she said, taking out her phone and swiping through the images. She chose a close-up of Morgan that was the most serene, as if she were merely asleep and not dead. "Is that your daughter?"

Ms. Chambers cupped the phone in her delicate hands like a precious gift. She stared at the screen. Mr. Chambers leaned solicitously over his wife's shoulder and frowned. "Yes, that's her," he said and looked away.

Ms. Chambers handed the phone back. "Would you like something to drink, Detective?" she asked with blank eyes. "Coffee, tea?"

"No, thanks, I'm fine."

"What happened to her?" Heather asked, her face drawn and ghastly pale.

"Heather," Mr. Chambers said gently.

"We don't know how or why she died," Natalie explained as gently as she could. "We found her in one of the dumpsters during our annual cleanup. We're doing everything in our power to find out what happened to your daughter, Ms. Chambers."

"Please. I'm Lawrence, and this is Heather," Mr. Chambers interrupted.

Heather whispered, "Oh my God."

"I'm so sorry for your loss," Natalie said, hating the inadequacy of those words. They were so stupid and scripted-sounding. So fucking brought-to-you-by-*Law & Order*.

Sorry? For my *loss*?

"I know how hard this must be," she continued gently, and Mr. Chambers put a protective arm around his wife. "But I need to ask a few questions." Natalie took out her notebook and pen. "When was the last time you heard from Morgan?"

"About a month or two ago," Mr. Chambers answered, while his wife stared off into space, attempting to process the awful news. "We weren't in regular communication with her. Not like we used to be," he said in a strained voice. "But we let her know she was welcome home at any time. We kept her room exactly the way it was before she moved out. Morgan's a very independent soul. She'd drop by maybe once a month to check in with us."

Natalie nodded. "What was she doing in Burning Lake?"

They glanced at each other.

"We don't know," he admitted.

"So she didn't share that information with you?"

"No," Heather said, trembling all over. "Somehow . . . we've all drifted apart."

"And she plays the violin?" Natalie asked.

Mr. Chambers nodded proudly. "Morgan was a child prodigy. An excellent soloist. I taught her myself. She had a very promising future . . ."

"You taught her yourself?" Natalie repeated.

"I'm a professor of music at the conservatory. She took a few classes with me when she went to school there."

"Which is why she never came around to see us anymore," Heather muttered.

Natalie rested the notebook in her lap. "Why is that? Was there a problem?"

"My wife thinks I'm too hard on Morgan," Professor Chambers explained. "That I demand too much from her as a musician. But I demand the same amount of commitment from all my students. I didn't treat Morgan any differently."

"So you teach the violin at the conservatory?"

"Yes," he said. "Morgan graduated with honors two years ago."

"And the last time you saw her was . . . when exactly?"

"The end of September," Heather said with guarded eyes. "She needed to borrow money again, so she came home and pretended to care about us before asking for five hundred dollars."

"Heather, please," the professor whispered harshly. Then he told Natalie, "Morgan works at the town library, and her salary can barely cover her monthly rent."

"Does she rent the apartment by herself?" Natalie asked.

"No, she has a roommate, Samantha Dreyfus." He gave Natalie the address—it was the same as the one on Morgan's driver's license.

"And she didn't tell you she was going to spend Halloween in Burning Lake?"

"She told us to get a life," Heather muttered hoarsely.

"Get a life?" Natalie repeated, feeling this woman's huge loss emanating from her like a viral infection. In clinging to these minor quibbles, Heather Chambers was still in denial that her daughter would never be able to blame her for anything again.

"She told us to get out of her life," Heather corrected herself angrily, her gold hoop earrings sparkling in the afternoon sun.

"Get out of her life—why is that? What led to this rupture in your relationship?"

"Will you please stop?" the professor barked at his wife, shards of pain in his eyes. "Detective, I think we've had enough questions for today, if you don't mind. Morgan was a wonderful girl. Full of life and laughter. I don't understand why this has happened. I guess I don't understand anything in this crazy world of ours."

Natalie looked at Heather, who was staring into space again, exhausted by her own bitterness. She asked Mr. Chambers, "Did Morgan have any enemies to speak of? Anybody who might've wanted to hurt her?"

"I can't think of a single person who'd want to harm Morgan," he said loudly, and Natalie felt a sharp sympathetic pinch, like a glass shard lodging underneath her fingernail. She paused to let their anger and confusion dissipate.

She picked up a framed photograph of Morgan from the polished wooden side table and asked them, "May I take a picture of this? Do you mind? We're still trying to locate witnesses . . ."

Heather nodded vaguely.

Natalie took a few pictures, then placed the framed photo back on the table.

Lawrence sighed hard. "I love both of my daughters, Detective. I'm very proud of them. There's a shelf in Morgan's room full of all the awards she's won over the years. She was incredibly talented, but after she graduated, I'm afraid she lost faith in herself. I don't know why. I don't know whether it was the company she kept, or her own inner struggles with self-confidence . . . but anyway, she let us know that she needed a little space, and so we gave it to her. But after a few years, the chasm kept widening between us."

Natalie found herself nodding. "You have another daughter?"

"Poppy. Also a gifted violinist. She's seventeen."

"What happened to provoke this alienation between you and Morgan?"

"God only knows. Kids at that age . . . we were just hoping she'd figure out what was bothering her, and eventually come back to us with a stronger sense of purpose." His eyes were bloodshot from straining to hold back the tears. "Anyway . . ." He sighed heavily, as if the world had just tumbled off his shoulders.

"I'm so sorry," Natalie told them. "I don't mean to pry like this."

"We understand," he said, speaking for both of them.

"Do you recognize this item?" Natalie took out her phone again and shared a screenshot of the silver necklace with the Wiccan symbol on it that Lenny and Augie had found in the dumpster.

Heather shook her head. "I've never seen it before."

"Neither have I," Professor Chambers said.

A heavy silence filled the house.

Natalie broke it by saying, "I'd like to take a look at Morgan's room, if that's okay."

Heather tied her silver hair back with a tortoiseshell clip and stood up. "It's right this way, Detective."

12

Morgan Chambers's bedroom was like a shrine to her past accomplishments. The walls and trim work were painted in pastel tones that were pleasing to the eye. The bed was neatly made, crowned with a collection of well-worn plush toys. The comforter was decorated with a pattern of musical staffs. On the oak bureau top was a ceramic jewelry box in the shape of a violin.

A pink music stand was propped in front of a full-length mirror, and adorning the walls were framed photographs of Morgan playing the violin, spanning the decades, from elementary school to college. The tall oak bookcase contained a multitude of awards, plaques, and trophies. Through the bedroom windows, you could see the misty mountain peaks beyond the crimson woods.

"I don't know how to tell Poppy," Heather Chambers said from the doorway. She glanced around the room. "What should I say? She adored Morgan."

Natalie nodded sympathetically. "Tell her . . ." She hesitated.

"Yes?"

Natalie wasn't supposed to say anything. It was against the rules, but fuck it. "Tell her that the longing and sadness will be there like the tide, rolling in and out, awakening and then quieting down. It will come and go, but eventually it won't hurt so much."

Heather ran her hands distractedly through her hair and checked to make sure all the buttons of her Ann Taylor blouse were buttoned up. The color had returned to her cheeks. "I think I'll wait until after you're gone," she said. "Before I tell her. Before I break the news that her sister was tossed away like human garbage." She reached for the doorknob. "You'll let me know if you need anything?"

"Thanks. I will."

Ms. Chambers closed the door behind her, and Natalie was alone in the room. She walked over to the closet, flicked on the light, and rifled through Morgan's clothes. She found the baby-pink skirts of a little girl and the leather jackets of a rebellious teenager. There were rows of shoes— wedge heels and flip-flops, rain boots and New Balance. There were artfully ripped denim jeans, microprinted dresses, yoga pants, and bloat-concealing sweaters. Clothes to fit all sizes and moods.

Moving over to the bookshelf, Natalie counted an impressive number of trophies, plaques, and blue ribbons. Among the awards was a crystal vase shaped like a violin and a plush teddy bear wearing a T-shirt that proclaimed, "Music Is Who I Am."

Natalie flipped on the track lighting and a pure, white light illuminated the leather task chair in front of Morgan's sleek contemporary desk. She picked up a dusty copy of Sylvia Plath's *The Bell Jar*. Tucked inside was a handwritten note from Morgan to her mother, apologizing for an argument they'd had. In heartbreaking fashion, Morgan had dotted all her *i*'s with little hearts. *"I didn't mean to hurt you like that. I'm sorry, Mom."*

Above the desk was a shelving unit full of conflicting influences— *Hunger Games* and Jane Austen, a whimsical figurine of an angel next to a *Bride of Frankenstein* action figure, a ceramic fiddle player next to a chipped dragon. On the wall was a poster of Jascha Heifetz playing the violin. In this room, Natalie sensed the sanity and insanity of an adolescent girl who longed for adulthood, but wasn't ready to abandon her childhood yet.

She suddenly heard the muffled sound of a violin playing. She opened the bedroom door and stepped out into the hallway. The bittersweet, haunting melody coming from behind the closed door at the end of the hall. Natalie followed the alluring sound to its source and knocked. "Hello?"

The music stopped. A few seconds later, the door swung open.

A teenaged girl with clear blue eyes and long auburn hair stood staring back at Natalie. She wore a white tailored blouse over black tights and a beanie that said "Bad Hair Day." She held a violin and bow with experienced panache and observed Natalie with solemn, critical eyes.

"Hello," Natalie said.

"Hello," came the dull-edged response.

"You must be Poppy."

"I must be." The girl stared. "Who are you?"

"My name's Natalie," she said, emotionally torn. On the one hand, she desperately wanted to ask Poppy a few questions about her sister. On the other hand, Poppy didn't know her sister was dead yet—and Natalie understood with gripping clarity what it was like to lose a sister. Besides, she wasn't allowed to interview an adolescent without her parents' consent. It was an awkward situation.

"Hey, you have a badge," the girl said, smiling sweetly.

Natalie looked down at the badge slung around her neck. "I'm a detective."

"Oh, really? What are you doing here? Is this about the dog?" Poppy asked.

"The dog?"

Her eyes rounded with excitement. "Our neighbor's golden retriever keeps running over here and digging up our garden. Mom's apoplectic. You know, 'OMG, my roses!'" She smirked with childish glee. "Her precious roses, right?"

"You should build a sandbox next to the garden," Natalie said. "Trust me, the dog will head straight for the sandbox every single time."

"Really? Wow, that's good advice." Poppy was framed in the doorway, smiling curiously at her. "Do you like classical music?"

"I had a friend once who played the violin. She told me that picking up the violin and bow was a sacred act."

"Really. Sacred? I like that. Did she ever play anything by Tartini?"

"Who?"

"He's this amazing composer. His name's Giuseppe Tartini."

"Never heard of him."

"Most people haven't, which is a shame." Behind her, Poppy's room was cluttered and stuffy-smelling. The shades were drawn and the curtains were closed. Natalie noticed little piles of things on every surface— books and magazines, sketch pads and stacks of sheet music, scattered pens and colored pencils. A wall mirror, an antique bureau, a messy desktop. Every inch of wall space was covered with pictures of Poppy accepting yet another award, along with family photos and ribbons, certificates, plaques, and newspaper clippings. "Tartini is incredible," the girl went on, her face pink with excitement. "That's his sonata in G minor I was playing. It's called *Devil's Trill* sonata. He wrote it in 1735. It's based on a really weird dream he had."

"Wow, that must've been some dream," Natalie said with a warm smile.

"More like a nightmare, huh? I performed it for my high school's Halloween concert last week."

"Well, you're very good."

"Am I?" she said, batting her eyelashes with comical exaggeration. "I thought I was masterful."

"You're all that and more." Natalie smiled, sharing the joke. "Sorry to interrupt your practice. I should be going."

"Thanks for the tip about the dog." Poppy smiled back. "Well, good-bye!" She nudged the door shut with her foot.

Natalie felt a headache coming on. She stood rubbing the back of her neck with soothing, circular motions and decided it was time to go talk to Morgan's roommate.

13

S amantha Dreyfus lived in a boxy apartment complex in a run-down area south of downtown Chaste Falls. Natalie could smell chemical fumes from the dry cleaning business next door as she took the cement steps up to the front entrance.

Samantha lived on the third floor. A slender brunette in her mid-twenties, she greeted Natalie in her pajamas and bathrobe. "Hi, can I help you?"

Natalie flashed her credentials. "Detective Lockhart. I'm here to talk about your roommate, Morgan Chambers. May I come in?"

"Sure," Samantha said, cinching her terry cloth robe tighter. She led Natalie into the living room—hardwood floors, bargain basement furniture, old-fashioned windows letting in lots of natural light. Mellow jazz was playing on the sound system. "What about Morgan? Is she okay?"

Natalie took a seat on the sofa, while Samantha settled into a worn armchair. "I'm sorry to break the news to you like this, but Morgan passed away last night."

"Oh my God, no." She shuddered. "Seriously? Morgan's *dead*? How? What happened?"

"We found her in Burning Lake this morning. We don't have a whole lot of answers yet. That's why I'm here." Natalie studied the delicate tattoo on her wrist—*yin-yang*.

"Oh my God, I'm devastated. She's my best friend. We met during our freshman year at the conservatory." She burst into tears.

Natalie looked around for a box of tissues but couldn't find any. She got up, went into the bathroom, found a box of Kleenex, took it out to the living room, and placed it in front of Samantha.

"Thanks," she said between sobs. "God, this is crazy. I can't believe it."

Natalie sat down again. "I'm sorry for your loss, Samantha."

Sorry. For your *loss.*

"What happened? Did she get in a car accident or something?"

"No. We're not sure about the cause of death yet," Natalie explained. "We're still in the process of retracing her whereabouts last night. Can you tell me a little bit about her? Fill in the blanks?"

"Sure." Samantha pressed a tissue against her reddened eyes. "Umm, where to begin . . . Morgan was awesome. Everybody loved her. She has a great sense of humor and she's really smart. I was kind of in awe of her actually," she said, tossing the crumpled tissue on the coffee table and plucking another one out of the box.

"Did she have any enemies to speak of?"

She made a face. "No."

"Take your time, Samantha."

"Everybody calls me Sam. No, I'm serious. She didn't have a bad word to say about anyone. Who'd want to hurt her?" She stared at Natalie uncomprehendingly, then shook her head.

"I know this is hard."

"Hard? It makes me feel kind of insane. I can't believe it. We just texted each other yesterday morning. She said she was having a great time."

"Did she drive to Burning Lake alone, or was she planning on meeting someone there?"

"She went alone, far as I know." Samantha took out her iPhone and showed Natalie a text message from Morgan, dated yesterday at 8:00 A.M. "She said she was meeting lots of cool people. See?"

Natalie read the text message: *It's a little creepy here, I guess, but really fun. The people are so nice. I'm feeling much better about myself already.* ☺ She handed the phone back and asked, "What does that mean—she's feeling better about herself?"

Sam scowled as if it were obvious. "We both graduated from the conservatory two years ago, and Morgan's big dream was either getting an orchestra gig or being a violin soloist. Most people don't realize how ridiculously hard that is, but the truth is . . . very few people ever make it as violin soloists with their own concert tour, signed to a record label. Even landing a seat as *second* violin in an orchestra is next to impossible. It doesn't matter how talented you are. The competition's brutal. Hundreds of applicants from all over the country show up for one position. So whenever there was an opening anywhere in America, Morgan would spend her last paycheck traveling and auditioning, and it practically killed her."

"I don't understand," Natalie said. "There are no orchestras in Burning Lake."

"No, look. It's hard to explain." Samantha grew frustrated. "She was becoming depressed about her situation. She'd been training her whole life for one of two things—either a career as a soloist, or a job in one of the country's best orchestras. That was her goal. She'd won all these awards in school, and everybody knew—they just *knew* she was going places . . . and when that didn't happen, it crushed her. She couldn't figure out what else to do with her life. You can't teach without a master's, and she was already behind on her student loans. She tried to write a Broadway musical once, but that fizzled out. She joined a string quartet last year, but they ended up playing mostly at funerals. That's how desperate she was. Freelance sucks. Low pay, zero benefits, always scrambling for your next gig. It got to the point where she figured . . . nobody needs another fucking musician. We're like a dime a dozen."

"So she had a freelance gig in Burning Lake?" Natalie asked.

"Not exactly. She entered that music contest . . . you know, the Monster Mash?"

Natalie nodded. Every year during the month of October, Burning Lake would hold a contest for the "spookiest" Halloween musical act as part of the festivities. This year, the Monster Mash contest had taken place last Friday evening in Percival Burton Park. It was a big deal. People would leave the bars to go watch. Natalie had been assigned to monitor the fairgrounds that evening, and so she had missed it, but in years past she'd enjoyed all the clever performances—things like the *Ghostbusters* theme song, "Season of the Witch," "Time Warp," "Werewolves of London," and spooky classical pieces that captivated the judges.

Now Samantha wiped her nose and said, "Morgan figured, if she couldn't make it into an orchestra, then maybe if she won something like the Monster Mash contest, she'd be picked up by a record label or get scouted for being part of a cool concert tour. At the very least, someone in the audience would be taping it, and then maybe it would go viral and she'd gain some notoriety that way. She said it was her last shot."

"Last shot? Why?"

"She was getting desperate." Samantha's eyes filled with tears again as she pointed at a glossy photograph on the coffee table. "That's us last summer."

Natalie picked up the airbrushed headshot of the two roommates, Samantha and Morgan, posing with their violins, looking like radiant bookends. "So you play the violin, too?"

"Uh-huh."

"But you said it was difficult. How do you cope?"

Samantha leaned back and crossed her arms. "Through a combination of luck and busting my balls. I lowered my sights after graduation. I'm a part-time teaching assistant at the conservatory now and a fiddle player in a local folk band. Now admittedly, 'fiddle player' doesn't have the same ring to it as 'violin soloist,' but I'm okay with that. I'm willing to compromise my dreams, whereas Morgan refused to give up. She wanted to be the next Jascha Heifetz. Period."

"So you compromised? What's wrong with being a fiddle player?" Natalie asked, putting the headshot down on the coffee table.

"Nobody wants to be a fiddler in a folk band, God forbid. It's looked down upon in the community. But I'm earning a decent living, so fuck it."

Her face sagged. "Look, I'm in shock about this. I hate myself right now, because I sort of encouraged her to go down there in the first place."

"To Burning Lake?"

"Yeah."

"It's not your fault," Natalie said carefully. "Don't take that on your shoulders."

Samantha shook her head mournfully. "Yeah, okay," she said weakly.

"So what you're saying is that Morgan figured that the Monster Mash contest was her best shot at fame and fortune?"

"When you put it that way, it sounds pathetic. Look, ever since she was little," Samantha said, "her father expected her to become a superstar, okay? There was no plan B. Can you imagine the pressure? It's either become the next Lindsey Stirling or Sarah Chang, or forget it—right? And so her failures after graduation embarrassed her. She thought her father had given up on her, because now he's pouring all of those same expectations into her little sister, and come to find out . . . Poppy's looking more and more like a superstar soloist. Just what Morgan had hoped to be. It was killing her.

"So she had to face reality and get a job at the library, which she hated. It was draining and exhausting, and she figured if she was too tired to practice anymore, then she might as well quit. And so, just imagine," Samantha said hoarsely, "after years of practicing five or six hours a day, and missing out on all the things you wanted to do . . . not being allowed to be a kid, not being allowed to act like a normal teenager. And then, after all that sacrifice and hard work, after graduating from one of the best music conservatories in the country . . . nothing happens. No stardom. No orchestra job. No help. No support. And the library gig was part-time. It didn't pay shit. Her next step was a nightmare. She was thinking about selling her violin to pay off her student loans. Talk about hitting rock bottom. But Morgan *couldn't* do that. She knew that it meant giving up on her dreams. So she figured she had to come up with a better solution."

"The music contest," Natalie said.

Samantha shrugged. "Last-ditch effort."

"Did she win?"

"No."

"That's too bad."

"I know."

Natalie wondered if losing the contest might've pushed Morgan over the edge. She wondered if they were indeed looking at a suicide, or perhaps an accidental overdose.

"But she was a finalist," Samantha said. "And there were only ten finalists up on that stage. She got to perform for an audience like she wanted."

Leaning forward, Natalie said, "Did it go viral? Her performance?"

"Not that I know of."

"Was she serious about selling her violin if that didn't work?"

Samantha shrugged. "She talked about it. Most people don't realize how much it costs to maintain your instrument. At least a thousand bucks a year. And her violin was worth thousands, so selling it could've helped her out financially. That's a ridiculously difficult decision. You know, like . . . you'll have to pry my violin from my cold, dead hands." She cringed. "Sorry, I didn't mean it to come out that way."

"That's okay, I understand."

"I told her to start doing podcasts or open a Patreon account or a GoFundMe, but she's a very private person. She was shy. Most guys mistook her shyness for confidence. They thought she was a snob. But Morgan wasn't competitive in any way. She was just passionate about her music. You wouldn't know it to look at her, but she was absolutely lacking in self-confidence. Her father really did a number on her."

"How so?"

"All that pressure to succeed. He was a violinist himself, you know. A failed violinist. Those who don't—teach. Right? My dad was more low-key. I didn't have the same pressures as Morgan did growing up. Her father was focused on mega-success."

Natalie nodded, reminded once again of her old friend Bella. From a very early age, Bella Striver had shown a passion for music, but her father—himself a former child violinist—rarely praised her for her accomplishments. Corbin Striver would browbeat his only child into practicing longer hours and call her a failure if she made a single mistake. "You must sacrifice *everything* for this!" he would shout.

Natalie took out her phone now and showed Samantha a picture of the silver necklace. "Do you recognize this?"

Samantha leaned forward. "No. What is it?"

"What about this tattoo? Do you know what this symbol means?"

Samantha studied it, then shook her head. "I'm not into witchcraft. I don't think people should mess around with that kind of dark energy."

Natalie put her phone away. "No jealous boyfriends? No enemies to speak of?"

Samantha frowned. "She was dating a TA from the conservatory for a while. His name's Josh Mendoza. He's the kind of guy who would constantly undermine her self-confidence by setting impossible standards. Sort of like her dad. They shacked up for eight or nine months a few years back. Then Morgan dumped him and moved in with me." Samantha shrugged, expressionless.

"Do they still see each other?"

"Just as friends. Once in a while."

"Has she seen him recently?"

"Not that I know of. She didn't mention it to me, anyway."

"Can I ask you a favor?" Natalie said. "Do you mind if I took a look around the apartment? I don't have a warrant, but if you'd consent to it . . ."

"Please do. If it helps, please take a look around. Her room's over there."

"Thanks." Natalie stood up and couldn't help thinking about Bella again. Her friend had occupied very little space. She could be quiet and introspective, but once you got to know her, you realized how snarky and funny she was. She had her own ideas about life. For instance, she kept a plastic fork tucked in her pocket at all times, because you never knew. She used to play her violin in the broad open meadow behind her house in the middle of the night. She wasn't afraid of the moonlit dark. She had a lucky hat, a light blue bucket hat that she wasn't wearing the night she disappeared. Her violin, however, disappeared with her.

14

Natalie checked out Morgan's small, square bedroom. There was a handmade quilt on the bed, plush slippers on the floor, a wrinkled jacket draped over a desk chair, several art prints on the wall—Chagall, Georgia O'Keeffe, Renoir. Wide old-fashioned windows with gorgeous natural light pouring in. An empty bag of potato chips on the bed. Books on meditation and mindfulness on the bedside table next to the cheap digital alarm clock—similar to Natalie's. A closet full of Lilly Pulitzer and Alice McCall dresses, along with ASOS and Bershka pants and blouses, and a mess of Crocs, Vans, UGGs, and brogues on the closet floor.

There was an old-fashioned music stand, a wooden chair, and a metronome set up in a corner of the room where she practiced. There were stacks of sheet music on the seat of the chair. Morgan's violin and violin case were absent—Natalie wondered where they were in Burning Lake.

On the IKEA desktop was Morgan's laptop, but Natalie would need a warrant before she could check out the hard drive and email accounts. Still, Samantha had consented to a look around, so Natalie walked over to the antique bureau and studied the collection of lip balms, lipsticks, sunglasses, and earrings on the bureau top. Next to the plastic earring tree was a book on Wicca Morgan had checked out of the Chaste Falls Public Library where she worked.

There was nothing more the room could offer her without a warrant, so Natalie drove across town to the Harrington Brock Conservatory to speak to Teaching Assistant Josh Mendoza. She stopped at the information kiosk, picked up a brochure about the conservatory, and got directions to Bishop Windsor Recital Hall.

Students were bundled up against the chill as they hurried across the charming, historic campus to their various classes. According to the brochure, admission to the conservatory was a challenge—thousands applied annually for three hundred and fifty freshman spots. The faculty boasted an impressive list of classical and jazz legends, including Grammy and Pulitzer Prize winners. The hundred-and-fifty-year-old institution offered undergraduate and graduate degrees to hundreds of gifted musicians every year.

The senior class orchestra was practicing for the Thanksgiving concert inside the rehearsal hall on the first floor. Natalie took an old-fashioned brass elevator to the third floor, where the soundproof rehearsal rooms were. The west wing of the building was reserved for the string instruments—violins, cellos, violas, basses.

Natalie heard a tapestry of muted sounds coming from the practice rooms as she headed down the long green corridor, then paused in front of practice room 3-F and knocked on the door. A young man holding a violin and bow answered. "Hello!" Tall and rangy, he wore wire-rim glasses and a casual outfit of jeans, sneakers, and a green pullover sweater. His violin case was open on a chair seat, and his sheet music was propped on the music stand.

"Josh Mendoza?"

"That's me."

"Sorry to interrupt." Natalie introduced herself, and he welcomed her inside.

"I was just practicing my Brahms violin concerto," he said with a smile. "Please, have a seat." His face became animated as he produced a series of dark, edgy sounds on his violin, which soon gave way to a rapidly rising, energetic melody, his fingers dancing expertly over the strings. He fumbled when he came to the end of a musical phrase, then stopped playing altogether. He sighed with frustration. "Damn. I've been working on my major concerto repertory this year, and I keep fumbling over that one knotty capriccio."

"Do you mind if we talk?" she asked.

"Sure." He put his instrument away in its case and studied her over his wire-rim glasses. "What did you say your name was again?"

"Detective Lockhart from Burning Lake."

He attempted a smile.

"Morgan Chambers passed away last night," she said, watching him carefully for a reaction. "I was told you two lived together a while back."

His face emptied of blood. "Passed away? Are you sure?"

"We found her this morning," Natalie said with a nod. "We don't have all the information yet. That's why I'm here."

"Oh," he said nervously. "Well, this is awful news."

"When was the last time you spoke to her, Josh?"

He gave her an anguished look, then sat heavily on one of the metal folding chairs. "What happened to her?"

"It could've been foul play. We aren't sure. That's why I need to ask you some questions. Where were you on Halloween?"

His eyes grew deeply suspicious. "Why are you asking me that? Do you suspect me of something?"

"It's a standard question. Part of the investigation."

"Where was I? I was in Chaste Falls all weekend."

"Did you know she went down to Burning Lake for Halloween?"

"She told me she was going to enter that contest . . . the Monster Mash. She was pretty excited about it."

"When did she tell you this?"

"We got together for coffee about two weeks ago." His face was deeply sad. "We split up more than a year ago."

Natalie nodded sympathetically. He seemed perfectly sincere—but liars could easily swallow their own bullshit. She crossed her arms and asked, "What else did you talk about over coffee?"

"Oh God. Whenever we got together, we'd have these tortured conversations . . . I mean she was so raw. So painfully aware of everything, if that makes any sense. Morgan took things too literally. I cared about her very much, but she wasn't the easiest person to get along with," he explained, sliding his glasses back up his nose.

Natalie struggled to understand. "Can you elaborate?"

"Morgan and I have very different personalities. She's overly sensitive, whereas I can be blunt. I pushed her to excel, both professionally and personally, just like I push myself. But she took my honest criticisms the wrong way."

"What honest criticisms?"

He turned his hands palm side up. "What can I say? She wasn't the genius her father always insisted she was. It was sad, actually. She wanted to be a violin soloist. That was her dream. Whereas I prefer to face reality. The competition in the field of music can be brutal, and Morgan wasn't prepared for it. I was trying to help her lower her expectations and be happy with who she was. Get a teaching degree, you know? But she was so hard on herself. She refused to let go of her dream."

"Is that why you split up?"

He sighed so hard she could smell the peppermint on his breath. "Look, Morgan was very dear to me. But we couldn't make it work. Living together was impossible. She told me I was the only guy in the world Gandhi would've punched in the mouth." He smiled at the thought, then he caught himself and straightened up. "I admit it. I can be tactless. Some people think I'm cruel. I'm not. I'm reality-based. That's just the way I was raised. But I've always couched my criticisms in loving language."

"So when you got together two weeks ago, did you end up arguing again?"

"Morgan asked for my opinion, so I gave it to her. She wanted to know what I thought about her musical choice for the contest . . . you know, spookiest Halloween music or whatever the hell it is. First of all, I told her if she wanted to be taken seriously, she shouldn't be entering something like that in the first place. But as long as she was going to go ahead with it, I suggested John Williams's "Dance of the Witches," but she thought that was too commercial. Then I suggested Berlioz or Mussorgsky, but she called them cartoonish. She said there's nothing the least bit scary about Bach's Toccata and Fugue in D Minor."

"What did she decide to play?"

"Béla Bartók's *Transylvanian Dances*, which he based on these old recordings of peasant folk songs . . . from Transylvania, of course. Morgan selected the second movement, which I've heard her play before. It's very dark and gloomy, almost a creepy piece of music. I told her she'd do better with *Danse Macabre* by Saint-Saëns, but she'd already made up her mind."

"Okay," Natalie said. "Then what happened?"

He shrugged. "She said she had an appointment at the clinic, so we agreed to continue our conversation later."

"What clinic?"

"At the conservatory. She was having a minor problem with her wrist and she wanted to take care of it before the contest."

"When was the last time you spoke to her?"

He shook his head. "That was the last time."

"No phone calls or text messages?"

"We both got busy."

"And you didn't go to Burning Lake for Halloween?" Natalie pressed.

He looked at her with great indignation. "No, I didn't. Why?"

"Where were you last night?"

He grimaced. "I rehearsed with the chamber ensemble all afternoon. And last night, I attended the department Halloween party here at the conservatory."

"From when to when?"

Mendoza shot her a resentful look. Paranoia descended. "I went straight from the music hall to the party at six o'clock and stayed until about nine. Then I went home. I slept in late this morning."

"Do you live alone?"

"Yes."

"In an apartment?"

"I rent a house on the outskirts of town."

"Did you interact with anyone after nine o'clock last night?"

"I don't know. I don't think so. But I can give you the names of everyone who saw me at the rehearsal hall and the party yesterday, if that's any help."

"Thanks." Natalie took out her phone and showed him the silver necklace. He'd never seen it before. Or the tattoo. "I'll take that list of names," she said. "Everyone you interacted with yesterday."

He found a piece of paper and jotted it all down. After a few minutes of thoughtful scribbling, he handed her the list, then glanced at his watch. "I'm supposed to join my chamber ensemble shortly."

Natalie nodded. "Look, Josh . . . is there anything else you can tell me about Morgan that might shed some light on the investigation? Anything at all?"

His shoulders sagged. "Chaste Falls is a small town. Everybody knows her dad, and they know Morgan hasn't realized her dreams yet, but they can't stop asking—why aren't you on tour? Why aren't you on TV by now? It's been completely devastating for her. She told me her life was one big ball of ego-crushing freelance gigs and ever-mounting debt."

"Was she suicidal?" Natalie asked.

He folded his arms. "All I can tell you is that the Morgan I know isn't into self-harm. She avoided hard drugs. She enjoyed a glass of wine now and then, but she wasn't a heavy drinker. The last time we spoke, she said she was feeling chaotic internally. She mentioned getting into therapy. She just wanted to find her power again. She said she was sick of feeling like a loser, and she wanted to turn her life around. She wanted to change her lousy luck."

"Does she know anyone in Burning Lake? Have any friends, colleagues, co-workers, or schoolmates there?"

Josh shook his head. "Not that I know of."

"Thank you." Natalie got up to leave.

"She was a passionate musician," he said, standing up as well. "Her bow technique wasn't exceptional, but listening to her play for the first time was an emotional experience for me. You weren't just hearing music, you were stepping into the soul of a wounded human being."

15

Natalie took the curving flagstone path toward the main building on campus, a Gothic behemoth topped with ferocious-looking gargoyles and covered in climbing ivy. Carved into the stone façade was a frieze of famous composers—Aaron Copland, Duke Ellington, Mozart. Inside were polished hardwood floors, arched doorways, somber oil portraits, and a pervasive sense of history. Natalie headed down the corridor toward the administrative offices. Inside the director's office, she was greeted by a middle-aged man behind a steel desk piled high with paperwork—his tired-looking eyes peered at her from behind a mess of curly gray hair. "Yes, can I help you?" he said in a petulant voice that didn't really want to help anybody.

Natalie introduced herself. "I called Director Brock about an hour ago. I believe that she's expecting me."

"Have a seat," he said. "I'll let her know you're here."

Natalie took a seat on a prickly upholstered chair and glanced at the donor wall with its plaques and framed photographs. There were so many faces she recognized—Burning Lake's Mayor Arnold Bryden and Chief of Police Roger Snyder; Coroner Barry Fishbeck; Brandon's father, Kenneth

Buckner II; Veronica Manes; Hunter Rose; and many other donors from Natalie's hometown. It wasn't surprising. The music conservatory was one of the best in the country, and Burning Lake regularly hired Harrington Brock grads and undergrads to perform at various venues during the busy month of October, as well as the summer months, when tourists flocked to the area.

Natalie's gaze finally landed on a large, expensively framed photograph of a pretty young woman posing with her violin. Most striking of all was her long red hair. Natalie asked the assistant, "Excuse me, who's that?"

He sighed, planted his elbow patches on his desk, and squinted at the wall. "That's the Maldonado violin scholarship for string players."

"She's very beautiful."

He nodded indifferently. "Elyssa Maldonado. That picture was taken in the late nineties, I believe, shortly before she died in a car crash. Her family set up the scholarship in her honor. Thanks to them, every year, three gifted young students will receive five thousand dollars toward their tuition."

Before she could ask any more questions, his desk phone beeped, and he picked up.

"Yes? Okay. Certainly." He hung up and said, "You can go in now."

The director was seated behind an impressive nineteenth-century mahogany desk surrounded by portraits of former conservatory directors. She was in her mid-forties, Natalie guessed, very attractive in a corporate sort of way, with a fashionable blond haircut, plastered-on smile, and faux-jovial manner that had an edge to it. Natalie suspected the director could be a real bitch if she wanted to. One eyebrow was higher than the other, giving her a look of bemused condescension. She shook Natalie's hand and said, "Detective Lockhart, so nice to meet you! Although it's very sad to meet under these circumstances. Let me introduce Sheriff Dressler. I took the liberty of inviting him to join us, I hope you don't mind."

Natalie turned to face Sheriff Dressler, a man of indeterminate age with salt-and-pepper hair, craggy features, and parchment-paper lips. It looked as if the sun had aged him, but perhaps it went deeper than that. He studied her with solemn, interested eyes. As they shook hands, he said, "Lieutenant Pittman called a little while ago and gave me the rundown, so I thought we should meet in person and talk about jurisdiction."

"Of course," Natalie said, irritated that Luke hadn't given her a heads-up. "But I'm confused. The body was found in Burning Lake, so . . ."

"Coffee, Detective?" Hyacinth Brock interrupted.

"No, thanks, I'm fine."

"Well, you're right about that," the sheriff told her. "I'm not arguing that point. But Morgan Chambers grew up here, she's part of our community, her family lives here, she went to the conservatory, you get my drift . . . it's just that I'd like to be apprised of the investigation as it unfolds. Regular updates."

"I'll keep you in the loop, for sure," Natalie said, nodding.

"We're a close-knit family here," Hyacinth said. A sign on the wall behind her said "Don't Lose the Forest for the Trees," and next to that was an oil portrait of the founder of the conservatory with a young girl on his knee, and it dawned on Natalie that Hyacinth was that little girl. Harrington Brock's great-granddaughter. The man who built this place, one of the best schools for music in the country.

Hyacinth's smile wasn't really a smile—it was a polite sneer. "Have a seat, Detective. How can I help you?"

"What can you tell me about Morgan Chambers?"

"She was a good student whose future looked bright. Her expectations may have been set too high, however. You already know her father is a professor here, I assume? His other daughter is exceptionally talented. Poppy has all the makings of a superstar. Anyway, all I know is . . . two years after graduating from the conservatory, Morgan appeared to have lost her way."

"That's what I've been hearing," Natalie said with a nod. "But she succeeded academically and musically at the school?"

"Our students are all dedicated, competitive, and extremely talented," Hyacinth said. "You have your stars, and then you have your section players. Now here at the conservatory . . . we see no difference between them. They all work just as hard. But regardless of where our students end up, it takes years of talent, focus, discipline, and versatility. You can't just sit back and think that an orchestra position is going to fall in your lap. Hard work, and then more hard work. *That's* what it takes to succeed in this business."

"So you don't think she worked hard enough?" Natalie clarified.

"Oh, please, I'm sorry if you misunderstood." The director reorganized her face into an affronted expression. "That's *not* what I was saying." It took a moment for her ruffled feathers to settle down. "Morgan had talent. She had advantages. She was gifted. In this business, it's all about experience, timing, and vision. We attract superbly accomplished musicians from all over the world. We've been designated an all-Steinway school, did you know that? We have one hundred Steinway pianos available for our students. Our chamber-music practice spaces are acoustically perfect. This is a state-of-the-art facility. Now," she went on, "a professional musician's life isn't easy. You're required to audition, and then if you're lucky enough to be selected, you'll spend a minimum of three hours a day rehearsing with an orchestra, and many additional hours of personal practice and preparation. There's a lot of physical stress involved. Musicians must be able to perform well under duress. The audition process is arduous. Grueling, to be honest. Not every student can handle it."

"I think I know what you're getting at," Natalie said. "You're suggesting Morgan Chambers wasn't entirely cut out for the competitive world of classical music."

She frowned. "It's true you need a certain temperament."

"And you're suggesting that her emotional state probably wasn't the best."

"Emotional state?" She shook her head. "I wouldn't know about that."

"Is there anybody else I should be talking to while I'm here? Teachers, students, staff? Anyone who might shed some light on who Morgan was?"

"I think her father's the best source of information."

"I've already spoken to him. He pointed me to Morgan's roommate."

"About her father . . ." Hyacinth said in a measured, circumspect tone. "He's a superb teacher, don't get me wrong. He sets the bar high for his students, and many have gone on to become successful violin soloists. But I think it's possible Morgan felt the weight of his outsize expectations on her shoulders. If anything, a lot of the source of her anguish and stress could've come from pressures at home. Feelings of inadequacy. But that's all I can say about that." The director's phone rang. "Sorry, I have to take this. Thank you so much for dropping by." She stood up and shook Natalie's hand. "If you need anything else, please don't hesitate to contact me. Here's my card."

Natalie thanked them both and left.

The sheriff followed her into the corridor. "Excuse me? Detective Lockhart?"

"Yes?"

He glanced back at the director's office and said, "Let's talk while we walk." They headed down the hallway together. "We'd like to have the body returned home as soon as possible. The Chambers need resolution. They want to bury her. I'm sure you understand."

"Yes, I do," she said, sympathetic but cautious. She wasn't happy with the shortness of the meeting and wasn't sure what was going on.

"The lieutenant said you haven't determined cause of death yet?" he inquired.

"No, but it's suspicious. Possible suicide or OD. Maybe foul play. We're not sure. We want to be absolutely thorough in our coverage, given the circumstances."

"I understand," he said. "But you need to know what you're dealing with here. The world of classical musicians, especially violin soloists and their enablers . . . well, it's like a beauty pageant. There's a similar mindset. You might meet with some resistance from the staff, but also from the families. They're all concerned about protecting the conservatory's reputation. And this investigation threatens their cloistered world."

Natalie stopped walking and asked, "How so?"

"What she said about pressure . . ." He held the front door open for her. "The truth is, a lot more graduates of this institution fail than you'd think. And the suicide rate for music students is relatively high. Some folks call it the gifted child curse."

"The gifted child curse?" she repeated.

"It's true of most classical musicians, but especially of the violinists. A gifted violinist has a special place in an orchestra. They also have higher suicide rates, but the conservatory will downplay the statistics. Nothing illegal, mind you. No cover-ups or anything. But it's bad for business, so the PR spinners come out in force whenever one of these incidents occur. The conservatory labels them 'accidents,' instead of what they sometimes are."

Natalie nodded. "Death by suicide."

"Correct. Now my predecessor . . . the sheriff before me . . . he was big on putting a positive spin on the situation for the sake of the community, since the conservatory not only brings prestige to the town but it fills the coffers. Tourism, musical events, real estate holdings, contracts with local businesses. Chaste Falls is thriving. You won't get much help from the kids' parents, either, because they're in complete denial about their contribution to the problem. Plus they often have more than one child studying the violin, so they'll call it an accident, too. They don't want to admit their kid was depressed or doing drugs. For example, if somebody falls after overdosing, they'll say it was a slip-and-fall, and the family won't contest it."

Natalie nodded, understanding what a bombshell he was dropping.

"Now mind you," the sheriff continued, "Hyacinth is a good person. She loves her musicians and she loves the conservatory. Her name is Brock, did you catch that? She's the great-granddaughter of Harrington Brock, and she's protecting her legacy from slander, is how she sees it. And so, when a graduate of the institute dies by suicide or 'has an accident,' she knows how to keep it out of the press. Some of these kids are true geniuses, true prodigies, who've won statewide and nationwide competitions, and she's all about saving face for the institution. And it's not just Hyacinth who wants this, it's the mayor and the town council and all the folks who've donated and attached their names to the institution for the prestige . . . you understand? A lot of local business leaders in town are heavily invested in the success of the conservatory, since it attracts tourism and investment. Without it, what've you got? Just a lot of woods and boarded-up textile factories. The Brock Conservatory is the lifeblood of this community. And the families of the deceased have financial and emotional investments. These families have sacrificed a lot to see their kids succeed up there onstage, playing the violin to adoring crowds. They dream about Carnegie Hall. You can't mess with the dream."

Natalie stopped in front of her car. "Okay, I get the picture," she said. In truth, she was feeling the same pressure as Sheriff Dressler. Burning Lake didn't want a dead body on Halloween, and if she could call it an accident, the chief would be happy.

"Anyway," he said with a smile, "I hope I can count on your discretion."

Natalie stiffened. She hated backroom dealing. On the matter of corruption, her father used to quote Nietzsche—*Whoever fights monsters should see to it that in the process he does not become a monster.* "Are you suggesting I lie about my findings?"

"No. Not at all." His chapped lips cracked along the lines of his smile. "I'm asking you to give me a heads-up so that I can prepare for whatever shit hits the fan."

"Okay." She hoped she was reading him right. "Because I'm not bending the truth for anyone."

"I didn't think you would," he said with a wry smile. "Look, you can trust me, Detective. I'm highly motivated to get to the heart of the matter. I'm not like my predecessor. Not even close. Now that that's settled . . . what's your next objective?"

She took out her keys. "I need to talk to her co-workers at the library."

He sighed. "Tell you what. I'll interview them myself and let you know what I find out. How's that sound?" When she hesitated, he added, "Like I said, Chaste Falls isn't your jurisdiction, and I'm assuming that since the investigation is in the early stages, it wouldn't be prudent to call it a homicide or a suicide yet, and that means getting a subpoena will surely take a while. So here's what I'll do. I'll talk to any witnesses you want, and I'll send you my reports. How's that sound?"

"It sounds like I have no choice."

"Oh, you have a choice. But your way might take a lot longer."

"Then I guess I should thank you, Sheriff." She opened the door and got in.

"Not a problem."

"Morgan's ex-boyfriend has no alibi for last night after nine o'clock. His name is Josh Mendoza. Here's a list of names of the people he claims he was with yesterday."

He took the slip of paper. "Great. I'll follow up."

She rolled up her window, but Sheriff Dressler wasn't finished yet. He tapped on the glass, and she rolled it back down.

"I've been meaning to mention how impressed I was with your work, Detective. I read about the Crow Killer case in that *New York Times* article. As fate would have it, I've got a couple of missing persons I'd like you to take a look at."

"Call my boss, Lieutenant Pittman. Go through proper channels."

"I did go through proper channels. I sent copies of those files to your chief of police months ago, and I never heard back. You're still in charge of the Missing Nine, aren't you?"

"All the detectives in the Criminal Investigations Unit are working on it, along with the Department of Wetlands and Woodlands," Natalie said. "We're still pulling together the pieces." They had to verify every case and confirm that Samuel Hawke had been involved with each homicide based on solid evidence—a tough thing to do when not all of the bodies had been recovered yet. The first seven victims were found buried on Samuel's property, but the rest were still missing, so they'd extended their range to the woods and surrounding property, along with areas of the state park that had been under Hawke's patrol. Once the other bodies were recovered, the local jurisdictions where the bodies were found would take over in coordination with the BLPD. Meanwhile, they were swamped with paperwork, since police departments as far away as Oklahoma kept sending in copies of missing persons files—men and women who'd vanished while visiting the Adirondacks.

"We're admittedly backlogged," she confessed.

"One of my missing cases was a transient, but the other was a young woman, and I think this will interest you. She was a violinist," the sheriff explained. "She went to the conservatory, and she disappeared from Chaste Falls about six months ago. I don't know if you've heard about Lily Kingsley."

"I read about it in the papers," she said, vaguely recalling the case. "I didn't know she played the violin. The CIU probably added it to the stack of possible Crow Killer victims at the time."

"According to family and friends, Lily Kingsley was a free spirit who wasn't afraid to hitchhike. She was last seen leaving a bar on the outskirts of Chaste Falls and getting into a long-haul truck shortly after performing the spring concert at the conservatory. Lily's parents offered a generous reward for any information leading to her safe return, but no kidnapping demands were ever made, and no witnesses have come forward. The body's never been found."

"I'll ask Lieutenant Pittman to follow up on those files you sent," she promised.

"Better yet, I'll make a deal with you," he said, leaning against her car door. "If you'll personally take a look at those two case files for me, I'll interview all the people in town who knew Morgan, and I'll send you my reports ASAP. Save you plenty of legwork."

"Are you suggesting a quid pro quo?"

"I wouldn't call it that. More like cooperation between jurisdictions."

Looking at him now, Natalie decided he was a straight shooter. "Okay," she said. "I'll get my boss to approve it and let you know by the end of the day."

He took a step back and dusted off his hands. "You know, when you look closely at some of the old buildings in Chaste Falls, you can see fossils in the limestone. For instance, the Smith Tower is made up of granite blocks that formed when the mountains first erupted. They're more than three hundred million years old, isn't that amazing? You can still see the melted iron and silica in the speckled granite."

She smiled. It was an interesting observation, but she wondered what his point was.

"We stand on the shoulders of giants, Detective. We live off the labor and struggle of our ancestors, and we don't even care. We think granite is granite, and it's always been granite . . . when it was once mud, thick and teeming with life. We ignore the old wisdom when we shouldn't."

"And what's the old wisdom I'm ignoring?" she asked.

"You? No, young lady. I'm afraid you don't miss a beat." He tipped his hat. "Have a nice day."

It wasn't until she'd crossed the town line on her way back to Burning Lake that the thought returned to her—whatever happened to Morgan's violin?

16

As she drove back to Burning Lake, Natalie let the anger pass, a slow-burning disgust that simmered and bubbled like a cauldron of frog's toe and newt's eye. *Double, double toil and trouble.* Bella used to complain that people didn't actually *see* her unless she was playing her violin; that playing the violin was the only way she knew how to get people to pay attention, especially her father. Corbin Striver never really "heard" his daughter unless she was practicing. Bella's violin was her voice.

Mr. Striver was gone now, having passed away six years ago, leaving Bella no one to rebel against and nobody to come home to. Corbin Striver had once been a rising star himself at the Berklee College of Music in Boston, but after failing at that, he owned a music shop in downtown Burning Lake and lived vicariously through his only child. Being a typical stage father, he forced Bella to perform at venues and pushed her to succeed. All that pressure only made her resent him more—but not the music. Never the music. Bella loved her violin so much she sometimes jokingly covered it with kisses. Her disappearance left a hole in Natalie's life, one that she hadn't managed to fill. All these years later, the mystery still didn't sit right with her. And Morgan Chambers's death was stirring things up.

Natalie swung her Honda into the parking lot behind the police station, eased into her spot, and got out. Despite the brilliance of the afternoon sky, the day felt grim. She plucked a few strands of hair that'd been tickling her face and tucked them behind her ears, then went inside, collected her mail, and took an elevator to the third floor, where she found Luke standing in the hallway next to the directory.

"Coming or going?" she asked, holding the door open for him.

He cupped his hand over his phone and said, "No, thanks. Hold on a second."

"No?" She stepped out of the elevator.

He was busy working his iPhone, ink-stained fingers dancing over the buttons, texting and taking phone calls, talking in staccato bursts. "Yeah? Okay. Go ahead with that." Finally he pocketed his phone and looked at her. "You're back. How did it go?"

"Long story."

"Lieutenant?" All of a sudden, they heard footsteps tumbling toward them, and Lenny Labruzzo came barreling around the corner with a frazzled look. "You need to come see this, Lieutenant. You, too, Natalie."

They followed him down the hallway into the unit, where the guys were clustered around Augie's desk. "Surprise!" they all shouted. They had a cake and everything. They started singing "Happy Birthday" in off-key unison.

"Oh jeez," Luke said, dumbstruck. Embarrassed.

Natalie was mortified. She couldn't believe she'd forgotten Luke's birthday. She never forgot—it was too easy to remember. The day after Halloween. November 1.

Her face flushed as she joined in the chorus. A long time ago, for her sweet sixteen, Luke had given her a dozen red roses, and it thrilled her adolescent heart. Ever since then, they'd remembered each other's birthdays, buying joke gifts or the world's stupidest birthday cards. She had the best excuse in the world today, but like Joey used to say . . . people won't remember what you did or said, they'll only remember how you made them feel.

Now Natalie scanned the room. There was Aimee Dreyer, the middle-aged department secretary, and detectives Lenny Labruzzo, Augie Vickers, Brandon Buckner, Peter Murphy, Jacob Smith, and Mike Anderson, along with Boomer Prutzman from downstairs, officers Bill Keegan and Troy Goodson, Dennis the dispatcher, and a dozen other familiar faces.

"Quick, L.T. Blow out the candles and make a wish," Lenny egged him on.

Luke blew out the candles on his birthday cake and thanked everyone.

"What did you wish for?"

"Can't tell you that." Luke smirked.

"Hey, Lieu," Augie said. "Forty's not old, if you're a tree."

"I'm thirty-nine," Luke corrected him.

"Oh my gosh," Aimee said, drawing her hand to her mouth. "They told me you were forty, so I put *forty candles* on the cake."

"His wish won't count then," Jacob said with a grin.

"You know you're getting older when you stop searching for the meaning of life and start searching for your car keys," Lenny joked, and everybody laughed.

Luke was grinning ear to ear, but his eyes were distant. Natalie knew that look. He hated being the center of attention almost as much as she did. Now Lenny opened his desk drawer, took out a gift-wrapped box, and said, "Something for the birthday boy."

Luke ripped off the bow, tore off the wrapping paper, and opened the box. Inside was a pair of blue boxers with a pattern of handcuffs on it. "Oh fuck you, guys," he said, and everyone laughed again.

"Okay. Here's the real gift." Lenny handed him a second box.

Luke tore off the wrapping. Inside was a coffee mug shaped like a donut. "Now that's more like it," he said with a relaxed smile.

"You know you're getting older when happy hour means a nap," Augie said.

"Can I file for harassment now?" Luke joked, tossing the boxers in the trash.

"Hey, gimme." Jacob fished the rejected gift out of the wastebasket, and he and Mike pretended to fight over them.

Then Aimee carved up the cake and handed out slices on flimsy paper napkins. People wished Luke a happy birthday before heading back to their desks.

"I can't believe I forgot your birthday," Natalie told him miserably.

He gave her a don't-worry-about-it shrug. "You've had a busy day."

She knew from experience that when you disappointed someone, you'd only make things worse by dwelling on it, so she let it go.

Lenny approached them, licking the blue icing off his fingers. "Natalie, when you get a chance, we found something on one of the surveillance tapes. The Lieu's already seen it. Whenever you're ready, I'll be downstairs." He headed out the door.

"What did they find?" she asked Luke.

"Go take a look. Then come back to my office for a debrief." He took his cake with him.

17

Lenny did his most important work down in the department's crime scene lab, which was situated across from the property room in the basement and didn't have any natural light. The lab was a large open space with plenty of workbenches and an impressive amount of state-of-the-art equipment, including a drying cabinet and a superglue fuming chamber with a fume hood. A grid of fluorescent lighting on the ceiling made everything look flat and cold. She found Lenny seated at his corner workbench where he wrote his reports. The workbench was crammed with computer equipment and half a dozen video monitors.

"So what've you got?" she asked, hoping for a breakthrough.

Lenny finished his cake, rumpled up the napkin, and tossed it in the trash. Then he scooped a pile of paperwork off the chair beside him and said, "Have a seat, Nat."

She watched while he typed in a command and pointed at a nearby screen. "Check this out. We pulled video from the liquor store across the way—you can see the mouth of the alley at an angle through the plate glass. At eleven forty-three P.M., a woman dressed as Wonder Woman heads east along the sidewalk. Here. At eleven forty-four she enters the alley alone. As you can see, she looks inebriated. Impaired motor skills. Swaying a little. Stumbling. Once she enters the alley, she never comes out. I've fast-forwarded the tape for the subsequent two hours, but she never exits the alley."

"Back up a minute," Natalie said, and he rewound the tape and hit play.

In the grainy security footage, the woman dressed as Wonder Woman seemed visibly distraught. She kept glancing nervously over her shoulder, as if someone was following her.

"Shortly before she goes into the alley, she panics and pushes her way through a group of people," Natalie observed. "See there?"

Lenny nodded. "Right. As if someone's chasing her. But nobody follows her into the alley. There's nobody pursuing her, as far as this tape goes. I had a couple of officers down here looking at the tapes with me. We checked two hours *prior* to the time stamp, as well as two hours *after* the time stamp," he explained. "That's a window of four hours. Now, we spotted maybe a dozen people going into the alley before she does, but they all come out again well before the time stamp. For example, there's a young couple that stumbles into the alley two hours prior to Wonder Woman, but then they leave the alley fifteen minutes later. And then, an employee dumps his trash at nine fifty-five, but he comes out right away. Doing his job. A drunk stumbles in around ten oh-three, a couple of teenagers go in there to get high, but they're all accounted for—meaning they all exited the alley well before eleven forty-four. Then afterwards, between midnight and two A.M., you have sixteen employees who are throwing away trash. But every single one of them comes back out within a minute or two of going in, and we've identified and interviewed all of them. They didn't see or hear anything unusual. Nobody in the alley, nothing unusual, no cries for help. They simply tossed their trash and went back to their jobs. We're still reviewing the other surveillance tapes we collected today, and we've gotten to widen our window with this one, but the guys are getting fatigued, so I've put in a request for more volunteers."

"Just to be clear," Natalie said, "you checked two hours prior to eleven forty-four P.M. and then two hours afterwards?"

"Yeah, basically nobody followed her in who hasn't been accounted for. And for at least two hours prior, there was no one lying in wait for her. We're going to keep looking, of course, but I need fresh pairs of eyeballs. Keegan's coming down shortly to review this tape farther back, and Petrowski will check it out between two and four A.M. It's always possible an offender was lying in wait, hiding in that alley for longer than two hours, waiting for some random person to attack," Lenny explained. "But I doubt it. And we haven't seen any proof of that so far. But still, just to be thorough, our goal is to go all the way back twenty-four hours prior to the incident and twenty-four hours after the incident, just to make sure our vic wasn't ambushed. But right now, it's looking as if she walked into that alley alone, and what happens next we don't know."

"Good job, Lenny. I'd like a copy of this segment of the tape."

"Sure thing. Hold on." He took out his phone and sent her the attachment. "Don't keep the lieu waiting."

She went upstairs to the third floor and knocked on Luke's door.

"Come in," he said. He was on the phone.

She took a seat in a wooden guest chair and studied his face, his inscrutable male feelings locked deep inside. His hair was the color of dark-stained wood, and his reading glasses made him look studious and solemn. There was a prowling inquisitiveness about him—an innate skepticism. He seemed forever poised to question whatever anyone had to say, one eyebrow arched.

Luke didn't have a lot of personal touches in his office—there was a worn catcher's mitt on his desk, a rubber band ball, Skye's watercolors taped to the wall, and a framed photograph of himself and his ex-wife from many summers ago when she was pregnant with Skye. They looked madly in love back then—you could see it in their eyes. Natalie felt an irrational twinge of jealousy. She wanted to be *that* in love.

He hung up. "The chief," he said. "He's like sandpaper to my raw nerves."

"What now?"

He shook his head. "Incompetence, hypocrisy, cowardice, ineptness, duplicity. Just the usual."

She smiled. The stark office lights dusted the steel cabinets with angled shadows. "So," she said a little awkwardly, "how's it feel to be thirty-nine?"

"Feels no different than yesterday, frankly." He smiled politely and waited for her to say something, but Natalie was all out of small talk.

"I saw the video," she said. "She looked exceedingly paranoid, constantly glancing back over her shoulder."

"And yet no one followed her into the alley."

"But she was clearly afraid of something."

He leaned back in his ratty office chair and said, "What did you find out today?"

She informed him about the music contest, the wrist injury, Morgan's failed attempts to get an orchestra gig, her relationship with her ex-boyfriend, her roommate's concerns, the library book on Wicca, and the rest. She told him about Sheriff Dressler and his offer to help with the case in exchange for their help with Lily Kingsley—another violinist.

"And Dressler thinks it's possible she was one of Samuel Hawke's victims?"

"Well, she disappeared six months ago, so she could've been his last victim. But she doesn't fit the profile. She wasn't a transient, and the only bodies they've found so far belong to the Missing Nine. It's worth looking into, but the violinist connection is what I'm interested in—a young female violinist from Chaste Falls. They both attended the conservatory, and judging from the pictures I found online, Lily Kingsley resembles Morgan superficially. Both are petite with long mahogany hair."

Luke nodded thoughtfully and put down his pen. "And you said Morgan came down here for Halloween?"

"For the Monster Mash contest last Friday night. It sounds like she was hoping her performance might create some heat. Go viral and get her a record deal or something."

"But she didn't win?"

"Apparently not. That's something I need to follow up on, along with a million other things." She opened her notebook. Her handwriting had deteriorated since high school, and it was difficult to read her own notes. Frustrating. "The witch sigil tattoo is an interesting lead. I'll drop by Cody Dugway's tattoo parlor and see if that's his handiwork, or if he knows who else might've done it. Lenny and his team are reviewing the security tapes, and we're still door-to-dooring. Morgan's ex-boyfriend had no alibi for last night after nine o'clock, so Dressler's going to look into it further. It's only half an hour from Chaste Falls to Burning Lake, so he could've driven down here."

"You think her ex-boyfriend was stalking her?" Luke asked.

"It's a possibility. Although he seemed relatively harmless."

"So you don't think this was an accidental overdose?"

Natalie shook her head. "Not after seeing the surveillance tape. She was scared to death of someone or something."

He gave a concerned nod.

"According to Dressler, a lot of these kids feel so much pressure to succeed that they become suicidally depressed. But Morgan strikes me as tremendously determined. Maybe the contest was her last hope, like her roommate said . . . but then again, it also gave her exposure."

"Exposure how?"

"To the judges and other contestants. Who knows? She might've made some good contacts that night. She might've been networking, trying to use her performance to leverage a job. We don't know yet."

Luke rested his hands on his desk. "The chief thinks there's a high probability that this was an accidental overdose. She was partying, she got drunk, took a few pills, and ended up dead."

"That's what Director Brock is hoping for as well," Natalie said, recalling the picture of the chief of police on the conservatory's donor wall.

"We're under a lot of pressure to solve the case quickly," he told her. "But I'm not going to interfere with how you run your investigation, Natalie. Just keep an open mind to all possibilities."

She scowled. "You think she crawled into that dumpster all by herself?"

"Maybe. You saw the tape. Nobody went into that alley after her, or before, that wasn't accounted for. That's a four-hour window. Maybe she was hallucinating from a bad drug combination? Which could explain why she removed her clothes."

"Maybe her attacker entered the alley three hours earlier? Maybe he was hiding in the dumpster? We won't know until Lenny has reviewed all the tapes and exhausted all possibilities. We have to open up that window to at least six hours before and after."

Luke gave a stiff nod, as if he didn't want to argue with her anymore. "You're right. It's premature to draw any conclusions."

She took a deep breath before leafing through her notebook. "You spoke to Dressler?"

Luke nodded. "I'm glad they're cooperating. Makes our job a heck of a lot easier."

"Some of these graduates from the music conservatory have meltdowns after their careers tank. The sheriff told me the rate of suicide for these kids is unusually high. It's clear Hyacinth Brock doesn't want the post-graduation suicide rates getting out to the media. Bad for business."

"So she's covering the conservatory's ass by trying to get ahead of the story."

Natalie nodded. "Meanwhile, nobody recognized the silver necklace, but she could've purchased it here in Burning Lake, and the Wiccan symbol interests me. She also had a library book on Wicca in her room."

"You think she was into witchcraft?"

"It's one of the leads I'm following." She closed her notebook. "How long before we get the tox screen back?"

"The state lab is prioritizing our request. They put a rush on it. In the meantime, Barry says there's no evidence of rape. The sperm in the condom was more than twenty-four hours old."

"What about the rape kit? Did he have any luck?"

Luke shook his head. "Test results were negative for semen or saliva. And the autopsy report was negative for abrasions, bruises, tearing, or forcible entry."

She sighed heavily, exhaustion tugging at the corners of her mouth. For a moment she felt all the pent-up rage she'd buried deep inside come rising to the surface, but those feelings quickly dissipated and turned into a hard resolve. She was going to solve this thing.

Augie knocked on the door and popped his head in. "Sorry to interrupt, folks, but Lenny just got a hit on one of the credit cards . . . we know where Morgan Chambers was staying over the weekend."

18

The **Sunflower Inn** was located on a quiet side street, just a ten-minute walk from the downtown cafés, boutiques, and museums. Built in 1820, this beautifully restored Georgian mansion was owned and operated by seventy-year-old Udell Pickle. Everybody called him Dell.

He answered the door and said, "Natalie, long time no see!" Dell's head was bald, his porous face sagged, and his eyes were as gray as the January sky. He was short and stooped, and always smartly dressed. Today he wore a crisp white shirt, a hound's-tooth jacket, pressed brown trousers, and a pair of Hush Puppies. He preferred the kind of soft-soled shoes that snuck up on you. "Excuse the mess," he said, ushering her inside. "Busy day after last week's chaos. The streets aren't the only place that need cleaning up post-Halloween."

The bed-and-breakfast was spacious and welcoming, with built-ins full of bric-a-brac and comfortable chairs and sofas. The air freshener smelled like honeysuckle. The young, mostly female staff was busy running up and down the creaking stairs with armloads of fresh linens and cleaning supplies.

"Let's go into the living room, shall we?" he suggested with a wave of his hand. "Most of the guests are gone. I call it the wham-bam-thank-you-ma'am season."

She smiled. The living room had speckled eggshell carpeting, large blocky furniture, and impressive views of the garden. The adjoining dining room's long oak table was set for happy hour.

"Have a seat. You don't smoke, do you, Detective?" He offered her one anyway.

"I quit."

"You did, huh?" He shrugged. "Suit yourself." Dell slid the glass ashtray closer to him. "Morgan Chambers was a delight. She booked with us for four days. I was shocked when I found out what happened to her. We all were. I was literally shaking."

"It's terribly sad," Natalie acknowledged.

"I won't ask you what happened, because I know you can't talk about it, Natalie, but rumors are flying. People are scared."

"We're doing everything we can to find out what happened."

He patted her knee. "Just like your dad. Keeping the streets safe."

Natalie smiled and took out her notebook. "When did she check in?"

"Belinda handles the check-ins. She's in the front office." He rubbed his chin and called out, "Belinda?"

"What?" she shouted back.

"Come in here a second."

"Hi there, Natalie," Belinda Pickle said from the doorway. Dell's blowsy middle-aged daughter had gray hair and a forehead nibbled with worry.

Dell's sigh sounded more like a hiss. "When did our friend Morgan check in?"

"Thursday," she said. "Around three o'clock."

"And she was supposed to check out this morning?" he asked.

"Yes, but then . . . you know." She shook her head sadly.

"Let me tell you, it came as quite a shock." Dell rested his cigarette in the ashtray and said, "She was such a nice person. A violinist at the Brock Conservatory. She was here for the festivities. She liked the doves outside her window, said they woke her up early, but that it was better than an alarm clock. She spent a lot of time looking at the brochures and asking for recommendations. She was curious about the Witch Museum."

"Speaking of which, Dad, did you know Harry Crenshaw slipped and fell last night?"

Dell's eyes widened. "You're kidding me. Not another casualty."

"You know Harry, right, Natalie? He manages the museum. Broke his hip. Once your hip goes, well . . ." Belinda shook her head sadly. "It's all downhill from there."

"What the hell is happening?" Dell asked rhetorically. "First Ned Bertrand has a stroke, then Jenny Marley passes away . . . you know Jenny, don't you, Natalie? She ran that dry cleaning establishment over on Dunham Hill Road. And now poor Harry breaks a hip. I should go visit him, Belinda."

"I'll take you to the hospital this evening, Dad."

"Maybe Death's coming for me next?" he said with a wink.

"Dad . . . you're never going to die. I won't let you."

"Ha. You hear that, Natalie?"

She smiled. They were never going to call her Detective Lockhart, so she didn't bother correcting them. They'd both known her since she was a little girl, when her father used to take her along with him on his beat. The lower half of Joey's face was sunburned from walking the beat from noon until ten at night. He knew these streets like the back of his hand. He knew every alleyway, every dead-end street, every business establishment and vacant building. Joey didn't just walk the beat, he strode, chest puffed, eyes alert, covering an area from Gerry's House of Style to Perlia Lane. His turf.

"When's the last time you saw Morgan?" Natalie asked him.

Dell rolled his eyes. "Gosh, I don't remember. We were fully booked, and it gets so busy this time of year . . . everybody has questions or special requests. There's so much to do. Some of the guests leave their rooms in a terrible mess. Things get broken or go missing. There's so much confusion, it's just . . ." He craned his neck. "Belinda? When was the last time you saw her?"

His daughter paused to rub the back of her neck. "Umm . . . yesterday around four o'clock, I think." The phone rang in the background. "That's for me . . ."

"Before you go," Natalie said, "what did she say when you saw her yesterday afternoon?"

"She didn't really have time to talk. She came into the inn carrying a couple of shopping bags and said she had to get ready to go out. I don't know. It was so busy. That's all I can recall."

"What kind of shopping bags?"

"One was from Murray's Halloween Costumes, I noticed."

Natalie nodded. It matched the label on Morgan's Wonder Woman costume. "Anything else?"

"No. Sorry." Belinda tilted her head apologetically. "I gotta take this."

Natalie watched her run off to catch the phone. "Which room was Morgan staying in?" she asked Dell, whose eyes shifted focus from the doorway where Belinda had just been to the marigolds on the coffee table.

"Suite Two B. Very nice, with an eastern view."

"I'd like to take a look, if you don't mind."

Natalie followed the innkeeper up a creaky flight of wooden stairs to the second floor. Suite 2-B was charming, with a four-poster bed, a brick fireplace, and a view of the rose garden. There was a small flat-screen TV mounted on the wall, a Keurig coffeemaker, and a white-tiled bathroom. The Sunflower Inn wasn't cheap.

"How much did she pay for the room?" Natalie asked.

"One fifty per night."

Natalie added it up. Six hundred dollars was a lot of money for somebody who was struggling to pay the rent, but that's what credit cards were for. Natalie had issues in that department as well.

"I'm not sure what to do with her belongings," Dell said now.

"Don't touch anything," she told him. "I've asked Detective Labruzzo to process the room for prints and trace evidence. He'll be here shortly with a search warrant. After that, an officer will pack everything up and make sure it gets back to her family. Did she have any guests while she was here?"

"Visitors?" Dell shook his head. "Not that I recall."

"Do you keep surveillance tapes?"

He seemed shocked at the suggestion. "Never. We value our guests' privacy."

The small bathroom was cluttered with Morgan's stuff—a hairbrush, toothpaste, deodorant, lipstick. Natalie found Morgan's suitcase and overnight bag tucked inside the closet. Her clothes were hung up neatly on their hangers. On the bedside table were Morgan's phone charger, her travel alarm clock, and another library book on witchcraft, which she'd checked out of the Burning Lake Library two weeks ago. It was due back tomorrow. Tucked inside the book was a promotional brochure for Halloween in Burning Lake, and there was a phone number scribbled on the front in blue ink.

Natalie dialed the number and listened to the automated response.

"The number you have reached is no longer in service . . ."

She opened the side table drawer and spotted a wrist brace. "Is this hers?"

Dell squinted. "We clean up after every guest, so I suppose it must be."

After searching the entire room, Natalie hadn't found a violin. "Did you see her take her violin out of the inn with her?"

"Like I said, Natalie," he said with a sigh, "it was a zoo around here."

"Okay. Has she ever stayed at the inn before?"

He shook his head. "She was a first-timer."

"Is her car still here?"

"Out back."

Outside, the fallen leaves rustled underfoot. The backyard was broad, with a couple of wooden benches and a mazelike path through the dying, sweet-smelling rose garden. The sun was about to set. The sky was pastel pink along the horizon, dark purple above.

Natalie found Morgan's green Kia Rio in the parking lot and called Augie to have it towed away to the impound lot, where it could be processed for blood and prints. She thanked Dell and Belinda for their cooperation, then drove across town to the public library.

The library was closed. She would try again in the morning.

Natalie rested her forehead against the steering wheel of her car. Exhaustion took hold. It felt like something awful was about to happen, only she couldn't control it. Her stomach twinged as she turned on the ignition again.

For some reason, "Happy Birthday" was playing on the car radio—part of an ad for health insurance coverage. How could she have forgotten Luke's thirty-ninth birthday? She retrieved her phone and checked her messages—nothing that couldn't wait. She saw things clearly for a moment through the fog of burnout. It was the kind of clarity that death can bring, brushing away the cobwebs and making room for reality. Morgan's life had ended tragically and pointlessly. That was today's lesson. Live your life fully, before it's too late.

She dialed Luke's number.

"Hello?"

"Hey, it's me."

"Natalie? What's up?"

"I'd like to take you out to dinner for your birthday. I thought maybe Lucia's . . ."

"Thanks, but . . ." He hesitated. "But I've got other plans."

"Oh." She tried to mask her disappointment.

"Rainie Sandhill invited me out to dinner," he said softly.

"She did?"

"Yep."

Silence.

"Natalie?"

"That's awfully nice of her," she said, feeling feverish. "Anyway, I just wanted to wish you a happy birthday again."

"Maybe some other time."

"Sure. Bye." She hung up and clutched the steering wheel, the tips of her ears burning. She drove home, feeling like the biggest loser on the planet.

19

The sun had set and the stars were out. Instead of going home, Natalie took a narrow winding road toward the old ruins that lay hidden on the edge of town. She parked her car in front of a crumbling stone-pillared gate, scooped a heavy-duty flashlight out of the glove compartment, and got out. The trek through the woods was spooky at night, weedy and dark. The place had a *Walking Dead* vibe to it.

The old theme park had been closed for decades by the time Natalie and her high school friends discovered it on the outskirts of town. They laughed hysterically at the big goofy cement figurines of giants and elves and twisted crones. Everything was covered in crawling vines and out-of-control ivy. Funland Village was so cut off from the rest of the world, they knew they'd found their special meeting place. Back in high school, Natalie had formed a club with Bella, Bobby, Adam, and Max. They called themselves the Brilliant Misfits and amused themselves by boasting about how talented they were, because it bolstered their morale. They were five smart, gifted kids who felt like total losers, but their club made them feel like superheroes.

Natalie stepped over the broken fence with its bullet-riddled KEEP OUT sign and entered a postapocalyptic playground where the rusty swings creaked in the wind. The decommissioned theme park was part of the vast state forest that spread into the Adirondacks and beyond. The boarded-up concession stand and abandoned ticket booth were covered in a tangle of vines, and the "sculpture garden" was populated with large, demented-looking creatures from *Grimm's Fairy Tales*—a headless Evil Queen, an eroding Snow White, Jack and his tumbledown beanstalk, a mossy-eyed Cinderella and her ugly stepsisters.

A few yards beyond Rapunzel's vandalized tower was the stone bridge where the five of them used to hang out after school, sharing joints and conjuring up their incredible futures. Part of the Bridge to the Future had collapsed into a heap on the forest floor, and as a result you could only walk halfway across before the future abruptly ended. Because of this, Natalie and Bella jokingly called it "the Bridge to Nowhere."

Now she headed up the crumbling stone steps and trailed her fingers along the guardrail, while ancient chips of paint flaked off beneath her touch. The mortar was disintegrating between the old stones. The bridge's floorboards were warped with rot. Above her head, the night sky was full of stars.

She paused at the precipice where the bridge abruptly ended, a few splintered boards jutting out over the drop. If you didn't mind heights, you could sit on the ledge with your legs dangling. It was like sitting on the edge of a cliff. Twenty feet down was a pile of rubble on the vine-choked ground. Scattered across the remains of the bridge were decades' worth of cigarette butts, discarded liquor bottles, condoms, and other detritus beneath layers of autumn leaves.

The place had once belonged to them exclusively—Natalie, Bella, Bobby, Adam, and Max. Five skinny rebellious teens. The absurd fairy-tale toadstools, cement elves, weird witches, and goofy-looking pigs made them roar with stoned laughter.

Now the treetops danced in the November wind, causing golden leaves to fall and drift like snowflakes. The figurines in the sculpture garden, which Natalie could see from here, appeared to be wading through a river of undergrowth. It reminded her of a haunted topiary garden—hedges trimmed to resemble strange beasts. She listened to the rush of wind through the brittle leaves—a haunted, pleading sound. Begging for forgiveness. Reprieve from the past.

After Bella went missing on the night of their high school graduation, a boy with behavior problems named Nesbitt Rose became the prime suspect. Nesbitt was innocent. He loved Bella and would never have hurt her, but the media hounded him and his family until one rainy night, three weeks after Bella disappeared, Nesbitt took his own life. That was tragic enough, but then, three months later, letters from Bella began to arrive, proving she was still alive. The case was closed.

In the aftermath, Nesbitt's brother, Hunter Rose, sued the police department and the local papers, blaming them for his brother's death. He turned his bitterness and grief on the small-town mentality that he believed contributed to Nesbitt's demise. The city settled, but it took Hunter years to get over it. Now he was one of Burning Lake's most prominent citizens, founder of Rose Security Software, a wealthy man with friends in high places. He pulled the strings and others danced.

When the police called off their search for Bella, it was a heartbreaking moment for the Misfits. At that point, everyone assumed she was dead. During the long hot summer that followed, it wasn't the same for the four of them anymore—not without Bella. Soon the Brilliant Misfits would be going their separate ways, heading off to college, but before they split up, they wanted to do something in her honor. They set up a website, intending to keep Bella's memory alive, but of course things never played out that way.

The four of them—Natalie, Bobby, Max, and Adam—grew closer then due to their shared grief and loss. If something like that could happen to Bella, then it could happen to anyone. Life was precious. Grab it while you can. Late in August, before heading off to college, they all made a pledge. Friends for life. Friends forever.

Funny, how things turned out. Adam was dead. She hadn't seen Bobby in ages. The only one she'd kept in touch with was Max. He used to play classical piano. Now he worked for his father's construction company and was advising Natalie on her home renovation schemes.

Natalie took out her phone and called him.

"Hello?" Max answered brightly as if he'd imbibed too much caffeine.

"It's me, Natalie. Got a minute?"

"Sure, kid, what's up?"

She had a flash memory of the last time she'd seen him—he'd come over to repair her leaky roof. He'd aged quite a bit since their high school days—a paunch over his belt buckle, graying temples, crow's-feet around the eyes—but he looked like the same old Max to her. "Guess where I am right now," she said.

"No clue."

"Sitting on the Bridge to the Future."

"Oh God," Max said with a laugh. "Brilliant Misfits, man. Fist bump."

She smiled sadly. "You heard the news, right?"

"About the woman in the dumpster? Yeah. It's freakin' tragic."

"She was a violinist. So I couldn't help thinking about Bella all day long."

"Funny how life turns out," he said gently. "Here you are, solving murders. And here I am, working for my dad. I never figured *that* would happen. Adam and Bella are gone, and Bobby's in Syracuse, working as a CPA, of all things. Christ, his SAT scores were off the charts. His math skills were college-level and beyond. How the hell did he wind up as a fucking accountant?" Max sighed heavily. "Remember the first thing he said to you?"

So much time had passed, Natalie couldn't remember.

"Your last names both had hearts in them. Lockhart. Deckhart."

"Oh, yeah. Right." She smiled, thinking about her teenage crush. Natalie had been a skinny punk wannabe with a growing feminine body she hid under layers of clothes, like Diane Keaton in *Annie Hall*. She didn't want to be "pretty." She wanted to be Dorothy Parker on acid. She wanted to be the female version of Jean-Michel Basquiat.

Back then, Bobby was a lanky, sensitive, dreamy-eyed youth with a cowlick on one side of his head that swirled his hair in different directions, and calm brown eyes that made him seem more mature than he actually was. He wore jeans put together with safety pins as proof he didn't care about fitting in, when he secretly cared a lot. The Misfits were all about finding a place to fit in. It just so happened to be with one another.

Bobby loved numbers and statistics so much, he used them to explain his love for Natalie—how many days they'd known each other, how many times they'd kissed, the geometry of her face.

On the night of their high school graduation, Natalie let Bobby finger her. Out of school and free at last. Their shy, slippery experimentation, a finger that went in a little further. Their awkward fumblings in the dark. Natalie figured she and Bobby would get married someday, but those feelings didn't last. Bobby was too sensitive, too passive for her tastes. Not ambitious enough. Not confident enough. After they headed off to separate colleges, Natalie broke up with Bobby over the phone. He sustained feelings for her all the way through college but eventually moved on. Now he was married with two kids and pretty happy, according to Max. Bella was gone. Adam was gone. Max and Natalie were single, but they didn't belong together. They were like brother and sister, always teasing each other and bickering about the small stuff.

"We were the Brilliant Misfits, right?" Max said. "But I was never that gifted, Natalie. I'm not brilliant. Neither is Bobby. He moved to Syracuse to become a bland corporate slave. We both gave up the dream."

She smiled. "Are you kidding me? You guys are legends in your own minds."

He laughed. "You're such a badass. Jesus, here you are chasing serial killers. I'm not worthy."

She rolled her eyes. "Yeah, I lead such a glamorous life. Up to my elbows in unicorn puke."

"You're right. I have no idea what it's like to be you."

"Anyway, I can't stop thinking about Bella. Where she is. What happened."

"Well, it is strange the way she disappeared without telling anyone, isn't it?" he said. "Not even you, her best friend. Before the letters started coming, Bobby and I figured Nesbitt must've done it. Or maybe him and his brother. Like maybe they killed Bella and buried her on the property," Max said. "But instead she ghosted on us. I guess you don't really know a person, do you? I mean, she never really explained anything in those letters, did she? Did she say why she left so abruptly like that, letting everyone think she was dead? Did she say where she went? And why? And what the hell? You split one night and don't tell your best friends. Then three months later, you send letters with pictures of yourself as if you're trying to prove . . . what exactly? 'Hey, I'm okay, you guys, I'm alive, but guess what? I don't care enough about any of you to explain what the hell happened to me.'" He sighed. "Anyway, I thought for sure she'd show up at her father's funeral six years ago."

"They had a complicated relationship," Natalie said.

"Complicated? You come home and pay your respects," Max argued. "But about the dead girl, Morgan . . . it's weird, Natalie, because I saw her perform at the Monster Mash on Friday night."

Natalie sat forward. "You did?"

"The whole point of the contest is to play the spookiest Halloween music, right? You've got a million pieces to choose from, but Bartók's peasant folk songs aren't what I'd call scary. They're fairly plodding. But she played with a lot of intensity . . . all elbows and swaying upper body. She gave it her best shot, and the audience was polite and respectful, but she didn't wow the crowd."

"Who won?"

"This violin soloist from Manhattan, Ava Dixon . . . she blew everybody away. I mean, it wasn't even close," he said. "First, the stage goes completely dark. This is an outdoor concert, mind you, and all of a sudden there isn't a peep. The audience is riveted. A single spotlight shines down, and three stagehands wheel out an old-fashioned tub on a dolly, and all around the tub is this white shower curtain. It's closed. You can't see who's behind it. There's a long pause . . . then you hear the beginning strains of *Psycho* by Bernard Herrmann. Oh man, this young violinist played like a storyteller. We all got chills. Then the shower curtain draws back to reveal the spitting image of Janet Leigh . . . all dolled up in a blond wig and a pink bodysuit with fake suds in all the right places, standing there in the shower, playing the violin . . . it was chilling. They used tinsel to represent water, and the audience is going wild. She's taking a shower, playing madly, when all of a sudden an Anthony Perkins look-alike in an old lady wig comes onstage and starts to viciously attack her, *stabbing* her . . . there's fake blood flying everywhere . . . and the violin is literally *shrieking* . . . and the audience is riveted. It was the star performance of the evening, no question. Hands down. She blew the competition away."

"Sounds amazing," Natalie said, thinking how hard it must've been for Morgan.

There was a click on the line.

"Hold on," Max said. "Gotta take this." He answered his call-waiting, then came back sounding winded. "Everything's a fucking emergency."

"Max, before you go, did anything unusual happen at the contest? Anything that might help me with the investigation?"

"Nah. I went to the contest and enjoyed the whole experience. I no longer beat myself up about why I quit playing piano, Natalie. Those days are gone. I'm much happier now. Sometimes you have to drop the pretense and just be yourself."

"Yeah," she said quietly. "Thanks, Max."

"Sure. Hey, call me anytime about the reno, okay? Take care of yourself, Natalie. Stay safe out there." He hung up.

Years ago, Bella had promised Natalie, "We'll never be separated, it's not possible. We're like barnacles. We'll be glued together forever. No matter what."

"No matter what," Natalie had promised back.

Little did she know that their promises would be broken and smashed forever, and completely lost in time.

20

Natalie woke up in the middle of the night and thought she heard music. Sad, sweet violin music. She sat up in bed and glanced out her window at the pitch-dark. There it was again—that eerie melody coming from the hills beyond the power lines. It ebbed and flowed, and the more she focused on it, the more distant and remote it sounded, until she couldn't hear it anymore.

Was she dreaming? Was it the wind in the trees?

She settled back against her pillow and tried to sleep.

Ever since Grace passed away last April, nothing else mattered in the middle of the night but the methodical, painful process of carpet bombing her memories and wiping out every last crumb of pain. Sometimes when she couldn't sleep, Natalie would get up and go downstairs and work on her caseload, until her head felt woozy and thick with facts. She would comb over the trace evidence—hairs, fibers, glass shards, leaf matter, soil samples, bits of random debris. She would stare at crime scene photos until her eyes throbbed and try to find that one elusive clue that might solve a case and guarantee a win for the good guys.

Sometimes, unable to process her losses, Natalie would close the case file, sit back, and sort through old memories like a Rolodex full of dog-eared cards. Luke, for instance, with his cracked leather holster under his left arm. In those rare instances when a detective's life was in danger and he was forced to reach for his weapon, Luke called it the "Pledge of Allegiance" draw. Because when you pledged allegiance to the flag, you placed your right hand over the left side of your chest. Whenever you were compelled to defend yourself, you pledged allegiance to your gun. He meant it ironically, but the reality was grim.

Ever since the tragic events of last April, Natalie had gone over the scenario in her mind, and yes, the chances of hitting the Crow Killer in the arm or the thigh were slim. There was always the risk of missing her target, and the odds of her surviving a subsequent attack while Samuel was even more enraged weren't good. Instead, she'd hit him center of mass, killing him. And she was glad she had stopped him. What didn't feel good at all was the knowledge that she had killed another human being, and that she would have less anxiety about it the next time. That felt shitty.

Outside the pitch-black windows, the world felt dead. A car drove past, its headlights casting creeping shadows. The shadows didn't go away. She sat up, parted the curtains, and looked out the window. Luke's Ford Ranger was parked by the side of the road, its engine idling.

Natalie expected him to get out of his car and come ring her doorbell, but instead he just sat there, alone in his vehicle. She wondered how his date had gone.

Leaping out of bed, she threw on some clothes and went outside to talk to him. "Hey there, stranger."

"Hello." He smiled but didn't get out of his vehicle.

"How was your date?"

He squinted moodily at her. "Was it a date?"

"What else would you call it?"

He shrugged. "Rainie's a nice person."

Natalie nodded, wondering what that was supposed to mean. He didn't sound super-excited, which made her feel happy. "So what's up?" she asked. "What're you doing here?"

"What else? Thinking about the case," he said.

"Well, I for one am glad you dropped by." She sat down on the cold lawn with her legs crossed. "I was about to wrestle with my insomnia for another hour or so. But the night air has revived me. Maybe I'll stay up for a while."

His body relaxed as he gazed at her. "I used to love my job so much, I couldn't wait to get out of bed in the morning. Digging around for the truth, arresting the bad guys. I took the worst cases—the shittier the better. The guys used to tease me because of the way I'd pounce on the phone. But I couldn't help myself. I was a CIU whore. I lapped it up." He paused. "That attitude almost ruined me. There's a price to pay."

She sighed heavily. "Why do I feel a lecture coming on?"

"I know all the symptoms, Natalie. First you start repeating yourself. Then you second-guess yourself. Next thing you know, you're drinking Red Bull and imagining vast conspiracies that only you can solve. Take the night off, understand? You need your rest—both mentally and physically. Go back inside, take a long hot shower, lie down, and at least pretend to sleep." In the moonlight, he seemed older, more worn down by life.

Natalie glanced at the stars. "I used to think Grace was so daring and brave. I had this illusion about her, because she dazzled me. But now I realize . . . she was kind of a chicken. She'd dare me to do things, and I never refused. Once, while we were browsing through Kmart, Grace spotted a discarded candy wrapper in one of the candy displays and dared me to pick it up. I did. I trusted her. I didn't realize there was a man standing behind me, and he thought I'd eaten the candy bar because I was holding a crumpled wrapper. He said, 'You don't want to grow up to be the girl who steals candy, do you?' I told him I didn't steal anything, and he called me a liar. All the while, Grace was laughing her ass off."

Luke smiled. "So your big sister set you up, huh?"

"More than once." Natalie crossed her arms and shivered against the chill. "It feels like I've spent the last six months picking up pieces of my life and realizing they weren't what I'd always assumed they were. Grace wasn't really the Grace I thought I knew. My father would've been heartbroken."

"They were my family, too," Luke said, studying her closely. "The Lockharts. Joey welcomed me into his home. Me, this messed up, fatherless kid.

You guys were my second family. The night Grace died, when everything went down the way it did . . . I wanted a drink so bad I could taste it. There was a worm in my gut that needed sedating. But I'd promised myself I wouldn't touch another drop, and I kept that promise. Alcohol doesn't numb the pain so much as it dulls the sharpest edges. But you can kill a man with a dull knife."

She looked at him in a different light—she'd never thought of that . . . that Luke had loved her family as much as she did. That she wasn't carrying around her grief alone.

"I wanted to give you whatever space you needed, Natalie," he explained, both hands on the wheel. "That's why I pulled away. You asked me to, so I did."

"Yeah, but it turns out I didn't need space. I needed the opposite. Only I didn't know how to ask for it, and hence . . ."

"Hence?"

She shrugged. "Hence, here we are."

He looked at her with soulful eyes. "Where are we, Natalie?"

"You tell me." She couldn't hold his gaze. She wasn't ready yet. She wasn't prepared to embrace whatever Luke was offering, or appeared to be offering. She wasn't ready for her fantasy life of love and marriage and kids and commitment . . . her heart was pounding. Because even if it only started out with hot sex and intense all-night talks, and then more hot sex, it would eventually lead to marriage and kids. She was positive about this. *Change the subject.*

"For the longest time," she confessed, "I've been in a dead zone . . . but lately I've felt glimmerings of life. And it's painful. Going from numb to awake. I'm outraged by my own blind spot with Grace, and now this. Morgan Chambers. Such a senseless death. It makes me think about Bella being gone all these years, and about runaways who've gone missing, and about young girls dying, and men taking what they want, and about people judging and shaming." She glanced up. "Now I'm babbling."

"No, you're not."

"I think it's Red Bull conspiracy time." She smirked.

"You'll do fine."

"Really? Because I've been thinking lately that this town must be cursed."

He shook his head. "I don't believe in curses, Natalie."

"Three innocent people were killed in 1712. Maybe we're all still paying for it? Metaphorically speaking."

"I don't believe in metaphors or curses."

She wiped her sweaty hands on her jeans. "What do you believe in, Luke?"

"Good intentions and bad intentions." He stared dead ahead at his headlights pooling across the road. "We're all capable of goodness, and we're all capable of evil. It's simply a matter of keeping your intentions aligned on the side of good and pushing away the bad impulses."

She realized she was afraid of him. Afraid of her long-repressed feelings for him. Something was stirring—if it had ever gone away. "Want to come inside?" she asked.

His mood darkened. "I don't think I'd better."

She rubbed the chill off her neck. "Look, I owe my friends and colleagues a heap of gratitude. Everyone's been so kind and thoughtful. But I don't know how to thank people." She smiled weakly. "I don't know how to thank you."

"You don't have to thank me." He looked at her briefly, then shook his head. "I'm proud of you, Natalie. Most people would've quit under the pressure. Now go inside. Get some rest."

She nodded listlessly.

"Good night." He rolled up his window and drove off.

Back inside, she turned off all the lights and went upstairs to her room, where she lay in bed like a brick, pretending to sleep. She felt sorry for him. She felt sorry for them both.

In music, there was no such thing as perfect timing, she'd once read—music skipped random beats once in a while. These silent notes were called "rests."

Sometimes the most important parts of a conversation were the things that were left unsaid—the rests between words.

21

Tuesday morning brought a slant of sunshine that turned Natalie's bedroom golden yellow. She wiped the crust out of her eyes, yawned luxuriously, and glanced at her clock. She'd managed to get a good seven hours' sleep.

Her phone rang, and she groped for it on the bedside table, knocking a box of tissues to the floor. "Oops. Hello?"

"Good morning." It was Luke. "We got the tox report back."

"Be right there." She hung up.

Natalie got up feeling refreshed, had toast and coffee for breakfast, then headed into town. She got stuck in traffic and was ten minutes late to the meeting. She parked in the underground parking garage of the county health building and took an elevator to the coroner's second-story office. She straightened her jacket and knocked on the door.

"Come in," Barry Fishbeck said.

She stepped inside. "Sorry I'm late. Traffic."

"No problem." Barry smiled warmly at her.

She took a seat next to Luke, who handed her a copy of the toxicology report.

"I was telling Luke," the coroner said, "what these findings mean. In addition to alcohol, it looks like Morgan Chambers had two drugs in her system. Ecstasy and GHB."

Natalie frowned. "The date rape drug?"

"Gamma-hydroxybutyrate." Barry nodded. She wasn't used to seeing him out of his lab coat. Today he wore a plaid short-sleeve shirt and brown corduroy trousers, and his face was etched with an untold number of deaths—one wrinkle for every slash of the scalpel or slice of the bone saw down in the morgue. "GHB is colorless, odorless, and tasteless, and therefore undetectable in drinks. It's sold as a liquid in a vial and has a slightly salty taste, so it would blend right into a cocktail. It acts as a depressant on the central nervous system. Similar to Rohypnol."

Thumbing through the tox report, Natalie said, "We're talking about a deliberate intent to induce a state of unconsciousness?"

Barry nodded. Behind his desk was an oak cabinet full of Victorian-era mason jars containing preserved body parts that were fairly common back when doctors were called quacks. Mellow jazz was playing in the background.

"So she must've been in a bar that night when somebody slipped her a roofie. How long does it take to feel the effects of GHB?"

"Not very long. Approximately fifteen minutes," Barry said.

"Which means she would've left the bar around eleven thirty, because clearly on the video, she was feeling the effects when she went into the alley at eleven forty-four."

Luke turned to Natalie and said, "You called it. She was running away from whoever slipped her the drug. Which would explain why she kept looking over her shoulder and pushing through the crowd."

"It wasn't nicknamed 'easy lay' for nothing." Barry picked up the phone. "Anyway, I've asked Russ Swinton to chime in on this, since he'll be able to tell us if anyone else tested positive for GHB over the weekend. Hold on . . ." He punched in a number, and after a moment Dr. Swinton picked up. "Hello, Russ. You're on speakerphone. Luke and Natalie are here."

"Good morning, Barry. Hello, everyone," Dr. Swinton said.

"Hello, Russ," Luke chimed in.

"Good morning," Natalie said a little self-consciously. They hadn't spoken since Sunday night, but this conference call made perfect sense. Russ was the best person to talk to regarding the effects of GHB, along with finding out if there were any Halloween emergency room visits involving GHB poisoning.

Barry leaned forward and said, "Russ, if you don't mind, I'd like you to explain to Natalie and Luke what you told me earlier this morning."

"Of course," the doctor said. "The combination of substances you described . . . GHB, ecstasy, and alcohol . . . can be lethal to a patient, depending on the dosages. There are any number of things that can go wrong. You can choke on your own vomit, your heart rate can slow down considerably, and if your breathing dips under fifteen to twenty breaths per minute . . . that's called respiratory depression. A fatal dose of GHB alone could involve any of the following symptoms . . . vomiting, seizures, profuse sweating, lowered body temperature, agitation, tremors, hallucinations, unconsciousness, fever, and even coma or death. If help doesn't arrive promptly, you will most likely die. GHB is a Schedule one controlled substance, and it's manufactured illegally."

"Have you had any emergency cases involving GHB recently?" Barry asked.

"Hard to say, since that particular drug can go through the system very quickly. Usually, by the time toxicology tests are performed, there's no trace of the drug left in the bloodstream. You were lucky to catch it this time."

"Have you had any patients complaining about any of the symptoms you described, Russ?"

"Well, if you look at the last three or four weeks," he hedged, "I'd say we've had our share of alcohol poisonings and overdoses. Unfortunately, that's typical for Halloween season. For instance, on Sunday night alone, we had two drug overdoses, four alcohol poisonings, a heart attack, a head injury when a man fell off a balcony, three minor traffic accidents, plus any number of scrapes, bumps, cases of heatstroke, food poisoning, and the like. I would have to review our records for a more accurate assessment, but it felt like a fairly typical Halloween weekend to me."

"Two drug overdoses?"

"Meth addicts."

"Are you sure?"

"Meth addicts think they're superheroes," he said. "They do crazy things. Opioid addicts behave like zombies. Date rape victims will experience periods of amnesia and loss of consciousness. These effects are amplified when combined with alcohol, and they can mimic alcoholic blackouts, which is also why they're so difficult to detect."

"So none of your recent patients suffered from GHB poisoning?"

"Not that I'm aware of. We would've treated any patient reporting such symptoms immediately. On Halloween night, no one reported having amnesia or suspected their drinks had been spiked. So I'd have to conclude that this particular case was unique."

Barry looked over at Natalie and Luke. "Any other questions before I let this gentleman go?"

They shook their heads.

"Thanks for your time, Russ," Barry said.

"No problem. Let me know if there's anything else you need," the doctor said and hung up.

22

Luke detained Natalie outside of Barry's office and said, "If she was given a date rape drug, that would indicate foul play. That's a whole new ball game. We need to pin down her time line. Follow up on the ink stamps on her hands. I'm assuming she got roofied in one of the bars or restaurants she went to that night."

"I was planning on dropping by the library this morning, since a book she borrowed was due today. Another book on witchcraft."

"Okay, you head over to the library. I'll take the lead on the time line. In the meantime, we still haven't located her phone, but I'm working on a subpoena for her phone records." Luke glanced at his watch. "Let's untangle this fucked up mess and find out what happened to her."

The hills blazed with an array of spectacular colors this morning—crimson, saffron, pumpkin orange. Flocks of migrating geese flew in V-shapes along the horizon, honking their way south. The public library was designed in the High Victorian style, with Gothic arches and medieval-looking turrets that reminded Natalie of Hogwarts. There was an east wing and a west wing. The stacks took up three levels of the main library, accessible by two circular wrought iron stairwells. There was a courtyard out back where you could sit in the sun or read on the stone benches.

Natalie found the associate director behind the circulation desk. He was busy pasting book pockets into recent acquisitions. In his mid-thirties, Patrick Dupree peered at her over his wire-rim glasses. He had neatly trimmed brown hair and a pudgy, formless face. Three years ahead of her at school, he was one of those unfortunates who were instantly forgettable. A cruel reality. "Hello, Natalie, how can I help you . . . I mean, Detective Lockhart?" He smiled warmly.

"How are you, Patrick?"

"Not great." He sat slumped in his stool, a box of tissues and a bottled water on the table in front of him. His eyes were red-rimmed. "Is this about Morgan Chambers?"

"You knew her?"

He nodded. He looked miserable. He unscrewed the bottled water and took a few sips, then plucked a tissue out of the box and blew his nose. "We met at a librarians' conference over a year ago and spoke on the phone quite a bit. She works at the Chaste Falls Library, and we have an interlibrary loan program with them. She borrowed a book from us . . ."

"This book?" Natalie asked, handing him the book on witchcraft.

"That's the one. It was due today. Morgan said she was going to swing by, and we'd go out for coffee. Yesterday, I heard all the rumors about a body in a dumpster, but I never dreamed it was her. Then I saw it on the news." His voice trailed off. He shook his head numbly.

"You spoke to her on the phone? What did you two talk about?"

"Mostly commiserating about our jobs. You know, librarian stuff. Moldy book donations from a flooded basement. Some perv changing the screen saver to a close-up of a penis. Morgan laughed it off. She thought it was funny. I told her she had a musical laugh. I think that made her feel better." He grew visibly upset. "I can't believe something like this could've happened to her. She was so nice."

"I know. It's really sad."

"We shared a passion for the Beat poets—not just Kerouac and Ginsberg, but the more obscure ones, like Herbert Huncke, Jane Bowles, and Lucien Carr. She was a huge *Lord of the Rings* fan, same as me. And she played the violin, and I adore classical music. Mostly we kibitzed about our jobs, though. When you work at a library, you're privy to a lot of strange behavior."

Natalie nodded, interested. "What kind of strange behavior?"

"Well, for instance, you've got your library masturbators," he said, lowering his voice. "Occasionally, I'll find an erotic book or magazine in the men's room . . . and you have to toss it out. We've banned all the masturbators from the library. And then there's the homeless population. There are a lot of . . . how can I put this? There are a lot of in-need people showing up at the library nowadays. I don't mean to sound insensitive, but they've got no place else to go that's as nice as the library. And they're pursuing knowledge and being productive human beings, and that's a good thing. Anyway, this one elderly lady likes to sit in the children's section and clip her toenails. Imagine that? It's very sad. We have to redirect her into the restroom, and she'll clip her toenails in there. Some of these people come in every day. But we never discourage them from using the library, even though the other patrons complain, especially moms with small children. Not that I blame them. So Morgan and I exchanged a lot of crazy library stories."

Natalie nodded. "What were some of Morgan's crazy stories?"

Patrick slid his glasses back up his nose and rested his elbows on the circulation desk. "There's a minister in Chaste Falls who has a thing for literary porn—you know, highbrow stuff like Henry Miller, Erica Jong, Nabokov. And apparently there's a wealthy, dignified lady who checks out the latest bestselling thrillers, only to return them with obscene comments scribbled in the margins. These are brand-new books, mind you. Completely ruined. To make up for it, she'll slip Morgan a couple of twenties, which more than makes up for the expense." Patrick shrugged. "Morgan says they've never canceled this lady's membership, since she sits on a lot of boards. It's an embarrassing fetish of hers . . . but you can tell she's grateful. She donates each year to the Chaste Falls library fund. She's one of their most generous contributors. It's just that she has this strange compulsion . . . anyway, we've got our share of nuts running around right here in Burning Lake. One guy will sit in the corner over there, crying and laughing. Softly, I mean. He doesn't bother anybody. And then there's a skinny young woman with no teeth who uses the photocopier every day. I don't know what for, but she eats snacks from plastic bags and makes a lot of noise. Others come here to sleep." He shook his head slowly. "I guess it's a peaceful place."

"Did Morgan mention any trouble she was having recently? At the library or in her personal life?"

"No, like I said, we were just beginning to get to know each other."

Natalie knew Patrick Dupree fairly well, the way people knew other people in small towns. He was an overall good guy. Helpful and considerate. He kept to himself. He was professional and caring. Whenever there was trouble at the library, he would call the BLPD for help, because he knew that the officers would handle the incident with discretion. "What about this book she borrowed?" Natalie asked, tapping the hardcover. "Did she talk about it at all?"

"Just that she was interested in witchcraft. Intrigued. I suggested this book by Corvina Manse, so she borrowed it from us. I explained to her that Corvina Manse is the pen name for Veronica Manes," he said. "It's almost an anagram."

"Almost." Natalie nodded. "Right. There's an *e* missing."

"Correct. This one's out of print, but it's quite interesting. *A Beginner's Guide to Witchcraft.* Veronica published it in her early twenties, before she stopped writing about Wicca and devoted herself to the practice."

Everyone in town knew who Veronica Manes was, although Natalie had never met her personally. Veronica was one of the better-known witches in Burning Lake. She was a priestess in a local coven—the oldest active coven in town, started in the mid-1950s. Veronica hosted quarterly moonlight rituals on her property and was the best person to talk to if you wanted to understand modern-day witchcraft.

"Morgan asked for Veronica's private phone number," Patrick said.

"Did you give it to her?"

He looked askance. "No, that's confidential." He leaned forward and touched Natalie lightly on the arm. "But I described Veronica's house on the east side of town. I didn't say which street exactly, but it's common knowledge, isn't it? Veronica's house has been written up in the *Burning Lake Gazette*."

"Do you think Morgan went to see her?"

Patrick nodded. "Oh, yes. I suspect she did."

23

Modern-day practitioners of pagan tradition didn't typically dress in Goth gear or have tattoos and nose piercings. Rather, the real witches of Burning Lake looked like regular suburban moms who wouldn't stand out in a crowd. You'd never guess they were witches. Most of the legitimate covens in town never advertised—it was strictly by invitation only, word of mouth. Members were mothers and working women, cashiers and teachers, grocery clerks and middle managers, farmers and business owners. Instead of a broomstick, they drove Nissans and pickup trucks and SUVs.

Veronica Manes lived in the historic Bell House at 8 Plymouth Street. Built in 1698, the two-story colonial had a five-bay façade with a central entry and a chimney on one end. Surrounding the house was an overgrown orchard. Thomas Bell, who'd sat in judgment of Victoriana Forsyth during the 1712 witch trials, had raised his six children here. His daughter married Minister William T. Manes, and it was only fitting that their great-great-great-great-great-granddaughter had become a witch, taking history full circle.

Natalie parked her car in the driveway and crossed the front lawn past a grove of spruce trees, stepping over a dense carpet of pine needles. The tumbledown house with its vine-softened walls and spidery, wrought iron gate had a spectral aura about it.

Veronica answered the door. The fiftysomething former author had long gray hair and wore informal, mismatched clothes—a blue turtleneck, a red cardigan, green stretch pants, beaded earrings, and white New Balance sneakers. "Hello, Detective. Welcome to my home."

"Thanks for seeing me on such short notice."

"Not at all." Veronica regarded her sadly. "I was about to brew a fresh pot of tea. Would you like a cup?"

"Love one."

"Let's go to the kitchen, then. It's the heart of the house." Her face was kind, with more than a hint of melancholy about it. She led Natalie down a colonial-narrow hallway into the cheerful, sun-filled kitchen, where it smelled of fresh strawberries and baked cinnamon apples.

"Would you like a piece of cake?" Veronica offered, pointing at the lopsided coconut cake under its plastic dome on the kitchen counter. "I made it myself."

"Not today."

"Dieting, are we?"

"Ha. Always."

"Hmm. That's the thing, you see. You're perfectly perfect just the way you are. All women are." Veronica took a seat at the kitchen table and poured two cups of steaming hot tea, then offered Natalie cream and sugar. "You wanted to know about Morgan Chambers. She came to see me last Thursday afternoon. Just dropped by. A lot of the tourists are craft curious, and some have figured out where I live. It's not hard to do. There are scattered websites and articles pointing the way, like bread crumbs. Anyway, I try to be as informative as I can. The term 'witch' carries a lot of baggage."

"I can imagine," Natalie said, sipping her tea, which was strong and aromatic. "Mmm. What is this?"

"Essence of bergamot. Eye of newt," Veronica said with a wink.

"Earl Grey." Natalie smiled, looking at the tag, then settled her cup in its china saucer. "And what did Morgan want?"

"Well, we talked a little bit about the contest on Friday—which was the next day. She was one of the finalists who were scheduled to perform. I told her it wasn't fair to discuss it with her, since I was also a judge in the contest. I have to remain objective." Veronica rubbed her hands together and sighed. "She seemed quite troubled. She wanted more than anything to succeed with her music. She told me her story. Her parents were very restrictive. Stage mom, tyrannical father. Great expectations, reality bites. She asked about casting spells, and I had to warn her—white witchcraft only." Veronica took an apple out of a bowl and held it in her tanned hand. "She wanted to join my coven, but of course we aren't accepting any new members currently. That's why we shut down our website. Too many people calling and begging to join."

Natalie took out the Halloween brochure she'd found in Morgan's room at the Sunflower Inn and asked, "Is this the coven's phone number, by chance?"

Veronica glanced at it. Nodded. "Used to be. We had to shut everything down. It became overwhelming. There are, after all, only two legitimate covens in Burning Lake, as you know, Detective . . . and unfortunately, we attract a lot of . . . I don't want to be unkind. Let's just say, we attract a lot of people who tend to project their fantasies onto us. I told Morgan there were plenty of unofficial covens in Burning Lake that are open to new members. I advised her to ask around. There are also plenty of small covens across the country, and thousands of solitary witches who communicate with each other online."

"What did she say to that?"

"She shifted gears a little and asked about specific spells for increasing success," Veronica said. "Spells relating to music and spells to boost your luck. I told her, you must use spells very carefully—especially if you're inexperienced. It's like putting surgical instruments into the hands of a child."

"Did you give her any other advice?"

Veronica shook her head. "I could tell she was troubled, and that can be a disaster when it comes to the craft. I advised her to read up on Wicca first. Study it. Start from scratch. It's more akin to a religious practice."

"What did she say?"

"She wasn't happy about it," Veronica said softly, putting the apple back in the bowl. "Like many young people, she was searching for easy answers. She pressured me for something . . . anything. I told her I don't do palm readings or hawk my kitschy wares. I told her she should stroll around downtown and visit the shops on Sarah Hutchins Drive, where she'd find plenty of willing advocates. She asked me—where do I start? I advised her to get her own sigil—you know, something she could create herself out of a desire to change her life and make things happen. It's a form of wishful thinking, but it's also an affirmation of a person's desire for growth."

Natalie took out her phone and showed Veronica the screen image of Morgan's tattoo. "A sigil. You mean, like this one? Do you know what it means?"

She shook her head. "No idea. Each one is as unique as a snowflake."

Natalie put away her phone and took out her notebook. "I understand you're on the committee that selected the participants for the Monster Mash contest. Who were the other judges?"

"Mayor Arnie Bryden, Owen Linkhorn, Hollis Jones, and Russ Swinton."

"Dr. Swinton?" Natalie repeated, a little surprised; she knew he enjoyed listening to classical music but didn't realize he was interested enough to participate in the annual Halloween contest.

"Quite the VIP lineup." Veronica nodded. "It was a good group this year. They all brought something to the table. Have you seen Hollis perform? He's a fiddler for Psilocybin in the Rye, a local folk band. They're very good. And Owen Linkhorn owns Pentagram Records, an independent label based in New York City."

"So, Pentagram Records . . . meaning that he's into Wicca?"

"No, he's just a smart capitalist who has a flare for drama."

"How many finalists were there?"

"Ten. All exceptionally talented, dedicated, and ambitious. Morgan coming to see me before the contest was against the rules, but I felt sorry for her."

"Did it factor into your final vote?"

"If anything, it worked against her, but I tried to be impartial. It just so happens that the winner took us all by storm."

"Why did Morgan lose exactly?"

"Technically she's very good. And she gave a passionate performance, but we were there to be entertained. I don't think she understood the concept of the contest. She was too serious, too caught up in the music. She gave what some might call an awkward performance. She played with such grim intensity that her performance was scarier than the piece itself. In short, she didn't bowl us over."

"What about the other contestants?"

"It was the usual blend of classical and popular theme songs. You know, Michael Myers came out and played the *Halloween* theme song. A string quartet dressed as sharks played John Williams's *Jaws*. Wednesday and Pugsley performed the *Addams Family* theme song. Of course, there were ever-popular classical pieces, such as *Danse Macabre* and Berlioz's 'Dream of a Witches' Sabbath.' Jerry Goldsmith's *Twilight Zone* . . . typical Monster Mash fare. The audience ate it up."

"But I heard the shower scene from *Psycho* blew everyone away?"

"It was magnificent. Talk about your star performances."

Natalie scratched her chin. "Do you think Morgan participated in any Wiccan rituals while she was here?"

"I have no idea," Veronica said. "But it was clear to me by her questions that she was ready to embrace the possibility of magic and its positive influence on her music. And I did see her talking to Cody Dugway after the contest was over. Maybe they discussed her sigil tattoo, the one you just showed me."

24

Natalie drove back to town with the windows rolled down, letting in a rush of crisp autumn air, and found a parking spot in front of Cody's Ink. It looked like an auto body shop inside, very masculine, with suck-it-up retro designs adorning the walls—skull and crossbones, sexy witches, snarling werewolves shouldering Uzis at fire-spitting dragons.

The place was messy and cluttered. No customers this morning. There were four vacant tattoo stations, and each station had its own privacy curtain, hydraulic chair, and leather tattoo stool. A sign on the wall said, "Don't Forget to Tip Your Artist."

"Detective Lockhart, hey," Cody said as he stepped out of the back room. He had a crude L-O-V-E tattooed on the knuckles of one hand, and H-A-T-E tattooed on the other. He followed her eye line and flexed his fingers. "You know what movie these are from? Robert Mitchum's *Night of the Hunter*." He picked up his ink gun. "I was a cocky kid who couldn't wait to start inking on human skin, you know? They make you practice on orange peels and pig ears first. Finally, my teacher said I was good enough to ink myself. There's a learning curve, you see. I'm right-handed. So the 'love' on my left hand is almost perfect. But the 'hate' on my right hand's messed up. I learned from experience, and now I'm ambidextrous." He tossed the ink gun from hand to hand, then set it down again. "How can I help you?"

"You've heard about the victim we found yesterday?"

"Terrible thing," he said, stroking the nape of his neck. "Wow. Very sad. We've never had anything like this happen before on Halloween, have we? I mean, people overdose or get drunk and try to punch each other and such. But this is creepy."

"You were seen talking to her after the Monster Mash contest."

"Yeah, that's right." He scratched the back of his head. "Isabel and I were hanging out after the contest, when she just walked over to Isabel and asked her where she got her cool tattoos, and Isabel pointed at me, so we talked for a bit. The next morning she came into my shop, and we did it all in one sitting. She paid cash. I have the receipt somewhere . . ."

"Is this the tattoo?" She showed him a photograph of the body art on Morgan's upper left arm.

He studied the image, then looked up. "Yeah, I did that. She came in with a vision and a dream, and I made it happen."

"Do you know what it stands for?"

"It's a sigil. Black and white. You know what a sigil is?"

"Sort of like a wish," Natalie said.

"Right, it's a desire for change. You state your wish as if it's already happened. Here, let me show you." He found a notepad and pencil and began to draw. "For example, let's say I wanted my sigil to state the intent of . . . 'I want to be protected.' Okay? But first, we shorten it. 'I want to be protected' becomes 'I am protected.' You make an affirmative statement. Proactive. *I want, I am, I will.* Next, you cross out all the vowels and any repeating consonants, like this . . . 'I am protected' becomes MPRTCD. Are you with me so far?"

She nodded, intensely interested in what Morgan's wish was.

"So these are your magic letters. MPRTCD. Next, you twist them around until they no longer resemble letters. You play with them and re-shape them, like a work of art. See?" He drew an elaborate design. "Once you're happy with the results, you stop manipulating the letters. Then you draw a circle around the entire thing. And voilà, there's your sigil. Unique to you. As individual as a fingerprint."

Natalie pointed at the photograph. "And what does Morgan's sigil stand for?"

"'I want to be a famous violin soloist.' First we translated that into, 'I *am* a famous violin soloist.' Which is reduced down to MFSVLNT. See? Like this. M-F-S-V-L-N-T. Twist them, turn them. Then draw a circle around it, and . . . voilà." His sketch was similar to the tattoo on Morgan's shoulder.

"May I take this?" she asked.

"Sure." He ripped out the page and handed it to her.

"Did she say anything about her stay here in Burning Lake? Was she upset about losing the contest? Anything you can tell me would be helpful, Cody."

"She mostly asked if getting a tattoo hurt, stuff like that. She seemed to enjoy the process, though, once it started. I play classical music. That helps people relax."

"Hey, babe," someone said from the back room.

Cody's left eyebrow arched. "Speak of the devil." He grinned. "We have company, sweet cheeks," he called out.

"They were out of your cigs," Isabel Miller said, breezing into the shop wearing jeans, ankle boots, and a Bart Simpson T-shirt. She had warm brown, wary eyes. "Oh, hello. Detective Lockhart, right?" She shook Natalie's hand. Her long strawberry-blond hair was pulled into a ponytail, and the morning light danced across her healthy skin. "Thanks for not arresting Cody the other night."

"No problem. What exactly happened back there?" Natalie asked.

"We were both invited to the party, but Cody was late, as usual. So I called and told him to get his butt over there, but I didn't think he'd bring his stupid friends along."

"I thought I could sneak them in the back door," Cody said with a mischievous giggle.

Isabel wrapped her arms around his neck and kissed him. "Everything's fine. I apologized to Mr. Rose for the commotion, and I got to keep my necklace." She showed Natalie a silver necklace, pulling it out from under the collar of her T-shirt, then tucking it back in and pouring herself a cup of coffee from the station near the register.

"Can I see that again?" Natalie asked.

Isabel produced the necklace again. "Pretty, huh? All the women at the party got one. Instead of a hand stamp or a gift bag, you got this. Classy. Real silver."

"Morgan Chambers had a necklace like this one," Natalie said.

Isabel's eyes widened. "Oh my God, we met her after the concert. Did you tell her, Cody? She was so nice. I told her how much I loved her performance, and it almost made her cry. She was at the party, too. I saw her there. She was dressed as Wonder Woman. Did you notice how many Wonder Womans we had this year? Or is it Wonder Women?" Isabel furrowed her brow.

Natalie tensed a little. "Did she come alone, or was she with someone?"

Isabel blanched a little. "Uh, Batman, I think. It was all a blur. I got wasted. I met a lot of vampires and Death Eaters and Zemos . . . and they were all very nice . . . but I wouldn't recognize them if I bumped into them on the street. Everyone was in costume, hiding their identities behind their masks."

"I hope I was helpful about the sigil," Cody told Natalie. "Are we about done here? I've got a ton of paperwork to catch up on. Busy October."

"What a great season, huh?" Isabel said brightly.

"One of the best, babe," Cody said.

"Except for how it ended." She looked at Natalie and shuddered.

"Did you talk to her at the party?" Natalie asked Isabel.

"Not for very long, but yeah. She said she flubbed the contest and was thinking about giving up completely and becoming a fiddler in a band, even though that was against her principles. She wasn't in the greatest shape. She was slurring her words and stumbling a little bit . . . I told her to go easy on the margaritas, but she said, hey, Halloween only comes once a year. She looked like she was having fun."

"Did you see her leave the party?"

Isabel shook her head. "No, I split before she did."

"I'll get you a copy of that receipt," Cody said, opening the cash register and sorting through the receipts. "It's in here somewhere." He rubbed the back of his neck. "I can't find it right now. Got a number where I can send it to you, Detective?"

Natalie passed him her card. "Thanks for your time."

"No problem." Cody winked at her.

Natalie handed Isabel her card as well. "If you think of anything else, call me."

Isabel nodded, then said, "Mr. Rose mentioned you."

Natalie took a mental step back. "Mr. Rose? He did?"

"He called you very brave. He said with all the superhero costumes, there should've been a Natalie Lockhart Halloween costume. He's funny. I like him."

"He's a fucking capitalist pig," Cody muttered.

"So are we, babe. What do you think this shop is? Charity?"

"Thanks again, Detective," Cody said, ushering her out. "I'll email you that receipt as soon as I find it."

25

Natalie drove over to Hunter Rose's house and parked in the gravel driveway. Her hands were clammy on the wheel. She smoothed a few strands of hair behind her ears, took a nervous breath, and got out.

The mansion reminded her of decayed aristocracy, nestled in the woods like a fairy-tale castle. On the eastern side of the property, the well-tended lawn gave way to a tennis court and small orchard. On the western side was a greenhouse and a detached garage for Hunter's vintage motorcycle collection. The interior of the house was composed of dark varnished paneling, tall echo-y ceilings and sinuous mahogany staircases. Natalie and Hunter had dated briefly one summer when she was in college and he was an aimless graduate student. They'd fucked on his parents' king-sized bed while the Roses were traveling in Italy, and afterward they ate Doritos out of the bag, while Hunter showed her where he used to ride his skateboard up and down the hallway and his brother Nesbitt had carved faces into the mahogany woodwork. Scary faces full of anguish.

She crossed the yard and rang the doorbell.

"Natalie Lockhart. What a treat." Slim and athletic, thirty-three-year-old Hunter cut an imposing presence in a black cashmere suit. He had thick dark eyebrows, a square jaw, and a handsome face. He hadn't aged much. "Long time no see." He gave her a self-conscious peck on the cheek and welcomed her inside.

She followed him into the large, antique-filled living room, where he offered her a mineral water from the bar. She accepted. It felt awkward. They hadn't spoken in years. She only knew they'd once been wildly, un-inhibitedly intimate. She remembered the excitement of being near him; she recalled the warmth of his skin, the magnetism of his body, and their core physical attraction.

A weak light came in through the north-facing windows—the ebbing of the afternoon sun through a veil of tangled woods. Hunter handed her the mineral water, then paused to light three candles on the fireplace mantel, and she couldn't help noticing that he lived like a medieval king inside his dark castle surrounded by private security.

"Nice violin," she said, noticing a cabinet full of antique musical in-struments.

"That's a German Stradivarius style, made in 1849. I have a New York dealer who acquires things for me."

"Acquires things?"

"Yeah," he said. "What's wrong with acquiring things?"

"Nothing. We all do it. Squirrels do it."

He smirked and sat on a velvet sofa opposite the beautifully uphol-stered wingback chair she was sitting in, sipping her mineral water. Nat-alie hadn't meant to fall into her old pattern, where Hunter would say something serious, and she would make fun of him, but old habits died hard. She set the glass down on an antique carved wooden table stacked with books. He already knew why she was there. They'd spoken about it on her way over.

"So you don't recognize her?" She showed him Morgan's picture ID.

He studied it for a moment. "No. But like I said, I heard about it on the news, and it sucks. She's so young." He handed it back. "Was she a tourist?"

"Her name's Morgan Chambers. She played the violin. She's from Chaste Falls, and she came down here for the annual Monster Mash con-test. This necklace was in her possession." She swiped her finger over her phone screen and showed him the silver necklace with its Wiccan pendant. "Isabel Miller told me you gave these out to your female guests on Sunday night."

"Yeah, that's right."

"And you don't recognize Morgan? She was dressed as Wonder Woman."

He frowned and shook his head. "There were a lot of Wonder Women, along with plenty of Belles and Ariels and Esmeraldas, a lot of beautiful women . . . so she may very well have been at the party. However, she wasn't on the invite list. I sent out over a hundred invitations, and some of the invitees brought guests. The silver necklace was a gift to all my female guests, anyone who walked through the door. But I don't recall meeting this woman."

"She was one of the contestants in the music contest."

He shook his head slowly. "I haven't gone to that in years."

"What about your surveillance tapes?" Natalie said. "I noticed there were several security cameras outside."

He shook his head. "I can't compromise the privacy of my guests."

"What about a guest list?"

"Sorry, but I can't share that with you, Natalie. Not without a subpoena." He studied her. "What exactly is it you need to know?"

"Who Morgan came to the party with, what happened to her while she was here, the exact time she left and with whom."

He didn't respond.

"Why is this such a state secret?" she asked, losing patience.

"Let's just say things got a little rowdy."

"Rowdy how?" When he didn't answer the question, she said, "Okay. I get it. There were a lot of important people at your party, and nobody wants their name getting out if things got a little rowdy. But I'm trying to re-create Morgan's time line—where she went, who she spoke to, how she ended up in a dumpster. I can get a search warrant if I have to, but I'd rather not waste the time. Your cooperation would be greatly appreciated."

He walked over to the bar, where he selected a bottle of wine and uncorked it. "My employees have all signed NDAs. Nondisclosure agreements.

However, I can ask around and find out if any of them saw this particular guest. I'll see what I can come up with, okay? If that doesn't help, we can talk again. In the meantime, I'll pull the outdoor surveillance tapes for you. You can swing by tomorrow—my security officer went home after an extra-long shift and I don't want to bother him."

She nodded, surprised by this sudden cooperation. "Thanks."

"The people I employ are discreet. All phones and devices were checked at the door. No pictures allowed. I want my guests to relax," Hunter said as the cork gave way with a muted pop. "We talked business. We drank. We traded gossip. We got silly. We celebrated Halloween. Care to join me in a glass of wine?"

"No, thank you," she said, wondering where the needle landed between silly and rowdy.

He poured a glass of red wine and sat down on a velvet-upholstered, carved wooden chair that looked like a medieval throne. "I was tested extensively as a kid, you know, and they found out that I had a Stephen Hawking–size IQ, which put me in rarified air. The top point zero three percent for kiddies with big brains. But ever since, they've found out that IQ tests for children aren't reliable indicators of how they'll do as adults. I could never live up to my genius-level IQ. It was complete bullshit." He shrugged and sipped his wine. "However, Dad expected me to be the Second Coming, or at least Einstein's clone, whereas I just wanted to be a normal kid. I got bored easily. I hated school. I hated homework. I withdrew into a made-up world, where I slayed dragons and explored outer space, but I did okay . . . because I was just smart enough for my teachers to give me a pass. College was a different story. I went into a full-blown panic mode when I realized Dad expected me to excel in a big way. But I was a classic frat boy fuckup. I drank and took drugs. I experimented. In my sophomore year, my father read me the riot act. He put the fear of God in me. Did I apply myself? Study harder? No. I took selfies at the library with a big pile of textbooks and sent them to him regularly, just to shut him up. In the meantime, I saw myself as defective, as if I'd been born with a tail. I felt like a failure. Like a phony. I used big words at a very young age. I especially liked 'ubiquitous' and 'euphemism' and 'infinitesimal.' But what happens if you're pushed to succeed, and then you fail? What if you fail and keep failing? Fortunately, my father left his entire fortune to me, so I was able to bide my time, and that made all the difference. Once I'd formed my first start-up company, the world opened up in a big way." He shrugged. "The rest is history."

"So you're saying . . . luck made you."

He nodded. "Arbitrary, unfair luck of the draw."

"And your father's fortune did the heavy lifting."

"Or you could say that my father's great expectations died with him. And when that happened, it eased the burden off my sad little rounded shoulders, so that I was able to achieve what I never could've accomplished if he hadn't kicked the bucket, yeah. You could say that." He took another sip of his wine.

The curtains were ablaze with late-afternoon light, as if the sky was burning.

He studied her a solemn beat. "You're judging me, aren't you?"

"No," Natalie said, blinking.

"You just blinked. That means you're lying."

"Actually, I blinked because my eyes are dry."

"'The eyes of men converse as much as their tongues,'" he quoted. "Ralph Waldo Emerson. Deny it all you want. I know what you're thinking, Natalie. You look at me and see a rich kid with your very dry eyes. You see a world of leisure and boredom, of partying and interchangeable sex partners, of fashionable clothes and money. A world full of power and prestige and status-seeking."

"Yeah, maybe," she admitted.

"You think I was coddled as a child. You think I'm one of those greedy fucks, those entitled brats, who's never suffered a day in their lives. Don't you? After all, I've never been hungry or cold or thirsty. I never had to take a minimum-wage job or put up with an asshole boss. But guess what? I get intimidated by people who embrace their own status fearlessly. What they wear, the money they flaunt, where they live, what kind of car they drive. I envy them their resolution and confidence. They seem quite alien to me. Because I don't care about status. Not really. All I care about is character and principle, old-fashioned virtues that were drummed into me by my dear mother when she was alive. However . . ." He polished off the dregs of his wine. "I'm also a realist—Dad's gift to me. I know that's not the way the world works. Morality and principles. Most people could give a shit."

"You're right," she said.

"I don't mean to sound like such a dick." He shrugged. "But my father didn't believe in raising a naïve, corruptible innocent. Why do you think he named me Hunter? I'm supposed to be a warrior. I was destined to rape and plunder. The world is a merciless place. I'm supposed to be merciless back."

"What about Nesbitt?" she asked. "Was he innocent?"

Hunter studied her for a long moment, and she knew she'd entered forbidden territory. "The police didn't think so."

"They were wrong," she said. "They later admitted it."

"Later? Or too fucking late?"

She didn't respond, but she recalled being proud of her father for not suspecting Nesbitt Rose of murder, like every other cop on the force at the time.

Hunter got up and walked over to the fireplace, where he stared at the flickering candles. "There are parts of this house I won't go into because they remind me of my brother. He used to ride his pedal car around in the third-floor hallway. There are scratches on the walls from where he'd turn the wheels too late."

"He was one of the last people to have seen Bella alive," Natalie said, in defense of the BLPD. "It's only natural that the police would want to question him . . ."

He spun around. "Oh, I *know* why they targeted my brother."

She nodded sympathetically. Unfortunately for Nesbitt Rose, he had a reputation as the town weirdo. Rumors abounded. When the high school was broken into and the gym lockers were vandalized, everybody blamed Nesbitt. When cats and dogs went missing, people accused Nesbitt. Of course, none of it was proved true. He was unfairly targeted because he was odd. He once brought a disgusting piece of roadkill—a dead raccoon—

into the school for show-and-tell. He liked to walk around late at night in the moonlight. People would spot him loping along by the side of the road in pitch-darkness, caught in the sweep of their passing headlights. His head would be down, studying his feet as he clopped along, arms dangling. His creepy eyes in the high beams of oncoming vehicles red and owlish. He was paler than normal, with short hair he cut all by himself with blunt-edged scissors. He liked to wear a striped Dr. Seuss–shaped floppy top hat made of felt. Kids called him the village creeper. Others claimed he was harmless. Some tried to defend him but eventually gave up. Nesbitt didn't want anybody's help. He lived in his own little world.

Natalie had never been afraid of Nesbitt Rose in school. She liked his weirdness and his offbeat individuality. She used to call his mumblings, "Messages in a bottle from Nesbitt Rose." With her friends, she would pantomime opening a bottle, pulling out a slip of paper, opening it, and reading his messages aloud. "Hello, world, what is the bat signal?"

Nesbitt was obsessed with people's fingers, and especially with Bella's fingers whenever she played the violin. She had the smallest, most nimble fingers in the world. He loved the music she produced on her violin, tucked under her chin, with that wildly swaying bow. It made him practically swoon with ecstasy. Bella claimed Nesbitt was her best audience.

After she disappeared that night, the four friends searched everywhere for her before finally calling the police. They kept thinking she'd show up and laugh at them. "Ha! Look at your faces!"

The police, including Natalie's father, Officer Joey Lockhart, interrogated the Misfits for hours. They were suspicious of the three boys initially—Bobby, Adam, and Max—who were all crying and sobbing and in shock. But the boys only wanted Bella to be found. Once their stories were corroborated, the police turned their sights on Nesbitt, whom Bella had been seen talking to shortly before she disappeared. Perhaps he'd been lurking in the woods, waiting to pick her off from the rest of them.

Soon rumors spread around town that Nesbitt had killed Bella Striver. Nobody knew why he would do that, or how he could've possibly gotten away with it when he couldn't find a pair of matching socks in the morning, or where he may have buried her, but that didn't stop the gossip from spreading like a malignant tumor. It got so bad that after three weeks of rampant speculation, Nesbitt ended his own life. Nobody realized how deep his feelings ran or how self-aware he was until it was too late.

But then something truly appalling happened.

After the police ruled Nesbitt's death a suicide, half the town accepted it as proof that he'd actually killed Bella. Hunter was furious. Their father was infirm at the time, and Hunter was Nesbitt's guardian, and out of a deep well of grief and fury he made a statement to the press: "My brother is innocent. He wouldn't hurt a flea, let alone Bella Striver. She treated him kindly. He loved her. She used to play the violin for him."

But that wasn't quite true. Bella had a cruel streak, and sometimes she would deliberately confuse Nesbitt just to see him sputter and blink. She liked it when he followed her around, trailing after her like an enormous slouching puppy. She especially liked it when he tried to hide from her and Natalie behind a slender birch tree, thinking he was invisible. She would burst out laughing and say, "Look at that! There he is, isn't he a riot?"

But Natalie appreciated his silly innocence, his raw integrity, and his gritty independence from the rest of the world's opinion of him. He didn't seem to care what people thought. But that turned out not to be true. He was very much hurt by other people's opinions.

When the police finally called off their search for Bella in early July, it was a heartbreaking moment for the Misfits. At that point, everyone assumed she was dead. It wasn't the same for them anymore—not without Bella. Then the letters began to arrive.

Bella was the most significant person in Natalie's life back then, besides Bobby Deckhart—the most important person in Natalie's universe. Everything she cared about had been torn away from her that night. The world changed when Bella ran away and let them think she'd been abducted or killed. Natalie lost her best friend forever. It was almost as bad as losing Willow eight years earlier.

"My brother had no alibi," Hunter said now, standing in front of the fireplace. "God knows what he was up to that night. But there's one thing I do know with all my heart and soul . . . it wasn't anything nefarious. And three months later, when those letters started coming from California and all over the southwest, proving that nobody killed Bella, that in fact she wasn't dead, that she'd left of her own volition . . . the whole town shrugged," he said darkly, the anger still very much with him. "He was a good kid, a kind soul, accused of something terrible. I think now, looking back, he had undiagnosed Asperger's or autism. He was somewhere along the spectrum. I've been reading about the syndrome, and it fits. Anyway, it's taken me years to get over it."

"I envy you," she said, and he looked at her sharply. "Your ability to move on."

He acknowledged her own pain with a nod. "You eventually come to terms with it," he said gently. "Life is fucking flawed."

She swallowed a hot mixture of agony, regret, and self-doubt, then shrugged, but her hands wouldn't stop shaking. "My grief has sent me underground. Nobody wants to talk about it anymore."

"Oh? There's a black market for grief now? Who knew?"

She smiled. She felt momentarily paralyzed.

He waited patiently, while she struggled with it.

Natalie stood up. "Anyway, thanks for the mineral water."

"No problem." He walked her to the door. "Swing by tomorrow, and I'll have those tapes for you."

She paused on the threshold. "By the way, I saw your donor plaque on the wall of the music conservatory in Chaste Falls. I didn't know you were such a fan of classical music."

"Nesbitt loved listening to Bella play," he said. "So I donated the money in his honor. See you tomorrow, Natalie." He closed the door.

26

The public entrance of the police station had an arched limestone doorway with two glass doors that swung shut behind you. The lobby was grimly functional, like a doctor's waiting room, except with brochures about crime everywhere. To the right was the dispatcher's area behind a large sliding glass window. To the left was a fire door that opened onto a staircase leading to the other floors. On the wall of the lobby was a floor-to-ceiling mural of the department's shield—*Burning Lake Police Department*.

"How's it going, Natalie?" Dennis the dispatcher asked.

"I have a pounding headache," she said, the pain between her eyes making her almost nauseous. "But hey, I'll survive."

"Need an aspirin?"

"Just took a few. Thanks, Dennis."

He nodded. "Chief wants to see you."

Down the hallway, past the squad room, the mail room, and the roll call room were the elevator banks. Just past the elevators, the corridor branched off to the right and left. A left turn took you down an L-shaped hallway leading to the holding cells and booking area. To the right, another L-shaped hallway led to the kitchen and restrooms.

Natalie rode the elevator to the second floor. Chief Roger Snyder's corner office overlooked the commercial buildings across the street. She hesitated before stepping inside. Luke was seated in one of two guest chairs, and both men were looking at her.

"Close the door, please, Detective," the chief said.

She closed the door and shook Snyder's hand.

"Natalie, I've heard nothing but good things about the job you're doing." He had an aggressive, bone-crushing handshake. His mouth barely moved when he spoke, but the words came out crisp and clear.

"Thank you, sir."

His desk phone rang. "Ignore that. Have a seat."

She sank into the only other available wooden guest chair. The air inside the office was stuffy and hot. There were photographs and certificates on the walls, along with an antique American flag in a modern frame behind the desk.

Chief Snyder was a barrel-chested man with a square, puglike face and a pragmatic smile. His gold-plated badge gleamed in the dying light of day seeping through the old-fashioned windows. "I was just telling the lieutenant here . . . we've received a list of partygoers from Hunter Rose's attorney. Mr. Rose is cooperating with us on this matter. And seeing as you've got your hands full, Detective, I've assigned Assistant Chief Gossett the task of handling this particular aspect of the investigation."

Natalie felt her cheeks grow warm. "I'm sorry? Which aspect?"

"The guest list," he clarified.

Natalie glanced at Luke, who refused to meet her eye.

Tapping her fingers on the polished veneer side table, she spotted an old photograph on the wall of Hunter Rose posing with the chief and Mayor Arnold Bryden, along with several town council members, in front of the headquarters for Rose Security Software.

"Arnie . . . the mayor and I went to Columbia together," the chief said, following her eye line. "We go way back. He only has the town's best interests at heart."

Natalie frowned—why did he feel the need to say that?

"Anyway," the chief continued, "I want to assure you, Natalie, that this in no way diminishes your role as lead detective in charge of the investigation, and nothing has changed essentially. We're simply lightening your load."

"Sir, with all due respect, I don't need my load lightened." She got a hard, dry feeling in her throat. Snyder was a busy man. A grinder. Cagily political. On the wall behind him was a sign that said, "Do What You Love and Love What You Do." Did he love fucking over his detectives?

"Anyway, I just spoke to Hunter's attorney," the chief reassured her, "and he's promised to get us those surveillance tapes ASAP. Assistant Chief Gossett will take care of that as well."

"Wait a minute . . . I'm sorry, sir," she said anxiously. "Both the guest list *and* the surveillance tapes?"

The chief nodded. "This will allow you to focus your efforts on other aspects of the investigation."

She frowned. Assistant Chief Timothy Gossett was an asshole. He was so well-groomed you could smell the store on him. His shirts were neatly pressed, his belt matched his loafers, his buckle was shiny bright. In his late forties, he knew himself and his place in the universe—he belonged with his head planted firmly up Snyder's butt.

Natalie sat back. "But isn't that an unusual step to take?"

He gave her a patronizing smile. "I have to respectfully disagree. The assistant chief will liaison with Mr. Rose's attorneys, and he'll examine the surveillance tapes and compare them to the guest list. We'll certainly advise you and Lieutenant Pittman of any pertinent findings, that's for sure."

"Well, okay, fine," she said. "To be honest with you, I don't care about the other guests at the party. I just want to know what happened to Morgan Chambers. Who she came with, who she left with, any altercations that may have occurred, I expect to be informed of it . . ."

The chief picked up an expensive fountain pen from his desk, fingers twitching. He spoke with tired authority. "Rest assured, we will leave no stone unturned. But according to the witnesses we've already spoken to, you'll be happy to learn that Morgan left the party unharmed. She had a few drinks. They think she called an Uber. Nothing happened on Mr. Rose's property. He's cooperating fully with us because he wants to put this thing to bed. His lawyers are cooperating a hundred percent with the investigation."

The puckered pockets of her brain hurt. Her head was pounding. Natalie studied the chief's square, inscrutable face and said, "An Uber? Who's the Uber driver? Do you have a name? Because just an hour ago . . . no, less than an hour ago, I talked to Hunter, and he said he was fine with me handling it. When did you speak to his lawyers?"

The chief held on to his pen and twirled it nervously between his fingers. "We've been communicating with Mr. Rose's attorneys since yesterday afternoon. They've decided to go through other channels. Things change. The point is, we're receiving his full cooperation." His face turned an unnatural shade of pink. "I hope you understand what's at stake here, Detective. Between the Crow Killer case and, well . . . let's just say the obvious. This town relies on tourism. We don't need the negative publicity. Half our annual income comes from tourism, and if this thing were to drag on too long, it might hurt us. The entire town. The mayor's main concern is that this story doesn't grab national media attention again . . . you know how that goes."

She lightly touched her forehead. "As long as you're not asking me to stop investigating all avenues of the case. Are you?"

"No, I most certainly am not."

She stared at him. "Because we can't change the facts to silence the media."

"This is simply procedural," he insisted with a grim smile.

"Because like I said, I can handle it."

"Nobody's shutting you down, Detective. We're diverting resources."

She nodded, feeling numb all over.

"In the meantime, let's try to resolve this case as quickly as possible."

She didn't like this turn of events, not one bit. But sometimes you had to let the Wookiee win—or at least you had to let him *think* he won.

"Good. I'm glad we talked." The chief tapped his pen lightly on the desk blotter. "I sincerely hope this addresses your concerns." He appeared to be smiling, even though he wasn't. "Feel free to drop by my office anytime, Detective."

She stood up. That was her cue to leave.

27

Bristling at the chief's decision, Natalie waited for the elevator doors to slide shut before she turned to Luke and said, "What the fuck?"

"Excuse me?" He blinked at her, but she knew he understood exactly what she meant. They stood for a moment watching each other's reaction. His eyes were more gray than blue under the artificial lights.

"You're babysitting me now?" she accused him, face flushing.

"It's not up to me. This was the chief's decision."

"And you went along with it."

"What else am I supposed to do? Disobey a direct order?"

Her head was pounding. "Why all the secrecy? What's going on?"

"There was apparently some nudity at the party . . ."

"Nudity? Like a sex party?"

"Not a sex party . . . it's just that people were drinking and doing business deals, and the chief wants to honor their privacy."

"So where does the nudity come in?" she demanded to know.

Luke rolled his eyes—whenever he got embarrassed he would roll his eyes like that. "The nudity was part of a performance piece meant for entertainment purposes only. Apparently, there was a reenactment of a Wiccan initiation ceremony. Risqué stuff, from what I hear. A dozen or so paid performers, attractive young men and women, going through the motions of an authentic ritual. Most of the guests didn't want to be seen enjoying such a spectacle. Including the mayor. It was almost as if Hunter Rose wanted to embarrass them."

Natalie suddenly understood. The Wiccan initiation ceremony was an important rite of passage, a spiritual cleansing where novices dedicated themselves to the service of the goddess. The sacred ritual was performed during the waxing moon. A coven would form a circle inside four white candles, pointing north, south, east, and west. Initiates would completely disrobe, and a nine-foot cord would be looped around each one, binding their arms behind their backs. To the uninformed, it looked like BDSM, but the ceremony itself was considered religious in nature, with a Wiccan priestess conducting the ritual using all the tools of the trade—bells, censers, goblets, libation dishes, crystals, and anointing oils. It was a solemn ceremony, not meant for entertainment purposes.

"So the chief is protecting the town's VIPs instead of doing his job?" Natalie said, feeling a pressure at the back of her eyes.

"He's doing what he has to do," Luke pushed back. "Politics is politics. I wouldn't go sticking my hand in that hornet's nest." He looked at her for a miserable moment. "We don't make the rules, Natalie. That's not our job, okay? Do you want my advice? Find a work-around. I'm not telling you to turn a blind eye, and I'm not telling you to disobey direct orders. I'm saying . . . follow all leads. Just understand what you're dealing with."

"What am I dealing with?"

"City politics. Corruption. People who can afford to hire whole teams of lawyers. People who could bankrupt you. Who could break you. And don't think they wouldn't try."

"Oh fucking fuck," she muttered, appalled.

"Look," he said in a voice full of good intentions, "fight the good fight. Just keep a low profile. It's poker. Don't show your cards. Be a little more circumspect. I'll pressure Gossett for updates and make sure he keeps us apprised, but it's your job to solve the case. With or without a guest list. With or without surveillance tapes."

Her head was pounding. The burden of this case felt like a grinding in her bones. "All right, so what's next?"

He smiled slyly as they stepped off the elevator together and headed down the hallway toward their offices. "As soon as I heard about the Uber ride, I took the liberty of calling Brandon's informant, Jules Pastor. He knows all the local Uber and Lyft drivers. I had him ask around and find out if there were any pickups of a Wonder Woman at Hunter Rose's house on Halloween night. Turns out an Uber driver picked her up from the party and dropped her off in downtown Burning Lake around ten fifteen."

Natalie stopped in the middle of the corridor. "When were you going to mention this to me?"

"As soon as you were finished chewing me a new asshole."

She crossed her arms. She was grateful and relieved. She should've trusted him. She should've known better than to blame him. "Dropped her off where?"

"Sarah Hutchins Drive. She happened to mention that she was meeting someone at Blondie's—you know that place?"

"Yeah, it's a popular jazz bar. But there were no ink stamps from Blondie's on Morgan's hands."

"Right. We couldn't decipher every single stamp, since some were blurred beyond recognition. I'm assuming Blondie's was one of the illegible ones. Anyway, according to Jules, an Uber driver named Stefan dropped her off a few blocks south of Blondie's due to street closures. You'll need to confirm that she made it there."

"Isabel Miller told me Morgan came to the party with a man in a Batman costume. Since we found her car parked behind the bed-and-breakfast, we can assume he drove her to the party, or she took an Uber to the party and met Batman there."

"I'm way ahead of you," Luke said. "Jules told me none of the drivers recalled transporting Wonder Woman *to* the party in the first place, so it's possible she might've ditched her date. Anyway, Stefan the Uber driver says he received a ride request around quarter of ten and picked her up in front of the residence fifteen minutes later on Hollins Drive. She was waiting alone by the side of the road."

"I'll head over to Blondie's now," Natalie told him. "Hopefully, they'll have her on their surveillance tapes."

"I'll go talk to Gossett and see if I can squeeze blood from a turnip."

Natalie cracked a smile. "Thanks, Luke."

"No problem. I told you I got your back."

She watched him head down the hallway toward his office, then went to catch the elevator. After Blondie's, she would drop by the hospital and get a prescription for this migraine from Russ Swinton.

28

B londie's was cool and comfortable with a vintage feel. Sticky, beer-tacky floors. Plastic flowers on the tables. Funky ragtime music on the sound system. A favorite watering hole for the locals.

Natalie knew the bartender. She'd gone to school with Gabrielle Dunham—Gabby for short. The skinny brunette was busy picking up after last night. She scooped a beer bottle off the table, held it to her nose, and sniffed. "Ugh. I hate beer, don't you?" she told Natalie.

"A bartender who doesn't like beer?"

"I tried a craft beer once. It tasted like piss."

"Beer always tastes like piss."

"No, I mean literally. As if someone peed in the bottle and put the cap back on." She made a disgusted face.

"But that's the whole point, isn't it?" Natalie said. "Beer is supposed to taste like piss. It's a guy thing." She shrugged. "You drink, you piss, you fall down drunk, mission accomplished."

Gabby laughed. "Okay, if you say so."

"Work with a bunch of guys for a while, and see if you don't start to enjoy a cold, clean beer in a sparkling mug. It's an acquired taste," she said with a smirk.

"Huh," Gabby said, setting the bottle on her cluttered tray and heading around the bar with it. "I get sick of the banter from jerks who are beer drunk."

"Beer drunk is different from other drunks?"

"Oh, yeah. Beer makes some guys think they're Mike Tyson. Wine is for ladies. You sip it slowly, but it gets you drunk faster. Vodka is for philosophers. Whiskey's for womanizers."

"Hmm. I like whiskey once in a while. Does that make me a womanizer?"

Gabby laughed. "Ha-ha. No. Women who drink whiskey are cool."

Stiff red curtains covered the windows. The bar was practically empty except for a couple of guys playing pool in the back room. On Friday and Saturday nights, the noisy kitchen served hamburgers and ribs, and the air grew dense with barbeque smoke.

"Who am I to judge, right?" Gabby said, lighting a cigarette and taking a hungry toke. Then she hunched her shoulders from an unseen danger. "Are you here about that poor woman who died?"

Natalie nodded. "Morgan Chambers. What can you tell me about Sunday night?"

"It was Halloween. We were busy as heck," she said, blowing smoke. "She came in shortly after ten and ordered a glass of white wine. I remember, because we chatted a bit. She said she was supposed to meet Hollis Jones here at ten, but I guess he stood her up. She asked if I'd seen him. I said no."

"He never showed up?" Natalie asked.

Gabby shook her head. "She seemed a tad upset. She was dressed as Wonder Woman. Did you notice? There were a ton of Wonder Women running around this Halloween."

"What about Batman. See any of those?"

"There were about a million Batmen and Spider-Men and Catwomen and Belles and Ariels and all sorts of Disney fucking princesses. All the employees were in costume, too. I was a sexy vampire." She wiggled her eyebrows.

"What time did she leave?"

"Oh gosh, Natalie. It was so freaking busy. Elevenish? I honestly can't remember. Like I said, it was fucking insane."

"So—eleven o'clock? Did she talk to anyone else while she was here?"

"Not that I recall, but I wasn't exactly standing still."

"How many glasses of wine did she have?"

"Two." Gabby studied Natalie for a moment. "What's the deal with Luke Pittman and Rainie Sandhill?" she said with barely concealed glee. "I heard they were seen together in a romantic corner of Lucia's the other night."

"Dunno." Natalie tried to prevent the flush from crawling up her neck.

Gabby drew smoke deeply into her lungs. "I thought you two were an item."

"Me and Luke? Nah. We're good friends. We were never an 'item.'"

"No?" Gabby waved a dismissive hand. "Sorry, I shouldn't have mentioned it. Small town—big ears. Right? Want a cigarette?"

"No, thanks. Did Morgan Chambers mention anything else?"

Gabby took out another cigarette and made a big deal of flicking her lighter and lighting the tip with a dramatic gesture. She put her lighter away and rested her hands on the countertop. "She made a few jokes about fiddle players. Like, what's the difference between a fiddle and a violin? I didn't know. She said, 'The number of teeth in your head.' I honestly didn't get it."

"It means she's a snob," Natalie explained. "It means she thinks fiddle players are beneath her."

"So why was she meeting Hollis Jones then? Isn't he a fiddle player?" Gabby blew out a plume of smoke. "No wonder he stood her up."

"And you didn't notice anybody else talking to Morgan?"

She shook her head. "Oh, wait a second. There was this zombie guy. She talked to him a few minutes, then brushed him off."

"Did you recognize him?"

"The *Walking Dead* guy? I don't know. He looked like a tourist to me. Not familiar. He kept buzzing around her."

"For how long?"

"I don't know. It was so fucking busy, like I said. Maybe a few minutes. This Halloween was totally ramped, wasn't it?"

"Could it have been Hollis Jones in a zombie costume?"

"No," Gabby said firmly. "I'd recognize that asshole in greasepaint."

"Why do you call him an asshole?"

Gabby rested her cigarette in the ashtray and swept the counter with her hands, catching a few toast crumbs in her palm. "Here's the thing. He's slept with half my girlfriends. He's a self-aggrandizing jack-off drowning in a lake of his own testosterone. I was tempted to warn her about him, but I've learned to keep my mouth shut. No good deed goes unpunished, right? Anyway, Hollis never showed." She shrugged. "So no harm, no foul."

"Are you saying he sleeps around a lot?" Natalie asked.

"That guy's a big-time slut."

"How drunk would you say Morgan was that night?"

"A little tipsy. A little fuzzy. Not falling-down drunk."

"So you wouldn't call her inebriated or incapacitated?"

"She wasn't trashed. She was okay. I could've served her again."

Natalie nodded. "What about the glassware? I'm assuming it's all been cleaned and put away by now?"

"A dozen times over."

"Anything else you can think of that was out of the ordinary?"

Gabby shook her head. "It was packed, like I said. Wall-to-wall flaming assholes, all demanding special drinks. Things I've never heard of before, cocktails they looked up on the internet, and here I am, taking instructions from half-wits, and everybody's shoving and pushing closer to the bar, shouting their drink orders at me. I'm just relieved it's over. Thank God for the parking lot."

"What's that?" Natalie said.

"You know, our quick getaway. Everyone in town knows we've got the fastest route out of Dodge," she said, writing down today's draft choices on the chalkboard menu. "Which is why I always park as close to the exit as possible. My shift ends at midnight, and I get home in like ten minutes."

Natalie glanced at the back door. "Do you have CCTV out back?"

"Nope, just the front entrance. Detective Labruzzo took everything."

"I appreciate your candor. Nice talking to you, Gabby."

"You, too. And good luck finding the creep who did this," she said. "We'll all sleep better."

Natalie left through the back door and stood on the edge of the dusty parking lot on Howard Street, which Blondie's shared access to with a handful of other businesses, including the Barkin' Dawg. Burning Lake had survived its biggest season. Only the locals knew the quickest, easiest way out of downtown during the entire month of October. Natalie had parked here herself on Sunday night for that very reason.

Now she realized—you couldn't plan a better escape route. The back exit of Blondie's had no bothersome surveillance cameras to worry about. You could spike your date's drink and then leave quickly and quietly, without getting stuck in traffic. Only a local would've suggested Blondie's as a meeting place on Halloween night.

But Hollis Jones never showed.

She got on her phone and told Lenny everything. "I heard you have the surveillance footage from the front entrance of Blondie's. We should be looking for Batman, a *Walking Dead* zombie, a musician named Hollis Jones, or anyone else who might've followed Morgan Chambers out of the bar on Sunday night."

"Sure thing," Lenny said, sounding dog-tired. "I'll add it to the to-do list."

"It's kind of a priority."

"Don't worry, Natalie. I'm planning on pulling an all-nighter."

"You and me both. Thanks, Lenny." She hung up and looked farther down the block at the back entrance of the Barkin' Dawg Saloon, where she, Luke, and Brandon used to meet regularly. Her head hurt. Tears sprang to her eyes, and she brushed them away. She decided to retrace Morgan's fateful steps out of Blondie's and toward the alley.

29

It was seven blocks from Blondie's to the mouth of the alley on Sarah Hutchins Drive. The sun was setting, and the sky ranged from pink along the horizon to purple overhead. The cleanup was ongoing, although the volunteer crews had thinned out. There were big piles of trash awaiting collection on every corner.

Natalie walked past boutiques, bookshops, restaurants, and bars, while the old clock in the town square tower struck six o'clock and the streetlights blinked on. Most of the businesses hadn't reopened yet. Their storefronts were dark, with a few exceptions—hardworking merchants taking inventory post-Halloween.

Natalie checked her watch. If Morgan had left Blondie's at around eleven P.M. on Sunday night and entered the alley at 11:44, that would leave forty-four minutes unaccounted for. On a normal day, at a leisurely pace, it was about a ten-minute walk to the alley at best. However, the size of the crowds would've slowed her down considerably. On the other hand, the crowds would've kept flowing, since the streets were closed to vehicular traffic. Only foot traffic was allowed. Therefore, there would've been no bothersome walk lights to wait for on Halloween's Eve.

Bearing in mind that Morgan was seen on tape pushing her way through the crowd—in other words, fighting against the tide—Natalie checked her watch and headed slowly down Sarah Hutchins Drive toward the alley, imagining hundreds of people around her. It took her fifteen minutes. That left twenty-nine minutes unaccounted for. Even if it had taken Morgan twenty minutes to get to the alley, that would've left a gap of twenty-four minutes.

So what happened between Blondie's and the alley?

Standing at the mouth of the alley, Natalie wondered what could've happened during those lost minutes. The dumpster was gone. They were still sorting through the garbage at the impound lot. She imagined the oblivious staff from local businesses throwing their trash away, tossing it in the top bin and leaving the alley, unaware that there was a body inside.

Natalie's phone rang, startling her.

It was Lenny. "The surveillance tape we pulled from the front entrance of Blondie's shows Wonder Woman, presumably Morgan Chambers, leaving the bar at ten fifty-four."

Natalie furrowed her brow. That was worse—now they had thirty-five minutes unaccounted for.

"So now, we're reviewing dozens of CCTV tapes from all the businesses on Sarah Hutchins Drive, following Morgan's steps and looking for any Batmen or zombies in the crowd around her. It's an eye-straining exercise, and we're all pooped. But we loaded up on pizza and Red Bull and energy drinks and Snickers bars, so . . ."

"You're my hero, Lenny."

"Now I can die happy." He hung up.

From the mouth of the alley, she looked back at Blondie's neon sign, seven blocks away from where she stood. Across the street was Rainie's New Age boutique, all lit up tonight. Rainie was talking on her phone at the back of the shop, bathed in a warm light. This was what normalcy looked like. Now she laughed flirtatiously and touched her hair, and Natalie wondered if she was talking to Luke and grew jealous. She had no right to be jealous, but still. She studied her own reflection in the storefront window, familiar lines of grief etched on her face. Jesus, she thought. Time to move on to the next stage—fighting spirit.

Natalie headed back the way she came. Seven blocks of prime real estate. The moon was high in the sky. The old-fashioned, wrought iron streetlamps lit the brick sidewalks. It was eerie with the crowds gone. A dampness invaded her bones. For a while, the town had transformed itself into a bewitched Halloween village. Now it was all over.

Earlier that day, Lenny had sent her a list of bars, restaurants, and pubs on Sarah Hutchins Drive that corresponded to the ink stamps on Morgan's hands. Now Natalie thought it was possible that Morgan had patronized another bar before making her final mad dash for the alley—that would certainly explain the thirty-five-minute gap.

She activated her phone and found two matches—a pub named Sir Martin's and the Barkin' Dawg Saloon. Both establishments were closed for business tonight. She tested the doors, but they were locked with the lights out.

As she approached Blondie's, Natalie walked past the bronze statue of the founder of Burning Lake, Thomas Latham, one of the magistrates who'd condemned Abigail Stuart to death. Light from a nearby storefront fell across his stern, puritanical face. She turned to face the only other business open on this side of the street tonight and spotted an antique violin in the storefront window. The sign above the front door read BERTRAND ANTIQUITIES.

30

A little bell jangled as she opened the door and stepped inside. Natalie was greeted by a ginger cat peeping out of a Victorian baby carriage. She gave the cat a pat on its fuzzy head and looked around. She and Bella used to come in here after school to ogle the historical witchcraft section, a locked cabinet full of ancient spell kits and handmade poppet dolls. Nowadays the store was mostly stocked with colonial paintings and high-end antique furniture—valuable things that Ned Bertrand found in people's attics, things they took for granted until he put a price on them.

The first floor of this beautiful old building was so crammed with antiques, it felt like a firetrap. Whenever she came in here as a kid, Natalie's eyes would glaze over after staring at so much wonder—heaps of rare books, a china bowl full of eighteenth-century reading glasses, a doctor's kit crammed with murky test tubes—treasures from all periods of history. Walking into the shop was like stepping back in time.

Twenty-eight-year-old Justin Bertrand—son of Ned, lean and tall—was fussing with something behind the register. Everybody in town knew that Justin had taken over the family business while Ned was recuperating from his stroke.

Hearing the bell jingle, Justin glanced up. "Sorry, we're closed." Then his eyes slowly focused. "Hey, Natalie. Long time, no see. I mean, Detective. Should I call you Detective?"

"Sure, that'd be great." She smiled warmly at him and walked up to the counter where they kept glass jars full of old marbles—tigers, chinas, crystals, bumblebees, agates. Justin was two years behind her at school. When she was a senior, he was a skinny sophomore riding his skateboard in the courtyard during lunch period. Now he looked like one of those young adults who lived in their parents' basement—a distracted, spiky-haired intellectual who dwelled in his own little world and didn't change his clothes often enough.

"How's your father?" she asked.

"As well as can be expected." Justin sat perched on the stool behind the cash register, just like his father had done for thirty years. "His physical therapist says he's seen some improvement lately. Anyway, I gave up smoking after Dad had his stroke. Want a piece?" He offered Natalie a stick of spearmint gum. "It's a halfway decent substitute for cigarettes."

"Nah, I'm good." She smiled.

"I can't wait for him to get better," Justin went on. "Running the show all by yourself is a lot harder than I thought. Electricity, gas, phone, internet, advertising, part-time employees. Our profit margin's surprisingly slim. You can have a good streak, but then all of a sudden nobody's buying. Winter's a slow period. Spring is better, but summer and fall are good for tourism. That's when we do best. I hope Dad will be ready to come back to work in the spring. Although his doctors are skeptical."

"Really? I'm sorry to hear that," she said sympathetically.

"He can't walk or talk yet, but he's doing okay. I knew something was wrong when he started to shake, right here behind the register. He looked really scared, and his mouth was all crooked. They said it was a major hemorrhagic stroke. There was brain swelling and everything. Dr. Swinton took good care of him in the ER, otherwise he might not have made it. Dad was in rehab for months before they let him come home. We've got a day nurse now who makes sure he's comfortable, gives him his meds, and helps him do his exercises. Just moving his fingers is exhausting for him. I can tell he's frustrated, but they're working every day on mobility, energy, and endurance."

"Glad to hear it," Natalie said. "I'm sure he'll get there soon enough."

"He's on the mend," he said optimistically.

She remembered visiting Joey in the hospital—it was horrible to see him looking so weak and thin. No more tests. No more treatments. Tears ran down the sides of his face. His body was shutting down, and yet he was awake and conscious. "Be the strength I need," he told Natalie.

It killed her that there was nothing she could do to help him.

"I'm worried about you," he whispered.

"Don't worry about me, Dad. I'll be okay. I love you."

He closed his eyes and never opened them again.

Now Justin Bertrand picked up the cat that was lacing itself around his legs and told her, "You used to come in here after school with your friends, didn't you? And now you're a famous detective."

"Oh God—famous? I hope not." Natalie felt herself blushing. She hated it when people asked her about the Crow Killer. How did you tell people you were happy you'd shot a man, but at the same time that killing another human being had stripped your soul bare? That you had to learn to live your life all over again? That your misery was all tangled up with the death of your sister and your family's fall from grace?

"My friend Bella and I used to head straight for the glass case full of poppet dolls and talismans. Whatever happened to them?"

He shuddered. "Oh, that. Bad karma. I got rid of the last of it after Dad had his stroke. I won't keep old curses in my store. I refuse to sell anything that's supposed to be haunted, not in my store."

"So you're superstitious?" she asked with mild amusement.

"Of ancient occult curses from Burning Lake? Hell, yes. Aren't you?" He laughed. "We used to have a Victorian embalming table, too, but we sold that to a rich guy with peculiar tastes."

Natalie had a flash memory of Justin as a scrawny teenager working in his dad's store. "You gave me a marble once," she said.

"I did?" He frowned. "I don't remember."

"Yeah, one day after school. Bella and I were in junior high, and you were here working with your father, and you gave us each a cat's-eye marble. You told us they were cat's-eyes, that's how I remember, since I know nothing about marbles."

"Well, I hate to break it to you, but that's an old sales trick. I was probably flirting with you, too." He laughed. "But the truth is we give away marbles and other inexpensive items for free. Advertising doesn't work. Word of mouth is how people find out about us. We're in a prime location. We get plenty of foot traffic. But the whole trick is to get people to come back. Repeat business. My dad says, if you give away something for free, most folks will develop a sense of loyalty. It's like winking while you give the customer an extra donut . . . you know, baker's dozen."

"Is that how that works?" Natalie said.

"Yeah, unfortunately. You have to use a few tricks, or else you're toast. Things can be good, and then wham. If the economy's bad, it affects sales. We have to buy reserves in advance to get through the hard times. That's why we've got a space in back for storage and furniture restoration. We own the second floor, too. It's jam-packed with inventory."

"Well, you've done a good job."

He shrugged. "It's a living. Like my dad says, we have done respectably well." He put down the cat. "Are you here about the woman they found in the dumpster?"

She nodded. "Did the police talk to you about it?"

"They've been in here a couple of times already," he said, closing the register drawer. "Detective Labruzzo wanted any surveillance tapes we might have, but I told him my father never installed a camera. We have a burglar alarm instead."

"Did you see Morgan that night around, say, ten or eleven o'clock?"

"No. Sorry. I closed up early. Six o'clock. Traditionally, we never stay open on Halloween, since we can't afford to have a bunch of drunken tourists or kids on a sugar high in the shop. You know. Bull, china. Too much breakable stuff."

Natalie nodded and said, "I noticed the violin in the window."

"Yup." He smiled. "That's a fake."

"Really?"

"A very valuable fake . . . made in 1895 to look like a Stradivarius." He held up a set of keys. "You want to see it?"

"Sure."

He walked over to the display window, unlocked the antique cherry-wood cabinet, and plucked the violin and bow off its stand. "People don't realize the value of the things in Grandma's attic." He turned the violin horizontally. "If you look inside through the f-holes, you can see a label glued to the back of the violin. Can you see it?"

She leaned forward and took a peek. "Yes."

"Anything before 1850, and the label should be made of paper. Not just any paper, mind you. It's called 'laid paper,' which is made from rags using a special process. The printing would've been done by hand with lead type. Anything after 1850, and you'll get 'wove paper,' which is made of wood pulp. Also, if it's pre-1850, the label should be the same shade of brown as the wood, with no curling around the edges. Otherwise you're looking at a counterfeit."

"And this one is a counterfeit?"

"A very rare counterfeit," he said, eyes lighting up. "It's worth a lot more than you'd think. Ironic, isn't it? That a fake can have real value?"

She nodded toward the front of the shop. "I noticed an appraisal sign in the window. Morgan Chambers was considering selling her violin. But you said she never dropped by. So she didn't see the violin or the sign in the window, and come in here asking for an appraisal of her violin? Not at any point between say . . . last Thursday and the weekend?"

"Nope. Sorry." He put the instrument back in the cabinet and locked it. "We haven't had any requests for appraisals in a couple of weeks, at least. Besides, I'm pretty good at remembering faces, and I've seen her picture in the news. We sell a number of antique musical instruments due to our proximity to the conservatory in Chaste Falls, so I would've remembered her for sure. But it's rare to get a walk-in. Most of our inventory comes from estate sales, auctions, and other dealers. Sometimes you get people who are looking to downsize. Yard sales, garage sales. It's all about finding inventory and transporting it back to the shop, then renovating, cataloguing, and researching it before you place it for sale."

"Sounds like a lot of work."

He grinned. "Yeah, but I like old stuff. I like buying and selling it. Once a year, Dad and I took a trip to the southwest or someplace like that, looking for inventory. He started this business thirty years ago. I'd call that a success, wouldn't you?"

"Totally." Natalie glanced around the shop. "By the way, who bought the Victorian embalming table?"

He smiled. "Ha. You wouldn't believe it. We have a few high-end customers who are always on the lookout for, shall we say, *unique* items. That historical witch collection you mentioned? I sold the entire lot to the same buyer."

"Really?"

"He paid a small fortune for it."

On a hunch, she said, "Hunter Rose showed me a German Stradivarius-style violin he acquired through a New York dealer."

Justin blushed. "Well, yeah . . . he got that from us. We've worked with his dealer for years now. Mr. Rose has a passion for old things. We're lucky to have a handful of serious local buyers, but I'd prefer to keep their transactions confidential. Do you mind me asking . . . what has this got to do with Morgan Chambers?"

"Don't worry," she assured him. "These are routine questions. Has anyone else purchased an antique violin from your store recently?"

"Sure. We get people in here all the time looking for that sort of thing. We also sell old flutes, trumpets, electric guitars, xylophones, you name it."

"Has anyone shown any interest in the fake violin in the window?" Natalie asked.

"A few people."

"Like who? Mr. Rose?"

"And Dr. Swinton, of course."

Natalie was taken aback. Russ had never mentioned an interest in violins, although now that she thought about it, he never talked about his private life. He knew more about Natalie than she knew about him. "Why do you say, 'of course'?"

"He collects them. Violins. He wanted that German Stradivarius you mentioned, but Mr. Rose snatched it up first." Justin nervously combed a hand through his hair. "Look, I don't want to get anybody in trouble."

"You won't. Dr. Swinton collects violins? I didn't know that."

"Yeah, his family has a number of classical musicians in it. His sister used to be a violinist before she died in a car crash, so he set up a scholarship in her honor."

"The Maldonado scholarship?"

"That's the one."

"Elyssa Maldonado is Dr. Swinton's sister?"

"Maldonado's her married name, I guess. She and her husband both died in that crash. Icy roads in the dead of winter."

Natalie had known Russ for years, but they'd always had a professional relationship. Doctor-patient. Detective–medical director. She'd never thought to ask him anything personal about himself, because she'd sanctified him as her physician. Now it sat uneasily on her shoulders. He obviously had a whole rich, textured life she knew nothing about, whereas he knew her body intimately.

"Thanks for your time, Justin." She turned to leave, but he tapped on her arm.

"I'm always on the hunt for new inventory, Detective, so if you ever clean out your attic, give me a ring. Here's my card. I'll make you a good offer."

"Thanks, I'll keep that in mind." She pocketed his business card and headed for the door.

31

Natalie's head was still pounding as she walked into the hospital ER. Two decades ago, she'd arrived at this very hospital suffering from acute panic. She vividly recalled the boy with the stick attacking her in the woods. She was nine years old when it happened. He was covered in red body paint, wearing a mask, and there was a savage look in his eyes. Samuel Hawke. When he chased her through the woods, all she could see was his red torso darting through the prison-bar tree trunks.

Dr. Swinton had treated her in the ER that day, reassuring her in his calm, low voice that everything was going to be okay. And it was. She trusted him. She'd trusted him ever since, and that was the reason she'd chosen him as her family doctor. Over the years, Russ had treated her for anything a general practitioner would've treated her for, referring her to various specialists he knew—gynecologist, allergist, dermatologist. It worked for her.

Last April, after Grace died, Dr. Swinton prescribed an antidepressant to help Natalie cope with her grief, and now he was in the process of incrementally decreasing the dosages to help ease her off the medication. He wasn't a therapist, but she confided in him. She trusted him.

It pained her to realize now how little she knew about this man, a lifelong bachelor. Rumor had it he'd been engaged once, but it didn't work out for whatever reasons. He was greatly respected in the community, on a lot of medical boards and a presence at local charity events. Besides that, she knew nothing about him. Zilch. He was one of the most private people she'd ever known. More private than Luke. More private than herself.

Now she stood in front of the reception area, sweat dripping down into her eyes, while one of the ER nurses said, "You're in luck, Natalie. It's super quiet tonight. He can see you right away." The nurse escorted her into an examination room and proceeded to take her blood pressure and perform a few tests.

Five minutes later, Dr. Swinton knocked on the door. "May I come in?"

"Yes." There was no need for modesty, since Natalie was in her work clothes, minus her jacket, with her blouse sleeves rolled up.

He breezed into the room in his blue scrubs. "How are you feeling, Natalie?"

"A little queasy. I have a bad headache, but I think it's because I haven't eaten all day."

"That'll do it." He consulted her chart. "Well, your blood pressure's good. Pulse rate, respiration, temperature . . . all normal. Any dizziness?" He put down the chart and checked her eyes. "Any blurriness of vision?"

"No."

He plucked a tongue depressor out of a box and tore off the wrapper. "Say ah." She did. He nodded absently and tossed the tongue depressor away. He palpated her neck. He used his stethoscope to listen to her heart. He took off his latex gloves and crossed his arms. "Tell me how you're feeling in general."

"Well, it's been a rough day," she admitted.

"So I've heard. Terrible news. Tragic." His eyes narrowed. "And you're in charge of the case?"

"Yes."

"Added stress can cause some of the symptoms you're experiencing— queasiness, headaches. But the discontinuation schedule is the more likely culprit. Your body's adjusting to the lower dosage of antidepressants we put you on. You may feel nauseous or have a loss of appetite. You may sweat excessively, flush, become light-headed, and have trouble sleeping. All these things are normal reactions. I want to continue decreasing the dosage as planned, but in smaller increments from now on. That should help." He picked up a prescription pad and jotted something down. "Let's keep you on your current dosage for another two weeks. Then we'll decrease it by twenty milligrams and see how it goes. I'm also prescribing a medication that will help with those headaches. Sound good?"

"Thanks." She took the prescription slips and tucked them away.

He signed off on her chart. "Come see me if you're feeling dizzy or having any trouble with your balance or vision, Natalie. All right?" He stood up to leave.

"Russ," she said. "I didn't realize Elyssa Maldonado was your sister."

His eyes grew solemn. "That's right."

"And you were a judge for the Monster Mash contest?"

He nodded stiffly. "This year."

"But Morgan Chambers was one of the finalists. And you never mentioned that."

His eyes narrowed with suspicion. "What's this all about, Natalie?"

She hopped off the exam table and put on her jacket. "I'll need a reference for a general practitioner. I shouldn't be seeing you for treatment anymore."

His jaw clenched. "Why not, may I ask?"

"Because you're connected to the case I'm working on."

"You're talking about Morgan Chambers?"

"Yes."

"Ask me anything. I've got nothing to hide."

"About the contest . . ."

"Veronica Manes asked me six months ago if I'd like to be a judge. I accepted," he explained. "I met Morgan about two months ago when she came into the clinic for a strained wrist, the type of injury that's very common to violinists." He shrugged. "It's an occupational hazard."

"Wait." Natalie looked at him as if they'd never met before. "What clinic?"

"At the Harrington Brock Music Conservatory. I volunteer there one evening a week."

"I had no idea you were connected to the conservatory," she said.

"My sister went there as a young promising violinist. After the accident, I started to volunteer my time. I do it because some of these kids are one injury away from having their dreams snatched away, and I don't want to let that happen. I'm sure my sister would've approved."

"So you treated Morgan for a strained wrist two months ago?"

He nodded. "Being a musician is like being a professional athlete. One significant injury can ruin your career." He put down the chart. "What else do you want to know about my relationship with Morgan?"

"Your relationship?" Natalie repeated, recoiling slightly. "Who said anything about a relationship?"

"There was nothing inappropriate going on, I can assure you." His eyes grew defiant. "She reminded me of my sister—dogged, determined, disciplined. I was moved by her passion for music."

"So now you're saying she wasn't just a patient," Natalie clarified. She couldn't believe he was painting himself into a corner like this.

He licked his lips nervously and tried again. "I escorted Morgan to a Halloween party," he explained. "She wanted to meet Owen Linkhorn. He's the record producer who was on the panel with me. I told her I'd be happy to introduce her."

"Are you talking about Hunter Rose's party on Sunday night?"

"Yes."

Natalie considered this for a moment. "Did you introduce her to the producer?"

"He didn't show up. He may have come later, but Morgan left around ten o'clock. I left shortly afterwards."

"How did she get to the party?"

"I drove her there. She took an Uber back to town."

"After Morgan left, where did you go?"

"Me?" He cracked a small, self-deprecating smile. "Home."

"You went straight home?"

"I felt rather silly. Embarrassed. Morgan didn't actually say good-bye."

"She ghosted on you?"

"Is that what they call it nowadays?" He smiled sadly. "Not that I blame her. She's a lot younger than me, but . . . I felt an instinct to help her. I sensed she was in trouble somehow. Emotionally, personally. I wanted to help her by introducing her to Owen. But then he didn't show up."

"Did Morgan bring her violin with her?"

"To the party?" He frowned. "I don't remember. I assume she brought it with her. But now . . . Natalie. I'm concerned. Am I a suspect?"

"I'm just gathering information," she said, but it wasn't the whole truth.

Russ rubbed his forehead and looked around desperately. He glanced at his watch, but he would not escape lightly. "I've tried dating, but it never seems to work out. Not because I'm picky, but because they're so picky. It feels as if you're expected to do some kind of song and dance, and I don't know the tune. I can provide a woman with a good home and a good life, but I'm not sure what else they want," he said. "I'm a boring old man with nothing to contribute, I guess. Since when did I become a walking cliché?"

"What do you think Morgan was looking for?"

He shook his head and shrugged. "She was very ambitious. I admired her for that."

Natalie suddenly remembered a detail she needed to confirm. "Were you wearing a Batman costume that night?"

He nodded reluctantly. "Believe it or not. Guess I'm a midlife crisis fool."

She felt sorry for him. She also felt suspicious of his motives. Why didn't he tell her about Morgan right away? It didn't sit right.

"Thank you for your cooperation, Russ."

He nodded stiffly. "Sofia will send you a list of general practitioners in the morning."

32

The foothills above Roscoe Canyon were a Realtor's wet dream, with exclusive residences tucked behind ornate wrought iron security fences. Home to an eclectic mix of artists, real estate agents, and business owners, Roscoe Canyon was bounded on all sides by conservancy lands. Residents paid a premium for the mountain views, but Hollis Jones's digs were modest. While most properties in the area went for sums in excess of $1 million, Jones lived in a stucco cabin whose gateposts were crumbling.

Natalie rang the doorbell and heard a reedy voice say, "Hello?"

"Mr. Jones? It's Detective Lockhart."

Wind chimes dangling from the porch overhang made discordant music in the November breeze. Natalie heard footsteps and could see a faint outline behind the rusty screen door. A pale face. Spiky dark hair. Broken capillaries on a long, thin nose. An old robe worn from repeated washings.

"Can we talk for a minute?" she asked.

Jones gazed at her through the screen door, furrows of stress forming on his face. "How am I in trouble, exactly?"

"No trouble at all, sir," Natalie said. "I'm investigating the death of Morgan Chambers."

"Oh." He scowled. "I had nothing to do with that."

"May I come in? It's cold out here."

He balked, then conceded. He opened the door.

The furniture was a mixed bag, chosen for comfort over style. The twinkle lights strung across the living-room ceiling glowed like shy stars, while the wooden crossbeams cast cavernous shadows. The place was untidy, cluttered with newspapers and packages from Amazon. A teak shelving unit displayed vintage collectibles, and there were authentic-looking primitive masks hanging on the walls.

"Just so you know," he told her, "I was supposed to meet her at Blondie's on Sunday night, but then I ditched her for another opportunity."

"Why? What happened?" Natalie asked.

"The truth is, I met someone else."

"You stood her up?"

He shrugged. "Ava Dixon gave this amazing fucking performance. We hit it off. I'm going to see her next weekend. We may do a gig together."

"Did you call Morgan and let her know?"

"Nah. I acted like a complete asshole."

"So you just let her wait for you in a bar alone, and you never showed?"

"Right. But listen. I liked her at first, until she revealed her true colors when we saw each other on Saturday night. So I decided not to waste my time on someone like that."

"Someone like what?"

"Who thinks being a fiddle player is beneath her. She said she was looking for a gig like mine, but pretty soon she let slip what she really thought. As if playing the fiddle wasn't a worthy occupation."

"Did you dress up as a zombie for Halloween by any chance?"

He shook his head. "I don't go in for that shit. I was wearing my standard uniform. T-shirt, jeans, and a hoodie. Maybe a little mascara."

She disliked his arrogance, but he wasn't coming across as guilty of anything other than being a complete jerk. "When did you first meet Morgan?"

"At the contest. She came up afterwards and shook my hand. She was very bold, which I liked. We talked. She wanted to talk some more. I suggested we meet at the Shady Planet the following night. Ten o'clock."

"And you enjoyed her company enough to see her again on Sunday night?"

"She's sexy."

"But you stood her up."

"I met someone even sexier," he said.

"Where did you and Ava go?"

"I took her to Lucia's. Then we came back here and had a nice time."

Natalie nodded. "Can I have Ava's contact information so I can verify this?"

"Okay. But I didn't have anything to do with whatever happened to Morgan." He looked at Natalie. "By the way, what did happen to her?"

"Just get the information, please."

"Hold on." He went to fetch his phone.

When he came back, she decided to just throw it out there. "Have you ever used GHB or Rohypnol?"

"The date rape drug?" Jones laughed. "Are you serious? Me? Women fling themselves at me every night. I have to beat them off with a stick. Do you want Ava's number or not?"

33

Natalie buzzed through the supermarket—eggs, milk, a box of double-fudge cake mix, Cape Cod potato chips, Pete's dark roast coffee, and extra-strength Excedrin. She grabbed a box of Dove bars, then put it back. She tossed a box of cronuts into the cart and thought about the kinds of food Willow used to love. She used to keep junk food in the trunk of her car, the old Chevy Nova she called the Snooze-mobile because of its lousy acceleration. Tall, slender Willow adored the worst kinds of food— things you wouldn't find growing anywhere in nature, chewy lumps of chemicals wrapped in cellophane. Things you could keep in the trunk of your car for weeks and they wouldn't go bad. Food with absurdly long expiration dates. Food stripped of all nutrients. Food that bounced.

Natalie paused in the gift card aisle of the supermarket. She wanted to buy Luke something funny and goofy, reminiscent of their childhood, some private joke they used to share, like Monty Python's Ministry of Silly Walks. Luke used to imitate John Cleese's funny walks in the backyard, raising his long legs absurdly high, and Natalie would laugh so hard she'd double over, tears running down her cheeks. She couldn't find any Monty Python–themed birthday cards, so she hunted down the worst card in the rack. It was an old joke between them. Last year for her birth-day, Luke had given her a card with a dancing unicorn that spilled neon-colored glitter all over her when she opened it. *Corny the Unicorn Says Happy Birthday!*

God, it was awful.

Now it was her turn to return the favor. And she found just the thing. On the cover was an illustration of a glass half full of red liquid, with a bunch of heart-shaped balloons floating in the background. Inside the card, it said: *Glass half empty: Sorry I forgot your birthday! Glass half full: But I'm super early for next year! Happy Birthday!*

There was only one checkout lane this evening. Three people were in front of her. Natalie glanced at the tabloids and noticed a front-page story about the Crow Killer. She didn't dare pick it up. She couldn't stand the thought of reading another article about herself—one reporter had depicted her as a local hero whose sister was a cold-blooded murderer; another reporter dug into her family history and found that she was dis-tantly related to a notorious local witch from the 1800s. Not even Natalie knew that. In fact, she doubted it was true. The online stories were the worst, full of sensational misinformation and gossipy rumors, and she was relieved that the media had moved on for the most part. This article was the first of its kind in several months, and she wondered what the angle was. The case had been stalled out since August. Luke was handling all inquiries now, relieving her of the pain of having to answer more ques-tions about Grace.

She piled up her groceries in front of an acne-scarred young clerk, who smiled at her as he swiped her items across the scanner. He dropped every-thing into a membrane-thin plastic bag and said, "That'll be thirty dollars and twenty-two cents, ma'am."

Oh fuck, she thought, I'm a ma'am.

"I mean," he corrected himself, "Detective Lockhart."

She glanced at his name tag. "Thank you, Christopher."

"Sure thing." He had a wide, forgiving smile, and she briefly wondered how she knew her name, but then she realized he'd probably read about her in the tabloids on his lunch breaks. "Any news about the woman in the dumpster?" he asked, while she opened her wallet, took out her credit card, and inserted it into the payment reader.

"Sorry, Christopher, I can't talk about that. It's confidential."

"I only ask because my mom runs the Laundromat across the street."

"Oh," she said, nodding. "You must be Christopher Delgado, then." The Laundromat was called Delgado's Wash and Fold.

"You're sticking it in the wrong way."

"What's that?"

"Your card." He pointed it out, still smiling. "It goes the other way."

"Hey, I knew that. Ha-ha." Natalie smirked and reinserted her card. "Did the police talk to your mom yet?"

"Yeah, they asked her a bunch of questions. She doesn't know anything. But it made her cry." He rang up the receipt. "She remembers your dad, Officer Joey. When my grandpa first started the Laundromat, his burglar alarm kept going off in the middle of the night. And every time he'd call your dad, and your dad would come right over to check it out, even though they both knew the alarm was probably broken. Your father never seemed to mind, and they got to be friends."

"That's a nice story," Natalie said, smiling. "Say hello to your mom and your grandfather for me."

"I will." He handed her the receipt. "Have a good evening, Detective."

"You, too, Christopher."

"Stay safe out there."

Outside, the luminous orb of the moon had a soft red ring around it. This ring, Natalie recalled from her college ecology class, was composed of ice crystals very high up in the clouds, but some of the locals believed that a red ring around the moon was a bad omen. A pagan sign of negative influences coming your way. God, she hoped not. She shivered as she crossed the supermarket parking lot. It certainly felt as if negative influences had taken over recently.

She got in her car and drove home. The cleanup efforts were progressing at a nice clip, and they were further along than they'd been around this same time last year. Traffic wasn't bad. By the time she got home, a stiff breeze was up.

Natalie stood in silent contemplation outside the weathered, gray-shingled house while the wind blew through her hair, cooling her face. Five years ago, the trees across the street had been damaged by Dutch elm disease, and you could still see the blighted dead wood among the healthy trees.

A few leaves rattled across the porch, lifted by the breeze. Night gripped the woods in a shroud of fog. She stood in the front yard and thought about the deer coming into the garden last summer and eating all the flowers.

Hey, brat. Where you at?

The memory of her sister's voice hit her like a rock. She could smell Grace's orange blossom perfume. Sometimes her memories were so vivid, Natalie swore she could've held them in her hand and turned them this way and that. What to do with all these aching memories? How was she supposed to live with this new narrative?

A clammy, flypapery feeling enveloped her. Thank God Joey never found out about Grace. It would've broken his heart. He was pivotal in getting Justin Fowler sentenced to life in prison. He worked hard for a conviction. And now, to realize he'd been wrong all along—not only wrong, but misguided and clueless. To find out that one of his beloved daughters had killed his other beloved daughter—it would've absolutely crushed him. She was glad he died thinking he'd done the right thing.

Natalie figured that was what prayer was all about—asking forgiveness from the universe. This was why she kept so busy. She relished working late in the office, being the first to arrive and the last to leave. Physical and mental exertion didn't bother her. It was a feature, not a bug. Because as long as she was working, she wouldn't have to cope with her unfathomable grief.

Natalie gathered her groceries from the trunk. The lawn felt unnaturally spongy. Her fingers were ice-cold. She unlocked the front door and turned on the lights, taking gradual possession of the house. She put her groceries away in the kitchen, then moved through the downstairs rooms, holding herself as if her shivering bones might break.

Natalie had picked up a nausea she couldn't shake, and it burned on the floor of her stomach. Walking through these deserted rooms, she worried that somehow she didn't measure up—as an aunt, as a daughter, as a sister, as a cop. Ever since Grace's death, she'd believed that she could keep the nightmares at bay by weight lifting and jogging, training hard after work. Between the Exercycle, the treadmill, and Joey's old barbells, Natalie had put on a bit of muscle to make up for the weight she'd lost. Things died in her fridge from lack of interest. Once a week, she went through the leftovers and tossed everything out. Then she'd take another trip to the grocery store and stock up again, but she wasn't eating properly. She wasn't hungry. She was more anxious than hungry lately, and her face had taken on an angular, predatory look. Sometimes when she caught her reflection in the bathroom mirror, she was surprised by how different she looked. She gave off a disturbing don't-fuck-with-me vibe.

Now she started the coffeemaker, went into the living room, opened her laptop, and checked her emails. Her screen saver was an old photograph of the family—Joey, Deborah, Willow, Grace, and Natalie during happier times. Her father's police badge gleamed in the low light. All her life, Natalie had thought of the Lockharts as the good guys. To go from being perfectly normal, respected members of the community to being the type of family that spawned murderers was the worst kind of hurt there was.

Instead of finding peace and calm inside herself, instead of being able to forgive not just Grace, but herself, Natalie wanted to rip the world apart with her bare teeth, to locate the root of this evil and tear it to pieces. She wanted to burn it all down and start over—her childhood, the past, these bittersweet memories. She wanted to declare war on the unknowable, amorphous evil that had taken over their town, to face it, confront it, and destroy it. In the deep recesses of her body, Natalie wanted to reclaim her honor and win. She wanted to taste victory in her mouth. Only then would she be able to find any so-called peace.

By the time she'd finished her reports for the day, Natalie couldn't stop yawning. She sought comfort in the quilt she'd dragged down from the attic two months ago—Willow's old quilt with its pattern of Renoir-inspired dancers. She picked up the remote, turned on the TV, and watched a rerun of *Gilmore Girls*. She preferred late-1990s sitcoms that featured characters as glib and snarky as Lorelai and Chandler Bing.

She closed her eyes and saw the flush of Grace's cheeks as she stood on the edge of the cliff. *No, don't!* Grace spoke in a monotone. Her eyes ghosted like the deer in the garden. She stepped off the cliff and was gone.

Natalie sat up straight. She could feel a static discharge on the back of her neck as she remembered her old sketchbooks. She and Bella used to hang out upstairs in Natalie's room after school, where they'd make fun of their teachers and draw satirical pictures of their classmates and write embarrassing "confessions" in Natalie's sketchbooks. Then Bella would go home and practice her violin, while Natalie stashed everything under her bed for next time.

She hadn't looked at these sketchbooks in ages. She didn't even know where they were. But her pack rat mom kept everything—Protector of the Kingdom of Memories, Grace used to jokingly call Deborah. Their mother had saved every last scrap of the girls' homework, their letters, their diaries, and doodlings. She'd packed their childhoods away between layers of tissue paper underneath the attic eaves, where the paper wasps built their menacing nests.

The attic door creaked like the opening of a tomb. Natalie climbed the narrow stairs and pulled on the long chain that switched on the overhead bulb. The smell of wet insulation and mothballs hit her, and it made her skin crawl. The attic felt like a time capsule, trapped in amber. There were stacks of old photo albums, corroded kitchen appliances, glued-together pieces of furniture, old movie posters inside the umbrella stand, a rack of her father's police uniforms preserved in mothball-smelling clothing bags. She paused to rub the goose bumps off her arms.

Tucked under the rafters was a collection of boxes, long forgotten and thick with dust—each one labeled and dated in Deborah's careful handwriting. The top of Natalie's head skimmed along the sloped ceiling made of pit-sawed timbers as she crawled around under the creepy dark eaves, squinting at labels, and sliding out storage boxes one at a time. She pried off the lids and got a whiff of mildew or newsprint or oil crayons or wool.

She clapped the dust off her hands, brushed the cobwebs out of her hair, and sat cross-legged on the floor, her neck tensing as she pulled things out at random. She found a packet of old rolling papers inside Grace's Disney pencil case, a tattered butterfly net no good for catching anything, Willow's red vinyl purse full of absurdly bright lipsticks. She found things she'd forgotten about completely, like her funky *Reservoir Dogs* T-shirt and a compilation tape from Bobby Deckhart—Soundgarden, Pearl Jam, Nirvana, and for a splash of irony, Abba.

Then, like the surprise in the bottom of a Cracker Jack box, she stumbled across Bella's old letters tucked away in a box of stuffed teddies and old Barbie dolls.

34

Natalie hadn't read Bella's letters in a long time, but now she dug them out and read them in search of clues. She studied the snapshots. There were three letters addressed to Natalie altogether, postmarked from Los Angeles, Chicago, and New York City. Each envelope included a Polaroid picture of Bella that seemed to prove she was okay. She didn't appear to be intimidated or scared for her life or suicidal. In her letters, Bella insisted that she'd left town of her own free will. But there was something about them that irked Natalie to this day.

When Bella disappeared on the night of their high school graduation, both girls were on the cusp of exciting things. Natalie had gotten into Boston University, and Bella had received a generous scholarship package from the Harrington Brock Music Conservatory. But all Bella wanted to do was escape. "Let's travel around the world and stay in youth hostels across Europe." She'd marked up an atlas of all the places she wanted to visit. "I love the idea of Thailand, don't you?"

During their sleepovers, Natalie and Bella would confide their deepest secrets. "I don't want to play concertos," Bella told her once, "I want to *live* them. Let's have big bold lives, Natalie. Those old composers had the most amazing adventures. Bach played his violin in the middle of the Black Forest at midnight, and Mozart made fart jokes. Peter Warlock was into black magic, and Franz Liszt had affairs with married women. We could have affairs with Italian men. Italians are the best lovers, you know," Bella said, as if she knew. *"Avoir une bonne vie. Have a good life."*

Bella called Mr. Striver "my smother-mother daddy" and said he kept her in a box. "Not a literal box," she explained, "but a psychological box where I can't breathe. He's got my whole life planned out for me, and basically I'm going to be a violin soloist, whether I like it or not."

At the same time, Bella also stood up for her father. "He works so hard and cares so much, it makes me cry. He dreams about having this genius child, and I can't help thinking—what if he's right? What if I am a genius? I definitely don't want to be average. I secretly hope I am a genius."

"We're all fucking geniuses," Natalie said.

"Right." Bella laughed. "We're the Brilliant Misfits."

More than once, Natalie had witnessed Mr. Striver's overbearing attitude toward his daughter when she visited Bella at home or at Striver's Music Shop after school. He would say inappropriate things like, "Bella's violin costs more money than my car!" and he'd make cringeworthy jokes about the violin's f-holes. Bella would say, "Dad, stop. You're embarrassing yourself." He would remind Bella to smile. "Recital face! You have to have your recital face on, darling. Remember to smile!" Behind his back, Bella made monster faces and called him her stage mom with a dick.

The day before I decided to do it, to finally run away from it all, Bella wrote in one of her letters to Natalie, *Dad was in the kitchen making pancakes and listening to Prokofiev. His eyes were closed, and he was swaying to the music when I walked in. "Listen to this cadenza, Bella," he said. He had a glass of wine in one hand and a spatula in the other. Wine for breakfast again. Uh, yeah, Dad. "We're going to put a little meat on Bella's bones," he said.*

He ruffled my hair, and each time he dropped another pancake on my plate, he said, "Here you go, my angel. Eat up. Put a little meat on those bones."

I couldn't help rolling my eyes. "Dad-dy . . . stop it."

"Wha-at?"

"You're acting weird today."

"I'm in a good mood. What of it?" He laughed it off.

After breakfast, we practiced a Mozart concerto, and for some reason I kept flubbing it. I think it's because I just don't like playing duets with him anymore. He's no good at it. Especially when he's wasted. There is no expression in his music. It's just mechanical and dead. Halfway through, he screamed at me, "That's not right! Get it together! Where's your head?"

I felt nervous and wanted to stop, because he was acting a little erratic, but he wouldn't let me stop, and so we both had to keep playing this crappy duet over and over again. It was agony, because he kept yelling at me, when he's the one who sucks at this. And it made me feel bad to think that way. Sometimes I hate him so much—but then I hate myself for hating him.

That night, he came into my room, sat on the edge of my bed, and said, "I'm sorry, Bella," and I could smell the wine on his breath.

"It's okay."

"I'm too hard on you, sweetheart."

"No, Dad. It's fine."

"But look at you, going to the conservatory on a scholarship. You're going to be a star one day, Bella."

"Don't worry about it, Dad."

He nodded, and the bed shifted under his weight from the bobbing of his head. He finally got up, and I could feel the heaviness receding, and I was so relieved. He took his smelly wine breath and all his stupid, overbearing concerns with him and left the room, leaving me in peace. All of this would've been too much for me, if I didn't have a secret plan out of Dodge.

A secret plan.

Natalie reread the last sentence.

Bella had never explained in any of her letters how she'd gotten the hell out of Dodge. All she said was that she was happy now (this was twelve years ago), still playing her violin and at peace with herself. There was a hippieish tinge to her newfound freedom—*I'm more "me" than I've ever been; I've found peace and I hope you do, too; there's more to life than ambition and discipline; I'm finally embracing who I am.* Bella played the violin now because she loved it, she explained, not because she *had* to. She was satisfied, content, and fulfilled with her life, and she wanted the same for Natalie.

Natalie rubbed her fatigued eyes, then picked up the phone and called Max.

"Yello?" came the familiar response.

"It's Natalie. We need to talk. Do you have time?"

"Now? Sure," he said congenially. "I'm in the neighborhood. Timothy Harrison. I keep telling him, that tree branch is going to come crashing down any minute now. It's a liability."

"Now's good," she said.

"Be right over."

Five minutes later, the doorbell rang. Instead of flannels and jeans, tonight Max was wearing a white shirt, a bomber jacket, and black trousers. "Dude, what's up?" he said, breezing into the house and taking a seat on the living-room sofa. He was the kind of guy who was comfortable any old where. Outside, a moonlit fog curled through the woods.

"I want your opinion," she said, spreading out the Polaroids Bella had sent along with her letters, before they'd stopped arriving years ago.

Max picked up the Polaroid of eighteen-year-old Bella that came with the first letter. Bella was seated on the floor, leaning against a white wall and smiling at the camera. She seemed happy and relaxed, but too pale for the California sun. This was before cell phones and selfies. Bella had never mentioned who'd taken the pictures. They were all close-ups, from her shoulders to a few inches above her head, so you couldn't see the rest of her surroundings, just the white wall behind her.

The next two Polaroids were similar—close-ups of Bella leaning against a white wall—except that in Polaroid number two, you could see a strained sadness in her eyes. In Polaroid number three, Bella's eyes looked dead. To the contrary, her letters insisted she was perfectly happy with her vagabond life and having lots of fun adventures. She never asked Natalie about herself or the Misfits. She merely reassured her old friend that she was okay and sent Polaroids as proof of her existence. After about a year, the letters stopped coming.

"I remember at the time being satisfied that Bella was alive, although it left a kind of unease in me," Natalie confessed. "I figured she'd embraced a druggy lifestyle or something, which would explain the change in her appearance from picture to picture. The police processed everything, but they only found Bella's fingerprints on the envelopes and contents. She sent similar letters to her father, and it was persuasive enough that the police finally dropped the case. I let it go, too. But there's always been something about the entire incident that irked me . . . beyond losing a friend. Something about these pictures—her facial expression, the tragic lines of her face, or . . . something."

Max leaned over the grouping on the coffee table and studied them. Then his shoulders slumped and his stomach protruded like a beach ball underneath his button-up shirt. "She doesn't look happy."

"No. But I've been learning a lot about the violin culture lately . . . and it's given me more insight into Bella's troubled nature." She placed her hands on the curved wooden arms of her chair and said, "She used to run away a couple of times a year, and her father would panic. She'd tell me about his demands . . . how many hours he expected her to practice a day, what kinds of sacrifices she needed to make, how she couldn't ever be like the other kids. Occasionally, she'd run away just to blow off steam. I understand now what Bella was going through, what was causing her moodiness and depressions."

Max made an absentminded movement with his hand that distracted her. "Did I ever tell you about the time Mr. Striver called my dad for an estimate on the termite damage to his house?"

"No," she said, curious about this one-eighty.

"Well, the foundation was infested with termites, and some of the structural beams were compromised. I mean, let's be honest. Bugs were flying out of the walls. Mr. Striver just let the whole thing go to pot. So we called in an exterminator, and my dad did some repair work to the beams, but Mr. Striver refused to pay beyond a certain point, so we abandoned it with quite a bit more work to be done. Which is crazy. My dad tried to convince him to complete the job, but Mr. Striver couldn't see the whole picture. He might as well not have spent a dime, rather than stopping the work midstream. All those bugs just kept on reproducing."

Natalie frowned, wondering what his point was.

"Long story short, he exposed himself as a shortsighted guy. Someone you can't rely on for anything. Bella wasn't looking for freedom. She was looking for consistency. For stability. For the kind of parent who'd get rid of the termites once and for all . . . not let them take over the house."

"That's a good observation," she said.

"And after Mr. Striver died, a relative—a distant cousin or something—sold the house to an unknown buyer. It's in a blind trust now. Whoever bought it hasn't bothered to fix it up, either. You can hire an exterminator once a year, but the bugs come back."

"So it's vacant?" For the longest time, Natalie hadn't thought about Bella's old house, which was located across town near the old railroad tracks.

"Apparently. Like I said, a blind trust owns it. I don't know what the owner plans on doing with the property. Maybe they're gonna perform satanic rituals at midnight, who the hell knows? They paid a lot of money for it, too, so I hear. But there's no evidence they want to flip it. They're just letting it sit there."

Tucking this bit of information away, Natalie asked Max, "What do you remember about the night she disappeared?"

He sighed and loosened his collar. "Oh God, I don't know. Bella was this quiet, beautiful girl who spoke through her music, which was awesome. She was a sweet kid with a mischievous sense of humor. It was always a little weird to me that Nesbitt Rose, the Boo Radley of our neighborhood, had such a huge crush on her. Bobby used to call him pootard—remember? Cruel, but hey. Nesbitt scared people. He used to spy on us. Remember that? He'd skulk around town, terrifying everyone by carrying dead animals by their necks. At the time, I figured he must've done something to her that night." He darkened. "That night sort of ruined my life."

She rested her hands in her lap. "How so?"

"After Bella disappeared, I stopped practicing the piano. I figured that if something could happen to Bella, after all the hours she put in practicing, considering how hard she worked—you know? So I quit. I gave up on music. I shouldn't have, but I was young and stupid. Eighteen. What did I know? I partied hardy in college. Majored in business. I wanted to become a millionaire by the time I was twenty-five. I thought it would be a cinch. Thought I was a genius. Wasted my time. Women liked me—I don't know why. But I've never had any problems in that department. And so what did it all add up to, Natalie? I can't even remember *Moonlight* sonata all the way through. You believe that?"

Natalie frowned. "Max, what do you think happened to her?"

"For real?" He wiped the sweat off his brow and leaned forward. "I never bought into the idea she went to California of her own accord. I think she would've told us if she was leaving that night. Challenged us. Dared us. Why keep it a secret? Also, Bella never would've left you hanging, Natalie. She loved you. You two were like sisters."

Natalie nodded, but she knew that sisters could keep awful secrets from each other. "I agree it doesn't add up."

"Right after she disappeared, there were rumors going around that she got kidnapped by bikers. But you're the detective, Natalie. What do you think happened?"

She chewed on her lower lip and said, "Something's definitely 'off' about these Polaroids. In the beginning, she's smiling, but by the end, she looks devastated."

Max nodded eagerly. "Yeah, I noticed that, too."

"Those dead eyes. And the wall behind her," Natalie went on, "looks the same in every picture, despite the fact that each of her letters were postmarked from a different locale . . . almost as if it's the same white wall in each photograph."

"Yeah, you're right," Max said, studying the pictures on the coffee table. He landed his index finger on the first Polaroid. "Same white wall with the same crack in it."

"There's a crack?" She leaned forward and studied the images.

"Speaking as a contractor, over time, you can see the effects of gravity on the walls of a building. And it's unique to each wall, almost like a fingerprint. The weight of the floors above it, plus people and furniture will produce a 'turning effect,' also called a 'moment.' If the moment is large enough, the wall will collapse. But if the moment is small, then the wall will resist collapsing. Right here, you can see tiny flaws and cracks in the wall, due to tension and compression forces."

"Is it the same wall?" she asked breathlessly.

Max sat very still, studying the Polaroids. "It certainly looks that way."

Her phone rang, jarring them both.

It was Hunter. "Natalie, I have something to show you."

35

As soon as Natalie pulled into Hunter Rose's driveway, lightning cracked and torrents of rain poured out of the night sky. Drop after drop became a blur, then a downpour. Raindrops joining raindrops—splashing and flying to earth, forming rivery bands of water that threaded and braided their way downhill, feeding the wildflowers, feeding the oak trees.

She grabbed her umbrella from the backseat and hurried across the front yard, wind blowing in her face. She rang the doorbell, and when no one answered, she put her hands up to the glass and stared into the front hallway, where the shadows were tinged with shafts of muted light filtering in through the windows.

The door was unlocked. She took a tentative step inside, the old hinges creaking. "Hunter? It's Natalie." She paused on the threshold. The house was dead quiet. She picked up a queasiness she couldn't shake, and it burned in the pit of her stomach.

Behind her, a male voice called out, "Hello?"

She turned in the doorway and saw Hunter walking toward her through the rain. He held a big black umbrella and wore a long black trench coat, like a spy in a British drama. "Oh, there you are," he said.

"Sorry. Your door was unlocked."

"It's this way."

"What's this way?"

"Something my security guard found. Follow me."

She stepped outside and closed the door behind her, and they headed for the meadow on the western side of the property, beyond the garage where Hunter stored his collection of vintage motorcycles. They crossed an overgrown field toward the woods and spotted a deer in the rain. They watched as it paused with its delicate nostrils sniffing at the wind. After a moment, the deer tensed and bounded into the woods, its tail flashing white.

"What's this all about? What did your security guard find?"

"A person drove by my property tonight, while one of my security guards was doing his rounds. The driver slowed down and chucked a violin case onto the side of the road, then sped off."

"Are you serious?"

"You just missed Assistant Chief Gossett," Hunter told her while they walked. "He and a couple of officers have already assessed the scene. They talked to the security guard and took pictures of everything."

"Who's got the violin?"

"Gossett took it with him."

Natalie bit back her anger and asked, "Did your guard see the vehicle?"

"It was too dark and foggy. He couldn't make out the license plate, just a pair of taillights. He figured it was kittens."

"Kittens?"

"Sometimes people drive by the property and toss a bag of kittens into the woods. As you know, there are lots of farms around here. Farms with rats. Cats eat the rats. All those farm cats get pregnant and have litters of kittens. Instead of drowning them, the farmers will dump them on my property. I do charity work for animal organizations, so they know I'll take good care of them. But it pisses me off. People are lazy shits."

Natalie stopped walking. "Why did you lie to me, Hunter?"

He folded his arms. "Lie?"

"You were never going to give me those tapes. Why did you say you would?"

He watched her with quiet intensity. "It was a misunderstanding between me and my attorneys. They didn't communicate the information because, to be honest, I hate talking to lawyers. They're so fucking boring. I didn't realize you weren't in the loop when we spoke yesterday. And by the way, Natalie—why aren't you in the loop? Don't they trust you?"

She bristled a little. "No. They're protecting your party guests, but in doing so, they're slowing down the process and cramping my style."

"Well, if it's any consolation, my attorneys are sharing everything that's pertinent with the assistant chief. We're not holding anything back. But I promise to keep you in the loop personally going forward." He glanced around at the woods, then lowered his voice. "Some people will do anything to preserve their reputations. Part of the problem is that, well, Natalie . . . you're too high profile right now, because of the Crow Killer case. You're drawing too much attention to my wealthy, publicity-shy guests."

She rolled her eyes. "This case is drawing its own attention."

A dense forest of old-growth oaks, birches, and firs surrounded the property. The wind was gaining strength. He looked at her without smiling. "Do you remember Aesop's fable about the rabbit and the hound?"

"Is it the same thing as the tortoise and the hare?"

"No, this is different. Would you like to hear it?"

"Sure, why not," she said sarcastically.

"One day, the hound was out chasing a rabbit through the woods. After a while, he grew tired and gave up. He let the rabbit get away. But the blue jays were watching, and they mocked the hound mercilessly, laughing at him because the rabbit had outwitted him. But the hound replied, 'That rabbit was running for its life. I was only running for my dinner. That's the difference between us.'"

"So who's the rabbit?" she asked. "And who's the hound?"

"You're the detective. You tell me."

"Am I supposed to be the fucking rabbit in this scenario?" she demanded to know, but he ignored her and took a weedy path into the woods.

"It's this way," he said.

She followed him along the path, where wet leafy branches swayed in the wind, spilling big drops of rain onto their umbrellas.

202 ← ALICE BLANCHARD

"We know that Morgan went to your party with Russ Swinton," Natalie said, ignoring his mind games. "I need to know who else she talked to at the party. Who she engaged with."

"Do you know what imposter syndrome is?" Hunter asked her.

Again with the mind games.

Natalie nodded. "It's when a person doubts their own talent and accomplishments and believes they'll be exposed as a fraud. It's basic insecurity one-oh-one."

"The thing about powerful, wealthy men is . . . they aren't any more confident than the next guy. They aren't any less self-loathing. It's true we have more options, but not when dealing with things that normally come up . . . a rich man's toilet will back up, just the same as a workingman's. A rich man will wait on the phone for customer service just as long as a workingman has to."

"Or else you could hire someone to wait for you," she added.

"True. But it's still waiting."

"Why do you have this need to convince me you're like everyone else, Hunter?" she asked. "Comparing yourself to the workingman?"

He cracked a smile. "Because I can be paralyzed with fear and get night sweats just like anybody else. I can make mistakes and lose it all, if I'm not careful. It's true, what they say. Money doesn't solve everything."

"Okay, fine," she said irritably. "We've established you're an ordinary human being like Joe Schmoe down the block, only you happen to be hiding behind a team of high-priced lawyers. Got it."

He gazed at her with contempt. "I'm not hiding anything. I'm cooperating fully with the police."

"Oh, come on. You're covering up for your rich buddies. Helping to preserve their reputations. You just admitted it."

"You think I'm that predictable?"

She paused on the woodsy path. "I have no idea what you are."

"Seriously?" He paused for a moment, and she recalled the summer they'd spent together, when Hunter was a cool college guy with his straight-leg jeans and his John Lennon glasses and his dog-eared copy of *Nine Stories* by J. D. Salinger.

"Do you honestly think I lead a life of endless partying?" he said angrily. "A life of prestige and status-seeking? Oh, the sad struggles of the self-made millionaire. I'm not saying it's a burden to have money. The perks are amazing. I wouldn't trade it for anything." He waved a dismissive hand. "But I haven't exactly turned my house into party central. I think parties are for extroverts who want to show off or else reinforce the belief that they're fuckable. It's an ego thing."

"And yet every year, you throw one of the most anticipated parties in town," she shot back.

"Right. Because it's good for business. I need to impress these people and keep them receptive to my business plans. I hate politics, but it turns out that I'm good at it. Look, I understand I'm only where I am now because I lucked out. I was born to wealth. My father was a real estate tycoon straight out of a Monopoly game, with the twirly mustache and evil monocle and everything. He bought lots of prime real estate when it was cheap, and I'm basically set for life. Every year, my parties have gotten wilder, because the unwritten rule is you have to outdo the last one. The goal is to have everybody talking about it the following day. They look forward to it every year. But to be honest with you, I'm bored to death with my guests. They're shallow and uncurious, for the most part. The rest of the year, I lead a fairly quiet life. I read philosophy. I'm a snob. I collect paintings and rare antiques."

"So you're a self-reflective rich guy," she said. "Trapped in a web of his own making."

He smiled and looked away. "I don't control any of this. The cream doesn't rise to the top in this town—only yes-men rise to the top. It's disgusting. So I deal with it."

"Is that how you rose to the top? By being a yes-man?"

"No, I invented the best security software on the planet," he said. "But I can't afford a bunch of bureaucratic enemies. That's a death by a thousand cuts. Yes-men. Suck-ups. Call them whatever you like."

It was getting chilly out. She rubbed her shivering arms through the flimsy fabric of her jacket. "Who else besides Russ Swinton and Isabel Miller talked to Morgan Chambers that night? Do you have any idea?"

"I personally didn't notice. However, my employees have talked to the police about any interactions they may have witnessed, which means Gossett will have that information."

"What about drugs at the party?"

He shrugged. "We served Grey Goose, Maker's 46, and Veuve Clicquot rosé. Sapporo beer for guests with yeast allergies. An assortment of vintage wines. If there was any drug-taking, I wasn't aware of it. Here we are."

They stood on the edge of the woods facing Hollins Drive, where traffic was sparse this time of night. Hunter pointed out the underbrush by the side of the road where his security guard found the violin case, and there were broken twigs and muddy footprints scattered all around it. The site had obviously been disturbed by the security team, along with Gossett and his men.

She asked a few questions, and Hunter elaborated on the events that had led to the discovery of the violin. Then he sighed and said, "You look cold. Are you cold, Natalie?"

She hadn't noticed she was shivering until right this second. "A little."

He touched her arm briefly. "Let's go back."

They turned around on the path. "So I'm assuming Russ was on the guest list?" she asked on their way back through the woods.

"Okay, look. Morgan Chambers came with Swinton as his guest and left about an hour later," Hunter told her. "She called an Uber. That's all I know. That's every last bit of it." He stared at her. "And I can't imagine who could've killed her. I don't have any guesses as to who that could be. If I suspected someone in my circle of drugging girls . . . I'd never associate myself with them. I'd turn them in. Occasionally, at these parties you'll have a scene. People drink too much, it gets late. Jealousy, love triangles, it's all so boring. I don't know. Maybe I won't be throwing another party next year." He shook his head. "When I was in college, there was lots of craziness going on. This is nothing, really. This wasn't a sex party, or anything like that. I mean, there may have been sex going on somewhere inside the house, privately . . . just as there were probably people smoking weed or taking ecstasy. Shit happens. Not so shocking nowadays, right? But the thing with the Wiccan performance piece . . . I paid the artists very well. I have a big house, my guests are free to roam and express themselves. We had a lot of different performers, including a fire-breather, acrobats, and dancers. No lap dancers or strippers. It wasn't that kind of thing. Also, I'm not into the occult, but this is Burning Lake, and so . . . we had a reenactment of an occult ritual, accurate down to the smallest detail. It was, after all, Halloween. Now if you don't mind, I'm going this way."

They had reached the edge of the forest, where the path forked in two directions.

"I'm afraid we must part company," he said with solemnity, like a character out of *Jane Eyre*. She couldn't tell if he was joking or not.

Natalie tried to see the world through Hunter's lens—an upside-down world full of power encased in an idyllic wooded enclave among the powerless. Many years ago, when Hunter was in high school and his parents were never around, he threw the best parties and invited all sorts of kids to hang out in his backyard, drinking beer and dancing to the music bleeding out of the house. Natalie and Bella never got invited to these parties until they'd reached the end of their senior year. Natalie had a flash memory of Hunter rolling a joint in the living room—he was in college by then, and Bella couldn't hide the fact that she'd always had a huge crush on him. Hunter sat back on his haunches and sparked up. He picked a bit of weed off his tongue, then handed the joint to Bella. "Age before beauty," he said, but instead of mocking him back, Bella sat frozen with adoration. Natalie glanced at Bella's impassive face, snatched the joint from Hunter's hand, and took a toke. "Who's the snarky little bitch now?" she said, and Hunter cracked a delighted smile. "Thank God you girls have come of age," he said.

"One last thing," she told him now. "I'm not the rabbit. I'm the hound running for his next meal. Whoever killed Morgan Chambers . . . *that's* the one who's running for his life."

Hunter smiled and nodded. Then the rain took him.

36

Natalie called Luke with an update, and he promised to call her back with more information as soon as he'd spoken to Gossett.

On the way home, she drove past Dr. Russ Swinton's house. He lived on the northwestern edge of town in an old farming community where the corn grew tall in the summertime and cattle dotted the hillsides. As you approached Mercy Lane, the forested hills gave way to farmsteads and orchards, weather-beaten barns leaning into the wind.

About a mile down the road, she spotted a mailbox with SWINTON painted on the side. She felt a dull throbbing in her chest as she pulled over to the side of the road and let her confusion pass. Swinton's house was isolated. He lived alone. He had access to pharmaceuticals, as well as to drug addicts who came into the emergency room. Russ had withheld important information from her. He came across as guilty, as if he were hiding something.

She hated herself for suspecting him. She'd trusted him for years. But now that she thought about it, there was a slight creep factor. Once, when Natalie was in college, she'd bumped into Russ in a Boston sports bar. He was sitting with a bunch of other well-dressed doctor types, and they were teasing the waitresses. It turned out he was there for an emergency medicine convention, but there was something disturbing about seeing him drunk and sweaty and laughing with his friends at the harried waitresses.

Still, she thought, the evidence was thin at best. Besides, it wasn't possible. She'd known Russ ever since she was a kid, and he'd always come across as a stable, caring professional. He'd treated her for a bad case of poison ivy once; another time for food poisoning. He'd been there when the boy had attacked her in the woods. Dr. Swinton had calmed her down, resting his broad hand on her shoulder and looking into her eyes, and what she saw was kindness, genuine concern, and an absolute faith in his ability to help her. He'd been part of the background of her entire life, a steadfast ally, someone she could always count on. This had to be a mistake. Another false lead.

Back home, Natalie felt a little weak-kneed getting out of the car. She hadn't eaten all day and was hungry and exhausted. She crossed the yard, wind blowing wetly against her face. The rainstorm had moved on, but the air was thick with humidity. A few brittle leaves rattled across the porch, lifted by the damp breeze.

She collected her mail, unlocked the door, and reached for the lights. She dropped all her stuff in the living room. The kitchen counters were cluttered with flyers, an opened mayonnaise jar, unpaid bills, and insurance forms. The breakfast table was dusted with crumbs. She threw away the mayonnaise, opened the jiggly kitchen cupboard, and took down a jar of peanut butter. Natalie preferred eating peanut butter standing up with a spoon, because it didn't count that way.

The kitchen floor was uneven. The cracked linoleum made popping sounds when you walked across it. The kitschy curtains were patterned with wild stallions. Her dad used to love those old black-and-white cowboy movies on TV. Gary Cooper, Jimmy Stewart, Clint Eastwood—never any doubt about who the bad guy was.

Natalie put away the peanut butter and went downstairs, got on the treadmill, and listened to her playlist. She wanted to be ruthless. She wanted to catch a killer. She wanted her life to have meaning.

She worked the treadmill hard and fast, breathing deep from her diaphragm. She checked her time. She toweled the sweat off her face. The bottled water tasted flat. She could still smell the crime scene in her hair—that sweet, putrid aroma that soaked into your pores.

She took a hot shower, her thoughts growing muddy and stagnant. They were knee-deep in the case, not yet fully immersed. They weren't even up to their thighs yet. It was nice to think you might get lucky this time, that you could solve the case quickly, that the suspect would reveal himself early on. But it was just wishful thinking.

Natalie got dressed for bed. It was only nine o'clock. She felt a wind-swept hollowness inside her body and lay awake, playing with the thin silver bracelet Ellie had given her to remember Grace by, engraved with Grace's name in tiny elegant letters. She twirled the silver band around her wrist, wondering if it was too late to call her niece.

On an impulse, she tried calling Ellie, but there was no answer. She didn't bother leaving another message. She thought about Bella.

Maybe the past was trying to tell her something?

Upstairs in the attic, Natalie tried not to kneel on moldering insect husks as she pulled the storage boxes out from under the eaves. She found her old LEGO Wild Hunters, television plug-in games, Roboraptors, Mattel's My Bling Bling Styling Head, Smart Charms, and a fleet of broken balsa wood flyers.

She found her mother's old wire-rim glasses. She hesitated a beat before putting them on. She looked at the world through Deborah's eyeglasses, trying to see what life was like back then. To see the whole world—their house, the town, Willow, Grace, Natalie, and Joey through these blurry lenses.

Her mother had been thin-armed and beautiful. She smelled like a snuffed-out candle, slightly waxy. She never went to a salon in her life. Once in a while, Deborah would ask Grace or Willow to trim her hair, which she'd pull back with a scrunchie. She was a creature of habit. She had breakfast at six in the morning. She ate scrambled eggs on Monday, oatmeal on Tuesday, buttered toast on Wednesday, pancakes on Thursday, et cetera. She read the newspaper from front to back while she ate. She started recycling long before it was fashionable. She saved the Sunday *Times* and grocery bags, folding them up and stacking them one on top of the other. She saved flimsy plastic bags, coffee cans, and glass bottles. She recycled as much as she could, which was truly admirable. She would fill the dishwasher until every inch of it was crammed with glassware, and when she couldn't slide another butter knife into it, then she'd run it on economy.

The attic smelled like wet insulation. An oppressive humidity saturated the air. Natalie heard the dull buzzing of the paper wasps overhead as she tunneled farther underneath the eaves, where the ceiling was so low it was like crouching inside a dollhouse. The particleboard walls had been torn down, revealing the bare struts and joists. She slid out another heavy, dusty box. This one contained old toys, paperback books, and a musty baby blanket.

Natalie sat back on her heels and heard a soft scrabbling sound. Mice had left their droppings everywhere. There were little holes in the insulation where the mice had gnawed through, searching for secrets. There was an abandoned wren's nest in the rafters. Her father Joey once told her, *A secret is like a magic mirror, with endless layers of illusion. People will do anything to keep their secrets hidden from the world, but also from themselves. They'll bury them under layers of delusion, ego, and denial. We're like archeologists, Natalie, digging through the painful past. You have to be careful, because some people will do anything to keep their secrets hidden. If you pick up a stone, it might be the truth, or it could be a lie. Whatever you assume is fact, isn't always. Pick up a stone and peer underneath, and sometimes worms crawl out.*

In her line of work, facts were often accompanied by worms—those horrible wriggling truths people couldn't stand to acknowledge. Finally, she found a box full of her old sketchbooks and carried it downstairs.

37

Natalie spread her sketchbooks across the living-room floor and stood studying the pencil drawings, watercolors, and pen-and-inks. She didn't know what she was looking for but remembered coming home after school and sitting cross-legged on the bedroom rug, her long brown hair lying flat against her spine like a second set of vertebrae, while she drew pictures of all the things she loved—her best friends, her sisters, her mom and dad, this house, the backyard, birds, flowers, insects landing on the windowsill. She also painted nightmares—gargoylish creatures tearing into flesh, zombie monsters drooling in the midst of a postapocalyptic wasteland. She would lean over each clean sheet of paper and gaze at its blankness, her eyes narrowing with concentration until inspiration struck. Suddenly, she would dip her brush in the water and run the fine bristles over a small disk of color—red or blue or green—and start to paint. She used swift, deft strokes and let the colors blend together. Sometimes she used a pencil or pen and ink. The medium didn't matter. Getting her vision down on paper did.

Now she noticed a pencil sketch of one of the witch trees of Burning Lake. When she was ten years old, Natalie decided to carve her and Luke's initials into the bark of her favorite witch tree on the edge of McKinley Forest. As legend had it, if you carved your deepest desire into a witch tree, then over time, as the tree grew taller, the bark would slowly swallow up the carvings until they became indecipherable, and only a witch could read them.

Natalie went over to the bay window. Rain clouds had gathered around the moon, which shone like a pale dish of milk. She could barely breathe. What did she want?

Natalie wanted the thing that eluded her the most. She wanted love. She wanted happiness to surge through her—raining, crackling, gorgeous flashes of lightning. Orange fire. She wanted the sun to rise in the dead center of her soul.

Now her phone rang, and she fumbled for it.

It was Ellie. "Aunt Natalie?"

Joy ran through her. "Hey kiddo, how are you?"

"Sorry I didn't call you back, but I've been super busy lately. I also heard about the woman in the dumpster, and it made me think of Mom. And I sort of couldn't deal with it. I hope you understand. Otherwise, I would've called you right away . . ."

"I understand completely," Natalie said.

"Do they know who did it yet?"

"We're still investigating."

"My therapist told me not to dwell on negativity," Ellie said softly. "I'm supposed to compartmentalize my thoughts. Like, I have a special time when I think about Mom. I'll carve half an hour out of my schedule and sit alone in my room and light a few candles. I have this little antique cabinet Dad bought me, where I keep all of her stuff, you know? Her bracelet with the four-leaf clovers, her gloves, that book of poems she gave me—stuff like that. I'll sit with the lights off and think about her. And then, after I blow the candles out, I'm supposed to resume my life. To not think about her anymore. But sometimes the past will leak into my day, and I'll have to run to the restroom and hide in a stall and bawl my eyes out." She laughed. "It's embarrassing, but it happens."

"I wish I could see you," Natalie said. "Maybe when this case settles down . . ."

"That would be fun. I'll take you to my favorite haunts. Anyway," Ellie said with a sigh. "I'm not supposed to think about it the rest of the time. Because if I did . . . if I let myself think about it, I wouldn't be able to cope. You know what I mean?"

"I know exactly what you mean. That sounds like a good plan."

"How was Halloween? I really miss Burning Lake."

"Oh, you know. The usual chaos. It was insanely ramped this year," Natalie said. "How's school? What classes are you taking?"

"History, French, creative writing . . . a few generic college-prep courses."

Natalie smiled. "You mean, math? I hated math."

"Aunt Natalie, I have a boyfriend," Ellie blurted excitedly.

"You do?"

"Yeah. Dad wants to lock me up in a castle tower until I'm twenty-one."

"Your father's a smart man," Natalie said with a smile.

"His name is Asher. I really like him, Aunt Natalie. We kissed on Halloween."

"Oh?" she said lightly, feeling sweaty all of a sudden.

"Yeah, Dad freaked out about it, too. But don't worry. We're taking it nice and slow. Asher's in a rock band. He's so talented. We're inseparable, but not in an unhealthy way."

"So what you mean is . . . you're growing up, huh?"

"You always said that when two people love each other . . ."

"Oh, please don't quote cool Aunt Natalie to me," she said half-jokingly, wondering what Grace would have thought about all this. "Just be careful, sweetie. And if you ever need to talk about, you know, stuff . . ."

"Don't worry, Aunt Natalie, I know all about 'stuff,'" Ellie reassured her. "And Dad already offered me his shoulder to lean on. So I'm good. But I'll call you if I have any questions, okay?" Ellie said, as if Natalie were the one who needed reassuring.

"How is your dad?"

"He's great. His job is incredibly stressful, but he always finds time for us to spend together, and I love him, even though he's always changing our vacation plans." She laughed. "He makes sure that once a week, we go out to dinner and a movie, sort of like a father-daughter date. And he listens to me. He doesn't just pretend to listen while glancing at his phone, like Phoebe's father. Phoebe's my new best friend. She wears glitter on her face, and she used to be a cutter. She let me feel her blading scars once. We share the same therapist, but it's much easier to talk to each other. Adults don't understand what it's like . . ."

"Right, because we were never kids," Natalie said.

"Snark!"

"Well, it's true, isn't it? You forget, I have my own adolescent angst I'm still carrying around."

"That's why I trust you. You get me."

"You can always tell me things, Ellie. I'll give you the best advice I can."

There was a long pause before Ellie said, "I really miss her."

Natalie nodded slowly. "Me, too."

"But we have to believe, right? That she's in a better place? Asher has been helping me cope. He comes from a religious family. He's helping me pray for Mom."

"I'm glad to hear that," Natalie said. "I want you to find peace with this."

"Have you?" Ellie asked. "Found peace?"

"I'm trying," Natalie struggled to say. "I'm looking for it everywhere."

"Good. I hope we both find it."

"Me, too, sweetie."

"Okay, well . . . I have to go now."

"Okay."

"Love you, Aunt Natalie."

"Love you, Ellie. Call anytime."

Her niece hung up.

Natalie grimaced at her phone. She couldn't help feeling as if she'd somehow blown it—said the wrong thing, not said the right thing. While she was putting her phone away in her bag, she accidentally cut the tip of her finger on an open safety pin. You'd think that such a tiny cut wouldn't hurt so much. She sucked the tip of her finger and couldn't shake this ominous feeling. It clung like a cold sweat.

She stared at the eggshell-white walls, smudged with fingerprints. When she was in high school, Natalie used to rip the sketches out of her drawing pad and tape them to the white walls of her bedroom, then sit on her Haitian cotton–covered bed and admire her drawings as if they were prize-winning orchids. But then, after a few minutes, she would start to hate them. She couldn't help comparing herself to all the great artists she admired. She'd rip them all down, and the tape would pull little bits of paint off the walls. White didn't stay pure for very long. Children didn't stay young for long. Walls didn't hold up forever. All it took was a moment.

Now another one of her drawings caught her eye—a simple pencil sketch of Bella with her right hand bandaged in gauze. Bella was making a mock-sad face, and Natalie had written underneath, "Bella's boo-boo." Why did they make light of it? How did Bella get the boo-boo? Did her father grab her wrist by accident? Or was it muscle strain from overpracticing?

She turned the sketch over, but there was nothing written on the back side. On the front, Natalie always signed her name in the lower right-hand corner, along with the date. This one was dated a few months before their high school graduation.

She retrieved her phone and called Luke.

"Natalie?" he answered.

"I don't want to be here right now," she confessed. "In my house."

"Are you okay?"

She didn't know how to respond to that question. It was raining hard. The wind rattled the windows.

"Do you want me to come over?" Luke offered.

She hesitated. It was so tempting. "Never mind. I'm okay. Let's talk tomorrow."

She hung up, then gazed out the windows. The rain made ever-changing streaks of amethyst on the glass. Lightning flashed. Shadows trembled on the walls. She didn't want her niece growing up in a world where women died alone in dumpsters. She couldn't stand it anymore. She grabbed her jacket, scooped up her keys, and left.

38

The bad weather had surged into the hills. Everything was faded and indistinguishable in the rain. Luke greeted Natalie at the door.

"Are you okay?" he asked.

She'd gotten soaked running in from the car. Rain clung to her skin.

"You're wet," he said, stepping aside. "Come on in."

She followed him into the living room, where it smelled of pine cones. She dropped her bag on the floor, plopped down on a gray-speckled sofa, and said, "Did Gossett tell you anything yet?"

"They're trying to identify the violin. They've asked Sheriff Dressler to investigate, see if Morgan's family or her roommate can ID it. In the meantime, Lenny's processing the violin and the case for trace. Maybe we'll pick up prints."

"And no one saw the make and model of the car?"

He shook his head. "Apparently the security guard only saw taillights in the fog."

Natalie ran her hands through her hair and exhaled hard. "I talked to my niece tonight."

Luke nodded patiently.

"She's growing up so fast."

"But that's a good thing, isn't it?"

She looked at him, feeling raw and vulnerable. "I'm afraid, Luke."

"Of what?"

She shrugged. "Self-destructing."

He sat down beside her. "Six months ago, your life got flipped over. You suffered a huge loss. And now this case lands in your lap. Listen, you've behaved heroically, Natalie. Unfortunately, people like to punish their heroes. You're exhausted, that's all. Who can blame you?"

She squinted at his bookshelves with a pained smile. He owned Norman Mailer's *The Executioner's Song* and Doris Lessing's *The Golden Notebook*. The sofa sagged in the middle. The entire living room was lit by two anemic floor lamps. There were messy piles of paperwork and case files scattered about. Soft music played on the bargain-basement sound system. She picked a paper plate up from the floor. "The place seems more of a shithole than usual."

He put the plate down and said, "Talk to me."

She gave him a self-pitying smile. "You care."

"Of course I care."

She sighed with her whole body. "We used to make spazzy faces, you know? The three of us—Grace, Ellie, and me. Whoever made the funniest face won. We'd bake brownies and play Monopoly, and we promised one another that one day we were going to bring the telescope down from the attic and look at the stars. But there was never enough time." Tears welled in her eyes. "How could I have missed your birthday?"

"Doesn't matter." He shrugged.

"Doesn't matter? I'm like the world's worst friend."

"I don't care about my birthday," Luke insisted.

"Damn. I forgot to bring your card with me. I bought you a card."

He smiled. "It's the thought that counts."

"It's the absolute worst card I could find on such short notice."

He smiled, amused. "I can't wait to see it."

She sat back morosely and crossed her arms. "When Zack and I first got together, things were different. He was different. I was different. But over time, our flaws became magnified. And one day we realized we had nothing in common. It broke my heart."

"I'm sorry."

"Luke?"

"Yes?"

"I'm cold." She was shivering.

A long silence followed as they studied each other. There was a strange tension in the air between them, an unbearable feeling of "something" in the room with them. A hidden truth. She could sense them both trying to push past the discomfort and reach for each other, but it wasn't working. Their timing was off. With Natalie and Luke, it was one misfire after another. She hated these agonizing beats of silence. Of words left unspoken.

"It's getting colder at night." He picked up a blanket from the sofa and draped it over her shoulders. "Coffee?"

"Please."

"Two spoonfuls of sugar, right?"

"And lots of cream."

He went into the kitchen and fetched them both a coffee.

A few minutes later, Natalie was warming her hands on the steaming mug.

"I noticed something tonight . . . an old drawing of mine," she told him. "Bella had a wrist injury shortly before she disappeared."

"Is that relevant?"

"Two months ago, Russ Swinton treated Morgan for a wrist injury. Then he brings her to the party as his date and lies about it to me."

"Do you think the cases are related?"

"Or else I'm making random connections because I'm fucking exhausted. I've been thinking about Bella a lot."

His gaze was solemn. "That forty-eight-hour thing people are always talking about is bullshit, Natalie. No one can solve a case of this magnitude in a couple of days. If you think that's true, you're only setting yourself up for disappointment. More important, you have to ask yourself—will I be any good tomorrow?"

"Really?" Her eyes darted to the ceiling. "Because I thought I was doing a bang-up job."

He smiled warmly at her. "Be patient. Don't try to read the tea leaves just yet. Put your blinders on and trust the process. The evidence will lead us to the truth. Don't fight it. It'll come."

"Use the fork, Luke," she joked.

"Old jokes for old friends."

She shook her head. "It is an old joke, isn't it? Jesus, am I that lame?"

"Look, I'm counting on you," he told her firmly. "Don't fuck things up."

"I won't," she promised.

"You need to take care of yourself. There's plenty of time to talk in the morning. In the meantime, go home and eat some protein. Then get some rest."

She put her coffee down. "I can't go home. I won't be alone in that house."

He nodded solemnly. "I understand, but you can't stay here."

"Why not? Why can't I sleep on your sofa? It's very comfortable." She patted the lumpy cushion.

"Natalie, I'm your boss, your supervisor . . ."

"I promise I won't touch you," she joked, but she could tell instantly by his reaction that he didn't think it was the least bit funny. "Sorry," she said quickly. "I didn't mean it to come out that way. I was trying to make a joke. A stupid joke. Forgive me? But you have to understand, my house is full of ghosts. I won't go home tonight. I'd rather sleep in my car."

He watched her for a moment. "I want to help you through this. I'm aware of the fact that you were relying on Russ Swinton, and now you don't have his support. I'm willing to step in and fill the void until you start seeing another doctor, and by that I mean emotional support. Are you looking for a therapist, Natalie?"

"Yes." It wasn't quite a lie. She was thinking about looking for another doctor.

"Good." He stood up. "I'll light a fire and get you a pillow."

"My hero."

"Right," he said sarcastically. "Me and my superhero cape will be right back." He left the room.

She lay down on the sofa that smelled of him and closed her eyes.

39

Natalie got up in the middle of the night, thinking she heard someone crying outside. A plaintive, mewling sound. The wind blew through the house with a dull whoosh. She got up and stood on the back porch, but there was no one out there, wailing away. It was just the rain.

The house's roof dripped raindrops. The trees greeted the rain by tossing their arms enthusiastically, leaping and waving like drunken puppies. Strong, towering trees getting steadily more inebriated until—soaked to the core—they sagged and bowed and stumbled loosely in the wind.

Luke must've heard the back door open, because he came downstairs and stood next to her on the porch. Together they watched the chaos swarming around them—lightning and thunder, the wildness of nature that couldn't be contained.

It welled up inside her—an unnamable, unfathomable sadness. Life was tender and sweet and bitter. Even the good stuff was sad, because it had to end at some point. Some people drank or took drugs to numb themselves from all the emotions that stuck to life. Some people would rather be numb than covered in burrs.

"Beautiful, isn't it?" Luke said beside her. He wore pajama bottoms and a T-shirt, goose bumps rising on his exposed flesh.

"Powerful." She furrowed her brow.

"Before I fell asleep, I started reading Lily Kingsley's file."

She glanced over at him.

"Lily was twenty-two years old, a violin soloist who attended the Brock Conservatory. Just like Morgan. Her mother, Clarissa, was a former violinist. According to witness reports, she was a free spirit who wasn't afraid to hitch rides. Last seen leaving a bar on the outskirts of Chaste Falls six months ago. No kidnapping demands were ever made, no witnesses came forward. Her body has never been found." He crossed his arms. "An exboyfriend was a primary suspect for a while. There was also a pervy neighbor in her apartment building, a middle-aged man Lily had an altercation with about leaving his garbage in front of her door. The police cleared both suspects. One interesting fact—Lily was interested in witchcraft, and she looked a lot like Morgan. Blue eyes, long dark red hair, slight build, very pretty. Also of note, a few years before she went missing, she had Morgan's father as a teacher at the conservatory."

Natalie turned to him. "We need to find out if Lily had any injuries to her hands. Maybe she went to the clinic where Russ works as a volunteer."

"That would be significant," Luke said. "But circumstantial."

"The circumstantial evidence keeps piling up, though," she said. "Whoever slipped Morgan a date rape drug has to be local. He knew about the parking lot behind Blondie's. He has to be familiar with the area. He has to know drug dealers or have access to illegal drugs." She turned to him, anguished, and said, "Russ could've gotten GHB through his work in the emergency room. We need to see those surveillance tapes from Hunter's party and find out how soon he left the party after Morgan did. He told me he went straight home, but what if he followed her into town? We need to track his whereabouts that night."

"Okay, I'll get on it first thing," Luke reassured her. "In the meantime, what about your other suspects?"

"I still have questions about Lawrence Chambers and Hollis Jones. Also Morgan's ex-boyfriend needs more scrutiny . . ."

"Couldn't it be someone who's not even on our radar?" he suggested.

"Sure. Maybe the zombie at Blondie's. But Russ is being evasive, and the question is . . . why?"

"Regardless, you need to verify the alibis of Chambers, Jones, and the ex-boyfriend. We need to eliminate them if we want to narrow our focus."

"I'll call Dressler in the morning," Natalie said. "Have him find out if Lily Kingsley ever made an appointment with Russ at the clinic. We also need to find out if she participated in the Monster Mash contest last year, or years prior."

"Do you think there's a connection with the contest?"

"Could be." Her shoulders lifted with a sigh. "Russ was a judge this year. I don't know about last year."

"So your current theory is that Russ Swinton may have caught up with Morgan at Blondie's, where he slipped her a roofie, but before he could abscond with her, she ran away and hid in the dumpster?"

"Something like that."

Luke studied her silently.

She watched his calm, even breath clouds.

"Let's go back inside and get some sleep."

Back on the sofa, wrapped in a blanket, and listening to the steady sound of rain on the roof, Natalie managed to fall asleep.

In the morning, she opened her eyes and watched the sunrise bleed through the curtains. The fog, the rain had departed. She saw leaf shadows on the ceiling. She saw a pile of logs stacked next to the fireplace. She saw an old ax—he split his own firewood. She noticed an unplugged floor heater.

"Good morning," Luke said, coming in from the kitchen. She'd forgotten how good he looked in a T-shirt and jeans. "How'd you sleep?"

She yawned and stretched. "Never better."

He watched her with thinly veiled amusement. She liked his straight white teeth and forgiving smile. She studied his brushstroke eyebrows and the faint violet shadows beneath his intelligent eyes. "Coffee?" he offered.

She pulled the comforter up to her neck. "Yes, please. Strong, with lots of cream and two sugars, please."

He smiled and said, "Sure, have a little coffee in your cream." He went back into the kitchen, and a couple of minutes later, he brought her a cup of coffee.

She sat up and took a sip. "Mmm. Good."

"Distance is hard on relationships," he said. "It's sad to lose touch with a child you've known for years, and then suddenly they're gone, and communication becomes difficult. It's as if you're talking through two tin cans connected with string. It's especially hard when you can't see their facial expressions or sense their shifting moods. Losing touch is literal—you lose the touch of a hand, the touch of a smile. Eyes touching. It's a big loss."

She put down her mug. "So what's the solution?"

"After Audrey took Skye away to California with her, I didn't speak to my daughter for quite some time," he confessed. "I kept meaning to call, but she lived three thousand miles away, and I couldn't get the time difference straight in my head—do I call three hours ahead, or three hours behind? Whenever I got a few minutes to spare, I'd pick up the phone, but it would either be too early or too late. Finally, Skye called me and said, 'Listen, Dad, anytime you think about calling me, just remember what an ass you are. An "ass" is the same thing as a "behind." Got it? It's three hours *behind* in California. Just think of it that way, and everything will be cool.'" He laughed, and his body relaxed—and he looked suddenly more handsome than she'd ever seen him.

"That's awesome," Natalie said with a smile.

"So I told her, 'You've managed to insult me, while at the same time simplifying my life.'"

Natalie rested her gaze in the comfortable depths of his eyes.

"The point is . . . the next time you feel Ellie slipping away, just remind yourself how easy it is to reconnect. It's as simple as picking up the phone." He smiled warmly at her. They used to be so close. She craved that closeness now.

At the same time, it made her nervous and created a jitteriness in her soul.

"I should be going," she said.

"Are you okay?"

She nodded and smiled. "Thanks for the hospitality."

"Next time don't forget my birthday card."

"Deal." She smirked, then collected her belongings—shoes, bag, jacket.

He walked her to the door, where they paused on the threshold. "Natalie," he said. "Let me know how you're doing, okay?"

She looked at him quizzically.

"I mean . . . how you're handling it. I'm here to listen."

Her phone rang, and they both inched backward, slightly startled.

She fumbled in her bag for her phone. "Jeesh. What? Hello?"

"This is Hunter. We need to talk."

40

Farther north of downtown Burning Lake, beyond the patchwork of meadows, farmland, and forest, was a sprawling historic neighborhood of homes designed by such renowned architects as Stanford White and Frank Lloyd Wright, where the town's upwardly mobile professionals lived. Surrounding these posh, high-end estates were nature preserves and bird sanctuaries. It was isolated and beautiful, the kind of place where the tree branches scattered the sunlight in just the right way, like a Peloton ad.

Natalie parked in Hunter's driveway, then took the flagstone path to his front door. She rang the bell, and he greeted her warmly. Today he favored a Goth nerd look—skinny pants, black shirt, Harry Potter glasses, and black ankle boots. All that was missing was the black cat.

The drawing room had three bay windows with southwesterly views of the gardens. The paneling was tiger oak. The stained glass windows cast prisms of light on the Edwardian-style furniture. The restored mansion had retained all of its historic architectural features, and the place felt just as grand as the first time Natalie had set foot inside.

"Can I get you something?" Hunter asked. "Coffee? Tea? Fresh-squeezed orange juice?"

"No, thanks." She sat on an elegant blue velvet sofa. "What did you want to talk about?" The sunlight was too bright in here. Her mind was filled with all the things she had to do today. Her body was dragging. She should have accepted his offer of coffee.

"Glass of wine? No?" He went over to the bar, opened a bottle of wine, poured himself a glass, then set the bottle gently down on the bar. "On the night Bella disappeared, I volunteered to join in the search. We looked for three or four days. I helped them put up missing persons posters all over town. Nesbitt and I attended the prayer vigil. I contributed money to the reward. The police cleared me a long time ago, Natalie. I had nothing to do with Bella's fate, whatever that may be." His mouth grew pinched. "But it alters your worldview—that a person like Bella could vanish into thin air." He pinned her with his sincere gaze. "I'd like to show you something. Upstairs. I want you to see who my brother really was."

She hesitated a moment before accompanying him to the second floor, where the nineteenth-century reproduction wallpaper contained idyllic scenes of bluebirds and roses. They walked past the master suite, where she remembered fucking Hunter in his parents' ornate bed, and continued down the hallway to the very end, where a large door had a construction-paper sign taped to it that read BUSY—PLEASE KNOCK! in a child's blocky script.

"Nesbitt always kept his door shut. You had to knock three times before he'd let you in," Hunter explained as he opened the door.

The room was perfectly preserved. There was a single bed, a toy chest with jungle creatures painted on the lid, and a bookcase that held the collected works of Dr. Seuss and R. L. Stine. A wooden chair was positioned in the center of the room, with four black x's marked on the hardwood floor where the chair legs fit perfectly.

"He liked to measure the distance from the four corners of his room and find the exact center. He called it the middle-middle," Hunter explained. "He would mark the spot with a Magic Marker. It comforted him somehow."

Natalie followed Hunter inside. On the bureau beside an old-fashioned record player was a large glass jar full of pennies.

"I used to bring him pennies," Hunter explained. "I'd drop them in the jar because he liked the clinking sounds they made. If you handed him a penny, he wouldn't take it. He'd throw it on the floor. He didn't want to touch a coin, but once the pennies were inside the jar he adored them."

She smiled. There were little piles of stuff on every surface—old bottle caps, loose buttons, movie ticket stubs.

"My father spent a fortune on medical bills, and yet none of the specialists could tell us what was wrong—if 'wrong' is the correct word. Because, frankly, I didn't think there was anything wrong with my little brother." Hunter picked up a brown button from the bureau top and studied it for a moment. "One of the best pediatricians in the country diagnosed it as autism. Another specialist said my brother lacked 'emotional intelligence,' whatever that means. Another specialist said he had ADHD. My father wasn't satisfied with any of the diagnoses, but Mom was scared. She dropped Nesbitt when he was a baby and thought she might've caused brain damage. But the doctors insisted he was born that way. I don't care what people call it—autistic, mentally challenged, brain-damaged. I loved my brother. He was a character and a half."

Natalie smiled sympathetically.

Hunter gazed at the colorful zoo animals printed on the dusty curtains. "He used to keep his bedroom windows open at night, and it was always freezing inside his room. Every evening, I'd go around closing the windows, but every morning, they'd be open again." He rubbed his chin. "However, on the morning after Bella disappeared, all the windows were shut, and his bed hadn't been slept in. He must've been out all night doing God knows what." He rubbed his anguished forehead. "There was a time when I thought . . . what if he hurt her? What if everybody's right about him? Maybe my brother's a monster, like they say? Maybe I just don't see it? So, a few days later, I asked him what he was doing that night. The night Bella disappeared. As soon as I mentioned her name, he got upset and threw a tantrum. Bottom line, Nesbitt loved her. He missed her terribly. She was one of the few people who treated him like a human being." He held her eye. "You, too, Natalie. You were very decent to him."

She felt sick to her stomach. "And then the letters proved him innocent."

"Too late. Way too fucking late. He was gone by then." He shook his head sadly. "But for a short while, even I suspected him. To this day, I feel guilty about it."

"Funny," she said. "Because I blame myself for not suspecting Grace enough. I didn't have a clue what she and her friends were up to. I keep beating myself up, because if only I'd opened my eyes, maybe Daisy would still be alive."

He looked at her. "So we share this in common? This guilt?"

She nodded.

He held her gaze. "Do other people understand the loss, I wonder?"

"I'm sure some people do."

"Isn't it odd, Natalie. We've known each other for such a long time, and yet I never really understood you until now."

The silence stretched between them.

Natalie's phone rang. "Sorry, have to take this." She excused herself and took the call out in the hallway. "Yes?"

It was Luke. "Lenny pulled a print off the violin. It was Russ Swinton's."

Fear descended like a fog. "I'll be right there."

Hunter was standing in the doorway. "Before you go . . ." He took a USB drive out of his pocket and handed it to her. "The surveillance tapes for Sunday night. I hope this helps."

41

Natalie's stomach felt raw and unsettled as she headed down the hallway toward Luke's office. His door was open. The radio was on low, tuned to a jazz station. His whiteboard was covered with names, dates, and locations. They were piecing together a time line of Morgan's movements over the last three days of her life.

She stared at him. "So Russ is our prime suspect?"

He made direct eye contact, a concerned frown nestled in his lined, handsome face. "You need to go talk to him again, Natalie. Find out if he's the one who dropped the violin off on Hunter's property."

"Okay," she said. "We also need to pull surveillance tapes overlooking the parking lot behind Blondie's. If Russ followed her there, he would've parked in that lot. And then there's this." She handed him the USB Hunter had given her, and the two of them hunched over Luke's computer screen while he uploaded the surveillance footage.

The nighttime images were grainy and pixelated, but the cameras showed Morgan arriving at the Halloween party with Russ Swinton at 9:07 P.M. She wasn't carrying her violin case with her. At 9:50 P.M., Morgan exited the residence alone and waited down by the road. Still no violin.

Ten minutes later, an Uber driver picked her up. Russ Swinton left the party at 10:10 P.M. He drove away in his black Lexus.

"He said he went straight home after the party," Natalie said. "No witnesses."

"That's his alibi?" Luke asked skeptically.

She nodded. Her muscles felt sore as if she had the flu. She shook the hair out of her eyes. She didn't want it to be true. Every fiber of her being rejected the possibility of Russ Swinton's guilt. But it was her job to eliminate the innocent and identify the suspects.

"Go talk to him," Luke said. "Find out if he dumped the violin on Rose's property, and if so, why the fuck."

Fifteen minutes later, Natalie found Dr. Swinton working in the emergency room of Langston Memorial. She asked to speak to him alone, and he escorted her into his office. "What is it, Natalie?" he said, closing the door.

"I have a few more questions about Morgan Chambers."

He glanced at his watch. "I've got a few minutes." There was a restlessness to his muscles, a defensive look behind those guarded eyes.

"We found her violin last night. Somebody drove over to Hunter Rose's property and dumped it by the side of the road, but it was too foggy out to identify the vehicle. But this morning, we found one of your prints on the violin case."

An oppressive silence filled the room. Russ leaned back and folded his arms. "I have to confess . . . that was me. Morgan must've forgotten it in my car on Sunday night. I thought the police might suspect me of something, so I . . ."

"So you dropped it off by the side of the road in the middle of the night?"

"Should I call a lawyer?" he asked, and she remembered how reassuring he could be, writing prescriptions and declaring that everything would be fine. He had a good bedside manner. Now he seemed ravaged with worry.

"We lucked out finding your print," she told him, "because the rest of the violin and case were wiped clean. Did you do that?"

He gave a reluctant nod. "I know how bad this looks."

"Do you really?" she asked earnestly.

"But listen, I have my reasons. First, I had no idea that Morgan had left her violin in the trunk of my car until you and I spoke about it yesterday. So I went to check, and there it was. Then I realized the police might become suspicious of me, since I neglected to bring it up in the first place. But it was an oversight."

"I understand how tangled our thoughts become when we're under stress, believe me. How did your print get on the violin case?"

"Morgan showed it to me. She played Vivaldi for me."

"When?"

"This was Sunday night, before the party. At my place. Since I collect violins, she asked me to take a look and tell her what it was worth. In all the excitement, she must've forgotten her violin in my car. I didn't think about it until you brought it up yesterday. Then I panicked. I didn't know what else to do."

"You didn't think of calling me? Of calling the police?"

He shook his head. "I just wanted to get rid of it. Stupid, I know."

There was pressure at the backs of her eyes. "Did you ever treat Lily Kingsley for an injury at the clinic?"

"Who?"

"Lily Kingsley. She was a student at the conservatory up until six months ago."

"I must've treated thousands of students. I've been volunteering for years."

"And was Lily among them?"

He shifted uneasily in his chair. "Am I a suspect? Because I should probably talk to a lawyer before we continue."

"That's up to you," she said.

Russ glanced at his watch, and Natalie noticed the ink stamp smudges on the backs of his hands. "Did you go out to a bar or a club at any point last weekend?"

He stared at her with bloodshot eyes. "I didn't kill Morgan."

"You told me you went straight home after the party."

He sighed heavily.

She let the silence build between them. Listening to a suspect—asking a tough question and waiting for the answer—you let your silence do the heavy lifting. Most people wanted to unburden themselves.

"It was just a nightcap," he confessed, "and then I went home."

All sorts of alarm bells rang inside her head. She couldn't believe she'd caught him in another lie. "Which bar?"

"The Village Idiot. You can ask the bartender there."

"And then you went straight home? Are you sure?"

"Directly from the bar." He had a tight, guarded look around his eyes.

"Why did you not tell me this before? Why did you lie to me?"

He settled his shoulders against the broad leather chair and said, "I think I've cooperated enough. I think my next step should be to call an attorney. You'll have to excuse me, Natalie, but this is exactly what I was afraid of."

42

Getting a search warrant wasn't complicated, but it took time. In order to get a warrant, you had to fill out an affidavit listing all the credible evidence. You had to state your case plainly and clearly, then go to the town courthouse and visit the judge in his chambers. The judge would read the affidavit, ask questions, and then—if you'd done your job—sign the approval page. While Luke was busy getting a search warrant for Russ Swinton's property, Augie talked to the bartender of the Village Idiot, and Natalie drove up to Chaste Falls to find out if the good doctor had ever treated Lily Kingsley for a music-related injury.

Her hands wouldn't stop shaking on the wheel. She felt a roiling sense of shame in her stomach. How could she have missed the signs, the clues, the hints? First Grace, now Swinton. Was he guilty of something terrible? This man who'd been privy to her innermost thoughts for decades? This man who had counted her heartbeats?

She parked in the visitors' lot of the sprawling, landscaped campus and got out of her car. The waiting room of the conservatory clinic was just like any other doctor's waiting room—sterile and bland, with dated magazines on the coffee table, jackets and scarves smothering the coatrack, and a handful of students waiting for their names to be called. A medicinal smell filled the recycled air.

The perky-faced receptionist greeted Natalie with an overworked smile, her frazzled hair curling back from her damp cheeks. "Hi there, can I help you?"

"My name is Detective Lockhart. I'm here about Lily Kingsley . . . did Sheriff Dressler call you?"

She nodded. "Oh, yes. Hold on, please." The receptionist picked up the phone, dialed a number, and said, "Dr. Phelps? That detective I was telling you about is here . . . Detective Lockhart from Burning Lake. All right, I'll let her know." She hung up. "Dr. Phelps will be right out. Have a seat."

A few minutes later, Dr. Gary Phelps came out and introduced himself, then escorted Natalie into his cramped clinic office. He had bristly red hair and rosy cheeks and looked too young to be a doctor. "Sheriff Dressler said I should give you any information you need. So how can I help?"

"Did a student named Lily Kingsley ever have an appointment with Russ Swinton in the past, say, two years?"

He typed a few commands into his computer. "Hmm, let's see. Here we go. She came into the clinic over a year ago. She was scheduled to see Dr. Swinton."

"What was she being treated for?"

"Strain of the right wrist. Numbness and pain. It's pretty common among violinists." He shrugged. "An occupational hazard. We see a lot of tendinitis, carpal tunnel, pinched nerves in the neck. It happens when high achievers practice too many hours without taking a break. Sometimes it's due to faulty technique, but mostly it's from overuse. Tenos riotous, nerve entrapment, rotator cuff. We get them all. In Ms. Kingsley's case," he said, squinting at the screen, "treatment involved cold-heat, tissue massage, physical therapy, and the like." He smiled. "I usually advise our students never to take a summer job scooping ice cream."

Natalie smiled back. "How many follow-up appointments did she have with Dr. Swinton?"

"Let's see." He scrolled through the electronic file. "She came in twice a week for two months to see the PT. Treatment appears to have worked. Her final appointment with Swinton was in February."

"About eight months ago?"

"Correct."

"Did she have any previous clinic appointments with him? Before the injury?"

He took a moment to check. "No, it doesn't appear so."

Her shoulders sagged. Things were looking worse for Russ. She didn't want to ask the next question, but the words popped out of her mouth. "Have any other students besides Lily gone missing from the conservatory?"

"I don't think so. Not since I've been here, anyway."

"How long is that?"

"Six years."

"And how many patients has Dr. Swinton treated at the clinic?"

"Oh gee," Phelps said, his face scrunched with worry. "Hundreds, if not thousands."

"I'd like a list of names."

"Of our patients? Sorry, I can't extend that courtesy to you, Detective. We're bound by patient confidentiality. I'd need a subpoena."

"Okay, I'll work on that. I have one more question for you," she said. "Dr. Swinton was treating Morgan Chambers for an ongoing stress injury. I need to know the dates and times of each visit."

He hesitated. "Sheriff Dressler didn't mention Morgan Chambers in our phone conversation . . ."

"Our two jurisdictions are working together on the case," she explained. "We're cooperating fully, sharing information. If you'd like, you can call him. I'll wait."

"No, that won't be necessary . . . hold on." He typed in a command, then scrolled through the file. "I'm calling it up now. Okay. Her last appointment was four weeks ago on a Wednesday."

Natalie nodded. "How many appointments altogether?"

"Hold on." His fingers fluttered over the keyboard. "Let's see. It started three months ago. She was a walk-in for her first appointment, and Dr. Swinton was working the evening shift."

"He works evenings?"

"Yes, he volunteers one evening a week. You can tell he really cares, a busy man like him. He's a great guy." Dr. Phelps leaned forward and asked in a hushed voice, "Why? Is something wrong? What's this about?"

"Just routine."

Dr. Phelps folded his hands together like a worried parent. Most people sensed when you were being evasive. "I've known Russ Swinton for a very long time. He's a decent, hardworking guy who has a great rapport with the students. He's a dedicated physician. If I had a son or daughter who required medical attention, I wouldn't hesitate to put them in his care. And so I can't imagine . . ."

Natalie couldn't, either. She thanked him and left.

Back in the waiting room, the receptionist called her over. "I don't know if this helps at all," she said nervously, running her fingers over her mother-of-pearl buttons. "Some of these doctors can be such smug, out-of-control assholes, but Dr. Swinton will show up out of the blue to check in on his patients' progress. No one does that nowadays. None of these guys will take the time of day to see how their patients are doing after the fact. It's all . . . 'what about my golf game?'"

"Thanks, I'll keep that in mind."

But the receptionist wasn't done yet.

"My sister lives in Burning Lake, and she's a home care worker. He'll check in on his patients just to see how they're doing. At their homes. I'm talking about some of the patients from the ICU . . . he obviously cares about their long-term recovery . . ."

Natalie's phone rang just then. It was Luke.

"We have the subpoena," he said. "I need you over there to help execute the search."

43

Natalie, Luke, Lenny, and Augie spent the afternoon gathering evidence from Russ Swinton's house. The old-fashioned six-over-six windows overlooked the woods. The high-ceilinged rooms were tastefully decorated. They didn't find any dead bodies hidden away in the basement. No secret dungeons.

Natalie found a number of antique musical instruments—flutes, violins, and mandolins—along with a Victorian-era doctor's bag and surgical tools in a display cabinet. Above the mantelpiece in the living room was a picture of Russ's dead sister posing with her violin. There were more pictures of Russ's extended family—mother, father, grandparents, aunts, uncles, cousins.

Lenny powdered for prints in the living room, while Augie searched the house for trace and Natalie and Luke gathered up the computer records, telephone records, medical textbooks, and old patient files. A total of a hundred and twenty-three items were taken from the home, including several knives, a hammer, trash bags, different-colored fibers, and several long hairs collected from various surfaces, but the small quantity of blood they found in the first-floor powder room was the most relevant piece of evidence they'd found.

Outside, two BLPD officers were busy scouring the property with cadaver dogs, while Lenny processed the car—no blood so far, but an abundance of prints, hairs, and fibers.

As they packed the last of the boxes into the van, Luke got a call and turned away from Natalie, answering, "Lieutenant Pittman."

She watched his shoulders tense.

"Yeah? Really? Cordon off the area. We'll be right over." He hung up. "That was Brandon," he said, the change in his expression profound. "The cleanup crew found human remains in the park. Severed body parts inside a violin case."

44

New York's Adirondack Mountains were created by major events that had happened over geologic time—earthquakes, volcanoes, mudslides. Strip away the buildings and foliage, and you would find a dramatic landscape full of foothills and mountain peaks shaped by untold glacial freezes and thaws. Millions of years of upheaval had conspired to create what the place was today—a beautiful inland vista full of rolling hills, mountain ranges, and lakes.

Natalie followed Luke's Ford Ranger back into town. Percival Burton Park was the crown jewel of the Burning Lake parks system, located on the western side of downtown. Over a century old, the park was host to year-round community events and activities, including summer rock concerts and theatrical productions.

Natalie cut her hand getting her crime kit out of the car and sucked on her torn knuckles, tasting blood. Her blouse was soaked with sweat. She followed Luke across the street, and they entered the park together.

A ten-foot-square area of unimpeded lawn was cordoned off with yellow police tape. The Great Lawn was the site of the former Percival Burton mansion, which had burned down in 1905. The Monster Mash concert had taken place here a little under a week ago—Natalie could see where the scaffolding had been erected and taken down.

The sprawling Great Lawn was covered in trash that had yet to be collected—rumpled flyers, food wrappers, glow sticks, and other debris. A handful of officers were doing a grid search around the perimeter, on the hunt for any additional body parts. The cleanup crew—she counted seven volunteers—were standing next to an idling dump truck on an access road fifty feet away. Several of the volunteers wore T-shirts that read "Green, Lean, and Mean."

Natalie, Luke, and Officer Keegan formed a tight circle inside the cordoned-off area. They were looking down at the scuffed violin case on the ground. Natalie listened to a low dull pulse inside her head as Keegan hooked his thumbs through his belt loops and explained what had happened.

"A member of the cleanup crew found it," he said in his gravelly voice. "He was picking up leaves and debris when he spotted it."

"Did he touch it?"

Keegan nodded. "So did the first officer at the scene—Boomer Prutzman. He said it looked like a Halloween prank."

"They both opened the case?" Natalie asked.

Keegan nodded. "He had no idea what was inside. I also checked."

She was more than a little annoyed by the news. It meant they would have to eliminate prints and trace from those who'd handled the evidence, which translated into extra work and more delays. "Did you document everything?"

"Yeah, we both did," he said somewhat defensively. His face was red.

She didn't mean to challenge his professionalism, but Natalie was laser-focused on the task at hand, and she wasn't particularly good at hand-holding. Still, how you got along with your colleagues mattered. "Thanks, Bill," she said.

"Go talk to the volunteers," Luke told Keegan. "Make sure you get their contact information, and don't let anyone leave without giving a statement."

"Will do." He strode off, leaving them alone inside the perimeter.

"You do the honors," Luke told Natalie.

Her mouth was parched. Her exhaustion pulled at the muscles of her face. She noticed her hands were trembling—adrenaline or anxiety. She knelt down and studied the black oblong case. The pebble-textured vinyl cover was scuffed at the corners. She girded herself, then snapped the locks and opened the lid, bracing herself for the the stench of decomp, but there wasn't any odor. The body parts had been mummified. The skin was leathery and coated with layers of varnish. *Two mummified forearms, severed at the elbows, packed in tight; the mummified hands clasping a human heart.* She leaned back and tried not to gag. She felt the heat rising in her cheeks as Luke knelt down beside her and breathed softly in her ear.

"Looks like mummification," he said.

"The forearms and hands are slender. Female, most likely."

"Maybe Lenny can pull prints."

She studied the clipped, unpolished fingernails. "Most violinists like to keep their nails short, better for gripping the fingerboard. No nail polish. No fake nails. It's a point of pride."

"So we have another dead violinist on our hands?"

She stood up and crossed her arms. "This is obviously a staged message. We were supposed to find it. It was left here deliberately, don't you think?"

He stood up and brushed off his hands. "Okay, I'll bite. What kind of message?"

She glanced around the park. "Well, the concert was held here last Friday. You can see where the scaffolding, speaker stands, and light tower were set up. They haven't landscaped the area yet, because they've been waiting for the cleanup crews to finish picking up the trash. You can see where the stage was constructed for the concert, deep furrows in the ground where the scaffolding and tent foundations were. Seating would've been in this general area, in front of the stage and extending all the way back. I've been to the Monster Mash before. People are encouraged to sit on blankets or bring their own folding chairs."

Officer Keegan was talking on his radio, while half a dozen BLPD uniforms were walking the grid. Closer by, a female officer held on to a metal detector, sweeping it back and forth in a zigzag pattern across the ground.

They were looking for bullets, weapons, coins, or any other type of evidence that might be linked to the dump site.

Luke scratched the back of his neck. "So—we're standing where, exactly?"

"Center stage. Where the performances took place last Friday evening. If the setup is similar to last year's, then the judges' table would be off to one side. Over there." She pointed at the honeysuckle bushes. "The violin case is pointing in that direction."

"So he's sending a message to the judges?"

"It looks that way, doesn't it?"

Luke studied the scene. "Okay, but Swinton was one of the judges this year. If he's guilty, then why would he be sending a message to himself?"

"He wouldn't," she agreed. "Whoever did this left the violin case right here on the spot where the contestants would've given their performances. Which means we need to interview all of this year's finalists."

"You think one of them did it?"

"We can't rule it out."

He grew visibly aggravated. "You don't think Swinton is guilty anymore? Is that what you're saying?"

"You have to admit, this is a game changer, Luke. Besides, the evidence we have on him so far is circumstantial. I've known him all my life. People lie. People do dumb things. That doesn't prove he tried to abduct her. And now this."

"What if the blood in the wastebasket turns out to belong to Morgan Chambers?"

"It only proves she was in his house. It doesn't prove anything else."

A tree swallow swooped territorially above their heads. She could see the gears turning in Luke's brain, his shoulders beginning to slump with resignation. "All right. I'll have Augie compile a list of finalists," he said, taking out his phone.

She tried to imagine a scenario in which Russ Swinton could've hacked up and mummified a body. It seemed insane. And yet—what was that old cliché about serial killers? He was such a nice guy, according to the neighbors. Friendly. Quiet. Kept to himself.

Luke put his phone away. "Augie's getting started on the list, and I've authorized Mike to do the interviews. We're also pulling the cadaver dogs off Swinton's property and bringing them over here." He shook his head, his frustration peaking. "I still don't get it. What kind of a fucking message is this supposed to be?"

She hesitated to say it out loud. "I realize this is a leap, okay? But look. The two hands in the case are holding a heart. What does that say to you?"

"I don't know. I've got my heart in my hands?"

"I'm sure it's common to most performers, but after her auditions, Bella used to say, 'I played my heart out for them.'"

Luke gave her a skeptical look. "That's the message to the judges?"

She nodded. "'I played my heart out for you.'"

45

They parked their vehicles in the underground garage of an aging government building, then took the elevator down to the basement, where Natalie followed Luke into the chilly morgue. The body parts were laid out next to the violin case on a stainless steel table—two slender forearms holding a mummified heart. The faux-suede accessory compartments of the violin case were empty. On a nearby table was a cadaver—an elderly man who'd died of natural causes.

Coroner Barry Fishbeck lit a stick of incense to mask the odor of decay, but a morgue was a morgue. You couldn't disguise the fact. A Mozart piano concerto was playing in the background, and beyond the cedar-smelling incense, a foreign odor filled Natalie's nostrils. Decaying flesh, talcum powder, and disinfectant—the awkward, intrusive combination of smells that signified an extinguished human life.

"The victim's prints were viable," Barry told them. "She was in the system from a previous DUI, and we were able to make a positive match. It's Lily Kingsley."

Natalie's hands were balled into fists. She'd suspected all along that it could've been Lily, but the news hit her with dull shock. "Any idea how she died?" she asked.

The coroner shook his head. "I hate to be a Debbie Downer, but we may never know unless we find the rest of her, and even then. However, I still have a lot of testing to do—toxicology, X-rays, bloodstains, hair, and fiber. You know the drill. An attempt was made to preserve the body parts, as you can see," he said, lines in his brow deepening. "Nature's pretty good at breaking down corpses. When the blood stops pumping, everything begins to decompose, but you can slow down the process if you're determined enough."

"You mean mummification," Luke said.

"Obviously something was done. Ancient Egyptian techniques are taught in high school nowadays—how to mummify a chicken, for instance. It's pretty straightforward. Anyone can Google it. You soak the carcass in a saline solution and store it in a cool, dry place. The salt will absorb all the moisture, leaving the chicken dry and desiccated. It takes about a month. Then you apply coats of glue or varnish to seal the deal." He shrugged. "Boom. You've got yourself a homegrown mummy."

Natalie tried to subdue the thud of her heart. "If it works for chickens, will it work for a human being?"

"That's a little more complicated. For a human body, of course, you'd need a bigger container. Like a bathtub. Then you'd have to remove the organs and pack the body cavity with natron salt. The ancient Egyptians had a unique way of removing the brain through the nasal passages. I suppose this technique could be used today if you had the stomach for it. It also helps to place the body in a cold environment afterwards, like a freezer—that'll turn off any remaining bacterial or enzymatic action."

"What about embalming fluid?" Luke asked, and Natalie remembered the Victorian embalming table that Justin Bertrand had mentioned.

"That's a more elaborate enterprise." Barry lowered his face mask. "Hopefully, I'll have some answers for you after the autopsy. I'll put a rush on the tox report and let you know if I find anything."

Luke nodded. "Thanks, Barry."

Out in the hallway, while waiting for the elevator, Natalie turned to Luke and said without hiding her sarcasm, "I didn't see any embalming fluid in Russ's house, did you?"

"He's a doctor. How hard would it be for him to mummify a body?"

"But we found no evidence to support that on his property."

"I just found out he owns a cabin in the Adirondacks. We're working on a search warrant for it now."

The air had grown chillier. She felt grimy and exhausted.

"I spoke to Swinton's attorney about the blood drops in the bathroom," Luke said, holding the elevator door for her. "They claim he could've cut himself shaving. Lenny sent a sample off to the lab for DNA testing, but that'll take a while, so I've asked for a blood type. We should know soon."

"Even if it's Morgan's blood, that still doesn't prove anything."

"It'll prove she was inside the house, in case he decides to lie to us again. And who knows? Maybe there was an altercation. Remember those unexplained scrapes on her knees?"

"Or maybe she had her period or a paper cut or a bloody nose."

"Let's see what other evidence Lenny comes up with."

She nodded and rubbed her foot against her leg, feeling nervous and on edge. "What about Morgan's phone records?" she asked.

"I've assigned them to Jacob. He's out in the field right now, but the chief has approved us for overtime, so we're guaranteed another busy week."

"Did anything else show up on the CCTV?" Natalie asked. "The *Walking Dead* zombie or Hollis Jones?"

Luke shook his head and crossed his muscular arms. "We're still reviewing the security tapes from all of the venues, including Blondie's and the Howard Street lot. Nothing so far, but it's still early. You're talking hundreds of man-hours to go." He ran his hand through his slightly greasy hair. Luke's thick brown hair grew out fast, and it was getting to that in-between stage. "Why, Natalie. What are you thinking?"

She shrugged. "My cynicism is inbred. We don't always know the people we know. But I'm trying to understand what could've motivated Russ to act this way. His sister died in an accident years ago, but that's not enough of a reason to target violinists, is it? Sure, the connections are there—we can connect the dots from the clinic to the two victims, Morgan and Lily. He treated them both for wrist injuries. And the women share a lot of connections—they both grew up in Chaste Falls, were gifted violinists, attended the conservatory. Physically, they could be sisters—attractive, petite, early twenties, long red hair."

"Swinton had access to drugs," Luke added. "All those burnouts from the West Side OD'ing and being admitted to the ER. He must deal with narcotics on a daily basis. He could have easily gotten his hands on GHB. Besides, he lied to you repeatedly. That has to count for something, Natalie."

"But it would mean that his psychopathy lay dormant for most of his life," Natalie argued. "According to Sheriff Dressler, no other students have gone missing from the conservatory—only Lily Kingsley. There haven't been any reports of date rape cases involving female violinists. No rapes, no murders. We've been trained to look for patterns, and I see a pattern emerging, but it only started six months ago. First Lily, then Morgan. So the question becomes—what happened six months ago that triggered this?"

"Unless there are other violinists who've gone missing that we don't know about yet."

"Right," she hedged.

He narrowed his eyes. "What is it?"

"I keep thinking about Bella. Not that she fits the pattern. She doesn't."

"It was determined years ago that Bella Striver ran away from home."

"That's the consensus," she responded vaguely.

He frowned. "Okay, Natalie. But what?"

She told him about the Polaroid pictures taken of Bella in supposedly different locations, and what they revealed about the cracks in the wall.

"Max Callahan told you this?"

"It could be the same wall, which means we need to reopen the case."

"Fuck, Natalie."

"But like I said," she told him, "Bella doesn't fit the pattern. She doesn't look like the other victims and she never actually went to the conservatory. Plus, it would mean there was a twelve-year gap in the perp's psychopathy.

Twelve long years in between Bella's disappearance and what's happening now. It feels like trying to fit the wrong-sized piece into the puzzle."

Luke's upper lip curled away from his teeth. "Swinton and his lawyer are due at the station in fifteen minutes. I want you to go talk to our prime suspect, Natalie. See what he has to say. And find out if he ever treated Bella Striver for a wrist injury."

46

Natalie walked into the interview room and tried to gauge Russ Swinton's mental state. He didn't seem nervous, so much as tired. His eyes were bleary. He had his attorney with him. Shadows drifted across the floor. The days grew shorter in November.

She was glad Russ had representation. He would need protection because she and Luke were going to add up all the missing details and memory lapses. Russ would have to stay on message. The way the system worked, the truth didn't always come out and justice didn't always prevail.

Introductions were made. The attorney's name was Tim Hooks, and he emphasized the esquire at the end of his name. Everyone took a seat. Natalie began the interview.

"We found human remains in the park," she said. "Identified as Lily Kingsley."

Russ turned his glassy eyes on her. His face was raked with sadness.

"What's the question?" the attorney asked.

"Were you in the park at any time since last Friday when you judged the Monster Mash contest?"

"No," Russ told her. He didn't flinch or look away.

"At any time, did you place the remains there?" she asked.

"Certainly not."

"The bartender at the Village Idiot told us you had a couple of drinks on Sunday night," Natalie said. "But you said you only had a nightcap."

"A nightcap or two," Russ responded dully. "I don't remember exactly. I had a few drinks at the party also . . ."

"You don't have to explain," Hooks told him quietly. "Just answer the question, yes or no."

"Perhaps it was two drinks."

Natalie didn't get it—why would Russ kill a young patient in such a gruesome fashion after all these years of hiding behind a mask of normalcy? She could've understood date rape or abduction, but not homicide. Not the way those body parts were staged.

"Lily Kingsley had an appointment with you at the conservatory clinic about a year ago. You treated her for wrist strain. You sent her to a physical therapist and saw her for a follow-up appointment a couple of months later. And yet, when I asked you recently, you said you didn't remember treating her."

Russ slumped in his chair and looked at his hands.

"It's okay," his attorney told him. "You can answer the question."

When he looked at her, the muscles around his eyes twitched a little. "I've seen thousands of patients over the years . . . I don't remember every single one."

"You don't remember Lily Kingsley?" Natalie repeated. "I find that hard to believe, because she disappeared six months ago from the conservatory, and it was all over the news. Your colleagues must've mentioned it."

"I've never been particularly good with names and faces. They all become a blur after a while. I remember their files, though. If you showed me her file with a description of her injuries, I might've remembered."

"You lied several times about Morgan," Natalie said. "Why?"

Russ lowered his eyes. "I was embarrassed."

"Is that it? Because you told me you went home directly after the party," Natalie reminded him, "but then, later on, you said you went out for a drink. Then you changed it to two drinks. What is it?"

He looked up. "I had a couple of nightcaps."

"Why would you lie about that?"

"Like I said, I was nervous."

"So you know how bad this looks?"

"Yes." He sighed resignedly.

"And you have no idea what happened to Morgan Chambers that night?"

"No." He rested his shaky hands on the table.

"Do you know anything at all about her disappearance?"

"I swear to God, I'd never hurt her, for crying out loud," Russ blurted.

"Just answer the question," Tim Hooks said.

Natalie felt sorry for him. It was unfair, what she was doing—trying to trip him up, to catch him in another lie. So far he was guilty of having a midlife crisis and dating a young patient, and that was creepy enough, but it wasn't a felony. "What else can you tell me about the party? About Morgan?"

Russ folded his hands on the table. "She seemed upset that the record producer didn't show up for the party. I went to refresh her drink, and when I got back, she was gone. Someone told me she called an Uber."

"Who told you?"

"An employee."

"And how long did you stay after she left?"

"About half an hour."

"The tapes show you leaving ten minutes later."

"That could be." He shrugged. "I don't like parties when I'm alone."

Natalie decided to take a different tack. "You were a judge in the contest. Did you know any of the other finalists?"

"No."

"Did the judges mingle with the finalists, before or after the contest?"

"Mingle?" He shook his head, perplexed. "No."

"Did you notice any strange behavior? Anything the other contestants might've said or done?"

He chewed thoughtfully on his lower lip. "No."

"Did they all accept the judges' final decision?"

Russ glanced at his attorney, then told Natalie, "I don't understand."

"Just answer the best you can," his attorney advised.

"Well," Russ said, "you could see the disappointment on some of their faces. But nobody threw a tantrum or acted out, if that's what you mean."

"So if we talk specifically about the party, is there anything else that stands out?"

"No, nothing."

"Are you sure?"

He leaned forward and blurted out, "I didn't hurt her. You know that, Natalie. I'll admit I tried to cover up a few things out of humiliation and embarrassment. I mean, look at me. I'm a middle-aged guy dating somebody decades younger than himself, and that was a mistake. I won't repeat it. I'm a doctor. I'm trained to save lives. That's all I've ever known. Why would I hurt anyone? I liked Morgan a lot. She was a delightful young lady. You've known me your entire life, Natalie. You know I didn't do this. I'm completely innocent."

"Russ, that's enough," his lawyer told him. "Is there anything else, Detective?"

She decided to lay it all out there. "As a doctor, you're at risk for chemical dependence and substance abuse. It's been statistically proven. Have you ever had access to illicit drugs like GHB or ecstasy?"

"What?" He drew back. "No, certainly not."

"He's answered all your questions," the attorney said. "We've cooperated fully. I think we can conclude our meeting here." By interrupting, Swinton's attorney was only trying to prevent his client from sticking his head in a noose.

"One last thing," she said. "Did you ever treat Bella Striver for a wrist injury?"

"Who?" he said, looking befuddled.

"I've told you about my friend Bella who went missing on the night of my high school graduation," she said angrily. "I've mentioned her at least a couple of times. You don't remember?"

"He said he doesn't remember," Tim Hooks said, gathering up his paperwork and briefcase. He stood up. "Let's go, Russ. Thank you, Detective."

Natalie was heading back to her office when her phone rang.

It was Dennis the dispatcher. "Someone named Poppy Chambers says she needs to talk to you."

47

The day was getting chilly. Clouds were beginning to congregate along the horizon. Natalie recognized Poppy Chambers sitting on the sandy shore of the lakefront, bathed in a golden late-afternoon light. Her face was taut and moist, a few strands of hair sticking to her cheeks. She wore a pale blue parka, embroidered jeans, and blue Chucks.

"What's up?" Natalie asked, approaching the girl.

"I'm honoring my dead sister," she said solemnly.

Something was burning on the surface of the lake less than twenty feet away—it looked like a child's toy boat, little flames leaping from the hold.

"I built a papier-mâché ship and put Morgan's old violin inside," she explained. "Like the Vikings used to do. They honored their dead by putting them into long ships and lighting the ships on fire, then watching them drift out to sea." Poppy gave her a wary look. "Are you going to arrest me?"

Natalie smiled. "I've got a better idea." She sat down beside the girl on the gritty sand and said, "Let's watch it drift together."

Poppy hugged her knees to her chest, mesmerized by the orange-yellow flames reflected in the water. It seemed to relax her.

"Is that really your sister's violin?" Natalie asked, remembering that some of these instruments cost thousands of dollars.

Poppy shook her head. "Not the one she had as an adult. But the cheap one Dad bought us when we were kids. Toddlers have a tendency to bang instruments around, so this is the dinged-up violin we both started on. My father's not going to miss it, and besides, it belongs to us . . . Morgan and me."

"Sounds like a fitting tribute."

Poppy stared at the flickering boat, while Natalie studied the girl's un-disciplined hair. Her bracelets and geometric jewelry clanked and jangled whenever she moved. She was reminded of Ellie, and a wave of sadness washed over her.

"Did you drive down here all by yourself?"

Poppy nodded. "Just me, myself, and I." She stared at the small boat with its cargo of a child's violin, now burning steadily, orange flames leap-ing and reflecting off the surface of the lake. "They cremate the bodies and float them in India, too," she said. "Except they don't say a person is dead. They say she's attained a position in Vishnu, which is the land of the dead. Sort of like heaven. Do you believe in heaven?"

Natalie tensed a little. She couldn't help thinking about Grace, so slim and athletic, poised on the cliff above the lake, ready to jump. Ready to leap and perform a perfect swan dive. "I don't know," she admitted.

"But you believe in something, right?"

Natalie nodded—at least she wanted to believe. "I'm glad I could share this moment with you."

"I read about your sister," Poppy said with soft insistence. "She died in this lake."

It stung like an insect bite. Natalie could feel her face flushing. "Yes, she did."

"Are you over it yet? The grief? Because they told me there were seven stages of grief, and that once you've gone through all the stages, you can finally get on with your life."

Natalie struggled to answer the question. Her grief was still painful—it felt like sparks spitting from a fire. The truth was she could feel her own sorrow in the way her body moved under her clothes, like a dog twitching to run away, its coat rippling with anxiety. The truth was that grief was never quite done with you. It returned whenever you remembered even the smallest detail. Actually, small details were what grief was composed of.

"I'm doing better," Natalie lied, trying to be positive. "You'll get through it."

Poppy nodded hopefully. A few minutes later, she began to cry. Her shoulders shuddered. Her sorrow descended like fog coming off the lake. Natalie hesitated before resting a careful hand on the girl's back. The bones of her spine were as fragile as a bird's. Again, Natalie thought of Ellie.

Poppy wiped the tears off her face and whispered, "The Lord is my shepherd; I shall not want . . ."

Natalie listened to this earnest, heartfelt recitation rising into the golden sky. She could almost believe that Morgan, Grace, and Willow were up there somewhere, smiling down at them. *He leadeth me beside the still waters.* She listened to the words, perhaps for the first time. What waters were still?

They watched as the little boat's flames flickered out with a crackling sound as it sank into the lake. Poppy smoothed her locks back in place, then said in a clear voice, "I'm going to end up with all the Easter eggs."

"What do you mean?"

The girl sneered, her face growing ugly. "Morgan didn't have the guts to do whatever it takes to succeed, whereas I'm willing to crawl through broken glass. That's the difference between us. She wanted a soft landing."

It concerned Natalie—this bitterness, this hardness in someone so young.

"You have to be tough to be in this business," Poppy went on. "Hard-nosed. Thick-skinned. There's a joke going around the music department. What's the difference between a pizza and a violin?"

Natalie shook her head. "I give up."

"A pizza can feed a family of four. A violinist can't even feed herself."

She laughed—it was funny. "How sad," she said.

"But true."

Natalie's phone buzzed, and she turned it off, but it reminded her that she had a million things to do. They would have to track Russ's movements from the bar, see if he'd ever visited the park, find out if he'd once treated Bella for a hand injury, and search his cabin in the Adirondacks.

The girl lay down on her back and gazed at the cumulus clouds gathering overhead. "Morgan came home from school once complaining about a low A-plus. She was upset because it wasn't a *high* A-plus. She wanted to be perfect all the time. I kept telling her, nobody's perfect. If you think that way, you're going to fail. Because you're setting the bar too high for yourself. But she wouldn't listen to me."

"It's good you understand that," Natalie said evenly.

"Dad kept setting the bar higher and higher for Morgan. He was . . . how can I say this without . . . he was hard on her. He humiliated her in front of the class more than once. If anything, a lot of the source of her stress came from feelings of inadequacy. But Dad respects me because I'm not afraid to stand up to him and challenge his beliefs. Morgan wanted his approval more than anything. She wanted the approval of all the adults in her life. I learned from her failures—what not to do."

Natalie looked at her. "So your father . . ."

"He's fine."

"But you just said he humiliated her."

Poppy laughed. "I didn't mean it that way."

"What way?"

"Just . . . never mind."

Natalie was used to witnesses backtracking. People often blurted out the truth, and then felt guilty about it. We all got used to our comfortable delusions.

"Did Morgan ever mention Dr. Swinton to you?" she asked.

"Only that he was a judge in the contest, and that he was super nice to her. She called me once when she was here. She said she got invited to this cool party, which she was really excited about. She couldn't wait to meet all these cool people."

"When did she call?"

"Sunday morning, I think."

"Did she mention any names?"

"She said Hunter Rose was hot. It was his party, I guess. He's that software guy, right?"

Natalie nodded. "Yeah."

"She was so excited that she went out and bought an outfit she couldn't afford. Most of her credit cards are maxed out. She said she was going to hook up with this musician guy after the party. She called him the fiddle player."

"Hollis Jones?"

"Yeah, I think so. Anyway, she said he had lots of connections and knew all the ins and outs of being in a folk band. She said there was this record producer she wanted to impress, too. One of the judges. He was going to be at the party. She was excited about meeting all these interesting people. She said it was a great opportunity to advance her career. She sounded so happy, but then . . ." Anguish constricted her throat.

Natalie waited a beat before asking, "Anything else?"

Poppy scratched her chin. "She said some guy was going to show her his Stradivarius. I think it was the record producer . . . she couldn't wait to play Vivaldi on it. Can you imagine getting your hands on a real, honest-to-God Strad?"

"Are you sure it was the record producer?"

"Maybe the fiddle player. She had so much going on."

"What else did she say about the fiddle player . . . Hollis Jones."

"Just that they got together on Saturday and smoked some weed." The tears had dried in sticky tracks down Poppy's face. "She said they had a good time, and she could almost imagine them doing concerts together, you know? Dueling fiddles. Ugh. I mean, Morgan used to hate the idea of becoming a fiddle player, but then she can get a crush on a guy in like . . . two seconds." Poppy shook her head disapprovingly. "I can't imagine playing a duet in a folk band. Jesus."

"And you think it was Hollis who was going to show her the Stradivarius?"

Poppy squinted up at the overcast sky. "I remember her being really excited, because I mean, how many people get to do that? Play a real Strad? She said she was going to send me video of her playing, but then . . . it never happened."

Natalie nodded sympathetically. How heartbreaking—these memories. Last words. Last conversations. A swirling wind pushed against their backs and played with their hair.

Poppy sat up and brushed the grit off her hands. "I've been meaning to ask you where Morgan's violin is."

"The police have it. They're still processing it."

She sighed with frustration. "When can we get it back?"

"I'm not sure. Do you want me to find out?"

She nodded. "We need to bury her with her violin. It's only right."

"Of course," Natalie said. "I'll do my best to find out for you, okay?"

Poppy smiled and got to her feet, brushing grass stains off her jeans. "Well, I'd better go now. It's getting late. Thanks for sitting here with me."

"It was nice. I'm glad I didn't miss it." Natalie stood up. "One more thing. You initially said that it was the record producer who wanted to show Morgan the Stradivarius. Do you still think it was Hollis?"

"Honestly?" The girl shook her head. "I don't remember."

48

Sarah Hutchins Drive was empty and quiet this afternoon. The Halloween trash had been picked up and the cleaning crews had moved on to other locations. Most of the shops were closed. Tomorrow or the next day, businesses would reopen, but for now the town was in recuperation mode.

Natalie walked past the alley toward Blondie's. The temperature had dropped, and the air was nippy for November, more like December air. Rainie's New Age boutique was closed. The Laundromat was closed. A couple of bars and restaurants were open for business, but there was no foot traffic to speak of.

Her phone rang, and she picked up. It was Luke.

"The blood in the wastebasket is AB negative, same as Morgan's blood type," he said. "We also found a long red hair with a root on the sofa, but it'll take a couple of weeks to get the DNA results. Meanwhile, we're processing the warrant and coordinating a joint execution with the state police for Swinton's summer cabin. This could be a gold mine."

Natalie glanced around at the deserted street. "What about the list of finalists for the Monster Mash contest?"

"Augie's compiling it now. I'll have him send it to you shortly."

Her eyes grew hard. "Listen, I just talked to Poppy Chambers, and Morgan told her someone was going to let her play their Stradivarius violin. None of the antique violins we found at Russ's place were Stradivariuses, were they?"

"I don't know. I'd have to check," Luke said.

"Send me pictures of them, would you? I'm on Sarah Hutchins Drive, and I'm about to talk to Justin Bertrand. I figure he'll know anybody locally who owns one. Maybe he can shed some light on this for us. Send me those pictures, and I'll ask him about Russ's violins, while I'm at it."

After a pause, Luke said, "I don't doubt your instincts, Natalie. Just keep me apprised." He hung up.

The interior of Bertrand Antiquities was dark except for a globe lamp illuminating the back of the store. She could see Justin shuffling through some paperwork behind the counter. She rang the bell and he looked up, surprise flitting across his face.

After a moment, the front door swung open. "Hey, Natalie," he said, looking dapper in a plaid shirt and khakis. "We're closed today, but come on in."

"I have a few questions for you about violins."

"No problem." He motioned her inside. "This place is a ghost town, huh? Post-Halloween doldrums. I kind of like it, though. Peace and quiet. Coffee? Tea?" he offered, escorting her to the back of the store.

"No, thanks. This won't take long."

"You sure?" He ducked behind the register. "I've got spearmint. Not only is it delicious, but it helps reduce stress. It's high in antioxidants." On the counter behind him was a teakettle on a hot plate, along with packets of sugar and nondairy creamers in a bowl.

"I'm good. I just wanted to know . . ." Her phone rang, irritating them both. "Excuse me a second. Hello?"

It was Augie. "I'm sending over the list of finalists now. Check your emails."

"Thanks." She pocketed her phone.

"Everything okay?" Justin watched her inquisitively.

"Yeah, police business," she said dismissively.

Dusty air blew out of the vent above their heads, and the Post-it Notes on the wall behind the register bristled in the mild breeze. The cat was cleaning its whiskers on top of a faded rocking horse. The rest of the antiques shop was hushed, as if it had been doing something mischievous before she'd come in, and now it was frozen and still.

"Well, Natalie, you lucked out," Justin told her. "We almost missed each other. I was about to head home. Dad's nurse quit."

"Really?"

He shrugged. "It's the third one in six months. My father can be a handful. He's got a will of iron. If he doesn't want to do something, then nobody's going to make him. Stroke or no stroke. He's as stubborn as the day is long. He used to terrify me . . . well," he hedged. "Not terrify. I mean, he was strict. There were rules you had to follow. If you didn't, there was hell to pay. Anyway, what brings you here, Detective?"

It was the first time today he'd called her detective, not Natalie. Her intuition prickled. "I was wondering if you knew anyone who owned a Stradivarius," Natalie said.

"A *Strad*?" Justin repeated with a scowl. "You're kidding, right? Those are extremely rare. There are only about six hundred and fifty in existence, and they come with a provenance. They're worth a couple million each, sometimes more."

"So nobody local?"

Justin rubbed his chin thoughtfully. "Well, Mr. Rose would love to get his hands on one. So would a lot of people. But it's far more common to see imitations for sale."

"You mean fakes? Like the one in your window?"

"That's right. They started making replicas after Stradivari died. There are some excellent imitations floating around out there, and then there's junk. Most of the replicas were churned out in German factories in the nineteenth and twentieth centuries. There are literally thousands of them. I'd say the majority are inferior products, but a certain percentage are exceptional in their own right. It's those antique replicas I'm interested in."

"So the one in your window . . . ?"

"Is a fine example." He locked up the register. "Most people can't tell the difference, because it's so well constructed. The shape, the quality of sound it produces. Spruce for the top, willow for internal blocks, and maple for the back—that's exactly what Antonio Stradivari used to create his violins."

"But you wouldn't call the one in your shop a Stradivarius, would you?"

"No. That would be unethical. Besides, enough people can tell the difference."

"Has anyone bought an imitation Strad from you that might be able to pass for the real thing?"

"You mean, like . . . if they wanted to fool someone?"

"Yes."

"Well, like I said, Mr. Rose has an imitation Strad, but it's got a label from Germany. That's a red flag right there."

"Anyone else?"

"Mr. Linkhorn has one from nineteenth-century France that's exceptional." He scooped up his keys and said, "Let me show you something." He walked to the front of the shop, opened the cabinet, scooped up the violin and bow, and began to play.

He wasn't half bad, Natalie thought. He chose a sweet, lyrical piece and gazed at her with probing intensity. Then his eyes flicked away, and he slid the bow across the strings with such elegance and precision, she felt transported to another place and time. It was the sort of music that made your soul ache. He seemed to be sending all his loneliness and longing out into the world. When he finished playing, his gaze came to rest on Natalie's face.

"That was beautiful," she said. "I didn't realize you played the violin."

"It's just a hobby," he said self-effacingly. "My mother taught me when I was a kid. I was in the school orchestra for a while. I was planning on taking it further, but then . . . I broke my arm." He shrugged. "That's life, right?"

Something prickled at the back of Natalie's neck. "When did this happen?"

"Umm, let's see. I was in the ninth grade. Once you have a serious injury like that, you can forget about a professional music career. Now it's just my passion."

"And your arm is fully healed?"

"It wasn't easy to retrain myself. Not without a lot of blood, sweat, and tears. I had to switch from right-handed to left-handed." He placed the violin and bow carefully back in its case. "But I was determined. I never gave up. Funny thing, though."

"What's that?"

He paused. "As soon as I could play again, I broke my other arm."

"Really."

"Weird, huh?"

Her stomach dropped. She remembered the long-ago day Justin had given Natalie and Bella their free marbles. First he placed the two orange-and-black tigers over his eyes and made a funny face. Then he explained how glass-blown marbles were made. While he was showing them, he accidentally knocked the glass jar over and spilled marbles across the floor of the shop. His father reacted poorly, grabbing Justin by the arm and yanking him sharply with such force, Justin had cried out in pain.

"How did you break your other arm?" Natalie asked.

"One winter, I was shoveling snow in our driveway, when I slipped on an icy patch and landed wrong. *Snap.* Just my luck."

She put on her most sympathetic expression, while her body grew slick with sweat. "*Two* broken arms? Wow. That's kind of hard to believe."

"Isn't it?"

"And yet you still play the violin."

"The second time, it took a lot longer to heal, but I kept at it. I'm as stubborn as the old man, I guess. But I never regained full control of the instrument. That's why I call it a hobby now. You can't compete on any professional level with those types of injuries. So I just play for fun."

Natalie had a flash of Lily Kingsley's severed arms inside the violin case. "And you broke both arms within the span of—what? A few years?"

"That's right."

"And yet you persevered regardless. That takes guts."

He nodded slowly. "Guts is one word for it." He snapped the violin case shut, then picked up a stack of paperwork. "You've probably heard this before, but I consider it a gift. Sometimes bad things happen, but they make you grow. All this talk about 'adulting' is so much bullshit, if you ask me. So much of that is simply accepting responsibility and moving on."

"That's a good way of looking at it." Her body grew still as stone.

"Anyway, Hunter Rose bought two imitation Strads from me . . ."

"Two?" There was an acid taste at the back of her throat.

"Yeah, he's been trying to buy an original for years through his New York dealer."

"That's interesting. What about Russ Swinton?"

Justin shook his head. "He can't afford it. I think he's pretty happy with his Stainers and Vollers."

"I want you to take a look at something. Are these all Stainers and Vollers?" She activated her phone, opened Augie's attachment, and swiped through the images. "We found these antique violins in Dr. Swinton's house."

He looked down at the screen. "For the most part, yeah. No Strads there."

She put away her phone. "Nobody else owns one? Owen Linkhorn? Hollis Jones?"

"Well, Mr. Linkhorn's a collector of rare instruments. He'll ring me up to see if I've come across anything interesting. But he doesn't have a Strad as far as I know. Anyway, I should be going. My father's alone in the house . . ."

"I understand. Just one more question." Natalie felt herself edging into high alert. She recalled the scene in the store again—Ned Bertrand lashing out at Justin for spilling marbles on the floor. Shouting at his son "You stupid brat!" and grabbing him so violently by the arm, he could've pulled it out of its socket.

"But you're so good at playing the violin," she said. "It makes me wonder why you haven't performed or competed. Or am I mistaken? Did you enter the Monster Mash contest this year? One of the detectives sent me a list of finalists, and I'm wondering if you're on it."

Justin checked his watch. "Yeah, I entered this year for fun. But I was eliminated in the first round. I never made it to the finals."

She shook her head. "Why didn't you mention this to me before?"

"You didn't ask. Besides, it's embarrassing to lose. Nothing to brag about."

"But, see," she said, "it raises a bunch of questions. Like, did you meet or talk to Morgan Chambers while you were auditioning? Because she was a contestant, too."

He shook his head vaguely. "I don't think so. There were so many people there."

"You would've remembered talking to her. Right?"

He shook his head. "I didn't talk to anyone."

She knew instinctively he was lying. She swallowed a prickle of fear. "Your father . . . I'm assuming he didn't approve of your violin playing?"

Justin laughed derisively. "Now that's an understatement."

"But your mother approved, because she's the one who taught you."

"She was a classical violinist before she married my father. She passed on her love of music to me. Dad thought it was for eggheads. They used to fight about it."

"So the first time you broke your arm was—right around the ninth grade?"

"Dad and I went hunting and I shot a buck. We injured it. We followed the blood trail through the woods. We tracked it to a steep trailhead, where I fell down a ravine."

Natalie was careful to hide her disbelief. "It's funny, because I just remembered something," she said. "When you gave us those marbles, Bella and me—I remember you accidentally knocked the jar over, and marbles spilled all over the floor. Your father was quite upset. He grabbed your arm . . ."

"He thinks discipline is important."

"Was he rough with you a lot?"

He stared at her, appalled. "What's that got to do with anything?"

A bitter taste filled her mouth. "One last question. Have you auditioned for the Monster Mash contest every year? Or was this your first time?"

"First time." He shuffled through the paperwork on the counter.

"Why didn't you try out last year, too? Or the year before? Was it because your father wouldn't let you?"

"I don't know," he said brusquely, glancing at his watch. He looked up. His face softened and sagged. "I told you, he had a lot of rules."

"But not anymore," Natalie reasoned. "Not since he had his stroke. He's too sick to stop you. He can't speak. He can't move. He can't prevent you from performing. He can't grab you by the arm or break your bones."

Justin's hands were hidden behind the counter. She didn't like that. She could feel her gun in its holster, snug against her rib cage. How to reach for it without arousing a counterreaction.

"You said music was your passion," she went on. "It must be difficult being judged for that. I'm wondering what it feels like to stand in front of a group of judges and perform for them, knowing they might not like it. Knowing they're assessing you. How hard that must be . . . to play your heart out and know you could get a thumbs-down. I just heard you play, and in my opinion, you're very good. That you could get eliminated after the first round doesn't seem fair."

He watched her closely, as if he were trying to catch the lie. His hands were still hidden from view behind the counter. Fear coated her tongue. Her heart began to tic at the base of her neck.

"Let me see your hands, please," she said.

He didn't move.

She shifted ever so slightly, and her leather pancake holster squeaked.

His eyes widened.

Natalie sensed they were circling around the truth. A glaze of sweat broke out all over her body. She went for her gun, but she was too late. He'd already reached under the counter and was swinging the baseball bat freely at her head.

Natalie managed to duck, but the bat clipped her on the side of the skull and she went down. Her vision spun. Her knees caved. She felt the impact like a door slamming shut. Like a dead bolt locking.

49

Natalie woke up. *Where the fuck am I?*

She was lying on her back, gazing at the ceiling.

She sat up groggily and looked around. There was blood on the floor—a constellation of drops with crenelated edges. She touched her head. There was blood on her fingertips. Fear grabbed her hard.

She stumbled to her feet, then drew her service revolver and released the safety. "Justin?" she called out. The door leading to the back of the shop was open.

Natalie entered the back area, which was jammed with midcentury modern chairs, Art Deco bookcases, and eighteenth-century commodes. She squeezed past old advertising signage, Depression-era glassware, and funny-looking kitchen appliances from the 1950s, then burst out the back door and stood on the sidewalk that overlooked the public parking lot on Howard Street—the same asphalt lot that Blondie's backed on to. The quickest route out of Dodge.

A scenario flashed through her head: Justin met Morgan at the auditions, where he bragged about the Stradivarius in his shop, convincing her it was real and offering to let her play it sometime. They exchanged phone numbers. When Hollis Jones didn't show up at Blondie's on Halloween's Eve, Morgan called Justin from the bar, and they arranged to meet in his shop, which was practically next door. Once there, a little tipsy, she sipped an herbal tea that he'd spiked with GHB. Something must've spooked her, because she escaped about thirty minutes later, pushing her way through the crowd on Sarah Hutchins Drive and running away from Bertrand Antiquities, afraid for her life. As the GHB began to take effect, she ducked into the alley, crawled inside a dumpster, stripped off her clothes in her delirium, and died from a lethal combination of drugs and alcohol.

Natalie glanced around the lot and noticed that Ned Bertrand's reserved parking space near the back entrance to the shop was empty. She holstered her gun and raced for her car, which was parked a couple of blocks away.

In a town like Burning Lake, everyone knew everybody else, either personally or through a friend or mutual acquaintance. People talked. Natalie knew things about the Bertrands. For instance, she knew that Amy Bertrand had died in a car accident years ago and was drunk when she crashed into a telephone pole. She knew that most folks respected Ned Bertrand for his charity work and his annual gumball contest. His old white Chevy pickup truck full of dusty antiques was a fixture in this town. She also knew where the Bertrands lived—in a lovely, blowsy Victorian on the east side of town—and that after college Justin Bertrand moved back in with his parents and started working in his dad's antiques store.

Natalie scooped up her police radio and called it in. "Dispatch, do you receive? This is CIU-seven."

"Received, CIU-seven."

"I'm on Clementine, heading for Hyacinth. I just had an altercation with Justin Bertrand. I think he's headed home. Send backup to 92 Hyacinth Lane. I'm headed there now . . . ETA two minutes. Also put out an APB on his vehicle, a white Chevy pickup truck, I don't have the plate number, but the title belongs to Ned Bertrand."

"Received," Dennis responded. "Calling for backup now."

She plopped the radio back in its cradle on the dash, while fear crept through her. When you sensed your life was in danger, everything inside of you tensed. You became primed for fight or flight. Police training had given her an edge, alerting her to her own physical reactions, teaching her how to counter the adrenaline rush with rational decision-making. Now she steadied her breathing, slowed her racing heart, and focused on the task at hand. At the corner of Clementine and Hyacinth, she took a left and drove for another mile or so until she came to the end of the road.

Natalie pulled over to the side of the dead-end street and sat for a moment, feeling a static discharge on the back of her neck. The proud old Victorian was surrounded by towering oaks and blazing Japanese maples. The white Chevy pickup was parked in the driveway. The nearest neighbor was at least forty yards back. Across the street were more woods. A white picket fence surrounded the property, hearkening back to simpler times.

Steeling herself, Natalie drew her service revolver and released the safety, then crossed the yard toward the weathered front porch, where she rang the doorbell. There was no answer. Her heart beat erratically as she knocked. "Justin?" She glanced around the property at the well-tended lawn and lush overgrown gardens. "Justin?" she called out. "It's Detective Lockhart. Open up!"

Still no response.

The property had transformed itself from idyllic to eerie in a matter of seconds. The big oaks and maple trees stirred uneasily in the breeze. Her hands were freezing cold. Her feet felt like lead weights. She noticed an impression in the blue cotton seat of the Adirondack chair and wondered if someone had been sitting there recently.

She tried the door, but it was locked. She cupped her hands over the glass pane and peered inside. A muted light filled the living room. She broke the pane of glass with the butt of her gun, reached inside, and unlocked the door. An alarm went off.

Natalie entered the house, calling out, "Police! Come out with your hands up!"

The house showed its age with its creaking floorboards and drafty old-fashioned windows. The kitchen was fairly neat and tidy. There was a half-finished mug of coffee next to an open laptop on the breakfast table. The screen was asleep. Natalie tapped the space bar, and it blinked on.

A split-screen display revealed six different angles of the property. In one of the display panels, Natalie saw herself standing in the kitchen with her gun drawn. She looked around for the security camera, but it was well hidden. She moved swiftly past the granite countertops and chrome appliances, shouting, "Justin? It's Natalie Lockhart! Come out with your hands up!"

When she reached the living-room doorway, she paused to take it all in. A harvest-gold archway divided the living room from the dining room. A hazy late-afternoon light slanted through the mini-blinds on the western-facing windows. Two wingback chairs bookended the river stone fireplace.

"Justin?" she called out hoarsely, searching from room to room. After she'd cleared the first floor, she went upstairs where the dying light cast brilliant splashes of gold against the walls. She cleared each room one by one. At the end of the hall, the last remaining door was shut.

50

~~~

Natalie's hands tightened around the grip of her gun as she headed down the long hallway, stomach in free fall. She could hear strange echoes inside the house, like distant motors switching on and off. Mechanical sounds. Then a loud moan came from behind the door, and a chill spiked through her.

She aimed her weapon at the door, mind sheathed in velvet. She could taste her own fear. The door was painted midnight blue. "Police!" she shouted. "Come out with your hands up."

She stood listening to the low, deep groan. When it finally stopped, the silence that followed was disturbingly empty. Her mouth went dry.

She proceeded toward the midnight-blue door, sweat beading on her upper lip, her hair beginning to curl in licks and snarls. A washy haze hung in the air.

She reached for the glass doorknob. "Police! Back away from the door!"

There was a muffled whimper.

Natalie flung open the door and aimed her gun all around. It was relatively dark inside the stuffy room. She groped along the wall, found the light switch, and flicked it on. The room lit up.

Ned Bertrand lay underneath a white sheet on an ornate wrought iron antique bed facing the door. He was staring at her with red-rimmed eyes. You could tell he'd had a stroke. One side of his face sagged. He was sweating profusely. His nostrils were caked with blood. He looked terribly thin and sickly, with a jutting jaw and greasy white hair—a far cry from the dapper antiques dealer she used to know.

Natalie crossed the room, old floorboards creaking. A few hazy rays of sunlight filtered through the gap in the thick brocaded curtains. She almost tripped over a blood pressure cuff and an oxygen tank. The bedcovers were rumpled. There was a nasty smell in the air. She scrutinized his wrinkled, porous face. There were sharp lines of pain around his mouth. She fought off a wave of nausea and placed her hand on his arm. "Where's Justin?"

His open eyes conveyed nothing, expressed nothing. They were dark, tarry pits.

She squeezed Ned's liver-spotted hand. "Where's your son?"

Something stirred—a million bird wings beating the air.

Her head was pounding. She studied him closely. This poor man had irises like cracked marbles. He had weathered skin and hollow cheeks, and his breath smelled bad—a yeasty whoosh of air. The room was awfully hot. Everything was filtered through a veil of nausea. She tried to imagine Ned Bertrand breaking his son's arm not once, but twice. A cruel man breaking both of Justin's arms in order to prevent him from playing the violin like his mother used to. It was hard to imagine this withered old man hurting anyone. She couldn't help feeling sorry for him. There were small stains of vomit on his T-shirt. He was malnourished and dotted with bandages. He'd apparently been lying in this position for some time. The stench of rotting bedsores got to her. The smell of old piss billowed upward.

Now something sparked behind those eyes, and he grew agitated, focusing on Natalie with great intensity. His tongue wormed with all the syllables and consonants his chapped lips could not form. He struggled to get the words out, but all he managed was a hiss.

A whispery kind of creepiness prickled her skin.

The room grew hotter. She couldn't contain her revulsion.

Now his gaze flicked toward the doorway behind her.

Behind you.

She spun around.

51

Anguish squeezed Natalie's heart. Seated in a chair in between the doorway and bureau was the mummified corpse of Lily Kingsley. Her head was tipped to one side and the stumps of her arms flopped like a puppet with the strings snipped. She had leathery, varnished skin under the powder-blue T-shirt and skinny jeans, and she was barefoot, as if she'd been yanked unexpectedly from one location and dragged here against her will.

Natalie felt as if she was shrinking. She gripped her gun as if the corpse might spring to life at any second. She realized the horror of Ned Bertrand's situation. He could do nothing but stare at the mummified dead body seated in front of him all day long. He couldn't run. Couldn't scream. Couldn't tell anyone what was happening. Not even the day nurses. Justin obviously hid the corpse whenever they were here, but when their shift was over, it was just Ned and the dead violinist.

The home alarm had been whining steadily in the background, but now all of a sudden, it shut off. The silence was terrifying. Natalie's brain buzzed like a tuning fork.

She could hear a heavy door swung shut below.

Ned stirred and moaned with sick anguish.

She put a hand on his shoulder. "The police are on the way."

With a quick intake of air, she crossed the room and took a defensive stance in the hallway. Hands trembling, she hurried down the stairs.

52

Outside, the clouds were gathering force. She watched as Justin tossed a couple of bags into the flatbed of his truck and hopped in, starting the engine. He backed out of the driveway and screeched to a halt in the middle of the road.

She aimed her gun at his head. "Stop! Police!"

Their eyes met.

"Hands up! Get out of the truck. Now!"

He hit the gas and turned sharply, and she listened to the slap of the wind as he veered off down the street.

Adrenaline flooded her body in waves, like a motor revving and dying. Taking deep ragged breaths, she cut across the lawn and got in her car. By the time she keyed the ignition, Justin had disappeared in a vortex of dust.

She revved the engine and floored it away from the curb. She took out her anger on the road, accelerating hard and speeding past horse stables and stretches of forest. She took a left onto River Road, then climbed over a steep hill before dropping down into the valley below. She chased the white pickup as it sped toward Route 17, the highway out of town.

The clouds were thick overhead now, and a gritty wind pushed into the car as she whipped around corners, hands choking the wheel. They were heading for the Chumash Wash, a tributary that fed into the Cayuga River. During rainy season, the Chumash Wash was unfettered and free to run its course. Now it rolled dramatically past the old oaks and weeping willows growing on its banks. This rural area was full of wooded hills and meadows where equine and feed businesses thrived, and on either side of the road were swirling skirts of crimson leaves blown around by the wind.

As they sped toward the Wash, the road turned sharply and the Honda's discount tires hugged the asphalt. The forest gradually thinned out, giving way to a bevy of wildflowers growing along the banks of the big, slow-moving river. You could smell the fragrant autumn underbrush, cypress and sweetbriar. You could smell lichens and mosses growing on the wet river rocks. They'd passed the blue water tower and were heading for the old bridge on Winterberry Road, when the clouds broke with lightning and thunder rolled across the sky.

Natalie drove eastbound through a spitting rain. The pavement grew slippery, and she tapped the brakes lightly, cautiously, as she followed the pickup truck onto the bridge. She could barely see past the frenzy of her wipers and the hard rain hitting her windshield. She didn't see the delivery truck coming from the other direction until it was too late. "Fuck," she muttered, a deep panic threading through her voice.

What happened next happened very quickly. The delivery truck skidded over the slick grade, veering across the center divider line and forcing Justin to swerve into the scaffolding on the western side of the bridge. Horns blared. Natalie's Honda made a hideous squealing sound as she hit the brakes and lost control. The delivery truck wove back into its lane and sped past them, but it was too late. Justin had lost control of his vehicle and smashed it into the scaffolding, while at the same time Natalie hit the brakes and threw the wheel hard, trying to pull the car straight. But the car didn't want to go straight. She yanked the hand brake, and the back tires locked and lost their traction. There was a metallic crunch as she collided into the back of the white pickup truck.

As they spun around, the weight of the car shifted to the front as she desperately tried to control the slide, but the Honda impacted with the side of the bridge, and they both smashed through the scaffolding. Natalie's mind swam as a steel cable snapped like a slingshot. There were popping sounds all over, and then an awful crash. The impact pushed them over the edge. She was falling.

Natalie got thrown sideways, her seat belt digging into her flesh and clutching her tightly around the middle. She could see the water looming closer as they tumbled off the bridge. She was furious with herself for screwing up big-time. She clutched the wheel, while fright and shame swallowed her up.

The engine sputtered and fizzled as her vehicle dove headlong into the water. The fall was effortless. The car did a half turn and slapped against the water with such a powerful jolt, it snatched the air out of her lungs. She could feel the thudding relentless mechanism of her heart, like clunky windshield wipers whipping back and forth.

Then there was nothing but silence and bubbles.

53

Reality intruded. **Rude** and horrifying. Natalie could feel the blood pulsing through her temples while cold water embraced the car. She could hear the Honda's chassis groaning. The river was roaring. Life was a fragile thing. She had lost her grasp of the situation. Her mouth was bleeding—she must've banged it against the steering wheel, because now she could taste her warm blood.

As shock receded, she realized that the car was sinking rapidly into the river. She had to do something. Water came pouring in through the wheel wells, the trunk, and the cab. She could hear it funneling in from several openings into the car. She was stunned. She gaped ahead in horror—she was trapped inside a giant aquarium.

Natalie fought off her rising panic and tried to roll down the windows, but the electric circuitry had shorted out and the power wasn't working. The car was filling up fast. She could feel icy river water pooling around her ankles.

She popped her seat belt as the water level rose with astonishing speed. Eyes wide and uncomprehending, she grasped the door handle with trembling fingers and tried to open it manually, but the door was locked. She'd been instructed on how to escape from a submerged vehicle in one of her emergency classes years ago—you were supposed to take a deep breath and let the water fill the entire car. Only then, once the water had rushed in above your head and you were entirely submerged, could you open your door and swim to freedom.

Easier said than done. Nightmarish, in fact.

The ice-cold water was up to her knees now, and it shocked her senseless, until her instincts took over. Since the door was locked, Natalie had to break the driver's side window. She turned sideways in her seat and tried to break the window with one swift kick, but the safety glass was tough. She remembered the antitheft locking device she'd purchased at Home Depot and stashed under her seat years ago—a device she'd never used before—and now she reached for it, fumbling under her seat with frozen fingers. The water was shockingly cold and rising fast. She found the antitheft locking device and bludgeoned the window with it.

She had only minutes to spare. Fear foamed in her heart as she banged the device against the glass over and over again, until the window broke and a gush of water came pouring in. She girded herself as the water level rose swiftly around her chest and lifted her off her seat. Then she waited with extraordinary patience while there was still a pocket of air under the car ceiling. You weren't supposed to swim out until the water had entirely filled the car and the pressure was even. Once the vehicle was completely submerged, then you could escape through the broken window and swim to the surface.

Keeping her head inside the diminishing air pocket, Natalie kicked off her shoes and waited for the interior to fill up with water. Once the car hit bottom, very few air pockets would remain. She took a deep breath as the water line reached her mouth and nose, and suddenly she was plunged into darkness.

The car sank at a relatively steep angle. How deep would it go? Twenty feet? Thirty feet? The river was relatively shallow. As the car's heavy engine dragged it down to the bottom, she felt the front end hit the silt bed with a gentle thud and continued holding her breath as she waited for the car to settle. Waiting for the pressure to equalize both inside and out was excruciating, but absolutely necessary.

She couldn't see a thing. It was black as pitch on the reedy bottom of the river. Her body felt numb all over. Her lungs were about to burst. She slid her hand along the seat and reached for the broken window with groping fingers. There was still a small pocket of air at the top of the vehicle, and Natalie took a final quick breath before plunging into darkness again. Then she crawled through the broken window and swam as hard and fast as she could toward the surface.

Popping out of the water was like being reborn. She gasped for breath, coughing and sputtering, then turned around, buoyed by the current. She didn't see Justin's truck anywhere.

54

Natalie had no time to think. Instinct kicked in. She removed her jacket, sacrificing it to the river, then spotted a man on the bridge and waved at him.

The man showed her his phone and shouted something at her. She couldn't hear him over the roar of the river, but it looked like he'd called 911. She took a deep breath and dove underwater.

About twenty feet down, she spotted the white truck on the murky bottom. Justin Bertrand was stuck halfway out the driver's side window. He appeared to be unconscious. She swam over to him, grabbed him by the arms, and tugged hard, trying to yank him out of the vehicle.

His eyes popped open. He panicked and clawed at her face. Natalie tried to defend herself, but he grabbed her by the wrists and pulled her close. Years ago, as part of her training, Natalie had taken underwater lifesaving courses. As a rescuer, you had to be careful you didn't become a victim yourself. A drowning victim could panic and get you in a death grip, and then you'd both drown.

Natalie thrust her thumbs deep into the backs of his hands, gripped his fingers, and twisted them sharply outward. She could hear the crack of his finger bones as he shrieked and released her, and she swam backward through a swirl of bubbles.

The next fifteen seconds were a shitshow, but she finally managed to pull him out of the truck window. Once he was unstuck, instead of swimming to safety and in a blind panic, Justin grabbed her by the arms and pulled her toward him again. He was stronger than her, fueled by terror. Using Natalie as leverage, he climbed over her shoulders and stepped on her head, propelling himself toward the surface, while submerging her further into the murky depths, leaving her disoriented and exhausted.

Natalie's wet clothes weighed her down. She could taste grit from the river bottom as her fingers felt around for things—weeds growing in the slimy silt, loose rocks. She tried to push herself up from the bottom but couldn't summon the strength. Her limbs were like wet noodles. Her shoulders sagged.

Almost out of air, she saw a blinding light, like the kind projected onto a movie screen after the film has broken. A purifying white light poured into her eyes, and a woman's golden hair fanned out in the water, like silky wings through shafts of light.

You're going to be all right.

Grace floated above her with a mysterious weightlessness. Natalie was filled with a sense of tranquility and peace. She felt her sister's warmth flow through her. Time stopped. Something ropey slithered past her.

Grace smiled one last time before dissolving into the reeds.

Wait, Grace. Don't go! What am I supposed to do without you? Natalie cried silently.

Live your life.

Live my life? Natalie thought. Now that I'm drowning? How can I live my life if I'm about to die? She strained to see through a prism of bubbles, but her sister was gone.

Natalie was falling—an endless tumble through the glistening depths. She had tapped out her last reserves of air and was about to give up and give in, when an arm reached out and grabbed her. A strong pair of hands tied a length of rope around her waist and hauled her up through the water. She could see the surface getting closer as her rescuer lifted her up, up, up . . . until the river burst above her head, and the overcast day's brightness nearly blinded her. It felt miraculous, like a new beginning.

The rescue worker carried her onto the shore, his hands slippery against her skin, beads of water flying from his head like cartoon sweat. For a while, there was only the sound of Natalie choking, coughing, wheezing.

"Easy now . . . nice and slow."

A strobing red light hit her on the side of the face. She heard urgent voices. Someone wrapped a blanket around her shivering shoulders.

"Hey." A silhouette hovered before her between the flashes of crimson. "Natalie? Are you okay?"

She recognized those intelligent eyes. It was Luke—floating somewhere beyond the haze of rain and sirens and commotion. He knelt down beside her. She could feel his hand, so warm on her cheek. "Hang in there," he told her.

A cacophony of sirens and screeching brakes.

Another pair of strong hands lifted her onto a stretcher. Something darted in the sky above—zigzags of lightning. The rain was coming down harder now, pelting her on the face and neck. A paramedic shielded her and shone a light in Natalie's eyes, blocking out everything and temporarily blinding her.

Several EMTs lifted the stretcher into the back of the ambulance, where a female paramedic took her vitals. Sand-colored hair and freckles, like a pixie. She wrapped a blood pressure cuff around Natalie's arm and monitored the data stream. Water in the lungs, even a small amount, could lead to a condition called "dry drowning," which was sometimes fatal. It had to be closely monitored.

Natalie listened to the soft tearing sound of Velcro as the cotton cuff was secured around her arm. She listened to the dull pump of the inflation bulb and the snakelike hiss of the air-release valve. "I'm fine," she insisted.

"Take a deep breath and relax," the EMT said, pumping the red rubber bulb, inflating the blood pressure cuff with air and releasing the hissing valve. She pressed the stethoscope to Natalie's chest and listened to the blood tumbling through her arteries. "Sounds good." She stopped and tore off the Velcro.

"Can I go now?"

"Lie still, Detective."

They gave her oxygen.

The ambulance sped away, heading for the hospital.

The setting sun bathed everything in an apricot glow.

Clutching the sides of the gurney, Natalie tried to sit up.

"Easy now. Lie down."

"Did you find him . . . ?"

They need to find him.

"Everything's okay, Detective," the paramedic told her. "The suspect has been apprehended, thanks to you. I guess this means you'll be in the tabloids again, huh?"

No. Not again.

Natalie could hear her own stubborn heartbeat. A shiver of dark acknowledgment ran up her spine. She relaxed into all seven stages of grief and began to cry, great sobs shaking her frame.

They wheeled her into the hospital, where she kept blacking out. At first, it seemed as if all the doctors and nurses were there inside the hospital room with her. Then she felt isolated and alone, with only the beep of the heart monitor lulling her to sleep.

Blackness and silence.

Periods of consciousness.

Silence again.

Finally, she opened her eyes. Someone was holding her hand. She wanted to tell this person something, only she couldn't get the words out.

They need to find him . . .

"It's okay," Luke said softly. "I'm here. You're going to be all right."

"I . . ."

"You're in the hospital," he said.

"But I . . ."

"Natalie? Are you okay? Can I get you anything?"

She wasn't sure what she wanted.

She closed her eyes and pretended to sleep.

EPILOGUE

November came and went.
      In December, the sky turned a deeper dark as it seamed effortlessly into the horizon.

In January, a howling wind blasted through the town and littered everybody's front yard with broken tree limbs.

In February, the trial began. Justin Bertrand expressed no remorse. He blamed his father for the two victims—Lily Kingsley and Morgan Chambers. Justin's lawyers claimed that the boy had suffered a lifetime of abuse at the hands of his father—including two broken arms—and that this had twisted his mind. They went for an insanity defense. In the end, he was sentenced to life without parole.

However, Bella Striver wasn't one of his victims. She was one of Natalie's loose ends. It frustrated her that she didn't have any answers when it came to Bella.

Recovery was slow. But as the weeks and months passed and nothing dramatic happened, people forgot. Life fell back to its normal routine. Day by day, as was their custom, the townspeople of Burning Lake managed to put the past behind them.

One night in mid-March, as Natalie lay in bed reading *A Room of One's Own* by Virginia Woolf, she paused to reread the line: "The beauty of the world has two edges, one of laughter, one of anguish, cutting the heart asunder."

That was so fucking true she wanted to cry.

Her phone rang, rescuing her from this lovely, horrifying sentiment.

"Hey, Aunt Natalie, it's me," Ellie said brightly.

"Hello, you." Natalie smiled and put her book down.

"So . . . next month, huh?"

"You're still coming, aren't you?"

"Yeah, of course. I wouldn't miss it for anything."

"I rented the boat."

"Dad's booked our reservations. We'll be staying at the Sunflower Inn."

Almost one year ago.

Had it only been eleven months since Grace had passed away? For a moment, Natalie felt battered and sore all over, as if she was lying on top of a shattered mirror. She experienced a flashback to her former life—a cast-off life full of grief and pain. But things were different now. She was safe and sound in her own bed. In her own home. The blankets were warm. Her fuzzy socks felt good on her feet. She listened to the rain on the roof. The dishes were all put away.

"Hey, guess what?" Ellie said. "Did you know there's a black hole at the center of the Milky Way?"

Natalie smirked. "So we're doomed, huh?"

"Eventually."

"How long do we have?"

"Well, it's twenty-five-hundred-million-million kilometers away. So I think we'll be okay for a while."

"But we're also spinning headlong toward the Andromeda Galaxy, aren't we? So in about two billion years from now, there's going to be a spectacular collision."

Ellie laughed. "I think we've got time to figure something out."

Ellie was sixteen, almost a woman in today's world. Natalie didn't want her niece to grow up. Not yet. Not in this crazy world. She wanted to protect Ellie from all the things she didn't understand herself.

"We took a field trip to the observatory," Ellie said, "where you can literally watch the galaxies collide and smash apart. Except it's happening in super-slow motion, so it looks incredibly beautiful and peaceful, like a ballet."

Natalie saw shadows moving on the hallway wall outside her room. He came to the doorway, hesitant to bother her, and mouthed the words, "You want coffee?"

She nodded and whispered, "Thanks."

"Who's that?" Ellie jumped in.

"Just a friend."

"What friend? You mean Luke?" she said excitedly. "Are you serious?"

"It's not what you think."

"No?"

Natalie didn't respond. She could feel herself blushing. She was being carried along by a swift current she had no control over.

"You asked me what infinity was, Aunt Natalie. It's got to be love, right? Because there's no end to it. Love grows in all directions. It evolves and keeps growing and spinning outward . . . like the galaxies. It's as infinite as the cosmos. And maybe it even ends in disaster, like Romeo and Juliet . . . but the ride is beautiful . . . love is beautiful. Don't you believe that's true, Aunt Natalie?"

"I think it's mysterious and unknowable."

There was a pause while Ellie muffled the phone to talk to her father. Then she got back on the line and said, "Dad says hello."

"Hello, back."

"I've gotta go. It's a school night. Homework."

"See you next month."

"I can't wait! Good night, Aunt Natalie."

"Night, Ellie." She hung up and sighed.

There were footsteps on the stairs. He came into the room carrying two mugs of coffee. He set them down on the bedside table, then crawled into bed with her, and Natalie studied the handsome planes of his face. His physical presence made her shiver.

He locked his arms around her waist, wove his fingers together at her hip bone, and Natalie stopped jiggling her foot and just looked at him.

"Well, you got me," Hunter said. "Now what?"

ACKNOWLEDGMENTS

Many thanks to the brilliant Alex Sehulster for her insight, inspiration, and clarity. Her perspective is invaluable to me.

Love and gratitude to Jill Marr, Andrea Cavallaro, Sandra Dijkstra, and the rest of the team at the Sandra Dijkstra Agency for their support and wise counsel.

It's a true privilege to be working with the always inventive team at Minotaur Books—Alex, Andy Martin, Kelley Ragland, Joe Brosnan, Sarah Melnyk, Kayla Janas, Paul Hochman, John Morrone, David Rotstein, Sabrina Soares Roberts, and Mara Delgado-Sanchez. I thank you. Natalie thanks you!

Doug, my love.

Big appreciation and thanks to the Twitter and Instagram writing communities, and to my spectacular readers—you make make me laugh, cry, and work harder, in that order usually.

Thank you everyone for your love of books.

THE WITCHING TREE

Available Winter 2021

1

⌐

Mornings were dark in March, cold and foreboding. Chilly floors, hurrying downstairs for coffee, shivering and gazing out the French doors at the purple-black sky. For Natalie, living with Hunter Rose inside his enormous nineteenth-century mansion was like curling up with a leather-bound Charles Dickens novel—deliciously comforting. She loved getting up early, before Hunter was awake, and sneaking downstairs to sit at the end of the absurdly long mahogany dining table, built for a family of twelve, where she had a magnificent view of the manicured backyard and the wild woods of upstate New York.

Last night there had been another snowstorm, but it was dissipating now. She gazed out the French doors at the gently falling snow. The backyard was pristine—like an untouched canvas. She could paint the day in any direction she pleased. The plows were making their rounds, and the utility trucks would soon be repairing any fallen lines. Order was slowly being restored.

Natalie relished the quiet of early morning, before Hunter was up with his scratching and yawning and exaggerated gestures of emerging from the cocoon. He was gorgeous to look at. Gorgeous to touch and explore, but this morning she didn't want that. She needed a separate space where she could think, because she had an important decision to make.

In the cradle of winter, March's lullaby, Natalie Lockhart was considering quitting the police force. She'd had enough of the dark side. Four months ago, she was almost killed by a twisted individual who liked to drug and embalm young musicians, and six months before that, she'd solved one of the biggest serial killer cases in the American Northeast. Now, the more time she spent inside the Rose mansion, playacting the lady of the manor, the more she kind of liked it.

And what was not to like? Dinner parties with fascinating people, weekend jaunts to Manhattan to buy art, and basically having enough money and time to do whatever she pleased. An opportunity to explore her creative side. When she was little, Natalie used to love to draw and paint. Hunter had offered her a large room on the third floor to use as a studio space. No more scraping by to pay the bills, no more broken dishwasher, no more waking up in the middle of the night because she'd forgotten something vital to the case she was working on.

Living with thirty-three-year-old Hunter Rose, the founder of Rose Security Software, had given Natalie a chance to hide out from the press. His personal security team was highly skilled at performing background checks on persistent reporters and serial-killer fanboys, screening visitors, and examining the mail. They used closed-circuit TV to monitor the house and grounds. There were alarms and panic buttons. The only thing missing, Hunter joked, was a designated safe room. And he was thinking about that.

Natalie was grateful for the protection. She hadn't asked for the notoriety. It was a fluke, an unlucky turn of events—her being in charge of two sensational murder cases within the span of a year. It would've given any other detective wet dreams, and yet it had happened while Natalie was trying to come to terms with the tragic death of her sister Grace and the shocking revelation about what Grace had done. And so it became Natalie's worst nightmare.

As a teenager, Grace Lockhart and her close group of witch-curious friends had killed Natalie's older sister, Willow, by ritualistically stabbing her twenty-seven times and pinning it on Willow's boyfriend, Justin Fowler. Justin had gone to prison for twenty years before the enormity of the truth had been revealed.

The horror and sorrow Natalie had experienced during this past year had calcified into disillusionment. It was like waking up from a bad dream, only to discover that you were still living inside the same bad dream. A hall of fucking mirrors.

Recently, tensions had eased for Natalie when the national media finally left Burning Lake for greener pastures, feasting on brand-spanking-new tragedies in other areas of the world. At last, she could breathe again. She could sit there and process her feelings and not feel resentful or defensive each time she stepped out her door.

Hunter, for his part, wanted Natalie to quit her job and pursue other interests—to draw or paint or take up photography, to run a marathon or scale a mountain. He wanted her to evolve, to become more of herself. A bigger, better, improved Natalie. And so, these early morning retreats to the downstairs dining room, with its ornate woodwork and incredible view of the backyard that was more like a manicured park out of *Downton Abbey*, were vital to her well-being. Because now, she had to decide whether or not to quit the force. And as of this moment, everything was up in the air.

With a determined sigh, Natalie opened her laptop on the dining table and started to type: "Dear Chief Snyder, Please accept my letter of resignation from the position of CIU detective, effective two weeks from today. It's been an honor to work for you, both as a police officer and as a detective for the Burning Lake Police Department. I will greatly miss all my colleagues. My only regret is that I was not able to better protect the citizens of Burning Lake. During the next two weeks, I will help in any way I can to make the transition as smooth as possible. Please let me know if there's anything specific you'd like me to do. It has been a pleasure working for you. Sincerely, Natalie Lockhart."

Her fingers lifted off the keyboard. She felt light-headed for a moment. Was she actually going to hand in her resignation today? Due to budgetary constraints, the town council had passed a motion that, starting in April, the police department would freeze all hiring. It would be in effect from April until the end of September. Natalie had another week or so to decide what to do, because she wanted to give the department enough time to train her replacement. She would have to make her final decision this week.

Footsteps overhead.

She sighed. He was up. She closed her laptop, brushed a casual hand through her hair, and smiled. She leaned back and gazed out the French doors at the falling snow.

Hunter came shuffling down the stairs, talking on his phone and issuing orders to his second-in-command, an older man who was clearly intimidated by the founder and CEO of the biggest software company on the East Coast. Hunter pocketed his phone and stood in the doorway, smiling broadly at her. "Damn, you look pretty."

She smiled. "You're such a charming liar."

"I tell no lies."

"How'd you sleep?"

"Like the dead. You could've driven a stake through my heart." Handsome and disheveled, he crossed the room with catlike grace—feline as a mountain lion—and lifted her out of her chair and folded her into his muscled warmth, breathing his sour-smelling morning breath in her face. "I've got a brilliant idea," he whispered in her ear. "Let's take the day off. Okay? Please? We'll watch old movies and fuck like bunnies and have French toast for lunch. Can't I tempt you?"

She gave him a wry look. "One of us has to earn a living."

"Actually, that's not true. You and I could both quit tomorrow, and we'd be fine until we're a hundred." He arched an eyebrow at her. "We *are* going to live to be a hundred years old, aren't we? That was the deal, wasn't it?"

She laughed. Despite her best attempts to have her own space in the morning, she abandoned all her worries and melted into him. Hunter was like a drug, and she wanted to do nothing for the rest of the day but live within the span of his hug.

"We could order that take-out pasta you like for dinner," he said, picking up her coffee mug and taking a few sips. "Mmm. You make the yummiest coffee." His bathrobe was open, and he was shirtless, wearing pajama bottoms and a pair of suede bedroom slippers that had seen better days. "You know, the pasta with the shrimp and fresh basil and aged parmesan . . . where's the delivery menu?"

"In the kitchen drawer with the others."

"Is that a yes?" he asked, drawing her close, the surface of his skin twitching like a racehorse. There was an earthy, peppery scent to his sweat.

She thought about what was waiting for her at the police station—an inbox full of paperwork, more notes to review, digital files to be archived, an accumulation of busywork. This winter had been slow going down at the BLPD. Most criminals didn't like the cold. "I guess I could take a mental health day," she hedged, warming up to the idea—no, scratch that, sliding into it like a hot bath.

"You *deserve* a mental health day. You of all fucking people. God, I love you." He kissed her face all over, making playful smacking sounds.

She squirmed and laughed, trying to escape his sloppy kisses. "Okay, but only if you make the French toast."

"Bah. Who needs French toast when I've got this?" He nibbled on her earlobe, then progressed down her neck toward her collarbone.

She became acutely aware of the blood pumping through her veins, the weakness in her knees, the magnetism of his body, and their core physical attraction. Sex with Hunter was frankly earthmoving. Her body was drenched in love chemicals, and her mind floated in an atmosphere of euphoria. Total brain fog.

Her cell phone buzzed, interrupting them. It rattled on the dining table.

"Don't answer that," he pleaded, drawing back and staring at her admonishingly.

The sound was so jarring this early in the morning that she swung out an arm while reaching for it and accidentally smacked her hand on the table. "Ouch!"

"Your physical grace never ceases to amaze me," he said with a wry grin. He took her hand and kissed it.

"Fuck you, I know what a klutz I am."

"How very charming of you to bump into things and then swear at me whenever I politely point it out. Double scoops of goodness there."

She tried not to laugh as she picked up her phone. "Hello?"

"Natalie, it's me," Luke said in a solemn voice. "Something's happened. I need you over here right now."

DH Dowling

ALICE BLANCHARD is an award-winning author. She has received a PEN Award, a New Letters Literary Award, a Centrum Artists-in-Residence Fellowship, and a Katherine Anne Porter Prize in Short Fiction. Her debut novel, *Darkness Peering,* was a *New York Times'* Notable Book and a Barnes & Noble Best Mystery book. Her work has been published in seventeen countries.